The Dragon Pool

A Novel

Diana M. DeLuca

The Dragon Pool ~ A Novel

Inquiries should be addressed to:

Seafield House

320 Exeter Avenue

Eugene, OR 97404

ISBN: 978-0-9960934-3-9 (paperback)

ISBN: 978-0-9960934-3-9 (ebook)

Layout and Design by Superior Book Productions

Contact SBP at Larry@SuperiorBookProductions.com

Dedication

In memory of those who lost their lives during the British occupation of India and in the aftermath of Partition in 1947.

Kalyani September 11, 1950

Unseasonal Rain falls in grieving tears.
Wind banishes webs from pining needles.
Water purges moss from ancient rocks.
All is as it is and should be
When the clever believe the customs of trees,
While the wise know the rituals of water.

— Sanye Patel, Poet Laureate of Kuthan.
Translated by His late Majesty King Raju II.
Used with the gracious permission of King Raju III.

Editor's note: As is the case with any translation, it is hard for a non-native speaker to understand the nuances evident to someone who has spoken a language from childhood. In spoken Kuthani, changes in pitch and tone affect the meaning. To be sure of a speaker's intention, it is necessary for the words to be heard or to be solidly placed in context. King Raju II has provided an accurate direct translation from Kuthani into English, but there is a limit to how much the English-speaking reader can appreciate all that Patel refers to in his poem. The word ritual, for example, in English means ceremony and prescription, but in Kuthani, when applied to water, it also implies the myths, beliefs, incantations, and uses associated with it. Similarly, the English word purge means to clean and remove and has a slightly negative connotation, but the Kuthani word implies a symbiotic and enriching partnership between, in this case, the rocks and water. When dealing with this beautiful and highly evocative language, it is always best to employ the widest possible interpretation.

Table of Contents

Chapter 1

Kuthan Palace, May 1999

RAJU SOÖNG III, KING OF Kuthan, stood frozen before the elaborately carved, double doors of the palace banqueting hall. They were all that stood between him and the horror. Two generations of his family lay dead inside, their bodies scattered amidst the debris of what had been a family gathering.

For the King, history was repeating itself. Forty years after seizing control of India in 1858, the British Raj annexed Kuthan, forcing six warring clans into administrative unity and maintaining order for over ninety years by authority of the British Majesty's artillery. When Britain left in 1947, the families resumed old grievances, including a dispute over a valley on the border between Mountain Thunder and Water Dragon clans. The result was the near total massacre of the Water Dragon clan at their family home at Kalyani, a name now synonymous with both the slaughter and the destroyed compound.

The threat of violence did not end until a confederation of monasteries set up a rudimentary central government governed by a new constitution, and directed their reform efforts to where they thought the evil lay—in the flawed, undisciplined minds of the country's population. For a while, Kuthan was so traumatized by Kalyani that people accepted and even promoted what the monks called the five virtuous ways. But now, looking at the splintered bodies, the King recognized that the monks' policy of decreeing virtue and imposing a constitution on the country had not worked.

The King stood rigid with clenched hands and nodded to a guard. He put on the thick face mask he had been advised to wear and watched as the doors were opened and the lights turned on. Immediately, he knew that the face mask was no protection. When he felt the nausea rise in his chest, he strode outside and ripped the covering from his face.

The Gurkha colonel, the head of palace security, told him what they knew. The palace had been locked down and was still being searched; palace medical staff had provided emergency care to the three survivors: his nephew, a child of seven who was unharmed; his sister, the child's mother, who was critically wounded; and one of the household servants who was attacked in the hall's inner corridor. The two wounded adults had been rushed to the hospital. The other six victims, his uncle Tranh, his aunts Dechen and Pema, and two cousins, Kiran and Kamal, along with the palace's Sikh head butler, had died at the scene.

"Where is my nephew?" The King managed to ask the Colonel who was head of security.

"He is in the palace, under the care of his nanny."

The King bit his lip and began to ask the pragmatic, terrible questions.

"Who has been inside?"

"Palace medical staff who checked for survivors, four of our security force, and the ambulance drivers. We preserved the scene, but our priority was helping the wounded."

"Of course," the King agreed. "There were six dead, you said."

The Colonel repeated his account, giving more details and taking the events one step at a time.

"The moment we heard the shots, all access points were sealed. Palace medical staff were the only ones allowed at the crime scene. Staff were told to shelter in place. Ambulances arrived within ten minutes. We assured your safety and began a systematic search for intruders. Every level of the palace was searched, including the guest hotel, the offices outside the walls, the basements, and the outside perimeter. We have found nothing yet."

"Why was no one posted around the hall?"

"These are your private quarters, Sir. You directed us not to have a presence here."

"You are right," the King said. "I apologize. What are the next steps?"

"We shall photograph the scene before the bodies are removed to the hospital mortuary. We need to know how you want us to proceed."

"Yes, of course," the King said. "Do you have what you need?"

The Colonel smiled grimly. "Before our Gurkha Battalion was seconded to the United Nations Peace Keeping Force, the British Army trained us to document war-crime scenes. We know what to do."

"I want guards at the hospital at all times." The King spoke with a stronger voice. "My nephew is now my ward until his father returns from the Consulate in Honolulu. Who is the servant that survived?"

"Anya, sir."

The King froze. Anya was his childhood nurse. Who would attack an old woman? He felt a warning cramp in his stomach and strode over to a large ceramic pot that held a young fruit tree. There, in a series of heart-rending gasps, he vomited until there was nothing left. He rested his hands on the rim of the pot and wiped his mouth with the back of his hand before he turned back to face the Colonel.

"The Governing Council must be informed." The King spoke as if he were talking to himself instead of his worried head of security. "Also, the Chinese and Indian governments." His voice trailed off as he turned to stumble his way back across the courtyard toward the palace residence.

The Colonel watched him go. The Gurkha oath to protect had not ended when he retired from the British Army. An attack on the royal family was an attack on them all.

Once back in his office, the King sat at his desk, still not fully comprehending what had happened. This morning, his family had gathered to celebrate his Uncle's Tranh's birthday. He had been at the party himself until he was told there was an urgent phone call from Beijing. He was in his office's soundproofed telephone room when it happened and had not even heard the shots.

He impatiently brushed away a tear. He knew what had to be done and grief could not be allowed to interfere. Once he notified those he must, there was the immediate question of finding out who was responsible. The country needed reassurance that the crime would be solved and justice served. But for this, he needed to put someone in charge whose impartiality and integrity would be unquestioned, someone experienced in criminal investigation, and someone with no obvious reason to conceal or misrepresent the evidence or its outcome. He could think of no one in Kuthan with this expertise.

Disconsolately, he stared out of the window and tried to think. He'd been close to only one criminal investigation in his life, the one involving the murder of Hawaii State University professor Harrison Whitworth in Honolulu. That inquiry went well, or so the Kuthani consulate in Hawaii told him. When he visited Hawaii after the crime had been solved, he met the man who led that investigation team. He liked him. He even remembered his name: Inspector Kajiwara. Another idea then burst into his mind. Why not bring that Hawaii team to Kuthan?

Almost immediately, he played devil's advocate. Why would Hawaii send their detectives when it was unclear how long they would even be out of the country? What if the US government said there was no lawful way to make this kind of loan possible? And, would the detectives even be willing to come? But then he brushed aside those questions, telling himself he would deal with them as they came up. Now there was no stopping him. He picked up the telephone and told his secretary to connect him with the US State Department in Honolulu. "Get them out of bed, if you have to," he said dramatically.

He sat back in his chair, glad to have something to do instead of just feeling shocked and helpless. While he waited, he practiced what he would say. Describing the situation as an emergency did not sound convincing. The word *emergency* was weak from overuse. Claiming that Kuthan faced an international crisis might work if he hinted at strengthening American-Kuthani relations. But that was far-fetched and might make Kuthan sound desperate for charity. Then it came to him. He would request a contract with Hawaii to borrow the four detectives that had been the Whitworth investigation team. The details could be worked out later and the impossible part might be that he wanted them here in two days. But balanced against that was the fact that Kuthan was willing to pay whatever it took to make it happen.

As the phone rang, the King took a deep breath and pictured the detective he wanted.

Inspector Kajiwara, if you have not heard already, you will soon know that members of my family have been murdered. We do not know who is behind this tragedy, or what might follow from it. It is a time of national grieving and international uncertainty. I shall do everything I can to keep the country stable, but I need people by my side that I can count on. The person who leads the investigation must be above politics. It must be someone with experience in this type of investigation and who has unquestioned integrity. Of the two, integrity counts most. I respected how you conducted the investigation into the murder of Professor Whitworth. My brother-in-law, the Consul, said you showed sensitivity and professional focus. I saw those qualities myself when I met you. I want you and your team to direct the investigation for us. I know it will not be easy working in a foreign culture and we will do everything to help. But, please, find the truth and, with it, help us to find our way forward.

Chapter 2

THE ATMOSPHERE WAS QUIET ON board the Gulfstream GV that Kuthan had sent for Inspector "Kaj" Kajiwara and his team, Detectives Jill Nakamura, Cliff Lee, and Kaipo Kahana. They were now well on their way, headed for a brief stop in Japan before crossing the Korean peninsula, flying south to skirt the Himalayas, and turning over northern India to approach Mongarthuā, Kuthan's capital city, from the south.

The King's brother-in-law, the head of the Kuthani Consulate in Honolulu was in the forward cabin along with three members of his consular staff. A curtain had been pulled across the aisle to give them privacy. The Americans occupied the rear two cabin spaces. The middle cabin was occupied by two communication specialists accompanying Greg Horne, the US State Department's Hawaii expert on Kuthan. The rear cabin space had more armchairs and, at the back, a small conference table. This was where Greg had summoned the team for a briefing on Kuthan and the South Asian region. The meeting would be a personally interesting moment for Kaj as this would be the first time that his partner Jill and Greg had worked together since they announced their engagement. He had no doubt of her professionalism. He wondered how Greg would handle it.

Greg looked more curious than unsettled as they settled round the table. He noticed that Cliff had brought a book on the history of the modern South Asian region. The book's spine was creased, showing that he had read it.

"What does that say about Kuthan?"

Cliff looked disappointed. "It's sketchy. The book focuses on India and Pakistan after the British left. Nepal's left out because it was never part of the British raj. All it says about Kuthan is the difficulty they had controlling Kuthan's resurgent warlord violence after the British left, and something about a hydroelectric dam that provides electricity to Kuthan and its neighbors, China and India."

"I'm not surprised," Greg told him. "Kuthan is a small player located between large and quarrelsome neighbors. But that dam is critical because it assures Kuthan's independence. Since China and India helped pay for it and use the electricity it produces, they'll send in troops if anyone attacks Kuthan. The tricky part, of course, is whether the troops would withdraw after the threat was over."

"Greg," Kaj broke in, "I know the history will be helpful, but right now can you explain why we had only three days before we had to get on this plane. Why us? And what's the role of the State Department in all this?"

Greg hesitated for a moment. "We don't know much more than you, Kaj. Kuthan worked it all out with the Governor's office. The King called us first and was very clear who he wanted. It was an unusual request, but we made calls for them and facilitated where we could. What I can tell you is the amount of work that went into making this happen. It's an unprecedented cooperation, and a lot of people on both sides had to scramble. Kuthan had to settle for three days to get you over there. Originally, they wanted you overnight. The King named you directly. He said he wanted credible and unbiased crime detection, but he also said he needed transparency because you'll be working with Chinese and Indian crime specialists. He's assured us that you will be free to do your jobs just as you would at home, but it's still a foreign country, and I'd advise you to remember that you aren't at home."

"Go with the flow?" Kaipo broke in. 'Is that what you're saying?"

Greg shook his head. "Perhaps learn and appreciate is more like it. The Kuthanis are an artistic, gracious people still recovering from a difficult colonial past. They had to rebuild themselves after the British left. It wasn't easy, and you'll see that for yourselves. The murders at the palace have shaken the country and there is deep grief for the losses. I was told to give you enough background on Kuthan so that you can work with or around them."

"Around them? What does that mean?" Kaj felt the prickle start on the back his neck. It was his personal warning signal wrung from long hours of solitary, sentry duty in Vietnam. In the jungle, it had meant monsoon rains hiding the sounds of a snake, a centipede, a tiger, or the enemy. He wasn't sure what it was telling him now. But he was already getting the feeling that the detectives would be on their own. For a moment, he had a pang of homesickness. Murders in Hawaii seemed much less complicated. He wished he was back home having a quiet dinner with his wife and perhaps playing with their new grandson.

Greg immediately backtracked. "What I meant to say is that you are to do your job without interference."

Kaj frowned deeply. "We don't need circuses," he said. "It was bad enough with the Whitworth case,"

"I know," Greg said. "But that was the murder of a Hawaii State University professor who had won a Nobel Prize. How often does that happen?"

"It was a zoo," Kaipo objected. "The media never shut down and the politicians wouldn't stay away."

"Not to mention the endless conflicts on the campus," Cliff added.

"Nothing like that," Greg promised them. "Whitworth was a big shot, and who gets killed by a bow and arrow on his own driveway? Kuthan doesn't have news feeds in their main city, and the palace has more control over the media than we did in Hawaii. Let me tell you some more about the country."

He passed out copies of a hand-drawn map showing Kuthan's boundaries and major regions.

"This map is rough and not to scale, but I've never claimed to be an artist. Look around the edges for the six regions. The capital city of Mongarthuā is located roughly in the middle. These regions are what's left of the warlords the British suppressed when they took control of Kuthan in 1898. The British based their administrative center in Mongarthuā on top of an old hilltop monastery. When they left, the monastery was renovated into a palace for the current royal family. Your crime scene is in a building across the courtyard from the family residence."

"Is there a map of the palace area?" Cliff asked.

"Waiting for you when you arrive. The palace said their officers secured the site and searched for intruders. They didn't find any. Now that has created obvious problems. If no one went in or out, everyone in the palace is under suspicion. They plan to tell you all this once you get there."

"Who provides the security?" Kaj asked.

"It's an ex-military group based at the palace, headed by Colonel Pradhan, a retiree from the Royal Gurkha Battalion of the British Army. Interestingly, he also heads Mongarthuā's centralized security system. That includes airport security, border control, and international customs, all run out of the palace. The Colonel apparently handpicks the guards. Most served with him. He's Nepalese and speaks excellent English from his years of living in England."

"That sounds like a private army," Kaipo said. "Could someone in that army have attempted a coup?"

"That's not been suggested. But, for my money, I'd rule out the old warlord families first. Several have caused trouble in the past. The Gurkha security forces, on the other hand, are famed for their loyalty."

"What kind of trouble?" Kaj furrowed his forehead as he studied the map.

"Look at Kuthan's history. Before the British army marched over the border from India, people's loyalties gravitated to their warlord families. These families all stayed quiet under British rule. After the British left in 1947, that's when the Mountain Thunder clan decided to finally settle an ancient dispute over a valley. They brutally attacked their Water Dragon neighbor to the south. There had been skirmishes in the past, but this time it turned into a massacre at a place called Kalyani. The Water Dragon family was almost completely wiped out."

"Was there any retribution for doing that?" Kaj asked.

"They were the dominant clan and still have a dodgy reputation. City people like to say that if there's trouble, look at the mountains. They mean look at Mountain Thunder, which is up there in the Himalayas."

Greg pointed to the map before he continued.

"The Lhotse family got rich by taxing traders on a branch of the old Silk Road. The family was so powerful that when they threatened to break away from Kuthan to join Nepal, people didn't doubt them. These days they mine gemstones and ranch yaks, but no one's forgotten that the Kalyani massacre was the reason for people appealing to the monasteries to impose order on the country. The other clans were afraid they might be next."

"Why the monasteries?" Kaipo asked.

"They were the only organized structure left in the country when the British left. In the face of impending chaos, the monks came up with a plan for governing that they imposed by cajoling and sometimes bribing the clans into accepting a new constitution. This plan called for national leadership by an elected king. Mountain Thunder was offered the valley they'd seized so they would accept the new constitution."

Kaj's eyebrows both rose. "They were rewarded for attacking Water Dragon?"

"Circumstances demanded it. If there were to be a national constitution, Mountain Thunder had to be brought on board first, whatever the cost. Justice had to take a back seat. But consider this. Who was left to object? The Water Dragon clan was almost non-existent, and the monasteries couldn't raise an army to fight Mountain Thunder. The priority had to be creating some form of government."

"And a monarchy was the best way to do that?" Cliff sounded skeptical.

Greg gave a slight shrug. "Elected monarchy, at least to start. The monks were used to hierarchy, and they may have been influenced by the British confidence that a monarchy encourages a moral, hard-working population that knows its place. But the monks' constitution didn't call for an all-powerful king. The position came with restraints in the form of a governing council representing the families. The most interesting part is that the first king they elected was King Raju I, one of the very few survivors of the Kalyani massacre. He was the grandfather of the current king."

"So, Water Dragon lost its valley but gained a kingdom? How does that compute?" Kaipo looked bewildered.

"I wouldn't call it gaining," Greg said. "The royal family needs to lead by consensus. This is no autocracy."

"What about the other mountain clan? The one closest to them?" Jill pointed to the map. "It says Snow Leopard. Did Mountain Thunder attack them too?"

Greg gave a small smile. "An interesting question. You might think so, given Mountain Thunder's reputation. But when I asked Darya Lhotse about it, she said that Mountain Thunder and Snow Leopard have never competed and have traded peacefully for generations. Snow Leopard people are Kuthan's intellectuals, professionals, and artists. The Kuthani poet laureate, Sanye Patel, was one, as is the King's girlfriend, a psychologist who works at the Royal Kuthani Hospital. Both Mountain Thunder and Snow Leopard describe themselves as the guardians of the mountains. Perhaps that's what they have in common. It may also be that good old motive—luxury and good living. Snow Leopard supplies the country with the comforts of home—art, furniture, sculpture, fine foods, and clothing made from their Kuthani goat fleece. It's fascinating to watch how that clan operates since they have some type of indefinable authority. When Snow Leopard opposes something, they don't exert any political power. They just say that their goats will not like it, and no one argues. It sounds quaint, doesn't it? But it works for them."

"What about the other families?" Kaj asked. "Did they have problems with the constitution?"

"Because of the dam, it's a rich country. The only protests have been about dam expansion. At the turn of the century, young men from the western families, Blue Pheasant and Water Dragon, protested that their land was being flooded by the dam's expanding reservoir. They were ignored. When the British proposed to build a larger hydroelectric dam to produce electricity, there were threats of violence. The British took those more seriously. They arrested everyone they could find, and the dam organized its own security force. The families on the eastern side, White Bone and Golden Tiger are farmers. They don't get involved much in politics unless it's about water issues threatening their rice paddies and tea groves."

Jill looked at Greg. "Didn't you say that we should look at all these families? Are you saying now that it's unlikely they would be involved?"

Greg shook his head. "No. You need to look at everyone. Things change. This is what State monitors for. The only major conflict in the region at the moment involves India, Kashmir, and the Sikhs, and there are Sikh temples in Kuthan. But nothing is clear and no one has claimed responsibility so far."

"If the King had been assassinated, would there have been a succession crisis?" Jill was starting to feel the time difference and the lulling motion of the aircraft. She tried valiantly not to rub her eyes.

"That's why I asked the palace provide a royal family genealogy chart although I didn't say it was to help you identify potential killers. The presumptive heir would be the current king's sister, Soniyaa, if she survives, or her son, Aki, depending on how Kuthan feels about women and children as heirs. But who knows? There may be some unknown protest group with an unrecognized agenda. There's plenty of emotion below the surface in the South Asian region, long memories fuel revenge, and two of region's countries, India and Pakistan, have not only fought wars but now have nuclear capability."

"Without a viable heir, would anyone benefit?" Cliff asked.

Greg could tell they were all fighting time and the softness of the chairs. He called for the cabin attendants and asked for coffee. Then he waited until it appeared and poured cups all around without asking.

"I have no idea, Cliff. Why would India or China want to shake up a neutral buffer state that has a dam they helped pay for and that provides their countries with electric power? And why would Kuthan want to upset international agreements that have made the country wealthy?"

Kaj noticed that Greg had not included the US in his list of possibly interested nations. He wasn't going to ignore it. "What is the State Department's interest in the region?"

"We want it stable and it's nowhere near that. China supports Pakistan's clash with India over Kashmir. Pakistan also blames India for supporting East Pakistan when it broke away to become Bangladesh. India, in turn, blames Pakistan for smuggling arms to fringe-group Punjabi Sikhs agitating for a home state they call Khalistan which would be based in Punjab. Nothing was really settled by Partition, the name they give to the British rush to get out of India. It left unanswered questions regarding boundaries and homelands. America already has its hands full with these hot spots. We don't need Kuthan creating another one."

"Then you think Kuthan could become one?" Cliff asked.

"Assassinating the royal family is not a good sign. Until we know who's responsible, we won't know what's behind it and we're not the only ones concerned. China has reassigned one of its Moscow consular staff to Kuthan. Meng arrives with their medical team tomorrow. Our first thought is that he's been sent to keep an eye on them. But that's only a guess or a hope. He may be coming to foment unrest. They already have an embassy in Mongarthuā that could watch their people. China is like the echo on long-distance calls. You wait for the second sound bounce, but by then the first party is yelling, 'Are you still there?' and hanging up."

"Who is he?" This time it was Kaipo whose forehead was furrowed.

"I met him when he was assigned to the Russian embassy in Washington. He's old school, operating somewhere back in the Cold War, a few James Bond movies ago. China always has its reasons, and it doesn't waste time on sentiment. The country is run like a hierarchical corporation. They raise what they call armies of people when they want something done, and they don't give up on someone who's still useful. He's an opportunist. If any of you has a vulnerability, he'll exploit it. But he's also congenial, even winsome. He has a sense of humor, which is unusual for the Chinese diplomatic corps. He wangles invitations to events at embassies that don't even ally with China. When he was in England, he got himself invited to a Buckingham Palace tea party. You'd think he'd been knighted from the way he talked about the Queen and Prince Philip. The Chinese probably sent him to Kuthan because he has extensive international experience. People like him. Just be careful."

Kaj leaned back into the deep plushness of the soft leather chair and took a sip of coffee. He had to wonder whether Hawaii detectives had any business working in Kuthan, let alone the region. He knew that Greg was probably wondering the same thing. But the State Department had no choice. The King's actions had taken the decision out of their hands.

"What do we know about the Indian team?" he asked.

"As you know, they're coming to do the forensics. It's led by one of their international stars, Dr. Emir Sharma. The Indian Consulate in San Francisco said that we and Kuthan should feel honored by his presence. He's the head criminal investigator for the northeastern region of India, consults everywhere, and has ties with various US universities, including your Hawaii State University. India also sent a New Delhi mobile crime lab along with the professional staff that runs it. Dr. Sharma is bringing a graduate student with him."

"Graduate student?" Kaipo's eyebrows rose. "That's a new one."

Greg gave a rueful smile. "I'm told he wanted to bring his entire graduate seminar as a field trip. Kuthan said it was not possible, so he settled for bringing just one. China is providing your medical examiners. They did not confirm their participants until this morning. We tried to find out what we could about them. Their bios are included in the files."

Greg picked up another folder and pushed it across the table.

"Both Chinese and Indian teams are very high level, but it's important to keep in mind their political disfunction. As I said before—and don't worry if you can't keep this all straight yet—they have disputes with each other over borders, and they back different players in the region. Things operate here like a circular revenge tragedy. They are also competitive. Both claim they could have mounted a team qualified to do both the forensics and medical investigation without involving the other one. And to be honest, there's suspicion about why the King imported American detectives. Expect a lot of curiosity in you and your team."

"Let me get this straight." Jill's voice rose. "You're telling us that we are investigating a major case in a country so lacking in infrastructure that we must rely on foreign investigators who are likely be antagonistic to each other and suspicious of us? Did anybody think through how we're going to do this?"

Greg gave a slight shrug.

"You'll have everything you need to do the job. Just before we left Honolulu, we received confirmation that the operations room you requested has been set up, and they were gathering the information packets you wanted. You'll have the protection of the palace. The King has definite ideas about how he intends to work with you. As you all know, the King has insisted that Kaj head the entire investigation."

"What does that mean?" Kaj said. "I don't know anything about their criminal justice system."

Greg heard the weariness in Kaj's voice and noted how tired the detectives looked. It was getting time to end this first introduction to Kuthan.

"Most crime in the country is domestic violence and property disputes and those get handled locally. As I said before, this collaboration is unprecedented for Kuthan so you can expect some trial and error. There has been silence from Beijing and New Delhi on the matter. That's why John and Chris are along on this trip. They're part of the security system we're putting in place around you."

Greg looked down the mid-cabin to where the two computer specialists sat hunched over their laptops.

"You haven't met them yet," he said. "John's a specialist in Chinese economic policy. Chris's focus is India. In addition, they're our experts on anything involving technology. I wish I had their talent, but they were raised with computers, and I wasn't. Incidentally, we don't usually deal with Kuthan on their home front like this. We use our embassy in Nepal to handle local issues. Otherwise, we work through the Hawaii Consulate. We will always be in direct contact with the Honolulu office, and our New Delhi embassy is on alert to pull you out rapidly if anything goes wrong."

Kaj felt his shoulders suddenly grow stiff. He hadn't had time that morning for his Aikido exercises, maybe that was what was causing it. In fact, in the past few days, he hadn't had time for anything beyond the mandatory health checks, reassigning his open cases, and packing for the trip. He hoped wherever they were staying would have enough room for him to resume his morning workout. He finally gave into a yawn, and it had the unfortunate consequence of causing the Hawaii detectives to copy him.

Greg gave a compassionate smile and took a gulp of his coffee. It would be a long time before he would have the chance to sleep.

"Let me tie this up. The palace has planned a meeting for you to meet the members of the Kuthani Governing Council in the morning. Representatives from the remaining five families will be there and whoever else they feel like including. The Indian team is already on site. The Chinese team arrives shortly after we do. Right now, things are chaotic. The Mongarthuā newspapers are full of nothing but the attack, and the international media is thinking about it."

"Who's making all these arrangements?" Kaj imagined the worst.

"Palace staff. But they're working under the same time pressures we are, so everything's fluid. We just learned that you and the Indian and Chinese teams will not transfer to downtown hotels as we first thought. You will be staying in the palace's guest hotel. Diplomatic personnel—Chris, John, and I—are to be housed off palace. That means we occupy rented quarters still to be arranged. The local Australian embassy is assisting us with that. Palace security will meet us when we land and will drive us all to the hotel. From there, we'll take taxis into town. Once there, we'll buy local Kuthan.com phones for you. If you brought your own, don't use them. The roaming charges will kill you. We'll preload our numbers on the phones, but be cautious if you plan to talk about anything sensitive. We'll deliver the phones to you at the palace."

"Is it OK to use them to call the States?" Kaipo asked.

"That's what they're for, as well as for reaching us. Always carry them with you. That way we can track you. Incidentally, your team, unlike the rest of us, has special permission to travel wherever you need to in Kuthan. We're limited to the city. When you're off site, palace security will travel with you. We're not expecting trouble, but we make contingency plans for countries where we don't have an official consular presence."

Greg drank the last of his coffee and refilled his cup. He offered the pot to everyone else but only Kaipo accepted.

"How big a problem are these travel restrictions?" Cliff asked.

Greg shook his head. "It won't affect you at all. It would be for anyone who wants to visit the Kuthan side of the Himalayas. They'd need a permit. But I have a contact in the local community. He's a friend who has his own sources. Now, I'm seeing more stifled yawns, so how about we bring John and Chris back here and let you go forward and get some sleep? Once reclined, the armchairs are quite comfortable."

Chapter 3

KAJ SAT BACK AND WATCHED as Greg's two young Asian experts carried their laptops to the rear, quickly plugged them in, and put on headsets. No one said what they were listening to, so Kaj assumed it had something to do with monitoring the region. Jill, Kaipo, and Cliff reclined the recently vacated seats, accepted pillows and blankets, and soon settled into whatever sleep they could find. Kaj, meanwhile, stretched his arms above his head and willed himself awake. He wanted answers and wasn't willing to wait for them.

"What are you really doing in Kuthan?" Kaj spoke quietly but emphasized the word *really*.

Greg frowned as he weighed Kaj's question.

"The US State Department has sent us to provide support and protection for your team. We will work with palace security and civic authorities while you are in the city. When you travel, we'll watch you to the extent we can. If anything happens to you, we're accountable."

"I don't think you offer this service to every traveling American, do you?" Kaj smiled quizzically.

Greg shook his head. "Of course not. Our embassies abroad couldn't possibly assign individual agents to every traveler. But in this case, you're working with the topmost leadership of a sovereign nation in a region of emerging world powers. We're particularly interested because of the history you have with the King."

Kaj gave an ironic smile. "History? Hardly that. Greg, you almost had me convinced. But let me repeat the question. What are you really doing, officially or unofficially, in Kuthan?"

"The same thing that the Kuthani Consulate is doing in Honolulu."

Greg's smile was almost cheeky and conspiratorial. Kaj went into interrogation mode: ask broad questions with as few words as possible and leave Greg to trap himself by second guessing what Kaj wanted to know.

Kaj's face was bland. "And that's what?"

"Keeping an eye on the region." Greg raised his eyebrows to look innocent.

Kaj's eloquent left eyebrow rose without being asked. For a moment he felt as if he were in a Hitchcock movie, sitting at a darkened table in Shanghai with assassins all round, cups frozen halfway to their lips, and necks craned to listen. But Chris and John were the only ones in the rear compartment, and they weren't looking up.

"Spying?" Kaj was almost nonchalantly.

"Not what you think." Greg was using the same technique right back at Kaj.

"Please enlighten me," Kaj said drolly. "Are you saying that the Kuthan Consulate is spying on the US?"

Greg sighed. "Everyone in this South Asian region knows exactly what everyone else is doing. We're competitors, except, dysfunctional as they are, they're united in politely keeping America at arm's length. They don't want us meddling. Politics is juggling on a high wire over here. The diplomatic thing is that we keep our eyes open and pretend that we don't know what's going on."

Kaj steepled his fingers and pressed them to his lips.

"I'm just a detective investigating a crime. To me, protocol is politics, and politics is quicksand. I'm not cut out for the diplomacy business."

As he said the words, Kaj could see Linda, his wife, smile and hear her say "just as well."

Greg disagreed. "That's a bit naïve, Kaj. By solving the Whitworth murder, you became a Kuthani hero. Whitworth was important to them. He'd set up their medical system, and, in loyalty to him, their first impulse was to close the consulate and go home. We didn't want that to happen, and they didn't really want to do it either. When you proved that the murderer was Mallik, an Indian émigré employed by their consulate, everyone was relieved. They were able to use your competence as their excuse to keep the consulate in Honolulu. Personally, I think that the King didn't want to give up his surfing.

But whatever the reason, you were the first person the King thought of to lead the investigation."

Kaj's face darkened with annoyance. "I'm not a hero. I don't need that burden."

Greg had heard Kaj say that before. He adroitly changed the subject.

"The King's not a fool. He studied at Oxford University and is part philosopher and poet, part politician and economist, and part pragmatist. Since Kuthan has a plush set of Hawaii offices in a place without a winter, I think they got the best of the deal." Greg held up his hand. "My opinion."

"Except for Mallik," Kaj reminded him. "Killing Whitworth must have caused a lot of trouble for Kuthan."

"Well," Greg replied slowly, "that's another thing. And there's something you need to know. A couple of things, really."

Greg glanced at John and Chris, but they were focused on their screens. Kaj then looked grim. Whatever it was, Greg had just confirmed Kaj's earlier suspicions about how much he was holding back.

"Mallik was their head of consular security, but he was not Kuthani. His family came across the southern border from India as refugees. These unofficial immigrants posed a problem for Kuthan because they were mainly Hindu and tended not to get assimilated. They settled primarily in the foothills where they earned had a reputation for stealing antiquities from abandoned monasteries. The current King's father thought if he hired them in the palace, they might become Kuthani over time. That's how Mallik was hired. Unfortunately, he became greedy and, as you know, joined the family business. When he killed Whitworth to hide it, he made a bad mistake. But it was even bigger problem for Kuthan. They didn't want to tell the King that his father's policy had been misguided. But they also didn't want it known that Mallik was their spymaster. He knew too much. So, they compromised. They let us jail him in the US, but it was a foregone conclusion that at some point Kuthan would want him back. And that's what happened."

"They asked us to release him? That would never happen." Kaj looked shocked at the idea.

"Well, it did. We know how it worked because we monitored his prison mail. He wrote to the King claiming that his tranquility was being destroyed. As predicted, Kuthan made the formal request, assuring us that he would serve the rest of his sentence at a remote monastery somewhere high in their mountains. The State Department didn't want to lose what little foothold we have in Kuthan. We agreed that Mallik could be flown home under guard."

"So, where is he now?"

Greg looked away from Kaj for a moment and looked back embarrassed. "We don't know."

"You don't know?" Kaj's eyebrows hit his hairline.

"We thought we handed him over to Singapore at Changi Airport, but then we lost him."

"How did he escape?"

"Again, we don't know. Changi Airport says that security footage shows Mallik being handed over to men in military uniforms. They kept their backs to the cameras. Mallik was last seen walking down a corridor and out of range. After that, nothing. To add to the mystery, Changi wouldn't let us personally review their security tapes."

"How long ago was this?" Kaj leaned forward impatiently.

"Three months. There have been no updates since."

"Why was the exchange made in Singapore? Singapore was where his smuggling operation was headquartered. He'd have contacts there. Why not Japan or Taiwan?"

Greg shrugged. "That's what Kuthan requested. We flew him commercial out of San Francisco with two escorts."

"Did Kuthan have anything to say about it?"

"The palace didn't respond to our queries. We were left to suspect that someone high up wanted Mallik to fall off the radar."

Kaj sank back into deeply felt exasperation. "When were you planning on telling me this?"

Greg shrugged eloquently. "Whenever it came up, I suppose."

"So, we have a criminal on the loose with a history of violence and a possible grievance against the Kuthani royal family for letting the Americans jail him? And you didn't think to tell us?"

Greg ignored Kaj's annoyance. "Unfortunately, yes. And from Singapore, he could have reached Kuthan by air or by ground through Indonesia and Thailand. It would be easy enough to slip across Kuthan's porous southern border. But if he wasn't flying, he'd need extensive help to pull it off. As far as whether he had anything to do with the attack on the palace—well, among other things, that's why you're here."

Kaj leaned back and closed his eyes in frustration. Was he really ready for Kuthan? He was still dealing with his own losses and fears. It was only when he saw the row of his father's 442nd regimental buddies at the funeral service that he really understood that Goro would never *monku* again about how Kaj neglected his yard.

He hadn't handled losing Goro well even with his sister, Aileen, there. She'd been alienated from them all for years, but, at the end, Japanese custom called her back. She flew overnight when she heard Goro was dying, and Kaj was glad for that. But calamities came almost faster than he could handle. After the funeral, his daughter, Annie, was rushed to the hospital for an emergency cesarian delivery.

Grief and anxiety then melded into the finality of death and the fragility of life. Under those burdens, the old nightmare came roaring back. His work with the VA counselors had made him aware of what caused the dream, but merely understanding didn't stop it: It was Vietnam. They were under fire and taking heavy casualties. He was in rice paddy with a youngster, new to the platoon, someone he was trying to protect. When the kid was hit, Kaj turned him over. But the kid's face had been blown off. That is when Kaj usually woke. Except this time, when he turned the body over, the face on it was Annie's. He jerked awake, heart pounding, tears pouring down his face, and sweat soaking his cold body. They had nearly lost her to complications when the baby was born and she would not be able to have another.

No, he was not in great shape. But when they told him that Kuthan had personally requested him and that the agreements had already been made, his on-going nightmares did not come into consideration. In fact, they told him he didn't have a choice.

Kaj looked at Greg sourly. He wasn't sure how much to trust him. If he had held back the fact that Mallik was free and might even be involved in the murder the Hawaii team was about to investigate, what else was he not sharing? It made him wonder if the US was somehow complicit in the attack on the palace. It would an unbearable betrayal if it were true: it would mean that all those young Japanese-American lives were lost defending a nation unworthy of their sacrifice. In that moment, he made a promise to himself. When he and his team found the killer—and they would—there would be no holding back the truth. He would declare it to the world, regardless of who was implicated.

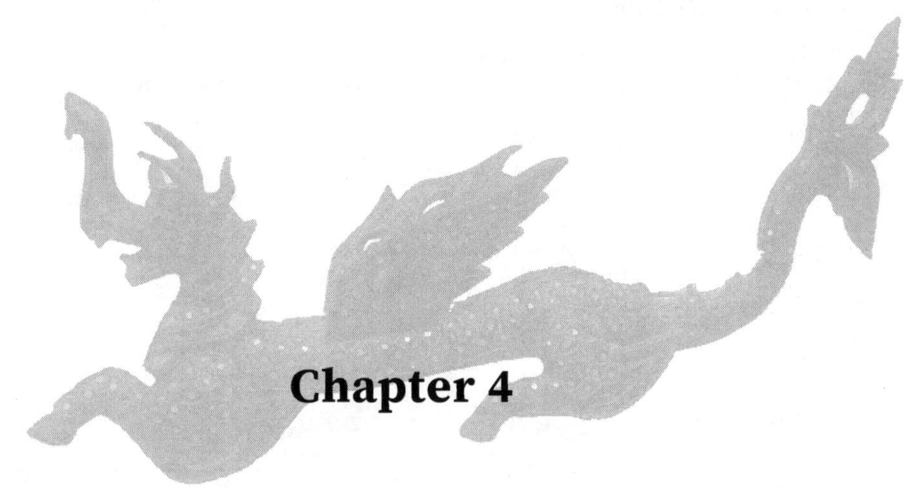

Chapter 4

THE PILOT'S VOICE SOUNDED VAGUELY British over the intercom as he woke anyone dozing. The crew had Indian and Kuthani members, and the long-ago colonial schools in both countries had done their job. The pilot sounded ex-pat Brit to Kaj's ear, and both India and Kuthan used British spelling and formal grammar.

"Please use this time to stretch," the pilot announced. "When we enter Kuthani airspace, we shall commence our descent into Mongarthuā, and the safety belt signs will display. We are directed to park at the corporate terminal. Entry formalities are to take place on board this aeroplane. The local time is 9:00 a.m. The altitude of Mongarthuā is 2000 meters, or just over 6500 feet above sea level."

Kaj glanced at Jill, wondering if she was thinking about her former fiancé, Steven Harkin, killed in a mountain climbing accident on Mount Rainier. Harkin had photographed the Himalayas for *National Geographic* and had loved Kuthan. He wanted them to be married there. Kaj was glad that circumstances or just plain coincidence made it possible for her fiancé Greg to be with her as she saw the country for the first time.

Jill was sitting upright with her face pressed against the window.

Kaj did the same, only his view was towards the rear of the aircraft. All he could see behind them were clouds.

"Can you see anything?" he asked her.

"Too high to see much. But I think I can see mountains in the distance, if they're not clouds playing tricks."

Kaj stood up and looked around the cabin. Despite the tragic circumstance, there was a controlled electricity in the air. The Kuthanis were nearing home, while the Americans were plunging into the unknown.

"Anyone mind if I catch a quick shave." It was more statement than question, and Kaipo didn't wait for permission before brushing past Kaj and heading back to the rear bathroom. Cliff gave a small yawn and put on his jacket. In the back of the aircraft, Greg and the two State experts were packing papers and equipment into diplomatic bags.

"Yes, it's mountains," Jill said. "That looks like Mount Masakatsu in the distance. The one with the double peak."

Kaj sat down and swiveled his chair to lean his face against the window. He could see the mountains, and they looked immense. Going up Mauna Kea had literally taken his breath away, but that was just under 14,000 feet from sea level. These Himalayan mountains were double that.

Greg came down the aisle and bent over Jill to look out of the window. He placed his hand protectively on her shoulder.

Kaj felt the aircraft begin the slow descent before the pilot announced it. Then Kuthan began to come into focus.

Mongarthuā, the capital city, was situated north of a broad fertile plain that stretched across the entire southern portion of the country. It was set against foothills that turned from green to dusty purple ending in a frieze of distant snow-capped mountains set against a brilliant blue sky dotted with pure-white clouds of ice crystals.

As the aircraft approached the city, it seemed to follow the route of a large, fast-flowing river far below them. Kaj assumed this was the Sindhu, one of the rivers that powered the dam and created a significant part of Kuthan's wealth. The banks were thick with lush jungle foliage, and white foam marked where the water raced over submerged rocks.

Rice paddies and acres of fruit trees soon gave over to farmhouses, and vegetable plots became suburban streets clustered around pagoda-shaped buildings with turned-up roofs and brightly painted walls. Patches of green suggested that residents liked to play golf. High rise buildings ringed the city center and what looked like urban sprawl spread across the outskirts and up hillsides. There was even a smear of beige smog on the horizon.

On final approach, they flew low enough to see that the houses had slate roofs and curving rafters. Most houses had a wooden, carved Buddhist spirit box next to the front gate, and nearly every house had a small city car parked on the driveway. The trucks had snub noses that looked more European than Asian. The city looked international, more like Singapore or Bangkok than the land of waterfalls, forests, and goats that the Consulate had presented in their Hawaii festivals.

The jet pulled up to a glass and steel building across from the main passenger terminal where parked aircraft bore the symbols of six different commercial airlines. Kaj didn't recognize any of them. Once the engines were cut, the Kuthani staff deplaned and disappeared into waiting cars. The Americans remained on board for the formalities of entering the country. Then they were escorted to Mercedes passenger vans. Kaj was glad they were not limousines. Greg had warned him that the Chinese government had gifted Kuthan with a pair of stretch-outs that might have come equipped with listening devices. The four detectives climbed into the first one, along with their luggage.

Because of its large size, the palace was visible from the airport. From a distance, it resembled a layered cake. Smaller buildings filled the lower terraces, while the main buildings occupied the very top of the hill. As they drew closer, they could see guards posted at the entrances to every level.

"How does someone get up there without being seen?" Kaipo kept his voice low and leaned toward Kaj as he spoke.

Kaj stared at the palace walls. "I asked for a map of the buildings and grounds, particularly showing anything like basements and sewers."

The van stopped in a courtyard in front of the guest hotel, a free-standing, three-story building with a pitched roof that directed rainwater out of the mouths of dragon-shaped downspouts. The building was within the upper palace walls yet outside the walled-off private residential space. A large white van with blue and orange stripes down the sides was parked next to the building, proudly announcing in English and Hindi that it was a New Delhi Mobile Forensics Crime Scene Investigation Unit.

Both airport vans emptied out at the same time, and Greg came over to join the detectives.

"The security officers in our van have your itinerary. An early lunch has been set up inside and, Kaj, you might want to grab a quick bite now before checking in. The King wants a private meeting before you start work. He's sending a car in half an hour. These two vans are headed back to the airport to pick up the Chinese medical examiners and their equipment. The meeting with the Chinese and Indian teams is set for when you return from your meeting with the King."

"Doesn't the King live in the palace?" Kaj's left eyebrow rose. He had wanted to visit the crime scene and meet with the security guards first.

"He'll explain." Greg gave a shrug that Kaj recognized. It said, "above my pay grade."

Kaj let his luggage be taken from him and was directed to a large room arranged cafeteria style with tables seating four people. It could have been part of any American hotel accustomed to hosting conferences. But there the resemblance ended. The buffet offered an explosion of vegetables and curries, but with little guidance how to choose.

Kaj walked down the line of food displays, feeling a little peevish. He was the only one there and there were no labels near the dishes. In the end, he went with what appeared familiar: a bowl of orange lentil soup, small dumplings sprinkled with cheese, vegetable noodles, and flat bread. He helped himself to a cup of coffee, hoping that the caffeine would carry him through to the evening.

He chose a table by the window and told himself sternly to settle down. Of course, the food and customs would be different. He was thousands of miles from home. What did he expect? He dipped his spoon into the soup, but stopped briefly when he felt the prickle reassert itself. This time he knew what it was saying.

This isn't Hawaii. You don't know the language. You don't know the customs. But this isn't the first time you've done your job without knowing everything. You fought a war that way, so you know you can survive ambiguity. Remember what they told you then. Keep your eyes open and your head down. You know the rest. Put one foot in front of the other as you go up the mountain. But remember, also, once you get to the top, don't look back down. Don't let anyone make you doubt yourself.

Chapter 5

Two palace security guards dressed in military fatigues smiled politely as they handed Kaj a bottle of water and ushered him into a green Land Rover. Kaj looked back uncertainly as they left the palace grounds. As an expert brought in from Hawaii, he thought it would look unprofessional if he appeared jet lagged. He fought urge to sleep, but as they drove out of the city, the time zone won.

After half an hour of driving on a well-kept road that cut through the foothills behind the city, they turned onto one that was crumbling from age and neglect. Kaj jerked awake as the tires complained about the transition. He saw they were entering the grounds of an apparently abandoned building. The structure must once have been elegant, but it was now overgrown with vines, bushes had obliterated a series of what must have been ornate terraced gardens, and a long-ago fire had left part of the walls with dark charcoal streaks. They parked alongside another Land Rover and two more guards.

Kaj noticed at once how drawn and burdened the King looked. The boyish charm and enthusiasm Kaj remembered from Hawaii had been replaced by a world-weariness that made him look much older than he was. This time, the King was not wearing one of his immaculate suits. He was wearing jeans with a loose silk shirt hanging over them. He looked almost Western except for his shirt's orchid pattern and braided buttonholes. He shook Kaj's hand and indicated their way along a path into the trees.

After a few steps, Kaj stopped to catch his breath. The King noticed and led him to a bench in front of an engraved memorial stone bearing a message in Kuthani and English. Kaj read the English version: "Unseasonal rain falls into grieving tears." Sanye Patel, Poet Laureate of Kuthan. In memory of those who lost their lives September 11, 1950." Kaj sat down with some embarrassment, not liking that the altitude had beaten him. The King stood slightly apart, staring back at the ruins of his family home.

After a few moments, the King resumed their walk but led Kaj more slowly down the path until they reached a large lake where vine-covered, tree trunks lay fallen along the banks. The air was cooler and less humid than it had been in town, and a brooding silence hung like a mist, preventing any outside noise from penetrating the stillness.

The King stepped up onto a cracked stone terrace overlooking the water and invited Kaj to join him on a cement bench streaked by mildew.

"This lake is called the Dragon Pool," the King explained as Kaj sat down beside him.

Some moments of silence passed before he spoke again. "Are you aware of places on this earth that are called dead zones?"

When Kaj shook his head, the King continued.

"These are places where there is only silence. No sounds of birds or wind, and even voices are muted. Something terrible happened to make the land die from grief. This place is called Kalyani. I saw you read the memorial. Do you know what happened here?"

Kaj looked somber. "Your clan, Water Dragon, was massacred."

The King stared into the dark, lifeless water. "That is what the history books say. Sanye Patel is our most famous poet. Every school child in Kuthan knows his poem, *Kalyani*. Our teacher told us to find a line that might have meaning for our lives. I chose the line, 'the wise know the rituals of water.' It seems silly now."

Kaj sensed a hesitation in the King's voice.

"Are the history books correct?"

When the King did not reply, Kaj stared somberly at the pool. Without thinking, or even knowing quite how he knew, he blurted out a response to the line of poetry the King had quoted.

"You tried to let the water flow quietly around the rocks. You looked for peace, but now you feel your ideals have been betrayed."

The King turned his head sharply to look at Kaj. "Do you think I am wrong?"

Kaj continued to stare into the pool, waiting to form his answer.

"No," he said finally. "But I live in a world where many people think that violence will solve their problems. I deal with inhumanity. I'm the one who tumbles the rocks out from riverbeds."

The King smiled. "Inspector Kaj, perhaps tumbling rocks is also the way of water. I think you may have lost your faith. My fear is that I am losing mine as well."

The two men sat silently until Kaj felt it was up to him to break the silence.

"Tell me about Kalyani and why you expressed reservation about the history books."

"Did I?" The King replied. "I had not realized that my thoughts were so transparent."

"I'm not sure your thoughts are transparent, but your feelings are."

The King smiled. "I must work on that. But Kalyani is both simpler and more complex than the history books say. Kuthan was ruled for centuries by warlords who carved the country into family regions or clans. No one is ever nostalgic about those years. Eventually the families became tired of fighting and an uneasy truce began to emerge. Some things had gone on so long, though, that they seemed incapable of being settled. One of them was the ownership of a valley."

"The one between Mountain Thunder and Water Dragon?"

The King nodded.

"The British had a policy of suppressing whatever got in their way. When they gathered Kuthan into their raj, they united Kuthan under one administration. Their purpose was to control the trade passes through the mountains from China, and they promised that any disturbances would be severely punished. For the years of the British Raj, the two clans went silent because no one wanted to find out what the British meant by *severe*.

"But then the British left in 1947. That is another date we all know. August 15, 1947. One day there was a ceremony in Mongarthuā, they played *God Save the King*, took down their flag, and were gone. They left us with schools, hospitals, roads, railways, and the dam that was eventually to produce enough electric power to make us wealthy. But they also left us without a functioning central government or any way to build one. Once they decided to leave, they wanted to leave immediately with no thought about what would happen to us. There was nothing to stop the dispute between Mountain Thunder and Water Dragon from coming back to life."

Kaj did not tell the King that he already knew the history. It was his way of testing the accuracy of what Greg had said on the plane.

"After Kalyani," the King continued, "people turned to the monks for help because they were the only group organized enough to impose order and discourage Mountain Thunder from taking more land. As with all religious governance, the monks developed a system that was moral, authoritarian, and intolerant. They developed and imposed a set of virtues they believed would build Kuthan into a peaceful, unified nation. But to give them credit, whatever their impulses, they recognized their own limitations. They were not trained to govern a country so they built a constitution and dealt with the clans one by one. Mountain Thunder was the greatest threat to peace in Kuthan, so that's where they started. Mountain Thunder could have the disputed valley if they supported the constitution. Water Dragon was not asked, but there were so few survivors they were in no position to object. The other clans agreed for their own reasons. In 1957, the constitution was accepted."

"And it was to be a monarchy?"

The King nodded. "The monks were familiar with strong central administration, and they knew how it worked. But the king was to be elected and to operate with a governing council representing the families as well as the monasteries."

"Your grandfather was the one elected."

"Yes. He suspected his election was a form of apology for Kalyani. He was fifty when he was chosen. He had lived through the political upheavals in India and wanted to encourage a Western-style financial system. I was seven when he died. I remember him as a solitary man who never laughed. He dropped our clan affiliation and turned the administration of the remaining Water Dragon lands over to the city. In the last years of his reign, when his health began to fail, he relied heavily on my father. Together they began substituting civil political authority for that of the monks. My father succeeded him in 1980. He was the one who worked with Professor Whitworth to build the hospital and medical school in collaboration with Hawaii State University. He had a progressive vision for our future and was able to achieve some of it, but he never recovered from losing my mother. They said he suffered a stroke but I think he died of heartbreak and overwork. He was only fifty-five. I came straight home and continued the work he started."

"You are the third in your line," Kaj said respectfully.

The King nodded. "Our dynastic name is Raju Soöng in honor of my grandfather."

"Going back to your grandfather's decision to give up your Water Dragon land, may I ask if anyone resented that?"

The King gave a small shrug. "The remnants of my family survived because they were out of the country when Kalyani happened. I think they understood that if Mountain Thunder wanted to claim more Water Dragon land, it would be best if they dealt with the city and not us. I have not heard anyone say he was wrong."

"Has anyone opposed replacing the monasteries with secular government?"

"As the old monks died, a new generation took over, and we were able to work with them. But there may still be some monks who resent their weakening public role."

"Would the monks have reason to attack your family?

"If they did, it would mean abandoning the virtues they promote—tranquility, gratitude, and justice among them."

Kaj looked down at the lake's muddy, brown water. The pool seemed lifeless—there was no movement or pond weed, not even sediment settling under the surface, no sulfurous smell of bacteria and rotting vegetation, and no shadows on the surface even though the sun was high. Yet the pool must have circulation or after nearly fifty years, it would be covered with algae.

"How does the pool look when it's alive?" Kaj asked the question more to prompt the King's explanation than for his own information. Hawaii had its own mystical places, and he knew what they were like.

"It was once a lovely place. On festival days, children flew dragon kites and people walked in the gardens and wrote wishes on red and gold paper to place in the trees, asking the dragon to tell their fortunes. It was said that if the dragon had messages for them, it would call them back to the pool. I have never seen the dragon. I am told it is a strange creature composed of parts from different animals symbolizing that it represents all living things. I'm told that only a hero can bring a dead land back to life. Do you happen to have a spare Western hero?"

Kaj laughed bitterly. "You wouldn't want our heroes. Ours kill dragons."

Kaj felt a slight shiver at the depth of the King's sad gaze.

"No one comes here now except me, and the buildings have been left to decay. I see it as a message for Kuthan. This land is not at peace."

The King changed the subject abruptly.

"Mr. Horne has told you why you are here?"

Kaj suppressed a shrug. He had no idea whether Greg had told him everything. Kaj wasn't even sure what *everything* meant in this case.

"He said you would tell me what I need to know. I was saddened to hear of your losses, Sir. He also told me that your political and cultural affairs make this investigation complicated."

Kaj's explanation was convoluted because, in a perfect world, he would have been fully briefed before he left Hawaii. Greg had admitted as much. But how could he be fully briefed on the crime when he hadn't seen the bodies or the crime scene? He was at a disadvantage right at the start of the case, and he knew it.

The King peered intently into Kaj's eyes. The area between the King's eyebrows furrowed into an expression of sorrow that disappeared as quickly as it emerged. Kaj felt the intensity of the King's loss and his struggle to contain it.

"China and India have differences, but they also have legitimate interest in protecting their investments in the Kuthani dam. They know that civil unrest in this country could threaten dam operations. Politically, I felt I must request their experts to avoid charges of a cover-up. But it is also why I request this investigation be as open as possible, and why I hope you can avoid open conflict between them. Ideally, I hope you can encourage them to work together. I know this is a lot to ask, but I face the possibility that one of their countries may want to destabilize Kuthan. I would like them to go home speaking well of their experience here if not of each other."

"Have there been any direct threats?"

"Until a few days ago, I would have said no. Today I am not sure of anything. I brought you to the Dragon Pool because it is one place I am sure we are private."

"If I'm hearing you correctly," Kaj said carefully, "You're saying that I should trust no one. I assume that includes anyone in the palace or outside."

"That is why I asked that you bring your own team. But I cannot guarantee that attempts will not be made to influence them."

"Is there any evidence of that?" Kaj's voice was brittle.

"No. But one must be wary under the circumstances."

Kaj nodded slowly. He understood that in the same position, he might also imagine enemies everywhere.

"Can you tell me what happened that day?"

"It was a birthday lunch for my Uncle Tranh. My aunt Dechen, his wife, was there with their son, Kiran. My other aunt, Pema, and her son, Kanchan were also there. They were all killed. My sister Soniyaa has survived, but she is in critical condition. Her son, Aki, escaped without injury, but I am told he is traumatized and silent. The staff were in the kitchen except for our butler, who is among the dead. An old family retainer, Anya, was in the passageway outside the door where she was attacked. I had been called away by my secretary who sent a message that there was an urgent message from Beijing that I must answer in person. I was in the secure room when the attack took place."

"What was that call about?"

"I never found out. There was no one on the line. Before I could try to call back, security guards came into the room and locked the door. After they told me what had happened, I realized that I might have been the intended target."

"Your secretary is the one who called you away? What is your secretary's name?"

"Ananda Dorji."

"Can you think of anyone with motive to harm you?"

The King swallowed hard.

"There has been talk about my getting married. I admit I have been thinking about it. My choices are limited. I may not marry someone from England or Europe because of the colonial history. If I choose someone from India or China, I raise political obstacles. Someone from America or Australia is too foreign. Yet, when I favor a woman from Kuthan, people say she is not royal enough or that I will favor her family. After Kalyani, the monks tried to create a culture of tranquility, but clearly, we have failed, and I am left with no idea of whom they think I should marry."

"But there is someone?"

"Yes." The King looked down and almost blushed. "Her name is Tashi Dema. She is Kuthani. We met when I was reading International Relations at Oxford."

"Was she also interested in politics?"

"To start, perhaps. But she came home to attend medical school."

"Do the clans think that by marrying a Kuthani woman you would change the power balance in this country?"

"I suppose they might, but who would benefit? We have little poverty and the British set how the dam proceeds are distributed."

"Are the clans still powerful?" Kaj asked. "I noticed that you refer to the areas as regions as well as clans and families."

"It is changing," the King admitted. "But we have been an independent nation for less than fifty years. Before that, the British used the clan structure if it was useful for administrative purposes but dismissed it or used the clans against one another if anyone caused them trouble."

"Does everyone working in the palace renounce their clans?"

"No. But we have tried to employ people equally from all five and the city."

"I see," Kaj said. "But with modern technology and the emphasis on international finance, isn't the city now stronger politically than the other regions?"

"That might seem so, but the families all trade in international markets. As a nation, we attempt to even out any regional advantages due to size and economy."

"And your lady is from which family?"

The King was smiling now. "She is Snow Leopard. That is the other mountain clan beside Mountain Thunder."

"Would your lady need to renounce her clan if she were to marry you?"

"By tradition perhaps, but not by law. I have not discussed it with her. Our more conservative thinkers might expect it, but there is much more at stake here than politics. We must prevent this violence from happening again. The monks' attempt to impose spiritual values was not enough. I am hoping that you can help me by sharing your observations. We need to know how we can move forward from this tragedy."

Kaj smiled quietly. "I'm not sure how much help I can give you. There are many others more qualified than I am to talk about how nations and governments work."

The King shook his head impatiently.

"That's not what we need. I studied their work when I was at Oxford. I heard them justify colonialism by talking about how they built roads and railways and hospitals. Even they admitted that those were built to serve their own needs. Before my father died, I had already made plans to come home. I was tired of the myth of empire. It looks different when you are the white man's burden. I do not want a Kuthani raj staffed by professional diplomats. I need people with integrity. I need people who can unify and see into the future.

Kaj's heart sank as he silently catalogued the baggage that he thought disqualified him from what the King was asking.

In America, we split vertically by geography and occupation and horizontally by money and race. We claim an ideal of inclusiveness that we honor only on national holidays. Our pursuit of profit is legendary, and our public life celebrates it. We demand individual rights at the expense of the community Kuthan is looking for. We support a popular culture that encourages solving our problems with a gun, and we have political parties determined to destroy one another. I don't think we've ever had a truly peaceful period in our history, and the great symbol of our culture is a bomb capable of blowing us all to pieces. Even worse, it seems we rely on the ballot box to continue our way of life without ever asking about the long-term consequences for the country.

"I think it's good for everyone to think about what the country values," Kaj said neutrally. "I promise you we will do our best to solve these crimes quickly."

"I know and appreciate that. But now you are here, there is the practical to consider. Where do you start and how can I help you?"

Kaj looked at the pool. He wished a dragon would come to the surface and give him guidance.

"Criminal investigations are not tranquil. People take offense and feel threatened. Until the crime is solved, these feelings are not the best foundation for building the unified national future you want. To solve the crime, we need your public endorsement for us to do this work."

"My staff will make your arrangements," the King said firmly. "That will remove any question of authority. I will also personally introduce you tomorrow at the public meeting. We cannot prevent the Chinese and Indian embassy staffs from visiting their citizens staying in the guest hotel, but we can keep the media away from you."

"Fair enough," Kaj said. "Media are often the larger problem. But we also need a regular channel for us to meet. We also need a way to provide regular information. A daily bulletin would lessen the need for anyone to approach the team. You want this investigation to be open to the extent possible, so any information is best coming from your office."

The King thought for a moment. "My secretary can be your liaison. If you feel we need absolute privacy, there is the secure room or this pool. Our newsroom can issue the daily bulletins. I like that idea. What else do you need?"

Kaj now asked the first of the many uncomfortable questions to emerge as the case unfolded. How the King answered would speak volumes.

"How much do you trust your secretary?"

The King looked merely thoughtful, as if he had already asked himself that question.

"Before this, I would have said completely. Now, I must say that I have no reason to believe I should not."

They both stood up at the same moment then, as if exhausted from the sharing. The King had been forced to admit that he must question the loyalty of those closest to him, and Kaj had seen the painfully tenuous position of a monarch who knows that someone may have wanted him dead. It was enough for a first meeting.

The King extended his arm toward the pathway, indicating the way back.

"I do have one more question." Kaj spoke slowly as they started back. "I heard today that Abhinav Mallik has possibly returned to Kuthan. Were you aware of this?"

The King stopped in his tracks. "Mallik? What about him?"

"I was told he might have been returned to Kuthani custody to serve out his sentence for killing Professor Whitworth."

The King's brows furrowed deeply and he shook his head. "I have not heard anything about this. Surely, you are mistaken."

"I'll look into it again." Kaj remained silent until they reached the crumbling parking lot.

Before he stepped into the van, Kaj looked back at the dense trees and tangled undergrowth they had just walked through. Perhaps it was the darkness and the silence, but he hadn't noticed before how the trees bent over as if they were listening. He did not believe in ghosts or spirits, but he had the uncomfortable feeling that they were being watched. He shuddered slightly as he climbed into the waiting Land Rover.

Long after the two men had been driven away from Kalyani, long after Kaj had been dropped off at the door of the guest hotel, and long after the King had returned to the dark place that spoke only of the permanence of death, an unaccustomed burst of wind whistled through the deserted trees and something disturbed the water in the Dragon Pool.

Whatever lay beneath the water did not break the surface. Instead, it sent ripples out in widening circles, stirring the pool's long-dormant sediment and creating tiny whirlpools that bumped against the shore.

If Kaj had been there to see this happen, he might have remembered the first line of the Bashō haiku, "The Old Pond": *furu ike ya*. He might even have added his personal interpretation to the poem's thought: *Old silence waits for action, just as winter waits for spring.* It was a sentiment of which his aikido master could be proud. It was a sentiment that Kaj was too tired to appreciate.

Chapter 6

A MIDDLE-AGED MAN DRESSED IN A loosely fitted shirt and vest worn over white baggy pants stood waiting in the entrance of the guest hotel when Kaj arrived back at the palace.

"I am Ananda Dorji, the King's secretary," the man informed him. "I am to show you to the conference room you requested."

Kaj agreed as graciously as he could. He had hoped to take a shower and call Linda. Obviously, those would have to wait.

Dorji led Kaj down the hotel's entrance hall to the bottom of an impressive flight of stairs leading up to the first and second floors. When Kaj stopped and looked up at them doubtfully, Dorji pointed to a hallway where a sign bore the single word *lift*.

"Altitude," Kaj said cryptically as they walked toward the polished brass plate and call buttons on the wall.

In the elevator, Kaj surreptitiously studied his guide. The man had the grayish look of the professional bureaucrat, the organizer of a life more important than his. No functioning office could operate without them, and the world of the wealthy and royal was littered with their names, including those who willingly fell on their sword for their employers as well as those who were forced to.

Dorji led Kaj to a pair of double doors on the third floor. He pushed them open and stood to the side of the wide doorway to allow Kaj to enter.

Kaj's first impression was of the main room's size. Four regular-sized hotel rooms could easily have fitted into it. Directly ahead was a bank of four floor-to-ceiling windows that provided a view of the palace walls, a large portion of the city of Mongarthuā, the airport now shimmering in the afternoon sun, and the distant, glistening mountains. An oversized television filled the wall between the middle two windows, with three large sofas set in an open rectangle in front of it and an oversized coffee table in between.

To the right of the entrance was a full kitchen with a counter, and next to it a dining table and chairs. Behind the table was a sideboard surmounted by a large painting of a horsetail waterfall that filled the frame. The artist had signed his name, *Lama,* with a bold flourish that defied the small size of the lettering. Across the room, another wall-sized painting by the same artist showed the foothills and snow-covered pitches of Mt. Masakatsu. Taken together, the paintings represented the exotic Kuthan that Kaj had been expecting. He knew that his police department per diem would never have stretched to a suite this size, but there was no doubt the room was his. His luggage was neatly placed on racks just inside the bedroom door.

Dorji walked over to the kitchen counter and put the room key card down on it, pushing aside a large basket of fruit containing rambutans, lychees, mangoes, bananas, and kiwis. He picked up a sealed manila envelope bearing the stamped symbol of the US State Department.

"Mr. Horne delivered this for you this afternoon. He insisted on placing it in your suite in person. I hope that was satisfactory." Dorji replaced it on the counter.

Kaj assumed that the package was the telephone Greg had promised.

Dorji then strode past the dining area, and opened a second door. This time, he stopped, looked back, and waited for Kaj to precede him.

This new room appeared to be a second bedroom to the suite but without the usual furniture. In its place were a long conference table, case boards along the walls, filing cabinets, and shelving. Best of all, Kaj noted a second door that opened directly into the outside hallway. People could enter and leave without walking through the main suite.

Dorji picked up a pile of folders and sat down at the conference table. He invited Kaj to take the place across from him and then pushed one of the folders towards him.

"Everything you requested. The envelope at the back contains the photographs taken before and after the bodies were taken away. These were taken by palace security."

Kaj removed the thick stack of pictures from the folder and laid them on the table. The photographs were clear, timed, and dated. They presented the bloody scene from multiple angles, including wide shots and closeups. Kaj studied them for some time before he returned them to the folder.

Dorji was not through. "We have taken the liberty of enlarging the palace maps and floor plans. We thought you might want to compare the photographs to them." He pointed to a stack of poster boards standing against a wall.

"Very thoughtful," Kaj said. "Are there any new reports on the survivors?"

"The Lady Soniyaa is stable, but she is still critical. Her husband, the Consul, who returned to Kuthan with you, is staying with her at the hospital. The servant, Anya, is most in danger."

"There was a child that was unharmed. We'd like to talk with him but would prefer to confer with a pediatric specialist first."

Dorji made a note of the request.

"What arrangements have been made for the Chinese medical examiners who will be working outside the hotel at the hospital morgue?"

Dorji took several sheets of paper from the folder in front of him.

"Colonel Pradhan, has arranged for their transportation and security. As requested, he will be at your meeting this afternoon to explain. There is also a list of attendees and an agenda for the meeting tomorrow."

A quick glance at the two pages of names told Kaj that the next day's meeting was becoming a full press conference. It reminded him of the press conference at the Hawaii State Capitol regarding the Whitworth case. His boss, Bob Wilson, had panicked because he thought he might have to respond to media questions deflected to him by the Governor. He could feel sympathy for him now.

Dorji continued with his briefing. "We have included contact information for palace and city offices and a list of palace employees and security personnel. Also, a duty roster shows who was in the palace on that day. You will also find copies of reports in our local media, translated when necessary."

Dorji put his head inquiringly on one side. "Is there anything we have overlooked?"

"Yes," Kaj replied firmly. "We need the King's telephone log for the last ten days. We also need a large map showing the approximate boundaries of the clans or families as well as a list of the guests staying in this guest hotel over the last month. Also, we need any information you might have regarding Abhinav Mallik, who once worked at the Consulate in Hawaii."

Kaj wasn't sure, but a shadow appeared to cross the man's face when he heard Mallik's name. Kaj's prickle began to stir. "Is there a problem?"

Dorji shook his head immediately. "I will see that you have everything."

"Mr. Dorji . . ." Kaj began.

"Ananda, please. I know that Americans are more comfortable with first names."

Kaj had the feeling that the man was determined to change the subject.

"Ananda," he nodded. "What happened four days ago? Tell me exactly what you remember even it if does not seem important."

Dorji's eyebrows both rose in what seemed to Kaj a plea for approval or understanding.

Approval about what? Kaj's prickle was now fully awake and on duty.

"I am sure you have heard that the King ordered a small party to honor his uncle. I made the arrangements but was not involved. There were rumors that he planned to discuss his possible wedding plans with his family, but the staff knew only that it was to celebrate a birthday."

"Did everyone know who the lady might be?"

"Oh, yes. The King made no secret of it. But I was surprised since I had heard that the King had asked her and she said no. Perhaps, though, she changed her mind. Ladies are known to do that now and then." Dorji looked down and gave a small, polite smile.

"Where were you when the shooting happened?"

Dorji's smile disappeared and his eyes flicked back to study Kaj's face. He answered slowly, as if measuring every word for its impact. "I was at my desk. The King returned from the hall and went into the secure room. That is where he takes international calls."

"Were you expecting him?"

Dorji looked down and shook his head.

"Did he say anything to you about why he had come back to the office?"

"No. He just said to forward calls."

"Were there any calls to forward?"

Dorji shook his head again.

"There were no calls for the King while he was at the party?"

"Dorji shook his head.

"Did you hear the shots being fired?"

"I heard a noise like fireworks. Then I heard shouting and went to the door. "The Colonel came running into the office and joined the King in the secure room. Later, the King gave us a list of people he wanted to talk to. I remained in the office until they said it was safe for the King to come out. Then I walked with him to the hall. It was a terrible sight."

"Weren't you concerned that there might still be active shooters who might have come to the office?"

"I felt it was my duty was to stay at my desk and protect the King."

Kaj looked at Dorji quizzically. Having someone lie was not an unusual problem for Kaj. In fact, he had never had a case where everyone told the truth. What was rare was the stark difference between what the King and his secretary had told him about the phone call that day. He gave an inward sigh and turned to look out through the windows at the distant mountains. The massive sheets of ice on the mountain faces were now turning cream and gold in the afternoon sun. For some reason, Patel's words came into his mind: "The wise know the rituals of water." Snow is water too. It made him wonder if he ever would understand.

"Have the Chinese and Indian teams been advised about meeting today?" he asked.

"Yes. They know. With your permission, we will set up a light supper for you in this room."

"Not in this room. Set it up in the main room next door. Only the investigative team are to come in here unless we request it. Also, please tell housekeeping not to clean this suite unless I expressly ask for service. Now, one last question. Where are the rooms of the Hawaii detectives?"

"They occupy the three rooms directly across from yours." Dorji pointed to the door that led to the outside hallway.

"And the others?"

"The Chinese doctors are in the next three rooms on the same side as the detectives. The Indian forensics team are in the five rooms on your side of the hall. For security, there will be no other rooms occupied on this floor."

"Thank you," Kaj said, "Please tell housekeeping that the same request for service applies to the Indian and Chinese teams. I think that's all for now."

Dorji stood up, clasped his hands together in a namaste, and almost ran out of the room.

Kaj looked around at the boards waiting to be filled in and the dossiers ready to be distributed and discussed. This was the police work he knew, but now made more complex by geography, history, and politics. He then spoke back to the insistent prickle, trying to reassure it.

I know. I heard it too. We'll investigate that missing phone call. But in context. This is just the start of the long road ahead. The good part is that we've arrived in one piece. We are professionals, and we will solve this crime, just as we always do. Then we'll go back to Hawaii and with any luck we will never again venture into politics, particularly not those of a country so far from home.

He stifled a yawn and went into the suite's kitchen looking for anything that might look like coffee. With cup in hand, he went over to the window and watched a pair of grey pigeons with bands of dark-brown speckles around their necks. They were sitting side by side on a ledge enjoying the afternoon warmth. The birds, at least, looked familiar in their shape if not their color. They had their backs to him and seemed to be looking out over the city of Mongarthuā, just as he was. Even the row of food carts just outside the walls seemed lulled in the afternoon sun.

The peacefulness of the view made a stark contrast to the horror of the crime-scene photographs he had just seen. He found himself wondering, and not for the only time, how such a terrible crime could have occurred in a place that was supposed to value tranquility.

Chapter 7

THE FOUR HAWAII DETECTIVES GATHERED in Kaj's conference room as the sun was setting, just before the Chinese and Indian teams were scheduled to join them. For Kaj, it was another moment for reflection, a place to draw breath before launching out into the unknown. Among other things, he wanted to make sure that his Hawaii team was settling in and safe.

Even though Kaj knew his detectives could take care of themselves, he still worried. Dr. Alvarez, his VA counselor, told him that his repressed anxiety was another legacy from the Vietnam War, along with the shrapnel in his leg. Alvarez even sounded like his aikido teacher: "Counseling and meditation only go so far. There comes a moment when you must 'see' yourself in a totally new way."

Linda, with the authority of being two years older than her husband, had her own theory. She was convinced that his anxiety was part of a predictable crisis. "Fifty isn't old anymore," she chided him. "Fifty is the new forty."

Kaj did not find either theory helpful. He was years beyond any excuse a fifties crisis could offer. Any suggestion that he should by now have found a new way to look back on his life just annoyed him. How long was he supposed to have talk therapy before the changes happened? He didn't want to write a book about his nightmares. He just wanted them to stop.

Jill was first through the door. She brought a business eye to the room's arrangements and immediately began setting up the evidence boards and maps in functional rows. She picked up the large posters Dorji had left and pinned them to the boards around the wall. Cliff soon joined her, and together they pulled chairs into place until they formed a reasonable replica of CID's work room at the Beretania Street headquarters.

"Did you have a chance to rest?" Kaj watched as Jill set up the poster of the palace grounds and circled a building with a marker.

"We requested a tour of the grounds while you were gone. The Colonel who heads palace security showed us the location of the crime scene."

She pointed to the circle she had just made on the map.

"It's located inside what they call the private residence, the royal family's living area. The crime scene is sealed, waiting for forensics to start first thing tomorrow morning. I told the Colonel you would want a thorough search of the surrounding area and that you'd explain more this afternoon."

Kaipo came in a few minutes later. What was on his mind was another matter entirely, although he had the grace to appear slightly embarrassed.

"We heard you have the royal suite. What's it like? I know Gail's going to ask. Hotels are her thing."

"Take a look," Kaj said. "But make it quick." He controlled his impatience because he knew Kaipo needed something to talk about with his girlfriend when he called her. Her family owned a hotel chain and this would be instant interest for her. Kaj knew he would have the same problem with Linda. What was there to say beyond asking how the grandbaby was doing? Kaipo needed something, anything, to drive away the awkward silences of absence.

It didn't take Kaipo long to scout the suite. "Only thing I've seen comparable is the King Kamehameha Suite in the Royal Waikiki. Impressive."

"OK," Kaj said, "tour over. Do you all have the cell phones Greg sent over?"

"Yep," Kaipo said, "and they're easy to use. Just dial 001 and the number to call back to the States."

"I called Greg on his Kuthan number, and it works." Jill looked equally satisfied.

Kaj mentally noted the number sequence to call Linda later that evening. "Are the boards set up?"

"Coming along. Starting to take shape." Jill handed a sheaf of papers to Kaipo who began writing labels on the tops of the boards to indicate the information to be recorded on them.

"The Colonel is bringing a projector. I told him to bring his own extension cords just in case. Good thing. I don't see any here."

Kaj looked around the room. As usual, Jill was creating order and efficiency. If they were climbing Masakatsu, she would be the one in the lead, installing and testing the fixed ropes. Cliff would be keeping the team together, helping them cross the crevasses while telling them how deep they were. Kaipo would be at the rear, encouraging weary stragglers to just keep on going. Kaj respected their strengths but sensed their struggles. Jill's efficiency shielded reticence, Cliff's organization covered wariness, and Kaipo's outward cheer hid vulnerability. Kaj hoped that Kaipo's girlfriend, Gail, saw the same things in Kaipo as he did.

"OK, let's get on the same page." Kaj took a chair on one side of the table while the others sat across from him.

"First order is to have introductions, then let the Colonel talk about the murder scene and planned security for the investigation. It will be trial and error how the different teams work as a group. Here are the basic assignments so far.

"Kaipo and Cliff, work liaison with the Indian forensics team for the first few days, see where they are and what they need. Tomorrow would be a good time to do a thorough inspection of the area looking for possible exits and entrances."

"Is someone from palace security going to go with us?" Kaipo asked. "The Colonel took us around the exterior premises while you were gone."

"Not identified yet. We can ask him. Start with the crime scene and work out. If you need more access, let me or Jill know, and we'll work with the palace.

"Jill, we need a liaison to the Chinese doctors, Same thing. Go to the hospital with them and see they are set. I've requested a meeting with a psychologist about the child survivor. I'll join you for that as soon as I get away from the public meeting tomorrow. If we need further technical support, Greg says John and Chris are available.

"Cliff, one extra for you. The palace has committed to issuing bulletins each day about the investigation. This is part of the King's push for openness. Tomorrow, we'll start daily team briefings in this room. That's where the afternoon bulletin information starts. The team determines what needs to be held back."

"The entire team? Every day?" Kaipo raised his eyebrows.

"That's my hope," Kaj replied. "We'll see what we get. That's how the King wants us to play it. Be prepared for things not to happen as we are used to. It will be up to us to make it work."

What Kaj did not share with the team was his increasing fear about how the Chinese and Indian teams would get along, let alone work together. Greg's assessment of their competing agenda sounded bleak and the King's doubts only confirmed it. How in the world could he be expected to form them into team when they throw rocks at each other over their borders? He forced down his doubts and prepared himself for whatever was coming through the door.

When he looked up, he saw the first of them. The Chinese delegation had arrived early, standing indecisively in the doorway until Kaj crossed the room to greet them.

The team leader seemed obvious by the deference granted her. Her hair was naturally grey but cut in a slightly bouffant style. Her dark business dress was softened by a light, tailored jacket that hinted at the white coats of her profession. Even her slight frown managed to suggest polite skepticism and confidence. Kaj had read her bio. Dr. Yunyi Nie, in the Western form of her name, had extensive experience as a medical examiner and professor of forensic pathology. She was also director of the national organization responsible for licensing Chinese medical examiners. Kaj wondered how much she, or anyone similarly prominent, had given up to achieve such success.

Next to her was a beaming man in a dark suit who seemed to be on tiptoes, leaning forward with an enthusiasm that reminded Kaj of Dr. Howes, Hawaii's Medical Examiner. Perhaps it went with the job itself. Howes had said he preferred uncomplaining clients. Kaj guessed this was Mr. Chengda Liu, the senior pathology technician. He looked like an earnest man, a rule-follower, who might be enjoying a vacation from his regular job.

Standing behind them was the second ME. Dr. Haoyu Xue was a lean man with a narrow face dominated by high cheekbones and a pair of large, trifocal glasses. He was professor of forensic pathology at a prestigious Beijing medical school. He was also a consultant to numerous law enforcement agencies and had just completed a workshop on forensic biotechnology in California. Kaj sensed austerity and obsessive perfectionism. Kaj wondered how this man would react once he learned what Kaj had in mind.

Kaj only had time to shake hands before a small knot of people arrived at the door, precise to the minute. The first through the door was a beaming Colonel Pradhan. He was dressed in army fatigues with a small beret that tipped to one side of his head. Somehow, Kaj had expected him to be very tall. In fact, the Colonel was shorter than Kaj's 5′10″ by several inches.

The Indian forensics team was right behind the Colonel. Kaj looked expectantly for Dr. Sharma, but there was no one there who looked remotely like a television star. Instead, there were three slightly disgruntled technicians and one much younger man whom Kaj assumed must be Sharma's graduate student.

Kaj addressed the man who appeared to be the team leader.

"Did Dr. Sharma travel with you?" he asked.

"No," the man replied. "He makes his own arrangements."

"Dr. Sharma prefers to fly," the graduate student broke in brightly.

"Undoubtedly, first class," the leader said under his breath, but perhaps a little more loudly than he had intended.

"Why not?' the graduate student burst out with eager eyes and youthful impetuousness. "Dr. Sharma is a god."

The team leader assumed a long-suffering expression while Kaj's left eyebrow twitched. "Were you on the flight with Dr. Sharma?"

"Oh no," the student said in something approaching shock. "I drove up with the lab. I sat on a fold-down chair in the back."

Just then, the god himself appeared through the doorway, without apology or explanation.

Kaj took a moment to study him as they shook hands. Where the rest of the Indian team were dressed simply in slacks and shirt, Sharma was dressed in a white long-sleeved shirt, white trousers, and a long black vest. His grey hair was close-cropped to his head, and he had an aquiline nose to rival that of Hawaii Forensics Director Eagle Bott, who once told the detectives that his name and nose were aristocratic. If Sharma were to make the same claim to nobility as Eagle-Bott, Kaj doubted anyone would argue.

"Good evening," Kaj said as he motioned for everyone to come to the table.

As they settled, the feeling of doubt was palpable. Nie's mouth was set in an unbending line. Xue looked bored and ready to object to everything. Sharma had a small, cynical smile, making Kaj suspect that the man was wondering why Kaj was at the head of the table and not him. The Indian mobile lab team looked mildly curious. The only one who looked excited was the graduate student, and that was probably because he did not fully understand the awkwardness.

Kaj took a deep breath and began.

"As you know, King Raju asked the Hawaii Police Department for assistance in conducting this investigation. HPD was glad to respond and the Criminal Investigation Division assigned us to the case. I would like to introduce the team to you.

"I am Inspector Kajiwara, and I have with me Detectives Jill Nakamura, Clifford Lee, and Kaipo Kahana. Between us, we have more years of experience in criminal investigation than we like to admit."

Only Colonel Pradhan smiled slightly, but he was about the same age as Kaj and probably more inclined to give a weak joke the benefit of the doubt.

"We are also," Kaj paused for emphasis, "the team that worked with the Kuthani Consulate in Honolulu to investigate the murder of Hawaii State University Professor Harrison Whitworth."

For a moment there was silence, and Kaj began to worry that his key revelation had fallen flat. Perhaps they had not known Whitworth's connection with the King's family.

But then everyone started to speak at once.

"A terrible loss," he heard Sharma say. "A tragedy," Nie corrected him. "A truly great man, a Nobel Prize winner," Xue said. Even the graduate student chimed in: "He spoke at our university. Brilliant." The sound in the room rose as anyone with any connection to Whitworth wanted to explain how. The exchanges went on for some moments. Whitworth, it seemed, often provided keynote speeches at international conferences and was a regular visitor to the South Asian region.

The chatter changed the room's atmosphere. The Whitworth case had bought the Honolulu detectives their place in history. The goodwill carried over when the prepared folders were distributed and people started looking through them. Kaj watched and wondered how much time Harrison Whitworth had bought them.

"Dr. Nie and Dr. Sharma," Kaj called out after a few moments, "would you introduce your teams?"

Nie gave a rapid, professional outline of her team's qualifications and looked over at Sharma with a satisfied smile. Sharma then gave a description of his own but rapidly turned to the Mobile Lab director, now revealed to be Bibek Agarwahl, and asked him to introduce the two lab specialists and explain their duties. They were Adil Achari and Prabal Choudhary, who, Agarwahl assured everyone, were the highly trained team who examined the crime scenes, did the lab analysis, and were factory trained on the operation of the mobile lab itself. Choudhary, in addition, had received advanced training in DNA collection and analysis, and Achari specialized in ballistics and blood trace evidence.

Sharma then leaned forward across the table and spoke with conviction about the major investment the Indian government had made in sending the mobile lab to the investigation.

"The New Delhi mobile lab is absolute state of the art. A plus plus. It is custom built and has the latest equipment: Photography, fingerprint, firearms identification, stereo microscopes, and biosensors. You must let us show you."

Nie raised an eyebrow and gave a small smile to Liu. Kaj guessed what she was thinking. Most of the lab's technology had probably been made in China. Fortunately, from Kaj's point of view, she said nothing.

"Dr. Sharma," Kaj said quickly, "you have a graduate student with you, is that correct?"

Sharma looked startled for a moment. He glanced at the young man on his left as if he had forgotten him.

"Yes, Sanjay Lal is one of my graduate students. He has his MS in forensic science. He is interested in international crime detection. He is here to observe and be useful while he finds the research question for his dissertation."

Sanjay leaned forward and nodded with enthusiasm. His expression suggested that he was overawed to be in the company of such distinguished professionals. He did not speak. It was clear he was not expected to.

The Colonel rose to his feet when Kaj called his name. He inserted a disc into the computer, and the crime scene filled half the wall behind him. Cliff and Jill went to the boards and waited.

"The King told us that he did not wish to have security personnel in the immediate vicinity of the palace residence."

The Colonel had hardly begun when he was interrupted by a disturbance at the door. He snapped to full attention when he saw who it was. Everyone looked around as the King walked briskly into the room. He was followed by a security guard who saluted the Colonel and then remained at ease in the doorway with his hands clasped, palms out, military style, behind his back. Jill immediately turned off the projector.

"Please sit down," the King said as he walked up to Kaj, shook hands with him, and looked around the room. The Hawaii detectives remained standing, aware that the King had made this appearance to give them his support.

"This is your first meeting, and I do not plan to take long. This may be my only chance to greet you in person until the investigation is over. I want to thank the People's Republic of China, the Government of India, and the US State Department and the State of Hawaii, for responding to our request. Kuthan is deeply grateful, as I am on behalf of my family.

"I know it was not easy to set aside your professional obligations to come on short notice. You are our guests, and if you have not visited Kuthan before, I hope that you can return one day under much better circumstances. In the meantime, we will do everything we can to make your stay comfortable. You are in the capable hands of Inspector Kajiwara and his team, as well as Colonel Pradhan and his security staff. I have asked Inspector Kajiwara to let us know if there is anything further you need."

He looked around the room for confirmation.

"I have made a special request of Inspector Kajiwara, and I will make it also of you. It is my wish that this investigation be made with the greatest amount of openness possible for the sake of our relations with your countries. I do not want this request to undermine your work in any way. I am sure that he will be discussing this with you.

"I will not take any more of your time. So let me thank you again for your presence and please know how much this nation appreciates your service"

"Thank you, Sir," Kaj said as the King shook his hand again, accepted the Colonel's salute, and left them to their meeting.

Once the King had left the room, the Colonel continued his presentation.

"There was no guard detail inside the private area at the request of the King. But there were guards outside the residence walls and close to the guest hotel. There were also security detachments at the main entrances to the lower office levels. When the shooting began, we implemented our emergency procedures and searched the area. However, we found no evidence of intruders. We assisted with the removal of the survivors and then photographed the crime scene before and after the removal of the victims. Security staffing at all entrances was doubled and has remained so. The palace remains on high alert."

The Colonel then began clicking through the pictures. He went slowly, showing the multiple pictures of each body, letting them see the position in relation to one another. The first body was identified as Tranh Soöng. Number two was identified as Ajeet Singh, the Sikh butler. Three and four were identified as Dechen, Tranh's wife, and her sister, Pema. Number five, was Pema's son, Kanchan. Number six, at some distance from the others, was Thranh and Dechen's son, Kiran. Then there were wide shots, showing the positions of the bodies from various vantage points. These showed the outlined positions of the three survivors, including the old woman who was the only victim outside of the hall.

"These crime scene photographs are good quality," Nie observed. Her tone implied that it was surprising.

The Colonel merely smiled.

"Yes, Madam," he replied. "The British Army trained us to document war crimes. We are well trained."

"How compromised is the crime scene?" Xue sat back in his chair as if wanting to doubt what he was seeing but not quite finding reason to do it.

"The only persons who entered without protective gear were the first responders. These were security officers and the palace medical staff. There was urgency in the search for survivors. After that, anyone entering for the purpose of documentation or removing the bodies was fully gloved and wearing protective covering. We kept careful records and preserved as much intact as we could."

"What were your preliminary observations?" Sharma asked.

"We could not rule out participation by someone already present in the palace," the Colonel replied carefully. "But we did not go further in our investigation as the King requested us to wait for your teams to arrive."

"Two of the victims were not part of the royal family," Kaj said.

The Colonel nodded. "The butler was the only palace staff present. The meal service had been concluded, and the serving staff were gathered in the kitchen. The other was an old-age pensioner in residence in the palace, living in a favor apartment because of her long service."

"Is there any indication what she was doing in the hallway?" Jill asked.

"We were told by the staff that she had been the King's nanny and liked to observe the family from a distance when they had gatherings. The staff considered her harmless and always prepared a meal for her."

Kaipo blinked a little in the bright projector light as he stepped out of the dark. "Colonel, is the palace equipped with external security cameras?"

"Yes, Sir. The cameras are located at the perimeter, inside the interior passageways, and at the main entrance doors and hillside offices."

"But not inside the private residence?"

"No," the Colonel admitted.

"Is that footage available?" Kaj asked.

"Yes, Inspector, we have downloaded it and I have brought a computer file with me. It contains the record of the entire day from every active camera on site. We have already looked at it but were not able to see any evidence of traffic or individuals we did not recognize."

The Colonel handed the disc to Kaj, who immediately handed it to Jill.

"Colonel, could you arrange for Detectives Lee and Kahana to tour the areas under the surveillance of these cameras tomorrow?"

"I will be glad to show them myself."

"Speaking of tomorrow, what are the arrangements for transporting the medical team to the hospital?"

"Palace vans and drivers are available at your convenience. For security purposes, two officers will always accompany any of you when you are off the palace grounds."

"We will want an early start tomorrow," Nie said. "We brought equipment that we need to assemble. I understand it was delivered to the hospital."

"My officers transported it from the airport and watched as it was secured. The hospital informed us that you will be using their facilities and personnel by prior arrangement."

Nie gave a small, smile. "Yes, we have agreements with the hospital and medical school. Not all of us have mobile labs to drive." She gave a small, sly smile in the direction of the Indian delegation.

"Such a luxury," Sharma said with a magnanimous nod.

"Thank you for your time, Colonel," Kaj said. "We will see you tomorrow then."

Kaj watched the Colonel leave before he turned to look at the assembled professional talent.

"I have some special requests of you," he said. "The first involves the way we work together. I want you think of the people in this room as a team. That means that, as we go along, we will be asking to you look at the case more broadly than through your own expertise."

"What does that mean?" Xue looked perplexed and slightly offended.

Dr. Sharma looked gleeful. "I think he means that medical examiners should talk with forensics experts. Even listen to us."

"The point is," Kaj interrupted, "that I will ask this group to work together in a different way."

Xue's cheeks had started to turn pink. He glared at Sharma. "I expected to do the autopsies and leave immediately. I have other commitments."

Kaj began to see evidence of what Greg had warned him. The narrow-faced, intellectual Chinese medical examiner and the dramatic, optimistic Indian forensics director had taken immediate dislike to one another. Greg's earlier words about working around Kuthan took on new meaning. Kaj ignored Xue's objection and considered his next words carefully.

"You heard the King's call for us to work openly. To honor that, the plan is for us to meet in this room every afternoon. We will use that time to report the day's findings and record them on these boards." Kaj pointed to the posters around the walls. "We will review the evidence together, advise the palace on what information can be released, and decide on next steps. This is how we honor the King's request. It was his family that was killed. He deserves that from us."

There was silence for several minutes.

"I volunteer," said Sanjay excitedly.

"Volunteer for what?" Sharma said dryly.

"To help. To do anything that you want. I want to study crime investigation of the future. Criminals do not respect borders. Investigations must be multinational. People must think beyond their specialties."

"Are you already writing your dissertation?" Sharma's voice was dripping with irony.

"Actually, he's right," Kaj said. "We are all outsiders here."

"This is not our protocol," Nie said. She sounded alarmed, as if deviating from established practice was threating in some way. "You are asking medical examiners to work directly with forensics clinicians and then discuss the findings with detectives."

"That sounds fair," Kaj nodded. "Out of the box, for all of us. Uncomfortable, perhaps, but making maximum use of experience and brain power."

"This is nonsense," Xue said.

Sharma raised his eyebrows with an amused expression. "We will be delighted to cooperate and collaborate with our esteemed colleagues from the People's Republic of China." Sharma bowed in their direction in case they had missed his sarcasm.

Kaj felt relieved that Sharma had not blown them a kiss. That would have landed like a middle-finger salute.

"We need time," Nie gave Sharma the withering look mothers save for children misbehaving out in public.

"Now, there is one more thing," Kaj said, deliberately ignoring her as he had Xue.

All eyes in the room turned on him suspiciously.

"I have no doubt that you will be asked by your home governments about how the investigation is proceeding. The usual direction is to treat everything with complete confidentiality. Well, I am going to tell you the opposite. You are welcome to report to your home governments."

Kaj smiled benignly as people looked at one another, some frowning, others with raised eyebrows.

"Just one request before you do. Please restrict what you say to facts and professional opinion only. Do not speculate."

The Chinese lab tech looked very worried. He spoke up for the first time. "What is the difference between *fact*, *opinion*, and *speculate*?"

Kaj spoke deliberately and slowly as if he were delivering the results of ground-breaking research.

"A *fact* is something for which you have evidence. For example: Today we performed three autopsies and recovered six partial shell casings."

He looked around the room knowing that there would be no doubt of the meaning of the English word. He moved on to the next.

"An *opinion* is your professional judgment based on evidence. You might say, 'In our professional judgement, we believe there were two weapons used'."

It was the third word, *speculation*, where he expected there might be trouble. He was right. Immediately upon hearing it, Liu broke in. "Is that the same as making a guess?"

"A little," Kaj conceded. "But it is based on experience so it is more a statement of professional judgement waiting for the facts. It would be something like 'We think the King may have made a mistake when he imported four Honolulu detectives to solve a murder when there were qualified people already in the region'."

It took a moment. Then someone gave a small gasp that was followed by a chuckle that others picked up around the room. They had got the point.

"Now," Kaj said as he deliberately cut off any further discussion, "I understand that a light supper of some kind is waiting for us in the next room. We should take advantage of it and get some sleep. We have a long day ahead."

Chapter 8

The Chinese and Indian teams lingered in Kaj's suite after claiming their supper boxes. But that did not mean the start of collegiality. The Chinese doctors sat at the suite's dining table while the Indian team collected at the low table in front of the television. It was clear that they were discussing Kaj's plan because now and then one of them turned around to stare at the other table. The Hawaii detectives walked around the room, mingling as they could. But the evening left no illusion. No one seemed clear on what was needed or even if they wanted to do it.

It was late evening when the room finally cleared and Kaj could call Linda. By that time, twilight played along the tops of the mountain range to the northwest. The light was a sliver of gold beneath a layer of luminous silver grey, and above it a blackness that even city lights could not penetrate. As the light continued to dim, masses of stars appeared in the unpolluted sky. Under these conditions, Kaj imagined that if he were awake and looked in the right direction, he would see the thick arch and colors of the Milky Way as he had never seen them before.

"What's the time there?" he asked when Linda picked up the phone.

"Five a.m." her sleepy voice replied. "It doesn't matter. I'm just glad to hear your voice."

"Me too," Kaj replied sincerely. Linda's voice meant a return to the familiar.

"Is this a secure line?" Linda's voice was clear now, and she was becoming her usual analytic self.

"Probably not. Greg says that everyone over here knows everyone else's business, so I assume we may be overheard. I don't care. I'll stand in front of the windows and make it easy for them if they've got long distance pick-up microphones. They should have. I saw some on sale at Radio Shack in Honolulu."

"If they bought them over here, I doubt they came from Radio Shack. Were you able to get any sleep?"

He knew she meant his nightmares.

"I slept on the plane going over and caught a nap this afternoon. I'm tired, so I expect to sleep tonight. I've taken it easy because I'm feeling the altitude."

"Just take care of yourself," she said.

The rest of the conversation was about the flight and the baby. It didn't matter to Kaj. It was just hearing her voice that made the call worthwhile.

He went down early next morning and found himself in the same downstairs room where he had eaten the dumplings and noodles the day before, except that it had been transformed. A series of long tables had been brought together to form an open u-shape at the front, and chairs had been lined up in rows in front of the opening. He counted five rows of six chairs. The tables now had microphones, name tags, notepads, water jugs, and glasses. A crowd was clearly expected, as two additional rows of single chairs for observers had been placed along the walls.

"Thought you'd be here early." Greg looked surprisingly bright for his lack of sleep. "Just wanted to tell you that we've been picking up chatter. It's the Chinese asking what Americans mean when they talk about *facts, opinion,* and *speculation.* Anything to do with you?"

"Could be. Just setting a few ground rules. Good things to keep in mind at any time."

"Well, you made an impact. Let me know. I'm willing to help although I function only as an advisor since you're working on contract to the King."

Kaj waited while the rest of his team caught up with them.

Jill looked around the room. "Did they say how many people would be here?"

Greg gave a small shrug. "The list keeps growing. The home embassies insisted on having their staffs here, and the media want to meet your team. It's typical Kuthan, though. It's much easier to be tranquil if you just say yes."

"I won't be saying yes without good reason," Kaj said with some emphasis.

"Which is why you're in charge."

"Mr. Greg," a cheery voice called out and a hand appeared to be shaken. "How is the spy business these days?"

Everyone instantly pivoted in place to face the speaker. With his round face and bland smile, the speaker resembled a classical Chinese painting. He could be the poet sitting under a tree, his legs crossed, his arms buried in the deep sleeves of his robe, and a scroll unrolled in front of him. His clothes were rumpled. Yet on him, the creased clothing somehow looked picturesque. A photograph of him ought to be labeled "Picture of the Crumpled Diplomat."

"Meng," Greg replied nonchalantly, "you've been in Moscow too long. You're starting to sound decadent."

Kaj looked at the man with interest. So, this was Meng. He looked harmless enough, except Kaj knew he wasn't. But the larger surprise was Greg. Kaj saw a new, suave Greg. Not 007, but clearly someone at ease playing out in the world. It made him wonder what Meng might have told the Chinese medical team about what to expect from Americans.

Meng's eyes crinkled. "Surely, *fin de siècle*? I am a modest fellow."

"And how was your flight?" Greg continued the banter.

"Much less comfortable than yours. We had turbulence from Chengdu. I hit my head on the seat in front of me. See the bruise? Kuthan did not send the royal jet for us. Ours was small, noisy, and smelled of fertilizer. Then they held us up at the airport for hours going through the autopsy equipment the good doctors brought with them. Unfriendly when we're trying to do a favor to this country."

"But you arrived safely," Greg observed.

"More or less. Certainly not the friendly skies."

Without waiting for any introduction, Meng extended his hand to Kaj.

"Inspector Kajiwara. A pleasure to meet the legend. I am known as Meng because my name is unpronounceable to Westerners."

He gave a self-satisfied chuckle suggesting that this was a favorite conversation starter, even if he was the only one talking.

"I understand you have a new grandson named William Goro. You honor your war-hero father. My condolences on death of your father, but my congratulations on your grandson. Grandchildren are so much nicer. You turn them back to their parents when they misbehave. I understand that you are in charge. I want to assure you that the People's Republic of China is pleased to work with you. Our medical staff will work with their colleagues as you need. And that is a fact."

He did not wait for a reply. He turned next to Jill.

"Detective Nakamura. I was saddened to hear that Mr. Harkin was killed in a climbing accident. I met him when he was in Beijing to photograph the Forbidden City. Beautiful pictures. I went there myself to see where he stood when he took them. I also understand that he climbed quite widely in the Chinese Himalayas. I was sorry for your loss. But I am glad also that you have found another good man."

Jill tensed, so Kaj quietly placed his hand under her elbow. Meng, however, had already moved on with his attention.

"Detective Kahana. Ah, I understand that you are a very good friend of Miss Gail Chen, perhaps even more? I am sure you know that her family is discussing a new Margate hotel in Shanghai. Much discussion, much planning needed, of course. How do you put it? Water must flow under the bridge? We will hope to welcome you both to China for the grand opening, if it happens."

Kaj stole a quick look at Kaipo. For once, Kaipo was standing mute with his mouth partly open. Under other circumstances, Kaipo's silence might have been amusing, but Kaj knew that Kaipo was deliberately protecting his private life because he was still dealing with the fallout from a difficult divorce. Kaj felt embarrassed at Meng's game of one-upmanship.

Then Meng's attention turned to Cliff, and Kaj did not know what to expect.

"Detective Lee," Meng began.

Kaj looked down and closed his eyes. Cliff was estranged from his South Korean family and did not like to talk about it.

"You have considerable family in North Korea. Did you know? They would love for you to visit them as a returnee."

If Cliff was disturbed by the news, it didn't show. In fact, he was the only one with a riposte.

"They would be welcome to visit me in Hawaii." He smiled almost cockily. "But would that be even possible? And if they did, perhaps they might like the Islands too much to want to go home."

"That's vintage Meng," Greg said as the man ambled off. "He's fishing for information."

"It sounds as if he has a lot already," Kaj replied. "He's made clear that he's in charge of the Chinese delegation. They asked his permission to work with us."

Greg nodded. "Not unexpected. Now they have permission, the doctors will cooperate. The nature of their society requires someone higher up to approve anything unusual."

"My family lived in South Korea for generations." Cliff sounded indignant.

Greg smiled. "He knows that, Cliff. He wanted to see if he could provoke you. Instead, you merely exchanged wits with him. That's the way to handle him. Welcome to a world of diplomacy that is not always diplomatic. Most of what Meng knows is public record, but he wants you to think you're being watched. A little intimidation out of the Chinese playbook. They expect us to have the same information on them."

"Do we?" Cliff asked. The question hung in the air.

The attendees began to arrive in almost prearranged knots of people. The media went to the chairs along the walls. Guests took the chairs facing the tables. The dignitaries and management teams arrived last and went to the head tables. Kaj had the feeling that they had come straight from a private meeting, probably with the King.

When everyone was seated, it was only a few minutes before the King entered the room along with the Colonel and two other security officers who stood off to the side, a visible reminder of the need for high security.

The King looked around for Kaj and gestured for him to join him at the front table. Every eye in the room turned to watch Kaj walk to the front.

"Good morning," the King said briskly. "I have three purposes today. The first is to introduce the members of the team investigating the attack on the palace; the second is to introduce the members of the governing council and representatives of the regions to them; and the third is to request your cooperation and assistance. Because this is a national emergency, I have asked that the investigation be as open as possible. Inspector Kajiwara, whom I will introduce in a moment, will have more information for you on how that will happen. I ask the representatives here to cooperate fully with his team."

The King looked along the tables on either side of him. "I want to thank the People's Republic of China for sending a distinguished team of medical examiners. I also want to thank the Government of India for sending a mobile lab and a highly qualified team of forensics specialists. I am told that these teams are already at work as we speak. Again, I ask each of you to give them your fullest cooperation and support.

"In order to coordinate these efforts, I requested that the State of Hawaii send to Kuthan the Hawaii detectives who worked with our Consulate to solve the murder of Dr. Harrison Whitworth. As we all know, Dr. Whitworth worked with my father, helping us build our medical services and open our first medical school in collaboration with Hawaii State University. He was a good friend to this country. I am grateful to the US State Department and the State of Hawaii for allowing Inspector Kajiwara and his team to be here."

Kaj noticed how the people at the table nodded agreement. He wondered if Hawaii understood how much influence and respect the State and its university enjoyed in Asia. He would not have known if he hadn't worked the Whitworth case, and he was an HSU graduate himself. It was only now, traveling outside Hawaii, that he could see the impact. Universities were strange things, inventive, flawed, and yet essential without always being credited for it. But then, that was true of HPD, wasn't it? The vital work of hundreds of un-sung crime-detection personnel was just assumed. It got wrapped up into two questions: how fast was the crime solved, and did the public like the sentencing?

"At this time, I would like to introduce Inspector Kajiwara and ask him to introduce his team. Then I will ask the representatives here to introduce themselves."

The King stood back and yielded the microphone to Kaj.

Kaj took a deep breath. There was no handing over the public speaking to his boss. He was the boss. He looked out at the sea of faces and set about making the introductions that he needed to.

He started by introducing Jill, Cliff, and Kaipo. He then repeated what the King had told them—that the medical and forensic teams were already at work—and introduced Dr. Sharma as the forensics director. Sharma stood up with a broad smile, looked around, and waved. Kaj also mentioned Dr. Nie, the director of the Chinese medical team who was already at the hospital commencing the autopsies. He explained that the palace would be issuing daily bulletins regarding the investigation to the media and then ended by stressing that the preliminary examination of the crime scene and that the victims were the immediate focus."

He was not sure whether the King welcomed questions, but he got one anyway.

One of the media representatives at the back of the room asked loudly what kind of information would be coming in the daily bulletins.

Kaj looked inquiringly at the King, who nodded.

"There will be a daily meeting during which the team will exchange and record information from the day's work. Unless the information is too sensitive to release, the results will be provided to the palace public affairs office and then issued to you as a bulletin."

Another question followed.

"Are you going to release information on these doctors and experts you're bringing in?"

The King stood up to control the questions before they could overwhelm the meeting.

"Contact the public affairs office. The information is available on request." He then turned to the man sitting at his right and asked him to introduce himself.

The names came and went as the process went down the table. Kaj knew he had the list and could refer to it later if needed. He paid the most attention to the Governing Council members, city officials, and administrators of various kinds, including from the monasteries.

The three groups were an interesting lot. The administrators from the city and lowland clans were mainly men in dark suits. The foothills clans and mountain clans were more colorful, and the monks stood out because of the vivid purple of their robes. Mountain Thunder was represented by the only woman, who gave her name as Darya Lhotse. She wore a long, wrapped skirt with a repeating diagonal pattern underneath a Western suit jacket, finished off by a pair of high-heeled shoes and a black leather Gucci handbag. There was no mistaking her among the black suits.

Once the briefing came to an end, indicated by the King standing up once more and starting to shake hands, Kaj found himself on his own. Jill had quietly dodged her way to the car waiting to take her to the hospital. Sharma, Kaipo, and Cliff had left together to go to the crime scene. Ordinarily, he would have gone straight to the crime scene himself, but he felt constrained by protocol. Only Greg and the Colonel were left to offer him any support. He waited stoically for what he assumed would be the cluster of people with varying reasons for wanting him to remember them.

As it turned out, most just wanted to give their condolences to the King and then affirm their support for the Hawaii detectives. Even the media was polite. He appreciated the connections that were offered, particularly when an older Australian pressed his business card firmly into Kaj's hand.

"Eric Strobel," he said. "Strobel Engineering Global Associates. We provide contractual engineering, project maintenance and design, and planning services to the City of Mongarthuā, the Dam Board, and the Palace."

"Buildings and roads?" Kaj asked. The man looked like an engineer with rimless glasses, an open jacket that looked slightly faded from long days in the sun, and a shirt pocket that looked as if it might contain a plastic protector. No sign of a pen, though.

"Anything the country needs. We're a family company, based in Sydney. My grandfather started it after he emigrated from England in 1930. In Kuthan, we've worked on high-rise buildings in the city, additions to the palace, snow-load bridges in the mountains, irrigation systems in the south, and, of course, the dam. If you need any help with your investigation, just give us a call."

As the numbers of well-wishers dwindled, Kaj noticed that the monks and the clan representatives had held back, with one exception. Darya Lhotse of Mountain Thunder had made sure she was the last to speak to Kaj. She quickly made her interests clear.

"My grandfather has something to say to you, and he expects to see you right away. He no longer travels, so you will have to come to him."

Kaj looked at her with bemusement. Darya clearly expected that her request would be met without question or hesitation.

"That will not be possible. The investigation is just starting. Perhaps another time?"

"Grandfather insists. He says you have heard the history of Kalyani and he needs to correct the errors." She glanced dismissively over at the Colonel. "Have him arrange it for you."

"I will have to see. . .," Kaj began.

"We shall expect you. Sooner rather than later." Darya gave Kaj a look that implied he ought to have realized that resistance was futile. "And that is the way it is."

She turned on her high heels and walked rapidly towards the door.

"Mountain Thunder can be quite commanding," the Colonel said admiringly as he watched Darya's dramatic exit from the room. "She is the force behind the family although Grandpa Lhotse is still the head."

"She wants me to drop everything because her grandfather wants to talk with me?"

"Not surprising. As she told you, he will want to tell you the story of Kalyani from their point of view."

"Are you suggesting that I go?" Kaj's eyebrows rose and his hair line jumped.

"Mountain Thunder generally gets what they want. If you don't agree, they will ask the King to send you."

Kaj gave an inelegant snort. "And he would? Are you telling me I must go?"

The Colonel gave his trademark smile, the one that crinkled his eyes and made him looked particularly good humored. "I strongly suggest it. Now, do you want to go tomorrow or the day after?"

"How does this work?"

"The palace will arrange a flight for you and anyone else you want to take. I will come with you. I always like to see the mountains. They remind me of home."

"I'm envious," Greg said. "Wish I could come too. But we'll keep track of you."

"I want another day to deal with the lower oxygen. Make it the day after tomorrow. Jill will come too."

Kaj's voice was heavy with resignation. He had wanted to interview Mountain Thunder anyway, but on his own terms.

The Colonel chuckled again. "They have a saying up there: 'And that is the way it is'."

"So, I hear," Kaj said with a frown.

Chapter 9

With the public briefing over, Kaj finally had his chance to see the crime scene. It was inside a large hall that looked like an add-on to another building. The mobile lab was drawn up next to it and Kaj immediately spotted Sanjay, who was sitting in the lab's open back door swinging his legs despondently.

"Hello," Kaj said to him. "Where is everyone?"

Sanjay nodded his head to the open doors of the hall. "The Colonel took your detectives somewhere to look at underground passages. Dr. Sharma and the others are inside. They told me to watch the lab. I do not know what for."

Kaj smiled. "Our officers do guard duty too. It gets boring sometimes, but it's part of the job."

Sanjay did not look mollified.

Kaj put his hand on the student's shoulder. "Tell you what. When you have a job title and an office, people will listen. That's all you need. Right now, as a student, it's your job to learn."

"So, you're saying that things will get better." Sanjay could barely conceal his scorn. "That is all I ever hear."

"I was told that too," Kaj said with rueful amusement. "I enjoyed hearing it as much as you do. But no one listened to me when I was a recruit, and a new police officer lacks authority. Give that officer some grey hairs and a title, and people respond. And not just people. Some people I know back in Hawaii wanted to raise sheep, so they brought in Australian sheepdogs to herd them. One was adult, the other a puppy. Even though the puppy knew how to herd, those sheep would not listen. But one bark from the adult meant nipped heels so the sheep did whatever the dog wanted. Right now, you're an amateur despite your degrees. But just wait. Things change in an instant."

"So, I am a puppy?" Sanjay even managed a slight smile. "Can I nip a heel or two?"

"Appropriately, young man. Only when it's appropriate."

Kaj laughed as he went over to the doors and peered into the gloom. He could see Sharma and the lab techs, all fully covered in overalls and masks, laying out grids and collecting samples.

It was Sharma who noticed Kaj. He left off what he was doing and guided Kaj back outside, where he took off his mask and took a deep breath of outside air.

"This is going to take days to process properly," he grumbled. "This scene should have been examined immediately. All we have now are the security pictures to locate the bodies. The footprints are a nightmare. Are they from the security guards? From the ambulance or morgue workers? From the killers? We must digitize the pictures, do overlays, and trace where the tracks lead to and from."

"Any theories so far?"

"We have recovered shell casings. We will have more tonight. We think that the attackers entered from the inside corridor." Sharma shrugged dramatically. "We are surmounted by difficulties. A whole hillside of them. But we shall overcome them, and we shall produce splendid results. You will see."

Somebody called Sharma's name. The insistence in the man's voice meant only one thing—something had been found. Both Sharma and Kaj were instantly on alert.

One of the lab technicians, came through the front doors and shouted something in Hindi to Sharma before turning around and returning into the building.

"It seems my promise is coming true," Sharma said. "Adil says he has found a blood trail leading down the inside corridor. If you want to see this, come through the kitchen area on the side of the building. We are finished there."

Chapter 10

Having decided to try a small nip on the heel of Dr. Sharma's authority by abandoning the mobile lab, Sanjay led Kaj through the suggested side door into a kitchen area left as it was when the shooting started. Food lay where it fell, dishes were piled in the sinks, and service trays were scattered in disarray on the floor and counters. It looked as if there had been a small explosion. Kaj did not envy whoever would have to clean it.

Sharma had taken a short cut through the crime scene and met them in the central corridor, where he had shoe covers, flashlights, and gloves. He scowled when he saw Sanjay but handed the items to him anyway.

Sharma pointed down the hall to a nondescript door that looked as if it opened into a broom closet. "Adil says he followed the blood trail down the hallway to where it ended outside that door."

"What's behind it?" Kaj asked.

"A storage room. Adil says the blood trail continues inside but suddenly ends."

Kaj and Sanjay followed Sharma down the passage, carefully avoiding the line of numbered evidence cards that marked the blood trail and the outline that indicated where the old woman, Anya, had fallen. The open door let them into a small room lit by a humming fluorescent fixture that revealed shelving along the walls. Serving dishes and boxes of cleaning supplies were stacked in the space, and, at first glance, nothing looked disturbed.

"Stay by the door, Sanjay," Sharma directed as he and Kaj went deeper into the room. "Adil says that one section of the shelving looks different and there are marks on the floor."

They both trained their flashlights on the floor and got down on their knees to look.

"There's a semi-circular scrape on the floor beneath the bottom edge of that frame, and it looks fresh." Kaj pointed to the marks.

"Adil thought these shelves might have been moved recently. That is when he came to find us." Sharma stood up and dusted off his knees. "Sanjay," he shouted. "You are young and full of beans. Get in here."

The section of shelving swung out easily when Kaj and Sanjay pulled on it. It revealed an opening in the floor with a fixed ladder leading down into darkness. A steady breeze of air escaped up from the dark. It smelled musty but not moldy.

"Someone needs to go down there." Sharma's observation was rhetorical because he left little doubt about who it was going to be.

Sanjay looked doubtful. "What am I looking for?"

"Anything you can find," his professor told him impatiently.

Sanjay sat down on the edge of the opening and tested the sturdiness of the ladder with his foot. He then took his weight on his hands and lowered himself down one step at a time. Sharma handed him his flashlight as he was about to disappear.

"What do you see?" Sharma demanded.

"Just got down," the answer came floating up.

"How far down are you?" Sharma yelled, probably a little more loudly than needed as the sound echoed in the dark below.

"I cannot touch the ceiling."

Sharma lay on his stomach to peer into the opening. Sanjay's bobbing flashlight illuminated what looked like rocky walls and rough cement floor that extended into the darkness underneath the hall.

"What can you see?" Sharma demanded again.

"Let me look around." Sanjay's beam of light grew dim as he explored. For a few moments, there was silence. Then Sanjay was back. "You need to see this," he called up.

"Tell us about it." Hearing nothing in reply, Sharma sat up and grunted with annoyance. "Who is able enough to climb down there?" It was another rhetorical question because Kaj was the only other person there.

"I'll do it." Kaj lowered himself into the opening. There was a scraping thump when he jumped off the final step.

For several minutes there was only silence and darkness until Kaj was back at the bottom looking up at Sharma.

"Sanjay's right. This area needs processing. The dust is disturbed. There is more possible blood trace. One of the walls has an opening. We'll see where it leads. OK, Sanjay?"

The flashlights faded as they walked away. Sharma sat on the edge of the opening with his feet on the ladder. He could not convince himself to venture down into the dark. That was what graduate students were for. He would have brought more of them if he could. He was rapidly becoming impatient when he heard a distant bang, yelling, and a commotion of multiple voices coming up from the darkness. "What is happening down there," he yelled.

Kaj was the first to appear, his face a pale grey in the light. Sharma moved aside from the opening to let him up.

"What did you find?" Sharma demanded.

"The area looks like a basement for this building. There is an opening in a wall that divides this building from the next one. Sanjay can tell you more. He linked up somehow with the Colonel and the detectives."

"Linked up? What does that mean?" Sharma looked appalled.

Sanjay was next up the ladder. His coveralls, his gloves, and hair were covered in plaster powder. He sneezed as he stood at the top and tried to wipe the dust of his face. He managed only to make it smear. In the weak fluorescent and flashlight lighting, he looked as if he had been sprinkled with flour.

"Where have you been?" Sharma demanded.

Sanjay was quite breathless. "There is an opening in the foundation wall. Behind it is a short passage full of rubble. I went down it. There was a sheet of wallboard at the end. I tapped it. It sounded hollow. I put my shoulder against it and it fell apart. Behind it, there was another tunnel with cables and lights in the ceiling. The Colonel and the two detectives were there. I fell on the ground in front of them."

Just then, to make matters even more complicated, the Colonel, Kaipo, and Cliff followed one another up the ladder.

"Everybody outside," Sharma said ferociously as the room filled up. "This is an active crime scene. Out. Everyone. Leave the lab something to process."

They walked back through the disarrayed kitchen and regrouped in the courtyard in front of the hall.

"Who wants to go first?" Kaj asked.

Cliff started. "The Colonel took us into a tunnel under the palace. It leads from the royal family's private residence to the security offices outside the residence walls. We were walking down the tunnel when we heard a cracking noise. Sanjay came through the tunnel wall and brought it down."

"Sanjay!" Sharma said mercilessly, "are you telling me you broke down a wall in a crime scene?"

For once, Sanjay did not look apologetic.

"I had to follow the passage."

"It is a good thing that Sanjay found the connection between the buildings," the Colonel said quietly.

Kaj looked directly and sternly at the Colonel. "Were you aware of this opening?"

"No. The main tunnel is on the map but not a passage leading under this hall."

"What are the tunnels meant for?"

"For escape if the palace was attacked."

"When was the last time someone was down there?" Cliff asked. "Wouldn't a boarded-up entrance be noticed?"

"We walked through that main tunnel immediately after the shooting. No one reported seeing anything that looked like an opening. We had no reason to look closely at the walls because we knew the security cameras had not been activated. They would have turned on if anyone had opened either the door in the palace basement or the one in the security building outside the residence walls. Those are the only working doors. I will look in the records. But I am sure the boarded up opening to this hall basement is not on our maps."

"There's fresh air under this building, so there must be some access to the outside. We need to find it," Kaipo said.

Sharma rose to the full height of his dignity.

"The tunnel is another active crime scene. It will be necessary to check with our mobile lab before any one walks through anything."

"Of course," the Colonel said respectfully. "I will order immediate research into the building plans for this hall. They should be on file. Would it be useful if we invited Strobel Engineering to meet with you? Their company built this hall."

"That would be very helpful," Kaj agreed. "We need more detailed maps of this passage system showing every possible outlet, no matter how small, no matter how inactive—windows, drains, everything. Kaipo is right. Fresh air is coming from somewhere."

"It should be on the original building plans," the Colonel promised.

"You said there are only two entrances to this tunnel?"

"Two active entrances. One is in the palace and the other is in the security building outside the residence area walls. There was a third, but it has been disabled. It was in the basement of the guest hotel."

"We need to process this tunnel and all the entrances." Sharma stressed the word *all*. "But, if possible, we need better access than going down a ladder."

The Colonel nodded. "The palace entrance to the tunnel will be much easier. That is where the detectives and I started out."

Sharma looked quite magisterial as he laid down his conditions. "This subfloor area and the connecting tunnel are crime scenes. Mr. Agarwahl must come with us. Sanjay, since you are now familiar with the tunnel and the wall you knocked down, you come as well."

Sanjay did not object and began shaking the dust off his clothes. Working a crime scene was more interesting than guarding a van in a deserted courtyard. He remembered what Kaj had said, and for a few moments, he felt that things might turn out as Kaj said they would. Perhaps he could even imagine that his bark was starting to sound less like a puppy's.

Chapter 11

THE COLONEL LED THE UNWIELDY group, now including two detectives, one inspector, one forensic director, one mobile lab director, and one graduate student, across the courtyard separating the crime scene hall and the palace residence.

A heavy double door admitted them to the residence's grand entrance hall, where the Colonel led them behind the expansive curving staircase leading up to the private apartments. Tucked out of sight was a door that looked as if it might open onto storage space for unused office furniture or cleaning supplies. But that was deceptive. Behind it was another door with a control panel of blinking lights and a panel of buttons. The second door opened once the Colonel punched in a code. When that door swung back, a bank of overhead lights came on to illuminate a flight of stone stairs and a passage carved out of the bed rock beneath the palace.

"Our movements are now being recorded," the Colonel said as they entered. "The cameras are linked to the lights. Both remain on until there is no motion detected. The lights have motion detectors set at regular intervals down the tunnel. That's to make sure that no one is accidentally left in the dark."

"Do all motion detectors trigger cameras?" Kaj asked.

The Colonel shook his head. "The cameras work only when the access doors are opened."

"And how much do the cameras record?"

"They are set for twenty meters from each of the two operational doors. About sixty feet. When the cameras are triggered, an alarm sounds that is monitored in the security office."

"That means there was no active camera at the point where Sanjay broke through the wall?"

"Correct."

"And the door connecting the guest hotel basement to the tunnel, does it also have a camera?"

"It was turned off." The Colonel looked grim as he admitted this.

"Detective Kahana will need the videos of any one entering the tunnel from either of the doors for the month prior to the shooting."

The Colonel nodded and then led them to the damaged wall where Sanjay had made his entrance.

Cliff pointed out the white debris on the floor. "This is where the wall collapsed into the tunnel and a dusty person fell through."

Kaipo studied the wall and the debris field on the floor. "It would not have been obvious. Someone had to know the opening was there. And there had to be some way the board was held in place. Someone also knew that there was no camera."

The Colonel agreed. "There was no reason to monitor this area because we did not know there had ever been an opening."

"Mr. Agarwahl and his team will find out how this happened," Sharma said with a generous sweep of his arm towards his New Delhi colleague. "We must walk carefully to preserve all the evidence for him."

Cliff shone his flashlight into the area behind the fallen board. It revealed only rubble and disturbed dust where Sanjay and the detectives had walked through earlier. He looked down to where the main tunnel disappeared into darkness.

"You said that this tunnel goes outside the palace residence walls?"

"Yes. It goes under the wall surrounding the private residence. It was meant to connect to the basement level of the hotel. But as far as we know, the hotel entrance has never been used. We disabled the locking system."

"We need to see it," Kaj said.

The Colonel once more took the lead and walked on towards the hotel. About halfway there, though, Kaipo felt a draft of air and started looking around.

"Wait a minute," he said. "There's a draft here."

He bent down and followed the invisible shaft of air until he found the source in a small grill close to the ground.

"What's this?"

The Colonel took out his map. "This one is marked on the map. It says 'flood control channel'."

Sharma studied the grill for a moment and seemed perplexed. "Mr. Agarwahl, what do you make of this?"

Agarwahl crouched down and shone his flashlight on it. "This type of grill is common. But most are installed at an angle so their weight holds them. This one is upright and has bolts."

Agarwahl shone his flashlight onto each of the bolts. "Prabal needs to perform a proper analysis, but I think these bolts may have been removed not long ago. There are tool markings. We must examine them under a microscope to be sure."

Sharma bent over to look at the bolts. "We need to know if this has been opened. But only a child can get into that space. We may need the robot."

Agarwahl reached out with both hands and took hold of the grill on either side. He had been merely intending to test how solidly the grill was attached, but instead of assessing the tensile strength restraining the grill, he lost his balance and wound up flat on his back with the grill still in his hands. He gave a loud grunt as it fell on him.

"Good God," Kaj said in the shock of the moment. "Are you all right?

Multiple hands pulled the heavy grill off Mr. Agarwahl, who sat up slowly, rubbing his ribs and wincing.

"It is a good thing you were not standing up when you fell backwards," Sharma said. "You could have broken ribs or hit your head." He picked up one of the now fallen bolts and studied it. "The threads have been sawed off. There is just enough left to hold it in place." He spread his arms in magisterial prophecy. "The attack on the palace was premeditated and planned."

No one disputed Sharma's conclusion. Kaj was relieved as he watched Agarwahl get on his hands and knees and slowly start to stand up.

"Which means," Sharma continued, "that it is critical that we know what lies beyond the grill."

He looked pointedly at Sanjay and said nothing further.

Sanjay hung his head. "It is not a big opening," he said, "What if I get stuck?"

"We will pull you out." Sharma smirked, knowing it would more likely be one of the others who made the rescue. Sanjay knew it too.

"Cliff and I will rescue you," Kaj said reassuringly.

Sanjay sat down on the floor and looked at the opening. He put his flashlight inside and slowly inserted his head and shoulders. It was tight, but he had clearance. He slithered reluctantly into the opening on his chest, inching along the rough floor, and sending back increasingly foreboding observations that suggested mounting panic.

"Cobwebs disturbed. Rat droppings. Rats are supposed to be lucky, aren't they? The Lord Ganesha likes them. No snakes so far. I hate snakes."

Then there was a long silence and darkness that made Kaj feel concerned. "Are you all right?" he yelled down the black tunnel.

A few minutes later, they heard scraping, accompanied by swearing about undefined somethings that were catching on other undefined somethings. Then Sanjay's flashlight and hands appeared. Cliff reached in and pulled Sanjay out. Once his feet were free, the student spun around to sit with his back against the tunnel wall, taking deep breaths that blew combined wallboard powder and tunnel dust off his chest.

"There's a rifle in there," he managed to get out once his breathing calmed. "The tunnel widens so I could turn around. I did not disturb the crime scene." Sanjay looked at Sharma when he said this.

"What kind of rifle? Automatic? Semi-automatic?" Sharma almost pounced on his hapless graduate student.

"That's what the robot explorer is for." Agarwahl put a kindly hand on Sanjay's shoulder.

"I didn't get close enough to see," Sanjay said plaintively. "It was dark in there. The torch did not give much light."

Kaj leaned in to whisper in the young man's ear while Sharma was distracted by shining his own flashlight into the opening. "You need to let people know you are claustrophobic."

Sanjay looked up at Kaj desperately, his eyes filled with a sudden, almost desperate pleading.

"Don't worry," Kaj said. "I won't say anything."

"This is another crime scene," Agarwahl said loudly. "We need to process the channel and grate."

Kaj turned to look at the Colonel and Sharma. "We also need to open the access door to the hotel basement. Whoever altered the grate might have come through the hotel basement. You said that you deactivated the hotel lock, Colonel. That would be for authorized users, right? There must be a master key so the system could be reactivated and the door reopened if it needed."

"There has never been reason," the Colonel began. But then he stopped. "These locks are electronic. It would require a security code to reactivate them. We were told they could not be broken into once they were turned off."

"Do you have a master code?"

"In the security office safe," the Colonel admitted. "But the company said it couldn't be done."

"But it can." Sanjay interrupted. "There was a security convention. Professional hackers said they had opened deactivated electronic locks. I saw the instructions. It can be done."

"I think I read the same article," Kaipo said. "Something called bumping."

"First things first," Kaj interrupted. "Before we start talking about breaking into inactive locks, we need to know that the door can be made operational. Will you do that, Colonel?"

"I will see to it." The Colonel disappeared down the tunnel toward the security building door, the lights in the tunnel coming on before him as he walked.

"How do you want to handle this?" Kaj asked Sharma.

Sharma looked at Agarwahl. "I defer to the lab. If the door to the hotel basement can be opened, they will process the scenes. They have the expertise and equipment."

Kaj noted Agarwahl's small smile and how it was promptly concealed by a professional blank expression, one that Kaj recognized. It made Kaj realize that Sharma and Agarwahl had not worked together before and that earning Sharma's respect was important. At the same time, he understood why Sanjay had battled so bravely to overcome his claustrophobia. In this part of the world, a gentle reciprocity kept the wheels turning and the competition muted. Sanjay had not wanted to tell Sharma no.

It took the Colonel some time to retrieve the code from the security office safe. The first they heard of his return was the sound of electronic buttons being pushed in repeated sequences on the hotel basement side of the door. The right combination did not come easily, but, eventually, the lock came to life with a green back-glow. The door then swung backwards. Agarwahl moved forward stiffly and shone his flashlight into the dimness. The Colonel was standing in a room full of what looked like furniture covered with white sheets.

"Someone has been in here recently," the Colonel said.

"Now we know the door works," Agarwahl said. "The next step is to see if Sanjay is right about opening the locks without using a code. We need technical experts to test the theory."

The words *technical experts* immediately triggered Kaj's memory of the flight from Honolulu. "I know some people who may be able to help with that."

"I want to work on it, too," Sanjay said immediately.

This time, no one disagreed with Sanjay, and no one implied that he lacked the experience. Sanjay's face glowed with the knowledge that he had something to contribute, but he looked anxiously at Dr. Sharma, seeking his approval.

Sharma was inclined to be generous in this instance. "All right, Sanjay. If you make yourself useful and are not in the way of the forensics investigation."

"Help is welcome," Agarwahl said immediately. "Multiple crime scenes require time to process." He then turned to Kaj. "Who are these experts? We need to coordinate access and documentation with them."

"We brought hi-tech people with us from Hawaii. Let me make a call and see when they can be available. If the locks can be opened even when the system is shut down, then we have a possible means of entry and exit." Kaj looked at Sanjay with a sympathetic smile. "We also know that whoever put these things into the drainage channel was probably smaller than Sanjay."

Sanjay managed a wan half-smile. He was sure he was going to have nightmares about being stuck in a narrow channel surrounded by rats and snakes. If it was the job of adult dogs to go into dark, narrow places, perhaps being a puppy was not so bad after all, at least for now.

Chapter 12

Under ordinary circumstances, the Colonel would have provided Kaj's security on the visit to the hospital that afternoon, but he was involved in the forensic investigation of the underground passages. It fell to Pradhan's second in command to chauffeur Kaj to where he needed to be. The new guard was a genial man with cropped grey hair who said he came from Pokhara and loved his years in the British army. He said his name was Abiral and that he had heard so much about Hawaii that he hoped to visit one day.

Jill was waiting for them at the hospital's main entrance.

"Any trouble with the morgue?" Kaj asked.

"Some, apparently, but it was settled. Dr. Xue was very particular about how the space should be set up. I'm not surprised. He's been subtly challenging Dr. Nie every chance he gets."

Kaj nodded. "The field of medical examiners must be very competitive."

Jill gave a rueful shrug. "Their lab tech, Mr. Liu, navigated the demands and has been doing the photography. Nie went right to work once the initial x-rays were done. Xue got started later."

"Nothing we need to do here then," Kaj said. "I want to check the status of the two survivors and talk with a psychiatrist about the boy."

"The two survivors are in Critical Care on the third floor, and we're scheduled to meet with a Dr. Tashi Dema about the boy."

"Dema?" Kaj hadn't shared the King's matrimonial challenges yet with Jill.

"Is something wrong?"

"There's some history here you need to know." Kaj's face took on its owlish look when he was about to demonstrate yet another strange coincidence. "I'll tell you on the way up."

Chapter 13

The waiting room in the Critical Care unit looked just as sad as in any Western hospital. Small groups of people huddled together, their clothing the usual combination of whatever they could find in the moment, all of them glancing up anxiously whenever the door to the interior ward opened.

It reminded Kaj of the day Goro had died. The finality of his father's death had made him question how much he had really known him, and how much his father, in his turn, had understood his own. Generations of men seemed to have been born, married, had children, and died while following some code of impenetrable formality about how fathers should behave. It was only when Goro was drinking that Kaj saw the lighter side, perhaps the side that Ai liked best in her husband, but that memory did nothing more than make him wonder how much any man can really know his father.

The Consul sat alone, just another crumpled participant in the fear and confusion that filled the room, looking as if he had slept on waiting-room chairs since getting off the aircraft. He rose to his feet when he saw Kaj and Jill.

"How is your wife, Sir?" Kaj asked.

The Consul looked around at the other people in the room and took them over to a private, glassed-in room meant for private consultations between families and doctors.

"They performed a craniotomy to relieve the pressure on her brain. She is sedated. That is all they have told me. They say I must be hopeful because there are small improvements. The next hours are critical. I am allowed to see her every hour for a few minutes. In the evening, I go to the palace to be with my son. But then I come back here. I want to be here when she wakes up."

Kaj looked at Jill. It was hard to know what to say. He was too accustomed to saying "we are sorry for your loss."

"We will be thinking of you and your family," Jill said. "And sending every wish for your wife's recovery."

The Consul nodded absently and looked out through the glass to the large clock on the wall.

"I can visit her in a few minutes," he said anxiously.

"We will not keep you, Sir. But we do need to ask about your son and whether he can answer any questions."

"My son is not well. I understand why you want to talk to him, but he is under the care of the best child psychologist in Kuthan. You should talk to her. Her name is Dr. Dema."

Then the Consul was gone, almost running toward the reception desk.

Kaj and Jill followed him slowly. Kaj wanted to ask about the condition of the other survivor, Anya.

"Are you family?" the receptionist asked him.

Kaj showed his Hawaii shield, although he doubted it would make any difference. Strangely enough, it did.

"I read about you in the newspaper," the receptionist said with mounting enthusiasm. "We were told to work with you."

Kaj smiled wanly. Celebrity is seldom helpful in a murder investigation, but in this case, it seemed to be the exception.

"What are able to tell us about her?"

"The manner of injury is listed as traumatic brain injury with intercranial hemorrhage."

"Does she have family here?" he asked.

"No one has asked about her. Someone is listed as next of kin, but no one has visited."

"Who is the next of kin?"

Kaj was soon reminding himself not to be surprised by anything.

"The person listed is Ananda Dorji. We do not have a contact number for him, though. That is strange."

"If you need him, call Colonel Pradhan at palace security and ask him to put you in touch. Dorji works at the palace."

The woman wrote the information down.

Kaj thanked her, feeling conspicuous but grateful she had not asked him for an autograph.

"Did Dorji say anything about being related to her?" Jill asked as they left, with Abiral in tow.

"If the palace is paying for her care, it may be just a business formality," Kaj said.

The label outside Dr. Dema's office announced her position as Clinical Specialist in Child Psychology and Professor of Psychiatry in the medical school.

The woman who opened the office door had a delicate oval face and dark hair that cascaded down onto her shoulders. When her face was at rest, there was a certain determination to her eyes and a resolution to her mouth. But when she smiled, her face lit up the room. Kaj wondered which one she really was.

She invited them into her office and closed the door, leaving Abiral to wait for them outside.

"Dr. Dema," Kaj began.

"Tashi," she corrected him. "Please have a seat. I am between clients. I have only a few minutes."

"We are investigating the crimes committed at the palace," Kaj began to explain.

"I know who you are." Tashi leaned back and crossed her arms.

"There was a child present at the shooting," Jill said tentatively.

"Aki," Tashi said. "I spoke with his father last night when he arrived from the airport. I told him that the boy needs to feel safe. His mother is here in the hospital."

"We know," Kaj said. "We have just come from the critical care unit and talked with his father."

"And what did he say?"

"He said to talk with you."

Tashi gave a small, knowing smile. Kaj immediately knew that their visit had been anticipated, and Tashi had told the Consul what to say. She had probably already made up her mind about him. He proceeded on that basis.

"When we work with traumatized children in Honolulu, our usual policy is to call in experts to help us," he said.

"And you hope I can make him magically better so you can interrogate him?" Tashi's tone went beyond ironic and strayed into mocking.

"We don't interrogate traumatized children," Jill said testily.

Tashi sat forward in her chair and stared at them. "Then why are you here? What is the point?"

"We are trying to find who killed his family." Jill did a remarkable job of sounding mild as she said this.

Tashi tossed her hair and swept it so it disappeared behind her shoulders. "I have visited Aki at the palace several times. He is shut down, and my professional opinion is that attempts to interview him will not be possible or in his best interests."

Kaj looked at her intently, considering how best to deal with the icy barrier she had created. "Have you worked with traumatized children like Aki?"

"Of course, I have or I would not have a professional opinion. But every child is different. Meticulous preparation is needed before a traumatized child starts to process what has happened. He must feel completely safe, and he needs an established routine. If you attempt to talk with him, you will damage him on both counts."

Kaj could see the mounting challenges, yet this child was his only conscious witness.

"Aki is a sensitive child," she continued. He formed a strong bond to his mother early and I am told that in his first year, he would cry if someone else beside her or his nanny tried to pick him up. Part of this is his own disposition, but, environmentally, it was made more difficult because his father was frequently absent. His response to stress is to withdraw. I must earn his trust and his care will be on-going. What he needs is for his mother to wake up. I am absolutely opposed to any pharmaceuticals, which I know is the Western solution."

"Not mine." Kaj spoke more emphatically than he had intended. If her cool reception was to protect the child from Western forms of therapy, she had miscalculated their intentions.

Tashi heard his tone and drew her own conclusions. "You have had therapy?"

Kaj felt his cheeks flush. There was nothing left but admit to it. "PTSD Vietnam."

"Then you may understand why there is a need to protect Aki."

Kaj was used to people's resistance or even fear when he showed his badge. He could see their point. A loud knock on the front door was not good news. Under other circumstances, he might even have agreed with her about Western therapy. He had refused pharmaceuticals, as much out of pride as distaste. In this case, though, he was about to have one more reason to be glad for his partner.

Jill saw the underlying tension and proposed her own distraction.

"How will you treat Aki?"

"By helping him develop what is called *resilience*. Basically, that means the ability to recover from trauma. As I said before, he must feel safe. Right now, he is non-verbal. I am drawing on Asian techniques of calming of the mind and envisioning recovery. He was trapped when his mother fell on top of him and probably felt helpless. As I said, the best outcome for him would be for his mother to wake up."

Kaj looked around the walls of the office. The area over Tashi's desk was filled by a large, framed print of two elaborately dressed Chinese court ladies riding horses. The first lady looked placid and serene. She was carrying a small crop to direct her stallion, which was looking with lustful longing at the mare being ridden by the second lady. The second lady was the most arresting of the two. This lady looked confident and self-aware, an expression that was mirrored by her mare, which was elegantly ignoring the stallion. The longer that Kaj looked at the painting, the more he thought the second lady looked like Tashi. He wondered if she saw herself in the painting.

"Is this hospital the primary treatment center for mental illness in Kuthan?" he asked.

"For the present," she told him. "There has been a lack of resources addressed to mental illness, particularly in children. This center was established by in 1982 after the medical school conducted a research project that showed a prevalence of suicide, particularly among women, and anxiety and depression among men in rural areas."

"Do you have any centers specializing in treating mental illnesses?"

"Not yet." Her voice was heavy with frustration. "And it is overdue. This hospital lacks facilities for long-term treatment. There is definite need. I keep telling them that." She did not define who "they" were.

"When I heard there was a little boy involved," Jill said, "I remembered that our HPD officers carry toys for frightened children. I wondered if it might help Aki to have something from America. I was not sure what animal he would be interested in. Seven seems too old for a teddy bear, but a dinosaur did not seem appropriate. Then it was impossible to decide, so I brought two."

Jill opened her shoulder bag and pulled out a soft bison and a slightly larger polar bear. "Do you think he might like these?"

Tashi stared at the two stuffed animals. Sensitivity was not what she had heard about American police.

"That is quite thoughtful," she said slowly, using a softened tone that suggested possible reappraisal of at least one of her visitors. She thought for a moment, as if looking for a compromise.

"I know the pressure you are working under, and I know how terrible this is for Raju, but I must do what is best for my patient."

"We do not want to interfere with your treatment," Kaj said.

Tashi thoughtfully fingered the polar bear for a moment.

"Well, perhaps, I can agree that if he wants to talk about what happened, and if he says something that I think it would be helpful, I will let you know. But I do not promise more, particularly not allowing you access to him."

"We understand," Kaj said, feeling more appreciative of Tashi than he had been a few minutes before. His immediate goal was to bring this first meeting to a conclusion while leaving room for something more. This boy was the only available witness to the crime.

"Have you worked out a way to bridge the Eastern and Western approaches to psychiatric treatment?" he asked.

Tashi sighed. "I see similarities if only in intention. People once believed that mental illness was caused by an angry neighbor or an invasive demon. In our more rural areas, there is an expectation than any treatment requires ritual. I watched a shaman treat a severely depressed patient by banging drums and going into a physical frenzy. I realized it was designed to meet expectations. In the West, the same thing is accomplished by displaying professional certificates on the waiting-room wall. Once the show was over, the shaman told the man to imagine pulling the curse out of his body. He then had the patient create a story of how he would be cured. Western talk therapy is not that different."

"You'd be prepared to use shamanistic techniques with your patients then?" Jill asked.

"To some extent, I already do. But, if I were setting up a psychiatric facility, I would certainly have a shaman on call. The shaman comes with the authority of community experience. Rituals are often conducted in front of neighbors and family. This creates context and visceral support. The Western practitioner works one-on-one, which is intellectual. There is room for both. A wise practitioner knows one size does not fit all—nor does one type of training. I would deal with what my patient believed."

Once they reached the street, Kaj looked back up at the modern, Western-style hospital they had just been in. He could not be sure, but he thought he saw Tashi standing in her office window looking down at them.

"What did you think?" Jill asked as they walked to the palace van.

"Of her?" Kaj gave a small smile as he turned away from the glass and steel building behind them. "I think she is tough and determined. But I must admit that every Kuthani woman so far matches that description."

"Every woman who has fought some kind of battle," Jill corrected him. "The Colonel told me that Darya's grandfather does not acknowledge that she runs the family business. He wants a man to be in charge. Tashi just told us that she cannot get the powers that be to set up a badly needed mental hospital. Even Dr. Nie must have her battles. She has title and position in a man's world, but the price she pays is dealing with the Xues."

"I was thinking that Linda might fit in here. She is the most tough and determined woman I know."

"Well, what has your wife battled?"

"Me, probably." Kaj regretted the flippant joke the moment he made it, perhaps because it was too close to the truth. It took him a few moments to realize why. It had made him remember how Aileen had talked about their parents after Goro's funeral: "Mom was the real heart of the family. Dad went out with his drinking buddies while she managed the family money, supervised us, and did everything else. He was the tortured hero, while she was the strong one keeping everything together. They must have found something rewarding in it, even a co-dependency, but she couldn't completely hide the scorn she felt for his supposed helplessness, the very thing she helped create. If you tried to change them, they would have both denied it."

His first reaction had been to protest her analysis. But now he could see a terrible symmetry. Had his experience with war and death condemned him and Linda to repeat those same roles? Was he the weakness to Linda's strength? Did she have secret contempt for the nightmares he brought home with him? He glanced up at the mountains, feeling that something had changed for him. He silently repeated the line from Patel's poem: *And the wise know the rituals of water*. Snow is water too, he thought again as he struggled to understand. Patel's words remained opaque, though, and the wisdom they offered was still beyond his grasp.

Chapter 14

It was late afternoon when Abiral deposited them back at the hotel. There was time only for a quick sandwich delivered by room service. Kaj was glad because he didn't feel like talking, and Jill wanted to use the time to check the workboards in the team room. As it turned out, only his own team plus the two Chinese doctors and Sharma and Agarwahl, showed up.

Plausible excuses were given. Mr. Liu was preparing the mortuary for tomorrow's work. Mr. Achari and Mr. Choudhary were analyzing the evidence retrieved from the crime scenes and the tunnel and Sanjay was assisting them. As Sharma pointed out, in New Delhi there was a large staff that could be pressed into action. In Kuthan, the team was stretched very thin.

"Dr. Nie. Your team completed autopsies today." It wasn't a question. Kaj made clear he wanted answers.

"We completed two. The morning was spent coordinating our electronic equipment with the mortuary's existing lab systems and then establishing our workspace requirements." Nie glanced at Xue. The look suggested that Xue had a hand in the delay.

"Autopsies commenced at 12:10 p.m. To be consistent with the crime scene photographs, we adopted the initial numerical protocol established by palace security. Our expectation is that the further four autopsies will be concluded tomorrow." Nie's tone indicated that her plan was more than a hope.

"My current report concerns the body identified as number one, Tranh Soöng." She pointed to the chart that showed the body's location.

Then she began and Kaj listened. The presentation was highly technical and very detailed, delivered with a professional polish that seemed compulsively complete. It made Kaj question who the report was meant for. It came to him just as she was finishing. There was no need to impress the Indian forensics team. Most of them were working in their lab. Liu, her autopsy tech wasn't there. She didn't need to impress the American detectives, who would want her to cut to the chase. That left only Xue. Kaj looked at the man. There must be history there, something beyond the dossiers that Greg had provided.

Kaj took from her report what he needed: Victim number one, the King's Uncle Thranh, had three bullet wounds, two through and through, with the fatal wound a bullet entering the heart and stopping it. The agency appeared to be an automatic or semiautomatic rifle.

Xue declined the competition, and went in a different direction entirely. He described his findings almost perfunctorily. Victim number two had two wounds to the neck and either would have been fatal. He concurred with the agency of a rifle. But then he went on to focus on the victim and what he was wearing.

He described victim two as a fifty-year-old bearded Indo-Aryan male wearing a turban, embroidered long shirt, narrow trousers, and embroidered slippers."

Kaj caught Cliff looking quizzically at Kaipo who seemed to have the same question. It seemed that Xue wanted to say something about the man beyond the dispassionate report of a near decapitation.

Xue did not let them hang for long. He concluded with the sober calm of someone reporting something where the only appropriate response would be silence.

"Visual investigation indicated heavy, healed scarring on the shoulders and upper and mid back. There was also evidence of badly healed fractures. This man was badly wounded at one point, and the injuries were severe enough to cripple him unless he was given first-rate medical care, which does not seem to have been the case."

Sharma was the first to emerge from the general shock that had engulfed the room. "How old were these scars?" he asked Xue.

"Fully healed," Xue said. "But the disability was permanent."

"So, he was Sikh," Sharma said.

"One of yours," Xue agreed. "You'd know that better than me."

"I wouldn't know if he was one of 'ours.' Sikhs live everywhere, including China. Foreign armies like to employ them."

"What's this about?" Kaj was starting to feel like the referee he didn't want to be.

Sharma gave a slight sneer. "Dr. Xue is implying that because this man is a Sikh he must have been wounded during protests for a Sikh homeland that they want to call Khalistan. The Indian army has put down several armed protests and the government considers extreme Khalistan protestors to be terrorists."

"I did not say he was a terrorist," Xue objected.

"Are you saying that the Sikh butler might have been a target or might even have been involved in the killings?" Jill asked.

"That's what he means," Sharma said. "Large numbers of Sikhs serve in the Indian army and have weapons. But they have also served in the Chinese army."

"That doesn't mean anything," Xue said nastily. "They have also served in the British and the US army."

"Where is this going?" Kaj said testily.

"If you want to consider all possibilities," Xue said, "we should look into this."

"And we will," Kaj agreed. "I will talk to the Colonel tomorrow."

Kaj turned then to Agarwahl and asked him to proceed with the forensics report.

"We took bullets from the walls, floor, and ceiling of the primary crime scene. We are reviewing these. The doctors also sent us bullet fragments. We now have new crime scenes." He displayed a map showing the recently discovered basement area of the hall and pointed out the various areas where bullet evidence had been found. Numbers had been assigned for easy identification.

"An AK-47 rifle was found. We have found that all bullets are consistent with that weapon."

"All? Including what we sent you?" Nie asked. "Was there only one weapon and one shooter?"

"That is a possibility," Sharma said, "but we must wait. There will be no definitive conclusions until all autopsies are complete. We also must wait until we are sure we can open an electronic lock after it has been disabled. This will tell us if the shooter used an access door in the hotel basement. We learned from Sanjay that it is possible. Much more knowledge to come."

"And Sanjay knows this how?" Xue's superior tone implied that he might relish emphasizing the difference in professional status between himself and a graduate student lacking in forensic experience.

Kaj stared at Xue. He didn't much like martinets, although he could live with them. Bullies he would not tolerate. Whether the absent Sanjay needed it or not, Kaj's internal urge to protect took over.

"Sanjay says that the information about opening the locks has already been published in computer journals. I have requested the assistance of two computer specialists we brought with us from Hawaii."

Now Kaj was in Xue's sights.

"Two government people?" Xue managed to embed a more obvious sneer into the word *government*. "I thought this investigation was to be above politics."

Kaj felt Jill's eyes bore into him. He also sensed Kaipo and Cliff shifting in their chairs. They knew his reaction to the word *politics*. It was comparable to when he heard the word *hero*.

"Politics?" Kaj languidly repeated the word and let his voice rise at the end of the sentence. For those who knew Kaj well, it was a rough-seas warning. The detectives exchanged glances and sat back in their chairs.

Kaj did not disappoint. "We are here because somebody may have attempted regime change by killing the Kuthani royal family. Isn't that the definition of politics? My first thought, Dr. Xue, is that politics existed long before any of us arrived. This afternoon, I asked if our experts could work with Sanjay on these locks. It wasn't politics. It was fact. This generation grew up with technology. It's their world now. If the People's Republic of China had sent computer specialists with your team, Dr. Xue, I would have asked for their help. I respect expertise wherever I can find it."

Xue was not about to give up. Kaj could not tell if the man was genuinely curious or just looking to be contrarian. Perhaps both.

"Why not use local locksmiths here in Kuthan?"

Sharma pounced before Kaj needed to answer. "How would we know that local locksmiths were not the ones who opened the locks to let the killers in? Perhaps you are not familiar with how electronic locks work?"

The question was obvious, the answer self-evident, and Sharma's tone scornful. Xue scowled in Sharma's direction at the implication he was not the best-informed person in the room.

"You forget that all new technology is made in China," Xue replied weakly. "Your mobile crime lab has all Chinese equipment."

Sharma was on a roll. "You forget that India wrote the specifications for the equipment and paid you to manufacture it."

"Enough, please." Kaj said firmly. "We are here because our governments believe we are the best that our countries have to offer."

Kaj looked around the room using his discouraged expression and willing the nonsense to stop. Both Sharma and Xue sat back in their chairs and studiedly looked away from one another.

For a moment, it looked as if it was going to be a miserable outcome from a meeting Kaj had hoped would promote collegiality. Being who he was, and as much to be mischievous as well as defuse the tension, he decided to use the darkest humor he could muster. It was a joke on all of them.

"The best they could find on short notice anyway."

Nie looked gratefully at Kaj and gave him a genuine smile. Even Sharma retreated slightly from his petulant indignance. Apparently, Xue had not caught the joke. He looked confused and suspected the joke was at his expense.

"The Inspector is right," Agarwahl said suddenly. "We should not worry whose people we are using. We should not forget our goal is to find out who killed the King's family."

Kaj looked at Agarwahl in surprise. Speaking boldly had not seemed the lab director's style. He seemed more likely to defer to Sharma.

"As long as we are not blinded." Xue said this nastily to cover his embarrassment. "Anyone on the security force could have opened that door. Why are they excluded from consideration?"

"They are not," Kaj replied immediately. "Detective Kahana is reviewing the surveillance cameras from the tunnel where the weapon was found. If anyone from the security staff entered the area from their side, there will be a record of it. The cameras are automatically triggered. As I say, we follow the evidence."

"And what about determining if the King or the butler was the target?"

"We know he was called away just before the shooting started," Kaj replied. "We have not yet confirmed who gave him a message about an urgent phone call from Beijing. His secretary, Ananda Dorji, denies sending that message and claims that there never was a phone call."

"Must we also question the King?" Xue asked the question politely for a change.

"We follow the evidence." Kaj's voice remained calm. "Detectives Kahana and Lee will interview the staff who were in the hall kitchen at the time. We also want to know why the King's old nanny was there. Tomorrow, I will follow up with Dr. Xue's findings and ask about the Sikh butler's history. Our team meeting tomorrow must be later. Jill and I have been summoned to a meeting with the Mountain Thunder clan."

Xue settled back into an uncomfortable acquiescence. He had not liked the thought that he was being laughed at.

"Dr. Sharma is there anything else that you and Mr. Agarwahl want to add at this point," Kaj asked.

"We will wait for the final autopsies. Information will come tomorrow. But we have information on the rifle. It is an old model. It could be a redundancy. It was heavily used and not well maintained. The mechanism of operation is unclean and Mr. Achari found goat hair and sand when he took it apart."

."What is you conclusion?"

"In the day, many armies used the rifle. Today there are newer models. The weapon should have been destroyed. Possibly it was sold on the black market."

"Are these older rifles easily available?" Cliff asked.

Agarwahl nodded. "A new weapon is very expensive. Major international arms dealers sell them. This one is cheap and available because it is old."

Sharma vigorously nodded his agreement. "We think we are dealing with amateurs. Paid assassins would charge enough for proper equipment." He looked around the room. "If they are any good at their job."

Kaj smiled at Sharma's attempt at humor. "But the rifle worked," he pointed out.

"It killed five people," Sharma agreed. "But it was lucky not to explode."

"Does the goat hair have any significance?" Cliff asked.

Kaj's eyebrows rose. "What are you thinking, Cliff?"

"I read somewhere that there are 300 species of goats. If it was a particular species, we might have an idea where the weapon came from."

"Probably the Middle East with sand and goats," Xue said dismissively.

"Many deserts and goats in China," Sharma said with a glint in his eye.

Kaj looked at the group around the table. Agarwahl and Sharma seemed the most at ease. Nie seemed still to be reserving judgment. But Xue was exuding what Tashi would probably call passive-aggression.

"Is there anything more?" Kaj deliberately didn't raise the question of the palace bulletin. That was up to Cliff. Hearing no objection, he stood up to bring the meeting to a close. Sharma stood up with the others but insisted on having the last word. It was another swipe at Xue.

"I agree with the Inspector and my esteemed colleague, Mr. Agarwahl. We must move beyond our politics. In my case, to be more collegial, I invite everyone to call me Emir rather than my formal title, Dr. Sharma." Sharma grinned, knowing very well that Xue would not allow himself the indignity of using Sharma's first name. Nor would he offer the intimacy of sharing his own.

Kaj felt glad to see the group walk back to their own rooms. He felt his shoulders start to release out of their defensive mode. It had been a tricky meeting, but he thought the worst was over. He wanted to call Linda.

He was just about the leave the room when learned he had been premature. He heard a quiet voice ask if he had a minute.

"What's your impression of Meng?" Cliff asked.

The Chinese spy was the last thing on Kaj's mind. "Greg told me what he does and the innocent act he puts on. Why do you ask?"

"When he started with that 'I know you' business, I didn't know what he was going to say when he got to me."

"I didn't either."

"That's what I wanted to tell you," Cliff said. "I am quite sure he thinks he knows who I am, and he wanted me to know it. My only question is why."

Kaj stared at him. Kaj never asked about his private life and Cliff never offered. If Cliff wanted to share something, Kaj had always known it would be only when Cliff was ready.

"Meng was telling us that he's the one pulling the strings for the Chinese delegation, which means that someone on that delegation is reporting to him. But a lot of the information he has is public knowledge. I thought you got off the lightest of us."

"Perhaps not," Cliff replied. "As Meng walked away, he winked at me."

"He winked at you?" Kaj's eyebrows shot up and his forehead jumped.

"No mistaking it."

"Why?" Kaj managed to get out.

"It gets worse. He left a message inviting me to dinner the day after tomorrow."

Kaj's face went into the fixed, disappointed stare that was his trademark. Cliff's went into the quizzical, doubtful look that was his.

"What am I going to do? I thought you needed to know."

"I do. But one step at a time. I doubt very much he wants you to spy for him. HPD lacks secrets worth the price of a dinner. Let's assume that he is being his normally obnoxious self."

Cliff managed a small grin. People tended to relax when Kaj went into planning mode.

"Don't directly accept his invitation but imply you're interested.'

"Even though I am not." Cliff looked indignant.

"We know that. He doesn't. So, trust me for a minute. Text him a message saying that you are intrigued. As simple as 'Intrigued. Where and when? Text back.'

"What if he agrees?"

Kaj began to get into the spirit of the chase. It was a welcome distraction from Xue's unpleasantness.

"I'm counting on it."

"You want to me appear to accept, but I don't have to go?"

"That's the general idea." Kaj smiled his reassurance. "I think the gentleman needs to be stopped in his tracks."

"So, you'll handle it? You're going to stand him up?"

"Not exactly. Give me the details when he shares them. Tell him you must have something close to the palace for security reasons."

"Where and when, then?" Cliff looked as relieved or as hopeful as the moment allowed.

"Right," Kaj replied. "As few words as possible. Don't talk to him in person. Let me know the details."

Cliff gave a relieved smile and Kaj returned it, knowing he now had something to tell Linda. Not about Cliff's situation. He'd never discuss that. But how many times would a Honolulu inspector have dinner with a Chinese James Bond? He wondered if Linda would even believe him.

Chapter 15

NEXT MORNING, KAJ, JILL, AND the Colonel found themselves the sole passengers on a DHC Otter twin-engine aircraft designed for high-altitude flying and short landings and take-offs. The flight's hold was full of supplies headed north to what Kaj expected to be a town of people accustomed to hard winters and isolation. He had formed this opinion from reading the Himalaya chapter in Cliff's book. "A dying way of life" is how the book had described the region. "Relying on traditional customs" it continued.

As the aircraft flew over the foothills, Kaj saw little to change his mind. The rich farms and trees of the temperate region along the border with India gave over to rolling hills dotted with hamlets set far apart. Then the ground became scrubby and the trees became bushes and willow thickets. He imagined it could only get more rural and the living harder as they approached the mountains.

The Colonel smiled reassuringly when Jill saw where they were landing and clutched the back of the seat in front of her.

"The pilots do this every day. Watch. He will nose down onto the runway, maintain airspeed, put the wheels on the numbers, apply the brakes, reverse the propellers, let the aircraft run up the hill, and then turn right into the terminal. As the British like to say "tickety-boo," or for you Americans, "a piece of cake."

"In Hawaii, more like 'duck soup'." Jill was not about to let go of the seat back. "You've done this a lot?"

"Enough. But this approach is not as difficult as landing at Lukla in Nepal. If you miss the turn to the terminal, you head into the mountain. If you take off too slowly, the aircraft dips into the valley and never comes up. Lukla is where climbers go for the Everest base camp. It is busy, so there is a control tower. This is a landing strip. They have visual or daylight rules. We must leave while there is still light and before the afternoon wind shears."

Kaj now understood why the King flew as if he were about to land on an aircraft carrier. He also remembered why he did not like rollercoasters. He stared at the ceiling and avoided looking out of the windows.

They came to a stop in front of a small stone building at the turnaround at the end of the runway. It had a wooden second floor surrounded by a bank of windows. A string of prayer flags fluttered in the breeze. Kaj wondered if the flags were prayers for take-offs or thanks for safe landings.

Almost before the engine was turned off, the cargo doors opened and the unloading began. Waiting trucks drove up to the aircraft and took away crates of vegetables and fruit, wooden boxes of groceries, bales of animal feed, and sacks of rice. Then just as quickly as they had appeared, the trucks were gone.

The Colonel was first off, and when Kaj and Jill finally stepped down from the aircraft, they saw him talking animatedly to Darya, who was leaning back against a black Mercedes van. There was no mistaking the vehicle's circle logo with the three-pointed star. It was no ox cart. He looked up at Masakatsu, feeling on his face the wind-swept dust from the mountains' scree slopes, exposed as ice fields melted in the early summer season. It was a chilled westerly breeze that had blown over snow

Darya was in working mode, wearing baggy trousers and a striped woven vest. Kaj watched as Jill put on her jacket. She had come more prepared than he was. But she was a California girl who knew the High Sierra snow country. He was a Hawaii boy whose only experience with snow came when he visited the telescopes on Mauna Kea. He had brought a jacket, but it was not fleece-lined like hers.

Darya ushered the three of them into the van and offered them bottles of water, the ritual greeting for anyone arriving from the lower altitudes.

"We are at 3,500 meters. That is 11,500 feet if you prefer."

She pointed to a pile of jackets in the cargo area at the back. Kaj took one gratefully and immediately noticed how the exertion of putting it on made his breaths come faster.

She drove them down the hill, heading west toward the town of Pahāda. The town was not visible until they rounded another hill and crossed a stone arch bridging a rushing, snow-melt stream. By now, Kaj realized that the guidebooks were either very dated or written for somewhere else. There were no goats with bells, no yaks wandering down the road, no ragged-looking dogs, no vendors with steaming caldrons of noodles, and no beggars on street corners—the images of mountain villages that the book had given him.

Instead, the town looked like the suburbs of Mongarthuā. The houses were built of stone blocks, all the windows were small but had double-paned glass, most had satellite dishes, and many had a small SUV parked beside them. As they drove past, everyone smiled at them, and children wearing embroidered hats ran alongside the slow-moving car, waving at Darya and looking curiously at the visitors.

Darya pointed out the British school, as she called it. "This is for the young children," she explained. "The older ones go to a school outside the city along with children from Snow Leopard, our eastern neighbors. The British set it up that way." She said this as if having the British set up the school system answered any possible questions. 'The British did it' seemed to cover both explanation and answer.

Once through the town, she sped south for about a mile and then turned sharply onto another paved road. A few moments later, she stopped at the top of a hill and turned off the engine. As soon as the passengers stepped out of the car, they could see why.

To the north there was an uninterrupted view of the Himalayan range. Both Kaj and Jill stood transfixed. The south face of Masakatsu was golden cream in the late-morning light. Even though the base was many miles away, the clear air made it seem as if they could reach out to touch the glaciers.

From this vantage point, Masakatsu was clearly part of a sea of mountains. To the east was Buthan's Mount Gangkhar Puensum, glistening like the frost of a morning not yet committed to winter. To the far west was the distant pyramid face of Everest. But Everest was only first among others of almost equal size and height. Today, lenticular clouds of blowing snow shrouded the gold ring around Everest's summit, turning the mountain's south face a silvery gray. To Kaj, Everest looked very bleak.

"We know we are lucky to have this land," Darya said. But I have given a father and husband to these mountains, and I do not intend to lose my son. He is in boarding school in Mongarthuā, where he will stay."

Kaj merely nodded. Seeing Everest made him think of a century of climbers, frozen marble-white on its slopes, their compasses, cameras, and ice picks still attached to their bodies. That image was replaced involuntarily by the memory of young men, their bodies blown apart, lying in black body-bags in rows under the Vietnamese sun. His chest tightened, sweat formed along his hairline, and his eyes stung.

He began the slow, deep breaths Dr. Alvarez had told him to practice during their EMDR sessions. He also heard his sensei's voice: "Don't get trapped in the past. Breathe to let it out." Kaj breathed deeply and, he hoped, inconspicuously. Let them think he was just adjusting to the altitude. Until now, he had not really absorbed what his aikido teacher meant.

"What are you thinking?" Darya asked him curiously.

Kaj fought his way back, and the moment passed. It was not something he wanted to share.

"I'm comparing Masakatsu to Everest," he replied evasively. "All those people who died trying to climb Everest just so they could say they were the first. Your Masakatsu does not feel like that." Kaj let out a deep, unobtrusive breath.

Darya looked strangely at him and then turned to look at Everest.

"That is why we do not allow anyone to climb on our mountain. We are the *rakhwala,* as they say in Nepal. The protectors. So, you are not one of those who believe that mountains exist just to be conquered?" She looked back at him quizzically.

Kaj shook his head. "I don't think of anything or anyone as needing to be conquered."

"And what about you?" Darya looked directly at the Colonel.

"I think mountains have their own truths. But climbing is a solitary undertaking, and I think people who climb them must be looking for something. I have climbed only out of necessity because they were in the way of where I wanted to go."

Darya stared at him for a moment and then shrugged. "We think Nepal gave Everest away for the tourist money. Do you feel you have lost your mountain?"

The Colonel smiled sadly.

"You have the advantage over us. Nepal needs money. If we had your resources, we could preserve our heritage like you. We never owned Everest. Tibet and China share it. But it is hard to have tourist money without having tourists."

"I know what you mean," Kaj said. "Statehood brought money to Hawaii, but also overcrowding and subdivisions that spread like lava. We import almost all our food, and we are losing the sense of community. I grew up in a different Hawaii."

Darya seemed not to have heard. Kaj watched as she focused on the Colonel with the prim authority of an English teacher correcting apostrophes.

"Do you agree that the money you gain from tourists climbing your Everest could pay for the bodies to be removed instead of encouraging more people to climb?"

Kaj was intrigued. Darya appeared to be trying to catch the Colonel's attention without knowing how to do it.

"I do not know," the Colonel replied. "Opening Everest brought money to Nepal. It made life better for the sherpas and for us village boys. It was the same with the British Army. Some did not like our young men competing every year to serve in the Gurkha regiment. But the British selected for merit, not because of caste or if our families had money. Because I was chosen, I traveled and could send money home. My son is now serving with the Gurkha Contingent in Singapore."

"You must be proud of him," Jill said.

"I am. I am also very grateful. I wish his mother was alive to see him."

Darya stared at the Colonel as if seeing him for the first time.

Kaj watched her with open curiosity.

"Gratitude is good," she said cryptically. Then she corrected herself. "You are up here for a reason. My grandfather wants to give you our history, and you must learn what he means."

Jill deliberately kept up with Darya's pace as they went back to the car. "You said that you never allow anyone to climb on your side of Masakatsu?"

"That's right."

"I knew someone who said he wanted to climb there. He seemed positive that he would be able to."

"That would not have happened," Darya snapped. "The only ones allowed to go up there are our yak herders and miners, commercial lorries from China, and dam workers who maintain the electric substation and transmission lines. We do not want tourists with their hotels and litter."

Jill looked as if she was facing a riptide of confusing currents and undertow. She dropped back to rejoin Kaj and the Colonel.

The four of them drove on until they reached a stone building with the usual, steep mountain roof. As he got out, Kaj looked around and saw the long-needled pines and scrubby rhododendrons that grew at this altitude. On the one side, they saw a large field with glossy black and variegated brown yaks. On the other, they found themselves looking far down into a green valley crisscrossed by the same stream that ran through the town.

Darya turned their attention to the stone building.

"My grandfather's father built this. He carried every stone on his back, and he built the yak pens. He wanted to build a family business. By the time my grandfather was born, he had done it.

She pointed to larger, more modern buildings further down the road. We have a cooperative of yak farmers. We supply yak milk, cheese, and butter to Mongarthuā. Yak milk is acceptable to anyone who does not eat beef, but yaks do not produce as much milk as cows, so it is precious as well as traditional. If you have tried yak butter in Kuthan, it was probably ours. But we also trade in gems around the world. We have international shipping facilities in Mongarthuā for our exports.

She led them around the house and stopped at the fence. When she gave a long whistle, three yaks started a slow amble towards them.

"The animals in this field are heritage stock. We keep records of their pedigrees to avoid inbreeding. We divide up the *dri*, the females, and decide which bulls to set among them."

She waited until the animals had reached the fence.

"Our family was here long before the British came to Kuthan. And for most of that time, even before history, there has been trouble between us and the Water Dragon clan."

Darya pointed down the valley. Her face was set and scornful.

"Every generation has seen conflict and death. We tried to be peaceful and share the valley, even though it has always been ours. We let them grow their gardens in plots there. All we asked was for our yaks to have winter forage."

She looked inquiringly at the Kaj and the Colonel.

"You have heard of the so-called massacre of Kalyani. My grandfather wants you to know that those stories are not true. He saw what happened. He will tell you about a yak named Marta and what happened to her. She was a prized breeder whose genetic line runs true. It still does."

Darya pointed to the yaks now standing in the shadow of the house. The three looked as if they had been expecting some reward. From time to time, they issued short, guttural grunts to indicate their disappointment. "Very spoiled, you are," Darya told the yaks. "One of those is from her line," she said to Jill.

"Which one?"

"The pretty one."

Kaj and Jill stared at the three. All they saw were three shaggy animals with shiny noses and curved horns, roughly three quarters the size of a Western dairy cow, with thick hair hanging down to their hocks.

"What makes a yak pretty?" Jill was not ready to admit to the imperious Darya that the yaks all looked the same to her. Kaj and the Colonel remained suspiciously quiet.

"Look for a square face, solid body, thick fur that is even, wide spaced clear eyes, horns evenly curved, and a well-developed hump."

"That one!" Jill said immediately and pointed toward a female leaning against the building.

"Well done," Draya said.

Darya looked triumphantly at the men. Kaj and the Colonel felt put on notice.

"My grandfather is expecting you. We need to go." Darya abruptly walked back to the van without looking back.

As they followed, the Colonel closed in on Kaj and Jill.

"If they offer butter tea, you are expected to sip it and your host must keep your cup full. It is acceptable to wait until the end and then drain the cup. But be prepared if you have not tried it before."

Kaj nodded thanks and held back to let Jill and the Colonel be the first to reach the van. He took one last look back at Masakatsu before he leaned toward the waiting Darya and spoke softly.

"Why was it so urgent for us to meet here today? It cannot be about yaks and history."

Darya tossed her head like one of the yaks and stared at Kaj with a slightly insolent smile.

"You have a lot to learn, Inspector. And my grandfather is the best one to teach you."

She slid the van door closed behind Kaj and then walked around and started the engine.

Chapter 16

THE FOOTHILLS OF THE HIMALAYAN range formed a dramatic backdrop to the Mountain Dragon family compound. The main structures were large stone buildings set deeply into a hillside that had been hollowed out to accommodate them. Each building had two rows of four windows. Anything or anyone wanting access to the buildings higher on the hill would have to detour around the lower buildings. Along the way were many defensible points. In more violent times, it must have functioned as a fortress.

Darya drove up to a clearing in front of the lower building, then accelerated up the steep driveway to stop in front of the two rear buildings.

"Grandpa is waiting for you." She pointed to a pair of heavy, carved wooden doors set in a building painted vivid orange with a yellow geometric frame around each door. It looked cheerful in the sunlight.

It was dark inside for the first few moments, but as Kaj became accustomed to the light, he saw that they were in a large reception room. The walls were covered by bolts of multi-colored fabric. A small shrine occupied an alcove by the door they had just entered. Further into the room, a sectional sofa and side tables were set in front of a large fireplace. The most spectacular part, however, was a round, low table set in front of the fireplace. The tabletop was a sunken dish filled with carved, golden animals and birds, topped with a thick pane of glass. Behind it, a large copper kettle simmered on a small heater.

Kaj assumed the kettle and mugs were part of the ritual offering of tea that they had been warned to expect.

Their host welcomed them by placing cream-colored prayer shawls around their necks. The shawls were faintly printed with geometric designs and the long-tailed letters of the Kuthani alphabet. Their unfinished short edges were wispy silk threads that rose and fell like waves.

Kaj accepted his with a polite namaste but took particular interest in studying the old man as they sat down.

Grandpa Lhotse had to be ninety, but his eyes were sharp and his gaze penetrating. Kaj felt the old man was looking past him to some horizon, scanning perhaps for the sacred, bluish-grey vultures circling a dead animal. He wore a scraggly moustache over his set lips, with grey stubble on his chin and a suggestion of a small, white beard beneath, but seasons of winter and altitude had turned the old man's skin into wrinkled leather and etched deep furrows between his eyebrows. He seemed a man who had suffered, but also a man who knew how to triumph.

Kaj's thoughts returned to the feeling of loss and death he had just felt seeing Everest. He wondered if Everest's dead might have resembled the old man if they had stumbled back to their base camp with snow-bleached hair, white-marbled skin, and fingers frost-bitten into icy twigs. Would they too have that faraway stare in their all-too-wise eyes?

"Sit, sit." The old man said that even though they were already seated. "Much to tell you." He nodded to Darya, who began to pour the frothy pinkish-grey tea into the mugs, carefully keeping the bottom of the teapot beneath the level of the tabletop as a gesture of respect.

The Colonel waited for the mugs to be distributed and for the host to lift his cup before he took up his own and took a small sip. That gave Kaj and Jill the cue to watch and wait. Once the Colonel set his cup down, Darya immediately refilled it. Jill then took a tentative sip before replacing her cup. Kaj took a sip of his. The tea tasted salty but also buttery, and the overall flavor was like hard, old, cheese with a tinge of barnyard. It would take time to get used to the taste.

Grandpa Lhotse let Darya refill his cup and then left it undrunk. He leaned forward and took a moment to stare into each of their eyes. Satisfied of whatever he was looking for, he sat back, folded his legs comfortably and started with what appeared to Kaj to be a practiced retelling of old wrongs.

"The massacre of Kalyani," he said with bitter scorn over the word *massacre*. "All Water Dragon dead? Well, what about Mountain Thunder dead? They do not matter?"

He stared directly at Kaj. "You heard about our dead?"

Kaj felt on the spot and considered carefully what he could say.

"I read the memorial at Kalyani," he said slowly. "Patel's poem spoke of all who died there. I thought that meant there was more to the story than the history books. That is what the King said."

Grandpa leaned forward eagerly. "He said that?"

After Kaj nodded, Grandpa sat back looking as if he were digesting unexpected but not unpleasant news.

"Darya told you our history? Always fighting with Water Dragon because the valley ours. You think not worth fighting for?"

Grandpa Lhotse's voice rose in pitch and his hands made wide gestures as if willing his visitors' agreement.

"Our yaks need valley in winter. Our *dris* calve there in June. We must protect our yaks. After the British leave, Water Dragon said good time challenge us again."

The old man now suddenly looked as if he wanted to spit. Kaj was not sure whether it was because of the British or because of the Water Dragon clan.

"The *dris* good mothers. But one refuse her calf. Usually, calf dies. But she was pretty yak. My son, Darya's father, was ten."

Darya broke in then. "Grandpa, he was sixteen."

"No matter," the old man said. "He likes animals. Always brings injured animals home to us. He says, 'May I have her?' She no live, we said. But he fed her warm yak milk, and slept in the sheds with her.

"She lived. He called her Marta. She was spoiled. Yaks have a temper. One day she broke fence and ran down into the valley. Everyone searched. Then shots down in the valley. Water Dragon workers killed her. They begin cutting up her body.

"We fought them and some were killed. Water Dragon ran away and Marta was brought back. My son saw her head and cried.

"That night, I call a meeting. We say enough is enough. As my father said, the devil must face his own tricks. Next day, I call for people to fight. Men come with arms, and a crowd went down. Not mercenaries. Water Dragon lied. Not Nepali. Only our clan, our herders. When Water Dragon saw us, they ran away. We chased. Then they shot at us. We fired back and we chased them and fired and fired until no more sound. We took away our wounded and dead. This is what I saw."

Grandpa took a sip of his tea and wiped away a tear.

"I told everyone that people from the city will come because of this. We put blocks on the road to stop them. We waited and waited. Months. Then it is spring. Then the calves are born. Two look like Marta. When my son sees them, he smiled. First time."

He wiped away another tear and hunched his shoulders.

"It was hot when they came. Our yaks and herders were in the mountains. A covered truck comes up driveway and stops. We go to our wall and watch. But there were no soldiers. Monks helped an old man from the truck. He had a stick and walked to our rock barrier. He sat down. The other monks sat around him. I remember the flags on the truck. I remember the monks in brown and purple robes. The old monk had a big voice:

'Akar Lhotse,' he yelled. 'Come down and talk.'

'Why should I? You go shoot me.'

'No guns here.'

'What in truck?'

The old monk yelled something to the truck. It backed down the driveway.

'Come down. Talk.'

'No.'

'Kuthan has a new government. We want to tell you this.'

'So what?'

'You will gain. New government says valley yours if you obey the government.'

'Is this a trick?'

'No trick.'

"The old monk stood up. The wind made his robes go into the air. Nothing underneath. We laughed loudly and he shook his stick at us. He turned around and pulled his robes up. Then he bent forward. We laughed again. 'The old fool,' I said. 'But good defiance.'

'All right,' I shout. 'I will come down. But big trouble if not right.'

'Only good things' the old monk shouted.

"We talk until late. We give the monks food and lodging. Next day they go back to the city. I hang a paper on the wall that says the valley is ours. I signed a promise to obey the new government."

Lhotse pointed to an elaborately framed document hanging on the wall beside the fireplace. It was written in the long-tailed Kuthani alphabet and had impressive seals on the bottom to indicate it was official.

Kaj frowned slightly and looked directly at the old man.

"Did the monk say why the Water Dragon clan gave up their claims to the valley?"

Lhotse had another rapid change of mood and looked suddenly shrewd. Up to this point, he had told the story of his clan jubilantly, as if they had won some sports trophy. He did not answer the question.

"Many lives lost over hundreds of years because of the valley. We would give more. But valley is now ours."

Kaj noticed the evasion and fingered his pottery mug. He had also noticed how the old man switched between broken English and then back to standard English. It seemed to vary according to whether the old man was feeling cornered. He took a polite sip to buy a few moments while he pondered his question.

"Why would Water Dragon give up their land, if they had been fighting you for centuries?"

Lhotse sat back and pouted. "No reason. Just offer."

"And you did not wonder?"

Lhotse sat forward suddenly. "I do not care. Perhaps the dam wanted more land. Do I think Water Dragon said they were wrong? No. I am not a fool."

He looked over at Darya. "Am I a fool?" He looked relieved when she shook her head.

Lhotse crossed his arms and stared hard at Kaj. "Everyone has a reason for everything. My grandfather said the Soöngs never gave an inch in a bargain."

"What do you think?"

Lhotse narrowed his eyes.

"We had our valley. All we wanted. Perhaps someone in his family did not like losing land. There is only one king at a time. What about the others. What was left for them?"

Kaj looked over at Jill, who met his eyes with an eyebrow lift of her own. Grandpa Lhotse had just implied someone from within the Water Dragon clan itself might be responsible for the palace attacks. It was not impossible. The world's royal families all had violent regime changes in their histories.

This time it was Jill's turn to plod on with the difficult questions.

"Do you think that is what happened?"

Lhotse's eyes narrowed as he turned to look at her. "Be careful when you ask that question. I am not accusing anyone. We are far from the city up here. We have no trouble with the government. Darya serves on the council. You asked me a question, that is all."

Kaj frowned. Something did not add up. "Sir, you and your daughter insisted we visit you just as we start an investigation. Why it was so important to you that we come now?"

The old man sat back against the sofa and uncrossed his arms. He gave them a knowing smile, as if trying to undo whatever damage his outburst might have caused.

"When trouble comes, people say 'Mountain Thunder did it'."

"Is that your reputation?"

"Reputation. Yes. That is it. I told Darya, that we should talk with you before you hear other people. You see us now. Are we heartless killers? Would we kill the people who gave us our valley? We are wealthy. We have no reason to harm the king, even if he is Water Dragon. No trouble for fifty years. That old monk, he knew. Why would we change that?"

Kaj looked stolidly at the old man. He was now convinced that Lhotse's fractured English was a deliberate misdirection, part of an act to convince Kaj that the old man was artless and straightforward. If that was the plan, it was failing. He began to move forward as he might in an interrogation.

"Do you know of anyone else who *might* want to harm the King or his family?"

The old man looked uncomfortable at Kaj's change in tone.

"People might say we wanted to harm the King," Lhotse's reply rose into a non-committal question mark that signaled insecurity and uncertainty. "They would be wrong."

"Falsely accuse you? Is that what you mean?"

Lhotse started the back-tracking and diversion that Kaj had seen so often in the police interview rooms.

"Not accusing. Just suggesting."

The old man could see that Kaj was not impressed. He paused for a moment and when he continued, his voice had an edge.

"Other clans are jealous of us. They might accuse us to do harm." The old man thrust out his chin as if he had scored great points against his rivals.

"Accuse you of what?" Kaj insisted.

The old man's voice took on a declarative firmness.

"We have not killed anyone. It is a long drive to the city. If we fly, everyone sees us. How could we attack the palace? My grandson, Batsa, lives in city, but he spends days selling jewelry, making packages, licking stamps. He has no desire to harm anyone. Why would he? He makes good living. He has forgotten the mountains and is soft. Mountain Thunder has done nothing. We have our valley. We have no anger."

Yet, Kaj noted, Grandpa sounded angry.

Lhotse stood up then indicating that the meeting was over. If they had been at the Beretania Street building, it would have been akin to the moment when suspects suddenly said they wanted a lawyer. Kaj felt they must have wandered further into Mountain Thunder's business than the old man wanted. Mentally, he put Darya's brother on the list of people who should now be interviewed.

They left the old man as the afternoon sun was starting to send long shadows and the sky was the color of turquoise and royal blue. The peaks of the mountains stood out like ice castles.

On the way back to the airport, Darya was surprisingly talkative.

"Grandpa is determined," she said. "He usually gets his own way. Only one time he didn't succeed."

Jill looked at her skeptically. "Oh?"

Kaj smiled slightly to himself. Darya had something to say. He wondered if this was a continuing part of Mountain Thunder's lagging charm offensive.

"I told you that the older children from Mountain Thunder and Snow Leopard share an upper school halfway between our lands. One of my friends was exceptionally bright. Grandpa decided that she should marry my brother and go to school to become a vet so we would not have to fly someone up here to treat the animals. But she was never interested in my brother. After the Dam Board gave her a scholarship, she went to study at Oxford. She came back to become a doctor, a human vet. Grandpa was disappointed. He was angry with my brother who was not interested in raising yaks and mining. He did not want to have the family business run by me—a woman. But my father died in a mountain accident and he had to accept what he could get. He still dreams of a grandson who likes mines and yaks."

Darya's lips formed a narrow line. The expression reminded him of how Tashi had looked at Kaj at the hospital. Both women seemed on guard, standing their ground.

Kaj looked at the Colonel, who had been silent during the whole trip and gave no indication that he had heard. Kaj had the strong suspicion, though, that the man was listening closely to every word Darya spoke. She drove them up to their waiting aircraft and left immediately after they had climbed in among the shipments headed south to the city.

"Oh my god," Jill said as she took her seat. "That smell. Yak cheese. I was warned about this."

Indeed, the cabin was full of an aroma that seemed a cross between strong blue cheese and dirty sock.

She furrowed her forehead in dismay. "The cheese smells ten times stronger than the tea."

Kaj leaned over the chair to talk to the Colonel in front. "Thank you for the warning you gave on the tea. We took your advice."

The Colonel's laugh filled the cabin. Apparently, visitor reactions to butter tea and yak cheese were a joke in the mountains.

"The tea is good for you. But drink it hot when it is cold outside. You will not be hungry all day if you have it for breakfast. Grandpa was hospitable with the prayer shawls and the tea. He behaved politely. You did as well."

Kaj found himself silently qualifying that assessment. He had found Grandpa Lhotse evasive and suspected that the old man found him rude, but he had to admit that he was applying his own professional biases. Most people did not think that being interrogated was polite.

It was only later in the flight, when the Colonel went front to talk to the pilots, that Kaj had the chance to ask Jill what she thought about Darya.

"She wanted to tell you that story," Jill whispered.

"I know. And I think we both know who she was talking about."

"Tashi. Who else could it be?" Jill's eyebrows rose in question. "Darya just suggested that Lhotse resents the fact that the King may be about to marry the woman the old man wanted for his grandson?

"It sounds very thin as a motive."

Just then the aircraft lurched and dropped a disturbing number of feet before recovering with a wild upward swoop. The Colonel hung onto the seat backs as he came back down the aisle.

"Welcome to the afternoon wind shears," he said as he strapped himself in.

Chapter 17

KAJ MADE TWO PHONE CALLS immediately upon coming back from the mountains. He made an appointment to meet with the King and then a more furtive call to Greg, who suggested that they meet at the tea cart just outside the gates to the upper palace. It was close enough that Kaj would not need a formal security escort.

The King took him into the secure room, which was not much larger than a bathroom. It had a small wood table with a couple of chairs and a telephone with multiple push buttons. Once the doors were closed, all noises from outside were gone. Kaj found it claustrophobic.

The King looked solemn and did not wait for any pleasantries.

"I have been informed that Anya has died. She was my nanny before I went to boarding school. My mother died when I was nine, and Anya gave me stability and kindness."

"That must be hard for you, Sir," Kaj said. "She was part of your past."

"An important part," the King agreed. "She loved me and my cousins as if we were her own."

"Did she have family?"

"She never married. During the holidays, she went home to Golden Tiger. That was her clan, but we were her family."

"Your secretary is listed on her hospital file as next of kin."

"Ananda?" The King thought for a moment. "That would make sense. We are responsible for her security and her hospital charges. Anya and Ananda are both Golden Tiger, so there is some connection."

Kaj silently noted the family connection that Dorji had not mentioned.

"Was your day in the mountains helpful?" the King asked.

"We were not expecting to be up there so early in the investigation. Darya insisted, and the Colonel suggested that we should go."

"I know. I told him to."

Kaj was not surprised. Did you tell him to come with us as well?"

"No. I just told him to provide security."

"Do you trust him completely?" Kaj tilted his head slightly to the right and just stared at the King.

The King frowned. "I have said how I feel about trusting anyone. But the Colonel has Gurkha pride and the loyalty of his men. Those are valuable assets."

"Old Man Lhotse gave us the countering story to the massacre of Kalyani. That included what happened when the Abbot convinced Mountain Thunder to endorse the new constitution."

The King laughed outright. "You mean the monk's baring of his soul? Our monks are large characters. They had to be. They were the only ones who could impose order at that time."

"Grandpa Lhotse told us that Mountain Thunder is misunderstood and people are wrong in automatically assuming they are troublemakers. It sounded possible if not plausible. But it is hard to overlook the systematic destruction they caused at Kalyani."

The King nodded. "Like most things, it is complicated. I wanted you to see Kalyani and then hear what Mountain Thunder had to say about it. They are not wrong. But neither was Water Dragon. I do not believe a yak caused all the later trouble."

"Grandpa Lhotse thought it special yak."

"Yes. He has the head preserved and its portrait on the wall somewhere in the house. Did he show you that?"

Kaj shook his head. "We did try his tea, though."

"Butter or chai?"

When Kaj admitted it was the butter tea, the King broke out another smile. "Rite of passage," he said, "Everyone must try it. It is quite possible to develop the taste. But I am sure you did not come here to talk about tea."

"I need to ask you to remember everything about the message telling you about the call from Beijing. You said that it was from your secretary. Did you see who gave you the message?"

The King put his head into his hands and started a slight up and down rubbing movement on his forehead.

"I am not sure. Perhaps one of the staff. It was a man. There were three or four male staff serving that day."

"One of the victims was your head butler."

"Yes. Ajeet Singh. A Sikh. He was the senior master of the servants. He would be called a head butler in England. A very dignified man."

"He was the only person killed in the room who was not a member of your family. Could he have been the one who gave you the message?"

"Perhaps, but I just do not remember."

"Can you remember the exact words you heard?"

"I was wanted in my office immediately for an urgent call from Beijing."

"Did he say he had been told to tell you that?"

The King nodded. "I think so."

"Did you mention this to anyone in the room?"

"I might have said something about the phone call to my uncle. I would not have said much if I thought I would return in a few minutes."

"When you reached your office, did you say anything to your secretary?"

The King looked up at Kaj in confusion. "Is this really important?"

"I think it might be."

"I walked quickly because the call was urgent and came straight to this room. If I assumed that the message had come from Ananda, why would I say anything to him?"

"You didn't ask him if the caller was still waiting?"

"He would tell me if the call had dropped. May I ask why all these questions?"

"We need to know more about that phone call. Just routine at this point. You told me before that you went into the secure room and found there was no one on the line."

The King nodded uneasily. "I had no chance to ask Ananda about the call before security officers came into the office and said there was an attack on the palace."

"And no one ever called back?"

"I suppose not."

The King frowned and stared at Kaj. They both knew there had to be something more. Without that call, the King would have been among the dead. As far as Kaj was concerned, in Kuthan there was always something more.

"I also need to ask you more about Ajeet Singh. Our Medical Examiners have reported that his body was scarred by what looked like military wounds or torture."

The King did not look surprised. "The Sikhs suffered when the British left. Ajeet and his father were visiting family in Delhi at the time when Indira Ghandi was assassinated. They were not involved, but they were caught up in the violence after she was killed by her Sikh bodyguards. Ajeet's father was beaten to death in the street and Ajeet was left for dead. I wish I could say that the violence has stopped, but radical groups still want a Sikh home state they call Khalistan and they do violent acts to keep their demands alive. There are expatriate groups in Canada and the UK that fund this movement."

"Did any violence like this happen in Kuthan?"

"I have not heard of any Kuthan groups supporting Sikh independence. I was told that arms are smuggled in from Pakistan to be distributed in Punjab. The Colonel would know more about that. But Kuthan's small Sikh community is based in Mongarthuā, not along our borders, and we have no history of ethnic or religious persecution."

"Then you would say that there is no anti-Sikh feeling in Kuthan? Nothing that would make a Sikh man working in the Kuthani royal palace become a target?"

"The Colonel would have informed me if he had information about that. But I would also talk to the temple director. Our Sikh community are the descendants of army clerks who remained after the British left. They have been the backbone of our civil service. I must make it clear, that not all Sikhs support the Khalistan movement, particularly not the violence."

When Kaj left the King's office, he pointed to the wagons outside the gates, said "chai," and slipped outside before the guards could stop him.

Greg had to pay for their teas because Kaj did not have Kuthani money.

"First, off," Kaj began, thank you for agreeing to loan Chris and John. Between them and Sanjay, they should be able to tell once and for all if electronic locks can be picked."

"My pleasure. Computer techies like to challenge electronic systems. Good thing they're on our side, except that I'm sure that the bad guys have the same motivated crew on theirs."

"It will be interesting to see if they can do it. Now, do you have any word on Mallik?"

"Still drawing a blank. No one admits knowing anything. We will keep on working on it."

"OK. But now another problem's come up. Meng's made a move on one of my team."

Greg looked concerned. "What kind of move?"

"He's invited him to dinner."

Greg frowned, "And?"

"Not sure. But Meng apparently winked at him during the briefing meeting the other day."

"Is this about Detective Lee?"

Kaj's stared at Greg, who just shook his head.

"You can run, but you can't hide from the government when it wants to know your business. We did full background checks on you all. If you remember, I warned you about vulnerabilities and Meng on the flight coming over."

"Is Meng gay? Is this a flirtation?"

"Hard to say. He says he has a wife and daughter, but no one's ever seen them. I wouldn't trust him one way or the other."

"I want to distract Meng and make him useful."

Greg shrugged and raised his eyebrows. "All ears. I've never seen that done."

"I told Cliff to accept the invitation, except I'm going in his place."

"Is that wise? It could be a trap."

"I had the hotel look up the address, and the restaurant is just down the hill. Security can wait outside."

Greg took a deep breath and started with the obvious objections. "And what do you plan to do with him?"

"Have him help me find Mallik."

"What makes you think he will?"

"I don't care if he does or he doesn't, but I think he will jump at the idea of showing the superiority of Chinese intelligence. It was his one-upping at the briefing that gave me the idea."

Greg looked doubtful. "You're in charge of this investigation and I can't stop you from doing this. But I can warn you that anything he does for you will come with a price tag. He will want something in return."

"I don't know what he can get from a Hawaii detective. I have no secrets to share. I hope that stroking his ego is enough."

"I think it's riskier than you think. But if you are determined, I will try to watch your back. I hope I never have to justify this to State."

"Speaking of State, I have a request for you. Will you ask them to release all documents regarding Mallik? Particularly, the letters of request from Kuthan. We also want anything you have on the exchange in Singapore."

Greg raised his eyebrows. "You suspect Mallik?"

"We suspect everyone."

"All right," Greg said, "I assume it's ASAP."

"Of course." Kaj looked at Greg with mischief in his eyes. "And, of course, you will want to know what happens if Meng comes through with something?"

"I'll be all ears," Greg agreed.

Chapter 18

It was time for the third team meeting and Kaj knew the danger. There was no longer any tomorrow. His plan to build teamwork was either going to succeed today or go completely off the rails.

Maintaining an outward optimism was not easy. During the last team meeting, he had silenced the dissent but not addressed the underlying issue. The Chinese team was openly skeptical of the Indian forensics team, and the latter was deeply resentful of the casual condescension. Sharma and Xue were neck-and-neck when it came to egos. Nie and Agarwahl were trying to stay out of it, although the latter would defend Sharma if needed. The crime lab technicians, Achari and Choudhary, and their Chinese counterpart, Liu, were keeping their heads down. Sanjay was doing the dirty work, but he had no clout. Everyone was doing their jobs but without much enthusiasm and certainly without any inkling of teamwork.

Kaj's current plan was to let the two sides work it out while he insisted on focusing on the job at hand. He'd seen these territorial disputes before. Matters usually came to a head at a moment when intervention seemed long overdue. In rare cases, simply working together straightened things out. He could live in hope that would happen, but he doubted it. He remembered a Shakespeare line, or thought he did: "a plague on both your houses." Correct or not, the quotation appropriately described how he felt about the situation.

"Good afternoon," he said brusquely as he called them all to order. "There is a lot to cover. This is a team meeting and not a lecture series, so feel free to ask questions of any of us as we go along. Dr. Sharma and Mr. Agarwahl, we'll start with your report."

Agarwahl pulled two of the evidence boards together at the front of the room. He pinned a large chart to each of them and then stood back.

The first was a meticulous map of the crime scene, drawn to scale with numbers and shapes representing the victims and different colored symbols indicating where bullet fragments and trace evidence had been retrieved. The second was a to-scale floorplan of the entire palace level, showing the aboveground buildings, the subterranean passageways that linked them, and a side-projection showing the connection between the crime scene, the palace, the guest hotel, and the security office.

As Agarwahl explained it, the crime scene map demonstrated two primary crime-scene areas. The first was at the head of the dining table, where the bodies of victims one through four—Tranh, the butler, and Dechen and Pema—had been found. The second was next to the hall's interior doorway, where the bodies of victims five and six—the cousins, Kanchan and Kiran, had been found. He acknowledged Mr. Choudhary's discovery of the blood trail down the interior corridor, and credited it with the discovery of the below-ground crime scene areas, which included subsequent processed areas in the hall basement, the tunnels connecting the palace to the outside security area, and the basement area of the guest hotel. He noted that the area around and behind the hall doorway was marked by scuffed, overlaying footprints, and bullet fragments were retrieved not only from the wall, which would be expected, but also from the ceiling. Ballistic evidence so far was consistent with the rifle retrieved from the drainage channel. Blood and DNA evidence was still under review.

"If the rifle was the sole weapon used, was there one shooter?" Nie asked.

"I do not rule that out, Madam," Sharma said cautiously. "But there were multiple fingerprints on the rifle that we are still working to identify."

"Did you make copies of these maps for us?" Xue demanded.

Sharma casually slid a folder across the table toward Xue. "Copies for everyone," he said. "In color," he added. "I am glad to share the excellent work of our crime lab staff."

Xue said nothing. He took his two copies and passed the folder on around the table. Kaj sighed inwardly while Sharma shared invisible handshakes with the crime lab team.

"DNA analysis will take time," Sharma said. He nodded for Agarwahl to continue.

"We said yesterday that the rifle was not in good condition. There was sand and goat hair in the mechanism. That may explain the chaotic pattern of the bullet trace."

Agarwahl stopped and looked inquiringly at Kaj.

"Any conclusions about the shooter?" Kaj asked.

"We've reported all we can prove at this point," Sharma said.

"I'm aware of that," Kaj interrupted. "What I want to know is what you think based on your own experience."

"What we suspect?" Agarwahl looked startled. "You mean that we might think that the shooter was an amateur and unfamiliar with the rifle?"

"Do you?"

"It's definitely possible," Sharma said. "But we need further evidence to make that definitive judgment."

Kaj persisted with his question. "Dr. Sharma, from your experience, what might you say—not can or should say—about the evidence you have so far?"

Sharma gave a gesture that suggested he was giving in reluctantly to someone else's worst impulses.

"All right. We might say that the bullet trace in the walls and ceiling suggest a shooter who is not experienced with the rifle and is not a professional assassin. Professional killers like economy and speed. We have seen mass killings with that profile. We think the shooter is an amateur."

"What do you mean by *amateur*?" Xue asked.

Sharma glared at Xue. "It means someone untrained, who has not served in the military, and may not have handled weapons at all. Not a weapons collector. Not someone who spends hours at a place shooting at targets. Is that clear enough?"

Kaj jumped in immediately to calm the rhetoric. "What is a *chaotic pattern*?" he asked.

"I'll let Mr. Achari answer that," Agarwahl said. "He's our ballistics expert."

Achari rose reluctantly from his seat and moved to the front as if he were walking to the guillotine. Sharma gave him encouraging smile as the man reached the front of the room.

"The rifle was not on automatic when it was recovered," Achari told them. "The rifle weighs 4.5 kilos, ten pounds, fully armed, and in untrained hands, the rifle jumps. The magazine holds thirty rounds and was empty. A pattern is chaotic when the bullets have no consistent pattern. The rifle may have worn parts or the shooter may stand improperly. We think the shooter was an inexperienced user."

Achari looked pleased with himself as he sat down, even more so when he caught Kaj's eye and felt the approval of Kaj's nod. Even Xue was quieted for the moment.

Kaj then looked expectantly at Nie for her autopsy report. This time her focus was on Kaj rather than Xue. She knew now what he wanted. Either that or she had given up on impressing Xue.

"The final four autopsies raise more questions than answers. Dr. Xue and I worked on victims three, Dechen, and four, Pema, and then worked together on five, Kanchan, and six, Kiran. We found that we must focus on the two males because they had considerably different wound patterns from the other victims. Our main question was why the bodies were separated from the others. We decided to perform their autopsies as a team with Mr. Liu."

Kaj's eyebrow rose when Xue stood up to follow Nie's lead. He had thought Xue would be resistant and Nie silent. Any change in the direction of cooperation, even if unexpected, was good. He wondered if Meng had something to do with it.

"We knew that the first four victims, the uncle, the two aunts, and the Sikh butler, were at the head of the table near where the King was sitting. The cousins, victims five and six, were further down the table, closer to the doorway where the shooter stood. We identified the first four victims as comprising the "main" case, and the final two as a "special case." When we looked at it that way, certain things became very clear."

Nie nodded to Xue to continue.

"Victim five, Kanchan, when he was shot, was standing to the front of the shooter but some distance away. Victim six, Kiran, had two bullet entries under the chin that penetrated the brain. Powder burns indicate that the rifle was held against his neck. He also had burn marks on both palms."

"Were you able to determine what caused those burns?" Kaj asked.

"They were in the center of each palm. It would be consistent with an attempt to take hold of something hot."

Kaj nodded thoughtfully. "Then we have a shooter in the interior doorway armed with an AK-47 rifle with 30 rounds in the magazine. We don't know yet if he was acting alone. We don't know yet a motive. But can we agree on how the shooter might have gained entrance to the scene?"

"Pending confirmation that the electronic look can be opened," Sharma said, "entry could have been through the hotel basement."

"That would mean," Liu said suddenly, breaking out of his self-imposed silence, "that the shooter knew about the party and who would be there. He or she also knew about the entrance from the hotel and about the drainage grate."

Nie's eyebrows rose as she turned her head to look at Liu.

Kaj noticed and began to relax. *This is more like it. That was a good conjecture. Come on, everyone. Start chiming in. Throw out ideas."*

Sanjay jumped in next. He spoke with the authority of being the one who climbed into the flood channel to find the rifle.

"The rifle was behind a grate in the tunnel. Someone small had access. A hotel guest? A hotel worker?"

"Someone able to smuggle a rifle into the hotel without being seen?" Kaj asked.

"An Ak-47 rifle can be disassembled and carried in a bag," Achari said. "But the shooter would need to reassemble it."

"A security guard?" Xue said "The guards are ex-military. They would have the training to do it."

At that point, and to Kaj's satisfaction, the exchanges became quick fire.

Kaipo: "Hotel and security staff need identification tags if the shooter planned to leave the hotel."

Sharma: "Perhaps he was given or stole one,"

Xue: "You're assuming that it was a male shooter."

Sharma: "I do not underestimate what ladies can do with a rifle. But, in my experience, mass murders are usually done by young men. I am willing to be corrected, though."

Kaj: "The shots start. Then what happens?"

Nie: "Everyone freezes. Noise. Confusion. Screams."

Sharma: "Three seconds—they try to get down on the floor. Five seconds—the first four are dead."

Achari: What about the last two victims. Do they try to hide?"

Sanjay: "Do they want to run at the shooter? Be heroes?"

Sharma: "Why was victim five shot standing in front of the shooter?

Xue: "Did he know the shooter? Did he think he would not be shot?"

Kaj: "Is there any evidence for that?"

Cliff: "It's a point. The last two victims were not sitting with the others. Did they know what was going to happen?"

Kaipo: "Did they think they could overpower the shooter? As Sanjay says, the shooter had to be small."

Sanjay: "And he would have to pick electronic locks to get in and out."

Kaj: "Potentially. We've not seen it done yet."

Achari: "What about the burn marks on victim six? Did he try to hold the rifle barrel and not know it would be hot. That might mean the victim also did not know much about the rifle. They struggle and the rifle fires. Is that how the bullets go into the ceiling?"

Achari: "Who was victim six?

Nie and Xue: Kiran

Sanjay: "Did the shooter mean to kill them all?"

Xue: "Why not?"

Sanjay: "If there was a plan, did the shooter follow it?"

Kaj: "What kind of plan? That's a big assumption."

Nie: "What about the old woman?"

Xue: "Was she an accomplice? Did she put the rifle in the tunnel?"

Sharma: "And crawl through the flood channel? I do not think so. Sanjay had trouble doing it, and he is young."

Cliff: "Why would the shooter hit the old woman? Why not shoot her like the others."

Choudhary: "No more ammunition? Magazine is empty?"

Agarwahl: "Who told the King to leave the hall?

Kaj: The King thought it might have been the Sikh butler."

Liu: "He didn't remember?"

Kaj: "He said all he could remember was that it was a man."

Xue: "Aristocrats do not notice servants. They are all the same to them."

Cliff: "How about another possibility? The staff said the old woman was a former nanny who often hid in a butler's pantry to watch the family. The staff gave her food and let her stay. Did she see something and try to warn the King?"

Jill: "Why didn't she go into the hall with the royal family to warn them?"

Xue: "It would not have been her place to do that."

Kaipo: "Could she have looked for someone else do it? The Sikh butler perhaps? Was that why he wasn't in the kitchen with the others after the dishes were cleared?"

Kaj: "Let's play with this for a moment. Did she tell the butler that she needs to get a message immediately to the King? Would he do it?"

Xue: "Possible. She is not important enough herself to give a message. She must say that the message came from someone else."

Kaj: "An urgent message from the King's secretary? Would the butler question that?"

Xue: "He has been trained not to question. But was the secretary involved? Did he lie about the phone call. Was he part of the plot but had a change of heart? If the secretary gave the message to the butler, he may not want to admit it."

Kaj: "How do we prove that?"

Xue: "Even the royal family should be considered. That is what you said. The Sikh. Everyone."

Kaj: "Yes. A possibility. A family member or a servant would be free to enter the inner palace walls without being questioned."

Sharma: "If a family member is involved, what would be the motive? Why kill an old man and a couple of older ladies?"

Xue: "Could the Sikh have been the target?"

Kaj: "There is one external possibility that needs to be up there on the boards. We learned recently that Abhinav Mallik left US custody. It is possible that he has returned to Kuthan."

Sharma: "The Mallik who murdered Professor Whitworth? How could that happen? I thought he had been sentenced to one of your prisons."

Kaj: "It seems that Kuthan requested his return. There was an exchange in Singapore and after that no trace of him."

Xue: "No trace?"

Kaj: "We have people looking for him. But there is no evidence to link him to the crime."

Sharma: "You are looking for him, though?"

Kaj nodded. "We have started inquiries. We are going to look at every possibility we have listed here. Are we missing anything?"

Sharma: "More results, more questions will come."

"And we will deal with them," Kaj said. "Dr. Nie, have you been advised that the King's nanny, Anya, has died?"

"Yes, the hospital called me. "Mr. Liu has prepared the mortuary for her autopsy tomorrow. Mr. Liu and I will conduct it. Dr. Xue wants to watch the attempt to open the door into the hotel basement."

"The lab will continue to analyze the DNA of the victims," Sharma said proudly. "Much more tomorrow." He gave his usual dramatic sweep of the arm. "Many more answers, I am sure."

Kaj looked around the table to see if anyone had more to contribute. Not seeing any hands, he began to conclude the meeting.

"Eric Strobel from Strobel Engineering will be here tomorrow morning. The Strobel company built the hall and the hotel. The Colonel has asked him to talk about the underground tunnels. Anyone here is welcome. Once that is over, we will see if electronic locks can be opened without a code."

"They can," Sanjay said happily.

Kaj smiled. "We'll see."

Only the detectives remained once the others had filed out. Their voices echoed in the hallway and gradually diminished as they walked down the stairs to their supper. For the time being, they walked as a group rather than two warring camps.

"Where are we all tomorrow?" Kaj asked once the voices had faded.

"Kaipo and I planned to watch the lock tests, then we're set to review the perimeter security tapes with the Colonel," Cliff said. "We can be there for the Strobel presentation, though."

"The hotel is releasing the visitor logs tomorrow morning," Jill added. "I have an appointment to pick them up and they will take me through them. That's my morning. The lock show is all yours."

"I'll follow up with the Lhotse family at their downtown jewelry store in the afternoon," Kaj said.

"I'd like to come with you to that, Kaj," Jill said. "Can we work something out?"

"I'll ask the Colonel to arrange it. Any thoughts on today's meeting while we are at it?"

Cliff raised his hand in a gesture that made him look as if he were bidding in an auction.

"It started slowly. I thought you were going to have to separate Xue and Sharma. Once you encouraged the brainstorming, it took off. The different viewpoints are interesting—not just professional but also cultural."

"Cultural?" Jill looked quizzically at Cliff.

"The Indian forensics team seems happy with their work. The Chinese team is detached and wary. But they were all paying attention, if only to each other."

"It was good to see the quieter ones like Liu and Achari start to participate," Jill said. "Even Choudhary. He's the expert on the DNA evidence."

"The DNA is going to be critical," Kaj agreed. "For a few minutes, they sounded like colleagues. If we want it to continue, we follow up on every suggestion and involve them where we can. No one's ideas are discounted, even if they come out of left field. We need a way to ratchet down the competition. It's useful when they challenge each other, but I'd rather they didn't do it by playing gotcha."

"Lots of history there," Cliff said professorially. "At the disputed borders, Indian and Chinese soldiers throw rocks. Better than grenades, but still very hostile."

"What happens if we can't get them beyond that?"

Jill asked the question more out of curiosity than doubt. If anyone could make a team out of these disparate people, it would be Kaj. But even he could not work miracles.

"Then we go with my version of Occam's razor." Kaj spoke more definitely than he felt.

"Occam's razor?" Kaipo frowned. "Wasn't that about taking the simplest solution when there were two competing theories?"

"Same principle. If they don't cooperate on the larger issues, we shave the problem down until we find a place where they can respect each other's expertise rather than try to top it."

"But can they leave the safety of their specialties?" Kaipo asked.

"One can only live in hope."

Chapter 19

WHETHER IT WAS ALTITUDE, THE persistence of jet lag, or just the challenge of trying to meld professionals into a cohesive unit, Kaj was exhausted and should have known better than to sit down in a soft reclining chair. One moment he was looking through the suite's windows at distant glaciers, and the next he was asleep. This time, though, he did not reexperience distant battle fields and young men dying too soon. Instead, he was an observer of something very different.

The man was walking along a narrow road somewhere in the mountains. It was a route he had followed many times before. He was returning from market, hurrying because it was growing late and he did not want to be walking alone in the dark. Suddenly, he heard voices and the clank of armor and horse tack. This was not usual, and he was afraid. He stepped quickly off the road, hid in the dense foliage, and waited for whoever it was to pass. After a few minutes, four horsemen came by, wearing heavy armor and brandishing spears that were red with blood. The leader had long, dark hair and crazed eyes.

The man knew that the dark man and his followers were evil, and he crawled further away, deeper in the forest. He did not want to go back on the road, even if the men had already passed by.

Deep in the woods, he found a pathway that ran parallel to the road, so he started down it, despite the growing darkness of both the trees and the sky. After a few minutes, he came across a clearing and saw a young child of about four sitting on a log with a wicker cage beside him.

"Hello," he said to the child. "Where are your parents?"

The child silently pointed to the forest behind him.

"Do they know you are here?"

"They told me to stay here until they came back."

"Will you wait here if I go to find them for you?" he asked.

The child nodded.

"Will you be safe?" he asked.

The child pointed to the cage. When he looked inside, he saw a bright pair of eyes staring back at him. It was one of the largest mongooses he had ever seen.

"He will keep me safe," the child said.

The man nodded and set off. It was not long before he came upon the scene of a massacre. Men and women lay mutilated in the ruins of what had been a camp. Death was fresh enough that the blood was still liquid. Immediately, the man knew that the horsemen had done this. Somewhere among the bodies must be the child's parents. He knew he would not ask the child to look.

He went back to where the child was waiting for him.

"Does your mongoose have a name?"

"He is called Jamaal," the child replied.

"And what is your name?"

The child hesitated as if he was not sure he should tell.

"Akela," he finally said.

"Well, Akela, I think you should come with me now. We will go to my house and wait for your parents. Is that all right?"

"They said I should wait," the child objected.

"We will wait at my house. They will know where to find you."

"What about Jamaal?"

"We will take him with us. He is your protector."

The man held out his arms and swung the child onto his shoulders. The child was surprisingly light. Then the man picked up the cage with the mongoose and the three of them hurried away into the woods. He made sure that they did not approach the place where the dead lay or the road where the horsemen might return. He did not stop until they reached his house.

"What do you have there?" his wife asked when she came out of the house and saw them.

"I found this child and his mongoose alone in the forest," the man replied. "I felt the need to protect him. I could not leave him."

"A mongoose?" The woman wrinkled her nose.

"It is called Jamaal and is his protector. He will not leave it."

"Where are his parents? There must be servants and retainers. Look how well he is dressed."

The man looked at the child as he had not before. He could see the quality of the clothing and a gold locket at his neck. This was the child of someone important.

"I will explain," the man said in a tone that forbade the woman from asking anything more.

"Come in," she said cooing to the child. "You must be hungry. And what does your mongoose eat?"

When the child was asleep, he told his wife about the horsemen and what they had done. "The child is in danger," he said. "Like the mongoose, we must protect him."

"He is the same age that our son would have been," the wife said. She went to a chest and took out the dead boy's clothes. "We can dress him in our son's clothes and tell him to pretend to be our son."

"Only until his parents come," he said.

"Of course," she replied. "Only until his parents come."

Kaj woke with the sense that the dream had stirred some memory, but he had no time to try recapturing it. The phone rang with a startling insistence. When he saw who was calling, he answered with a mixture of guilt and apology.

"You didn't call."

Linda's voice had an uncharacteristic accusatory edge. It took him a moment to calibrate his response.

"I made the mistake of sitting down when I got in last night. I just woke up." As if to punctuate his words, Kaj gave a yawn. "I was just about to put some coffee on."

"That's not funny. I was worried."

Kaj knew what she was worried about but did not want to admit it. He did not want to talk about his nightmares.

"I did not mean to worry you. It was a long day and the altitude got to me again. I'll try to do better in future.

"You sound different somehow," she said suspiciously. "Is everything all right?"

He did not know what to say so just stayed silent.

As she always did when a discussion carried the possibility of conflict, Linda changed the subject.

"How were the mountains?" Her voice began to settle back into her more usual upbeat tone.

"Massive, impressive . . ." Kaj struggled to find adjectives that sounded more original.

"But you wouldn't want to climb them?"

"People die up there."

"And how are things going?"

Not much different from a major case in Hawaii."

"You sound surprised."

"Not really. In the end it all comes down to the good old standbys: greed, revenge, lust, and envy."

Linda gave her sympathetic laugh. "What's happening today?"

"We have an engineer coming in to talk about how a building his company erected at the palace has a paper-thin basement wall that one of the forensics people fell through. Then we have three young men who hardly look more than twelve—to my old eyes anyway—who are going to demonstrate how to hack a supposedly impossible lock."

"Sounds like fun. They look like twelve, you say?"

"A young twelve. They are experts in computers. I think they probably knew more about computer programming when they were six than I ever have."

Linda laughed. "That's all right. That's why we pay them the big money."

"How are you doing?" Kaj asked.

"The baby's turned into real toddler now and into everything. He's even started putting words together into sentences."

"What does he say?"

It was her turn for a momentary silence. "Annie was hoping that he'd say something like 'I love you, Mama.' But he has a favorite talking bunny. You pull a string and it says something rabbity. He's been running round the house yelling 'I want carrots.' Not quite what she expected."

"She'll soon wish he wasn't so vocal when he starts with the questions."

Kaj wasn't sure where this conversation was going. It seemed strained. But then he was saved by the shrill call of the room phone.

"I've got to answer that," Kaj told her with a relief that came from somewhere he couldn't place. "I'll call you later. I promise."

The call was from Dorji wanting to make sure that he knew Anya, the retired royal nanny, had died. Kaj assured him that he did.

"I noticed that you were listed as family on her hospital records. Are you related to her?" Kaj chose not to tell Dorji that the King had already revealed the connection.

"Our grandfathers were cousins. But I had little chance to know her. Her life was always with the children at the palace."

Kaj felt the prickle before he could articulate it. *Wait a minute. You hardly knew her? If you had spent your life at Golden Dragon and she had been at the palace, that might make sense. But with both of you serving the same family at the same palace, that does not sound like a little chance even if she was older than you are. Something isn't adding up.*

Kaj decided that this was not the place or time. "Please accept my condolences for your loss," was all he said.

Chapter 20

KAJ SAT SIPPING COFFEE WHILE they waited for Strobel to arrive. Everyone with an assignment had gone, leaving Cliff and Kaipo on tap, along with Sharma, Sanjay, and Xue. Kaj looked at Xue and silently willed him to find something more interesting than provoking the Indian forensics staff. Perhaps that was too much to hope for, but he willing to believe things were possible.

Strobel and Colonel Pradhan came in together, and it was soon clear that the Colonel had done his homework. He placed a thick packet of plans on the table and then put a carousel of slides into the projector.

"In 1978," the Colonel began, "King Raju I directed Strobel Engineering Global Associates to design two buildings. One was meeting space for the new governing council, the other a guest hotel to house visiting council members. The present director of the Kuthan branch of Strobel Global Associates, Eric Strobel, is here today to explain these building plans and the design changes that were made over time."

The Colonel extended his arm toward Strobel and by that gesture implied he should start the presentation.

Strobel strode to the front of the room with an athletic bounce.

"I've met some of you already, but for anyone who doesn't know who we are, Strobel Global Associates built Kuthan's hydroelectric dam and we provide its on-going management and maintenance. We also contract for public and private construction. My late father, Richard Strobel, was the project director for all Kuthani palace projects in the 1970s. He kept meticulous notes regarding the construction of both the hall and the palace guest hotel that you are interested in. They were built at the same time. Fortunately, in 1985, our company locations were directed to digitize and centralize their records in Sidney. It was a safety precaution because of the growing number of unstable governments around the world. I was able to find the plans for the hall very quickly. The building you are asking about was identified in our company records as 'Kuthan Governing Council Meeting Project.' The specifications called for one large meeting space, council offices, meeting rooms, storage rooms, and limited catering facilities."

Strobel picked up a pointer and turned to look as a floor plan appeared on the screen behind him.

"If you notice, the original plans called for the meeting room to be on the first floor with a full basement area beneath. The basement was to serve as space for storage of council records. Access was to be provided by a staircase located in the corridor half-way between the meeting room and the rear offices to the back."

He advanced the next slide, which showed a rendering of the hallway and an open area where a flight of steps that led down into the basement. The slide after that showed the configuration of the basement with divided rooms and a series of windows set high the walls.

Kaj leaned forward to study the plan. It clearly showed an opening in one wall.

"Is that a doorway to the next building?"

Strobel smiled. "Let me get to that. It is complicated. But you're right."

Kaj raised his hand in apology, and Strobel resumed.

"Blueprints created from the original design were used for the pouring of the foundation. That foundation was completed on schedule in early 1980, except that just before work began on the upper levels, King Raju I died, and we received a design change request from the palace. The late king had wanted to keep the council meetings as close to the palace as possible. If the council members were housed in the hotel, which we were building at the same time, he wanted to use underground tunnels left over from the original monastery to provide access from the hotel to the council chamber. King Raju II, the present king's father, had a different vision. He wanted the meetings held in the conference room of the guest hotel so that council members would be housed in the same building where they would be meeting. The original hall would now become a reception space for state dinners and the royal family's personal events. He did not want underground access from the hotel to the hall."

The slide flicked to a schematic diagram of the original first floor plan of the hall laid next to the revised version.

"We were forced to make major design changes within the original footprint of the foundation we had already poured. Since the basement would not be needed for storage or offices, it was decided to leave it unfinished. The windows were either cemented in or converted to grids for ventilation. We were not given clear direction about the space that would have been occupied by the staircase to the basement. Originally, the staircase and opening were intended as a courtesy to the king who would be able to walk to the meeting across the courtyard, but without that purpose, it was considered a security risk."

"What was done in the end?" Kaj asked.

"Strobel Associates was told to solve the problem ourselves. According to my father's notes, the new King called the stairway and connection to the tunnel a 'hole in the wall' and told us to deal with it. My father wrote that he called in the other engineers working on the project, and they decided to create a storage room in the space but not to seal off the basement for perfectly good geologic reasons. Sealing a basement is not a good idea in the mountains because of radon gas. These were engineers after all. Also, what would happen in the unlikely event of a flood? How would the water be pumped out? They left an opening into the basement but put a trap door in the storage room floor for easy access. We were asked later to make the area less accessible. It seemed that the royal nanny was concerned because palace children had been exploring the basement. We removed the trap door and put in a moveable set of shelving to cover the opening."

"Do the notes say what was done to fill the hole connecting the hall to the tunnel?" Cliff asked.

"They filled the opening with plasterboard and left it at that. There were already cost overruns and this seemed the least of the construction problems."

"Is there anyone in your company who would . . ."

"Pass on the information about the opening?" Eric finished Kaj's thought. "No one is left in our office who worked for us then. Until our records were digitized, no one in our shop would even know where to start looking. After that, you'd have to know what to ask for."

Xue broke in at that point. "What about your central files in Sidney?"

"Security is the reason why we digitized and archived the records. We build essential infrastructure throughout the world and need to protect proprietary information from terrorist organizations or competitors. Access to the archives is closely guarded."

The room lights flicked back on as the Colonel shut down the projector.

"Colonel Pradhan has told us that these plans originally called for extensive camera surveillance in the tunnels."

Strobel nodded at Kaj. "I was not here when the decision was made not to install them. But my understanding is that there are cameras at the entrances in the palace and the security office."

He looked over at the Colonel for confirmation.

"The cameras at the hotel were disabled because no one believed that anyone could enter the tunnel from there."

"We'll find that out today," Kaj said.

"What about those children playing in the basement of the building. Did your father mention anything about them in his notes?" Kaipo asked.

"Yes, and I have copies of his notes for you. As I said before, the children's nanny told him the children were accessing the basement area through the trapdoor. My father says that moveable shelving was installed over the trap door to keep the four young rascals out—that is how my father described them. There were no further complaints in the file, so I assume that the solution worked."

"There were four?" Kaj asked.

"That's what he said."

"How many people would have known about this shelving and the trap door?"

"Obviously, the workers who built the shelving. The children, I suppose, and their nanny. Contemporary palace security would know, but that would depend on whether there were any records kept in the security files." Strobel looked inquiringly at the Colonel.

"I have not seen anything," the Colonel said. "I asked and no one remembers hearing about it. We went through the files and did not find any references to it."

"That doesn't surprise me," Strobel said. "My father's feeling was that the palace preferred the opening to be forgotten.

"Have you had projects in the Middle East?" Xue asked suddenly.

"One. We were brought in to build a water retention project in a high desert area near Kandahar. The circumstances became so dangerous that we had to contract with a private security company to pull our personnel out. An IED exploded outside the compound. After that, we refused contracts where we might get caught in a shooting war."

"Any goats there?" Sharma gave an amused glance at Xue.

"Goats?" Strobel looked confused. "There are goats everywhere."

"Are your guards armed?" Xue seemed to be trying for some vindication.

"They have small side arms. The only time I heard that one was fired was when someone disturbed a krait. They tell me it escaped unharmed."

"Lucky snake." Kaj said drily.

"Our engineers were the lucky ones. They tell me they are very poisonous."

Strobel looked around the room and stood silently for a few moments. There seemed to be a lull but he could feel the tension in the room. He closed his notes and his feet started to turn towards the door. "Is there anything else?" he asked hopefully. "Did I answer all your questions?"

Kaj looked around the room but saw no show of hands. Xue and Sharma seemed to have run out of ammunition.

"If you need me," Strobel said, "you know where I am."

Kaj looked at his watch as Strobel left. It was now more than time to find out whether supposedly impenetrable locks could be opened. If they could, then Kaj would not begrudge technological youth their victory over the doubting old guard. He knew his glee was unbecoming, but, secretly, he was cheering for the young upstarts.

"Who's up for locks?" he allowed himself to ask.

Everyone, it seemed.

Chapter 21

THEY MADE A STRANGE GROUP: Kaj, Cliff and Kaipo, Sharma, Agarwahl, Xue, and the Colonel crowded into the tunnel, watching to see if three determined young techies could work around, pick, hack, or whatever the current term was for disabling an extremely expensive lock system that had declared its own inviolability. The chase was on.

Chris, John, and Sanjay had bonded in the way of generational colleagues swaggering their way to rescue hapless clients who have done something silly, such as accidentally deleting their operating systems. In those cases, the mark of expertise was not just making the computer work again. That was a given. It was how fast they could do it. "It took me just five minutes" was the highest level of contempt.

Kaj, the Colonel, Xue, and Sharma could only watch. The process was less absorbing to them than the result. Kaj needed to see an opened door so he could confirm a possible means of access. The Colonel needed to know whether all the palace locks needed to be replaced. Sharma was probably there to keep an eye on Xue, who was determined to return the favor.

It was only Agarwahl who was essential. Nevertheless, there they all were, spread out in the barren tunnel waiting to see if there would be a major break in the case.

Chris started the demonstration by asking the Colonel to confirm that the door was locked and that all the codes had been deprogrammed. It reminded Kaj of the magicians of his boyhood. They started by demonstrating that the box was empty. They were creating illusions, though. Kaj needed proof rather than magic. A whole theory of the crime depended on it.

Sanjay held a light beam steady on the lock while John held up a small piece of shaped metal. Chris explained what they were doing as the process began.

"One of the great fallacies of electro-mechanical locks is the belief that they cannot be defeated. Every piece of technology is vulnerable. It just takes time. Colonel, you have a state-of-the-art system that has only been available for few years, but it has a fatal flaw. Someone can break in without tripping the electronic part. You shut down the system by removing access codes, but the central operating mechanism can still be accessed. The technological trick is finding the key and knowing the structure of the lock. Unfortunately, much of this information exists if you know where to look."

Just then, John inserted the small metal tool, jiggled it for a few moments with his ear to the lock, then straightened up and gave it a couple of knocks with a small hammer. There was a click and the door opened before their eyes. Chris and Sanjay cheered.

John looked around with a slightly bemused smile. "I've never been cheered for breaking into something before. I'm not sure I'm proud of it."

"My God." The Colonel looked in shock at Kaj and Sharma. "Is nothing safe?" He turned in confusion to John: "How did you learn to do this?"

"I did a computer search," John replied.

"There's even a video," Sanjay added.

Chris looked at the Colonel over his glasses. "We prefer to use computers for more ethical things. But better you know so you can strengthen your security."

"I could have used this information before," the Colonel said morosely.

"If you'd known, you would have kept the cameras in place," Chris agreed. "It was tempting to turn them off, but you were left without any way to monitor the area. I would reinstall them immediately if I were you."

"What you're telling me is that someone with that key and something to tap with breaks into any lock?"

"Not quite," John replied. "That key is special and specific. Whoever uses it needs special knowledge how to make it and the expertise to make it work. We had to work to find it. Usually, one comes with the original materials. You may not have realized its significance. That's what you want to lock away. It requires knowing how the lock works. But these days, with master computer hackers around the world, your best bet is to deploy multiple back-up security systems with overlapping domains: the locks, computers codes you change regularly, and security cameras. Even then, a locked deadbolt opens in two seconds with the right key."

Kaj glanced at the three young technocrats with their insider smiles. He was glad to see they were reveling in their work and even laying the foundation for future friendship. The future was theirs and he could only wonder what that was going to look like. He was not shocked at what they had done. But it made him wonder if the day would come when computers would make even detectives obsolete.

Chapter 22

It didn't take more than a few minutes after the grand opening of the lock for the Colonel and Kaj to collect Jill from the guest hotel and get them on their way to meeting with Batsa Lhotse at Mountain Thunder's downtown gem shop. It was the first time that the detectives had driven through the downtown area and they soon understood that Kuthan was a complex set of different worlds.

The modern high-rise structures they had seen from the airport were in what the Colonel told them was the business district, an area of about ten city blocks formed into squares built around fountains and leafy parks that could have been in any modern city, East or West. The district's glass and steel buildings displayed wealth and foresight, particularly of the kind that involve people who sign non-disclosure agreements.

The older part of the city was not that far away in distance but eons away in its cultural setting. The old town was a splash of bright colors and its alleys full of tables of artwork and household goods. Open-air cafes were everywhere, ranging from stands with pots of boiling broth and mesh sieves to others promising "divine, extra-special-deluxe" home cooking. Modern cars mingled with brightly painted trucks, people swooped by on mopeds, and triangular shaped tuk-tuks sounded their horns as they picked up passengers. Certain streets were blocked from traffic. Stands were set up there displaying Kuthan's produce. Every stand had someone yelling praises for the merchandise. Noise penetrated every corner, like the tobacco smoke that wafted across the road whenever the palace van stopped to avoid hitting a pedestrian.

Mountain Thunder had set up their downtown offices not far from this picturesque and historic part of the city. But theirs was another world, this time of high-end merchandise and luxury goods. The Lhotses' store was next to an art gallery that displayed a painting of Mount Masakatsu, signed by the artist, Lama, framed in a froth of gold-leaf that filled the window. On the other side of them, a boutique sold handbags and shoes tilted to reveal red soles. Mountain Thunder was announced only by the name in gold across the dark windows, along with the words, "by appointment only." It had an ambience that said this shop is expensive, internationally important, and worth every penny.

The Colonel escorted Kaj and Jill to the windows with the golden letters and left them while he crossed the road to join his staff at a small table in an outside café. The security guards ordered coffee and prepared for a lengthy wait.

It had not occurred to Kaj that a reservation might be required to enter the shop. He rang the doorbell doubtfully and watched as a camera swiveled to see who they were. They must have passed scrutiny because the door swung silently open, inviting them into to a fairy tale display of opulence. Customers sat in deeply plush armchairs sipping drinks while exquisitely clothed assistants brought trays of jewelry out to them. Everything sparkled as the detectives walked through the room, even the crystal decanters in the central, circular bar. Kaj glanced at the shop's guards who were eyeing them curiously. Kaj wondered if they too were veterans of the Queen's Own Gurkhas.

The man who greeted them with a namaste looked like Darya but his features were more defined and he lacked the robust mountain quality that seemed to accompany thin air and hard winters. He did not share his grandfather's far-reaching stare. He looked watchful in a different way. Somehow, Kaj could not imagine him and Tashi together. He wondered whatever had got into the old man to think that it could have worked.

"I am Batsa Lhotse. Please step this way to my office." Their host pointed towards a flight of stairs at the back of the store that took them up to a second floor with large one-way glass windows that looked down onto the sales room. It was all so impressive that Kaj did not notice that there was someone else in the room until Jill nudged him sharply.

He nearly crashed into Batsa as he stepped backwards.

"Darya," he said rather too loudly. "What are you doing here?"

"I came to town," she said nonchalantly as Kaj struggled with his surprise.

"How did you know where we'd be?" Jill took up the slack in the conversation.

Darya shrugged. "I made a good guess."

Before anyone could say anything farther, Batsa guided them over to a circular conference table and then ordered White Bone tea for them all.

"Who told you we would be here?" Jill sounded almost indignant.

"No one had to tell me. I gave you enough information for you to want to talk with my brother. I was prepared to wait until you worked it out, but you were very prompt."

Kaj did not look pleased at the manipulation. "You need to explain this," he said none too gently.

"I made some assumptions is all because I . . .' She stopped and looked at her brother. "We . . . wanted to talk with you privately and we knew Grandpa would insist on being present. I added on the business with Tashi to make sure you came here to talk to Batsa. But the main reason you are here is so we can talk about how things work with grandfather."

The tea arrived and they waited for it to be poured before Darya resumed.

"Everything he told you was true. But there is the past and there is reality." Darya looked at her brother. "Do you want to start?" He shook his head and gestured for her to continue.

"Our mother died young, so there was just our father. He was a gentle man, a kind soul, a lot like Batsa. But Grandpa wanted an heir, a mountain man like him. He insisted that our father work with the yaks. He was killed in an avalanche a few miles from home. Then there was talk of me going to Oxford with Tashi. I wanted to go. Grandpa would not hear of it. 'Absolutely not,' he said. 'Darya stays here and has babies. She does not need Oxford.' Then he came up with the plan that Tashi should become a vet and marry Batsa."

"How did you feel about this?" Kaj asked Batsa.

"I was one year younger than Darya and Tashi, and had no interest in being married. I applied to the Dam Board and they agreed to train me for a management position. Grandpa tried to stop me, but I said yes. The Board sent me to university in India and hired me when I came home. When I said I was leaving, Grandpa told me he never wanted to see me again. I took him at his word. I married a lady here in the city. After a few years of working for the dam, the Board told me that if I was interested, they would help me set up my own business in the city. I told Grandpa that I now had international experience and contacts and could set up our family business in Mongarthuā and expand it with global clients. He said no, of course."

"The Dam Board did not mind?" Jill asked. "You must have learned a lot about their operations while you were working there"

"The law says they must participate in economic development," Darya explained. "They sent Tashi to Oxford, all expenses paid. They supported Batsa with a program to encourage new businesses. Grandpa would not agree to let me go. Instead, he chose a husband for me. My husband was not a bad man. He was one of our mine managers, but he liked risks. I knew he would get himself killed one day. He took a company car and bet that he could drive to the city in record time. He was killed when the car went over a cliff."

Darya shook her head in frustration.

"Now I was left with a son without a father and a fierce determination not to let my grandfather run my life. Batsa and I decided we must run the business. We let him think he still was still in charge, but we managed the accounts. It was a secret at first. Batsa made the finances work properly. But then I told Grandpa he could still work with the yaks and the mines, but Batsa was to run the business. Of course, he said no. Then I told him 'You are responsible for our father's death. You forced me to marry, you are old school, and you are spoiled. You can work with us or we will work around you."

Darya gave a small, victorious grin.

"That shocked him. He could not believe that a woman would oppose him. I had learned about the business from my husband, so I told him: 'This is a new era. Work with what you have. Don't be a fool.' I also told him, 'You will not have my son to herd your yaks unless he wants to. If you want your dynasty, it will be Batsa and me, but not on your terms. Not anymore."

"And he went along with your plans?"

"Not right away. That would not have been grandpa. But the ranchers saw that Batsa knew how to get them paid on time. They also saw how much more professionally the business was running. Grandpa was forced to recognize that we knew what we were doing with computers. His heart was out with the yaks anyway and not in meetings or setting up spreadsheets. Even he could see that the old system of handshakes and scribbles on scraps of paper wasn't working. My little brother has built us into an international company, and he has two beautiful daughters. My grandfather has been proved wrong, but he is stubborn. Once again, he still wants me to remarry and have boys who will herd yaks."

Jill was wide-eyed. "He's selected another husband for you?"

Darya laughed and tossed her head. "He knows better than to try."

"Why is this family history important for us to know?" Jill asked with her usual directness.

Darya leaned forward as if to suggest she was about to share a confidence.

"Batsa and I have the same concerns as Grandpa. You must visit the dam. If you do not know it now, you will soon see how it drives our lives."

Kaj's eyebrow rose. Darya was becoming a bit dramatic for his taste. "Is that a bad thing? Many of your young people seem to have benefited from its programs."

"It is always difficult when so much depends on water. When there were plans to expand the dam and sell electricity, young men from Water Dragon and Blue Pheasant threatened to blow the dam up. They were all arrested, but it made people suspicious of the dam's motives. There was a rumor that the Dam Board had paid Mountain Thunder to attack Water Dragon at Kalyani so that there would be no opposition to their expansion. Grandpa tried to tell you that was not true. For him, the attack was caused by the death of the yak. He's back in the days of the warlords: attack him and his yak, and he exacts revenge or loses face. He also tried to tell you that some of the other clans had more motive than us to see the dam expand. That was true. The expanded dam was down below us, so it did not affect us or Snow Leopard. It was Water Dragon and Blue Pheasant who were to lose parts of their land to the dam expansion. None of the eastern families, White Bone and Golden Tiger, gave up anything. In fact, they gained because the British said the proceeds from the dam were to be divided amongst all the clans, not just those who lost their land. Can you see the trouble? Water Dragon and Blue Pheasant were the ones who lost land, but all the other clans would profit from the sale of the electricity. There could have been civil war.

The monks managed to keep the country together by creating a constitution and getting people to support it, but they knew if there was to be peace, there had to be a special leader. The King needed moral authority but without an army to attack anyone. Water Dragon had almost no followers left, so they were the only one that fit. The monks made sure that the Raju dynasty was elected. Kuthan and the monks were very lucky. The Soōng statesmen have looked to the future. India has not been so lucky. The violence never ends for them."

"Was everyone satisfied with this?" Kaj looked unconvinced. "Water Dragon accepted political power in return for its lost land. What did Blue Pheasant get?"

"Blue Pheasant had not lost as much land as Water Dragon. They wanted water quality. They were promised the water from the dam would be tested. The Dam Board has been very good."

"Then why does the dam need its own security force?" Jill asked.

"Patel's subversive little poem suggests something else," Darya said. "Someone may want to kill the royal family to gain control of the dam."

Kaj stared skeptically at Darya and her brother for several moments. "And why does that not apply to you? Couldn't you claim the throne?"

"They changed the constitution so that the monarchy is inherited. There is no way to choose a new dynasty. Batsa and I would have no claim, so it would have to be someone from Raju's family. We think that the killer may be someone who believes he or she has a claim to the throne."

"A pretender to the throne with a grudge and a private army large enough to just seize power?"

"Well," Darya said thoughtfully, "A private army may not be needed. Imagine that there's no one left. The monks and governing council may need to find anyone with a claim to the throne."

Kaj fingered his teacup. Kuthan was starting to sound as if it was back in the days of the warlords. His first thought was that Darya was spinning a conspiracy theory to distract the detectives from looking too deeply into Mountain Thunder. Yet, the reason for the election of Raju I sounded plausible, and because of the massacre, Water Dragon would certainly have the moral authority and emotional appeal. Elevating Raju might even assuage the other clans' guilt for accepting the dam money. But if Darya and Batsa were right, there had to be a Soōng relative waiting in the wings. The family tree the palace had provided gave no indication of that.

Kaj looked at Jill and almost read her mind.

How could this tangled web of motives and agendas be happening in a small kingdom supposedly dedicated to tranquility?

Chapter 23

WHEN KAJ REACHED THE MORGUE later that day, Nie was filling out paperwork and Liu and a pair of lab workers were cleaning the equipment and preparing it for the journey back to Beijing. Anya's body had been moved into a locker. Kaj asked if he could see her.

He studied the body after Liu pulled the drawer out. The wound looked black and sunken where her hair had been shaved to allow the attempts to save her life. Her skin was already starting to hint at the grey-green and mottled purple patches of death. But most noticeable was her expression. Whatever she had seen in the last moments of her life had frozen her face into a rictus of fear. She looked as if she had been scared to death. He supposed that the efficient Dr. Nie would have the last word on that.

"Did she regain consciousness at any point?" he asked Nie, who shook her head regretfully.

"The attendants said there was no conversation in a traditional sense. But there was one moment when she seemed to reconnect to her surroundings. That kind of moment is called *terminal lucidity* and it occurs shortly before death."

"And she had one of those moments?"

"She opened her eyes and said something that sounded like *camel*. Then she closed her eyes and became non-responsive. Shortly after that, they declared time of death."

"Camel?" Kaj furrowed his forehead. "Do camels make any sense to you?"

"None whatsoever." Nie spoke with the brisk, unemotional objectivity of her profession. "But they said she was struggling to talk, and they may have misunderstood."

Kaj watched as Liu pushed the body back into the locker. Unlike Nie, he had no alternative to working with human emotion. He knew that whatever terrified Anya was real enough that her last word had sounded like a warning.

"What do you make of it?"

Kaj was surprised when Nie glanced at Liu before she answered.

"Our examination confirmed what the surgeons reported. She died from blunt force trauma caused by a rectangular object."

"Consistent with the butt of a rifle?" Kaj asked.

"That would be consistent."

Kaj thanked them and walked away. When he opened the door to leave the morgue, he happened to glance back. Nie and Liu were engaged in what looked like a heated discussion, and Nie did not look pleased.

Chapter 24

KAJ HAD MORE QUESTIONS THAN answers this time when he met with the King later that afternoon.

"Something has come up and we need to ask you for an overview of your family history."

"What do you want to know?"

"We learned this morning that your grandfather contracted with Strobel Engineering to build the hotel and hall at the palace."

"He expanded the palace, yes, but he also supported the development of the hospital and the city downtown. He was a visionary. I think that is the correct word. My father continued his plans to create Mongathuā as a modern business center. I like to say that my grandfather started by building a government. My father continued his work by building an economy. I continue both their work by envisioning a unified nation. I see it as natural progression."

"Sir, may I ask about the circumstances when you became King?"

The King looked surprised.

"There was no question about the succession, if that is what you are asking. The line from my father to me was clear in the constitution."

"You were a young man, though?"

The King corrected him slightly. "I was reading international relations at Oxford. There was some thought that my uncle might preside over a regency to allow me to finish my university course. Instead, I flew home immediately."

"You told me before that your father was a relatively young man. Can you tell me more about him?"

"During my childhood, I seldom saw him because he was involved in helping my grandfather. He came to see us children whenever he could, but he was frequently out of the country."

"Did you see your uncle, Tranh, often?"

"I saw more of my cousin Kiran. He lived in the palace for a while and we had the same tutor."

"Now, Kiran's mother was not Water Dragon."

"His mother, Dechen, was Blue Pheasant, as was her sister, Pema and my mother, Aishwarya."

"Are there other cousins besides Kiran?"

"Yes, there was my Aunt Pema's son, Kanchan who also went to school with us in the palace. I do recall another boy when Kiran and I were young. But we were told he had been taken away. I never thought to ask about him."

"Do you remember his name?"

The King shook his head. "No. I am sorry. It was too long ago.

"Does the word *camel* mean anything to you?"

The King shook his head. "Is there some reason it should?"

"We don't know yet. Apparently, there was some possible connection with Anya."

"Anya was from Golden Tiger clan, so you might ask Ananda. If he does not know, he might know someone else who does. Perhaps they had camels on the farm at one time."

Kaj settled himself as he asked the primary question he had come to ask.

"Were you boys aware that there was a basement under the hall building?"

"Of course. Sometimes, we slipped away from Anya to go exploring in the construction site when the hall was being built. We found a trap door in a side room and went down a ladder under the building. When Anya found out, the trap door disappeared. I know it was dangerous, but it was exciting. After that, I was sent to boarding school and never tried to go down there again."

"Do you recall when Anya caught you?"

"Yes. One day Kiran and I had gone down the ladder but when we tried to come back up, the trapdoor had become jammed. We banged on the door for what seemed a long time before Anya found us. Anya was very angry, and I remember she must have banged her head on something because she was bleeding."

"Who else was there when you were freed? Was there another boy?"

"Only some security guards. I don't remember anyone else."

"Did anyone tell you what had happened?"

"No, Anya rushed us back to our rooms, and we were told never to go back there again. They did not have to worry. After being locked down there in the dark, we never wanted to."

"We think the shooter knew about that ladder and trap door and may have used it entrance to gain access to the hall."

"Really?" The King's eyes widened. "And you think it might have something to do with this missing boy? That is a terrible legacy for the building. I think we children were right when we said the building was haunted. If it was not true then, it is now. But it was so long ago."

Kaj gave one of his secretive smiles. "Not so long ago, Sir. From my point of view, you are still a young man with your whole life in front of you."

"I feel very old, right now," the King demurred. "Too much death, too much loss. I feel like rereading Tennyson's poem *In Memoriam.* I came across it while I was at Oxford. Like him, I would not ask questions if my family were to suddenly walk through the door."

"It's the finality of death . . .." Kaj willed himself not to finish the thought, but he felt the tightness grow in his chest. He took a deep breath and made himself focus on the King. He gave him the only comfort he could offer.

"We will find out who did this," he promised yet again.

Chapter 25

Because Sharma and Agarwahl both looked more than ready, Kaj invited Forensics to start that afternoon's team meeting. Sharma deferred in turn to Agarwahl and let him describe how the hotel door lock had been opened. The lab director did so generously, crediting Sanjay and the two American computer experts. The only reservation he had, he said, was that they had made it look too easy. He now had to look again at the locking mechanisms on the crime lab doors.

"We now have evidence for a possible entrance and exit to the crime scene, in addition to the ballistic and blood trace evidence," Sharma said, "as we promised." He looked at the Chinese delegation to make sure they were paying attention.

"You were there as well, Dr. Xue," Kaj said. "Were you satisfied with the demonstration?"

Xue spoke slowly, as if the words were being dragged out of him. "Yes. The door opened."

Kaj noted the almost reluctant acknowledgment. But that was all right. Sharma and the crime lab had not been deprived of their moment.

"Where do we stand with the DNA investigation?"

"We are working on that," Mr. Achari said. "Two days more."

Kaj then summarized Strobel's presentation for the crime lab staff who had not been there. He stressed the evidence of the building plans themselves: how the trapdoor access to the basement had been covered at the request of the royal nanny since a group of boys had found it.

"Did you find out who these children were?" Nie asked.

"Strobel's father said there were four of them. We think we have identified three: the King and his cousins, Kiran and Kanchan. They were of an age. We're looking for the fourth. I asked the King about it. He remembers another boy but not his name. Something must have happened because he remembers only that the boy was taken away."

"Taken away?" Sharma said. "That sounds strange."

"We're looking into it," Kaj assured him. "Dr. Nie, what did you find in the autopsy?"

"No surprises. Cause of death, compound, depressed brain injury caused by a catastrophic blow that drove bone fragments deep into the brain tissue. Given the amount of tissue damage, the factures, and brain swelling, along with her age, I am surprised that she lasted as long as she did. The injury was more than enough to kill her. We forwarded samples to the crime lab for processing."

"We're working on them," Agarwahl said. "We will compare them to tissue and hair retrieved from the recovered rifle stock."

"Keep us posted," Kaj said. "Meanwhile, we have arranged to talk with a director at the Sikh temple for further information on the butler. I believe that was your question, Dr. Sharma—about whether the butler might have been a target or even involved. Dr. Xue, you were also concerned."

Sharma and Xue both looked at Kaj without undue interest. He sensed that their interest in the Sikh depended on whether it provided fuel for them to harass one another. Well, Kaj, thought grimly, too late to back out now, gentlemen. He hoped their learning curve about the Sikhs and Punjab would be public and embarrassing.

"We have an appointment with the director of the local Sikh temple tomorrow. Since you both expressed concern regarding whether religious unrest might have been motivated the attack on the palace, I expect you to be there. I will look forward to hearing your opinion of what the director tells us."

Kaj's voice made clear this was an assignment, not a request.

"Of course," Sharma mumbled, looking as if the third wall between him and the world had suddenly crumbled.

Xue tried to preserve his dignity. "Yes," he said with a slightly stronger voice than Sharma had managed. "It sounds interesting." His face, however, did not reflect his words.

Kaj smiled internally and with a degree of pleasure at their discomfort.

Enough of this nonsense, gentlemen. You are scientists. It is time to move beyond the grubby nationalism that is the enemy of truth.

That is the message I want to send your governments. If you ask for facts, be prepared to go where they live. Be aware, though, that there is only so far you can bend truth before it turns around and mows you down. And, let me add, that your determination to use my investigation to fight your country's border wars is about to cost you a full morning of what I hope will a history lesson. Consider yourselves lucky that I am handling this in-house. I hope you both learn something from it.

Chapter 26

THAT EVENING, KAJ REPLACED CLIFF and slipped into the seat across from Meng, who worked hard not to appear surprised. Kaj rubbed his hands together and looked around at the various darkened booths. The occupants were indistinguishable, just dark shadows moving in unlit booths. Somewhere a flute was playing. It reminded him of the times when Goro played the *shakuhachi* flute he had inherited from his father. He played only occasionally and often sadly. When he played a certain Japanese tune, their dog, Fluffy, would howl. Kaj wished he had his father's talent, but his sister, Aileen, was always the musical one.

"Looks like a nice, private place. Is the food good?" It was a struggle for Kaj to keep from chuckling at the subtle disappointment in Meng's eyes.

Meng shrugged. "If you like curries and lentils. If you want caviar, you'll be disappointed."

"I trust your judgment," Kaj said slyly. "Order for us both, unless you already have."

Meng called the waiter over and ordered in Kuthanese. He looked quite pleased when the waiter nodded silently and went back into the kitchen.

"You speak the language. Impressive." Kaj was willing to allow Meng that small victory.

"Very rusty," Meng countered with a smirk. "I may have ordered yak testicles."

"I am sure they will be tasty. Now, Meng, I have a couple of favors to ask of you. Are you up for it?"

"That depends on what you want."

Meng folded his hands into his lap and appeared both innocent and crafty at the same time. It was an unusual ability, and Kaj noticed it with admiration. It reminded him of his own blank stare, the one that an academy instructor told him would be an asset in interrogation. "You could make even a drunk feel guilty," he said.

"I have two to start with. The first is that you stop trying to corrupt my detectives, and that means all of them. Not just my Hawaii team, but also the Indian forensic team and your own Chinese doctors. I have a good idea of what you've been up to."

Meng shrugged eloquently. "Have you heard the fable of the frog and the scorpion."

"Yes," Kaj replied impatiently. "They both died in the end."

"Before that."

"You mean the part about the scorpion having to live according to its nature? Do you consider yourself a scorpion?"

Meng leaned forward. "We are all scorpions. But some of us pretend to be frogs." He looked significantly at Kaj.

"And you think Americans are hypocritical frogs?"

"Wave a dollar bill in front of your country and you turn into a scorpion's nest overnight." Meng's lip curled into a sneer.

"See someone's land you want, and you just invade. Is that better?"

Both sat back while the waiter placed platters of food in front of them. Kaj stared at the mounded shrimp and rice and the lightly curried vegetables and momos. He recognized the food now.

Meng picked up a shrimp with his chopsticks and looked at it speculatively. "I like things that crunch," he said. "I have good teeth. They say if you have good teeth, you will have a long life."

Kaj looked quizzical. "I hadn't heard that."

"Did you know that in Nepal they eat with their hands. They scoop up their food with four fingers and push it in their mouths with their thumbs. Efficient, don't you think?"

Kaj positioned the chopsticks in his hand and did not reply.

Meng then picked up a piece of unidentifiable white meat. "Challenge!" he smirked as he put the entire chunk into his mouth.

Kaj used his chopsticks to do the same. If this meal was a contest, he was in.

"Goat brain," Meng said triumphantly after Kaj forced down the blob.

"Yes, but we prefer it pickled in Hawaii." Kaj had no idea whether that was true. He put down his chopsticks and looked hard at Meng.

"Meng, there is nothing to be gained by trying to undermine my team. You know that we release information daily, and we know your Chinese doctors keep you informed because I told them to."

"I know. Facts only. No opinions, no anecdotes, no speculation. I heard. Who are you fooling with this pretend honesty? What kind of game are you playing?"

Kaj sat back and looked at Meng with one of his blank stares.

"I do not have time for games. The King wants an open investigation, and I owe him that."

"Being a frog?" Meng took another mouthful of the food and allowed himself a superior smirk. He did not believe Kaj for one moment.

Kaj popped a shrimp into his mouth and bit down. He saw Meng's point about the crunch. It was crisp outside while the inside flesh was soft. He savored the experience for a moment before he resumed the conversation.

"Meng," he said, "I am a Honolulu detective. I do not play diplomatic games. I do not care about hot or cold wars. I am not trying to play James Bond. I have only one goal: to find a killer because I was asked to. What part of that is mysterious?"

Meng raised his bowl and sipped the lentil soup. "This is better than you'll get at the palace cafeteria."

Kaj picked up a fluted momo and ate it.

"All right," Meng said after a few moments. "I give you that you are an amateur, but an international investigation changes you. You now attract interest and attention, and not just from us."

"I don't welcome that," Kaj said testily.

"Do you think any of us do?" Meng laughed out loud. "We are the gray people, you and I. We do the dirty work of nation and empire, and they throw us away when we are expendable."

Kaj put down his chopsticks and looked hard at the man across the table.

"Have you ever served in the military and been in a shooting war?"

Meng shrugged. "I was in the Gulf when you invaded."

"You know exactly what I mean. Have you ever been on the ground with a rifle in your hands?"

Meng was finally forced to shake his head.

"Well," Kaj said, "let me tell you what that's like. You get orders you can't question. You're allowed no emotion when someone who was just talking to you gets his leg blown off. You become compulsive about not following the plans exactly because it means bad luck. You train yourself to ignore the body bags. You do not ask for help because it will go on your record and word will get around that you are trouble. And even worse, you become so used to explosions and gunfire that you're bored when they don't happen. That's expendable, Meng. Eating caviar in Russia is not."

"It is not all eating caviar," Meng replied indignantly. "At least you can trust your fellow soldiers. In Russia, there is no one to trust. You can buy someone's cooperation and then a higher bidder comes along and that person changes sides overnight."

"Which brings me to my second request. It concerns something that would be helpful. Kuthan is not a member of Interpol. China is, so the international databases are open to you. We need to locate a Kuthani named Abhinav Mallik."

"Where did you lose him?" Meng allowed himself to look mildly interested.

"Changi airport."

Meng sat back hard against the rear of the booth. "Singapore. Not so easy."

"You have an embassy there. And you must have personal contacts outside of official channels. China's usually so good at this sort of thing."

Meng leaned forward again and cradled his fingers speculatively. "Is he a suspect?"

"We just need to locate him."

"So why ask me?"

"Mutual interest. My take: You can appear to be doing something for your employer. Isn't that what scorpions do?

Plus, by helping Kuthan, you create good will for China, if that matters to you or them. We hear things too. We could always ask New Delhi—India's also part of Interpol—but I assume you have better sources in Singapore just as I assume you have something to prove to your bosses."

"I'd need more information," Meng said slowly, noting Kaj's ironic and slightly insulting tone. But Kaj had a point. Meng's eyes narrowed.

"I need time to think about this. I assume it is not going to come through official channels."

Kaj sat back and gave a dismissive snort.

"I am not about to deal with Washington politics.

"You have not informed your Greg and his government screen-watchers?" Meng looked triumphant, as if he was yet again demonstrating the superior Chinese capacity for surveillance.

Kaj deflated him immediately. "I told Greg that I intended to ask you for a favor."

"And what did he say?"

"That you're a scorpion."

Meng chuckled and changed the subject.

"And what do I get out of it? There are risks involved." He spoke now with a hint of honesty that told Kaj they were over the first hurdle and about to negotiate terms.

"I am not going to offer you state secrets, Meng, because I do not have any. Homicide detectives are very low on the food chain. But we do have a degree of honor. Do you have any left?"

"*Honor* is just a word."

Kaj put his head on one side and looked quizzical.

"Meng, I think you are a pile of—what do you call it in China?—*goushi.*"

Meng looked affronted. "Very impolite," he said. "That' is what you yell at bad umpires."

"I could have said *pigu*, but I don't think you are an ass."

"Where did you learn such words?" Meng demanded.

"Vietnam," Kaj replied blandly. "And I learned a whole lot more over there too."

Meng gazed down at the tabletop. He had forgotten for a moment that this Hawaii detective was a decorated war hero.

Kaj used his chopsticks to gather up more of the food. He had already decided the potatoes and spinach in coconut milk was his favorite. He would invite the team here for a final meal after they had solved the case.

"You have your pride if not your honor." Kaj looked at Meng across the table. "Are you ready to let screen-watchers replace you?"

"They cannot replace me," Meng almost spat out the words.

"One last adventure? Are you up for it? Or am I overestimating you?"

"So, who is this person you want to find?" Meng scratched his chin in a mixture of suspicion and calculation.

"Once upon a time he was the head of security at the Kuthani Consulate."

"In Honolulu?" Meng closed his eyes. "Mallik. That name. He was involved with the Whitworth murder. Now I remember. I thought you sent him to jail."

"We did," Kaj said grimly.

"And he escaped in Singapore? Are you sure you are not joking? I thought your prisons were better than that."

"He was not in our custody at the time."

"You were sending him home?" Meng allowed himself a superior snort. "I thought you sent people to your boys' camp in Cuba."

Kaj raised his right hand and waved away the insignificant.

"There was a formal request from Kuthan for his transfer. I don't know from whom. They claimed our prison was destroying Mallik's tranquility and he needed to serve the rest of his sentence in Kuthan."

Meng laughed out loud. "And they believed that nonsense? Or should I say that pile of *goushi*?"

"I have no idea what they thought. The first I heard of it was on the plane coming over here."

"And you have no idea who made the request?" Meng shook his head. "I thought you people were better than that."

"Point taken. I am working on finding out."

Meng finished off his lentil soup and pushed the dishes aside.

"I would want to know who made that request. It must come from the palace or someone connected to it. Everything official comes with an impressed dragon stamp. I would start with the palace."

"Are you interested in making those inquiries regarding Mallik?"

Meng looked at Kaj shrewdly.

"As long as you understand that I am taking a risk and may need a return favor in the future."

"Greg told me you would say that. I will have to deal with it."

"All right," Meng said. "Just for old times—my old times—I will look into it."

Kaj stood up then and looked down at the plates. He wanted to go back to his suite and call Linda before it was too late.

"You might want to ask for a to-go bag on that. It was good. I expect you to leave my team alone."

"For now," Meng replied. "But remember the value of a scorpion's promises."

Chapter 27

The Sikh *gurdwara* was a substantial four-sided building painted white with gold onion-shaped turrets. Each side had a recessed entrance with inner, scalloped arches painted in white and gold that seemed to recede as Kaj, Sharma, Xue, and the Colonel walked down the hallway. The arches ended at a simple doorway, leaving Kaj to wonder if they were supposed to represent something about how Sikh belief is internal. It would not be the first time he'd run across buildings where the architecture echoed whatever lay inside. This one stood out, though, for the beauty of white and gold that reflected the bright sunshine.

They stopped to remove their shoes, placing them in a cubby beside the entrance door, where another box held a tidy array of sandals and slippers. Even the shoes reminded Kaj he was a visitor, a stranger in an enigmatic land. When they walked through the doorway, they were welcomed and invited to wash their hands. A turbaned man offered them small, square caps to wear.

Across from where they stood, double doors had been thrown open, revealing another large room. A four-poster shrine stood on a raised platform beneath a round, concave alcove in the ceiling. Men sat silently on one side, women on the other. Kaj tried not to stare, but the gold decoration of the altar and the elaborate decoration of the ceiling made that difficult. He was glad when his greeter invited them to follow him down a corridor of doors to where the head of the temple directors was waiting.

The man who stood to greet them wore an impeccably folded, dark-blue turban, a blue-checked shirt, along with white trousers, and an orange coat. They sat around a low table and paused for a few moments while a tray of teacups was brought in.

"Thank you for meeting with us," Kaj said after they had taken a respectable number of sips of the hot tea. He was reminded of Grandpa Lhotse's hospitality, except this tea was very different, delicate, and more like oolong. Kaj wondered if it was White Bone tea, but there was no way to identify it.

"How may I help you?"

The question hung in the air, as Kaj did not have a simple answer.

"We are investigating the recent killings at the palace. I have brought with me Dr. Emir Sharma, who heads a crime investigation team from New Delhi on loan to assist us, and Dr. Xue, a member of the Chinese team of medical examiners. I have also with us the head of palace security."

"I know the Colonel," the man said with a nod.

"We are here to ask you about a victim, a Sikh member of the palace staff."

The director looked intently at Kaj, as if trying to determine what might be coming next. "Ajeet Singh," he said. "A good man. He lived truthfully. What is it you want to know about him?"

"The Medical Examiners reported evidence of very heavy scarring on his back. They advised us that these could have resulted from war injuries, or, if not that, from torture."

"Yes," the director replied. His tone suggested that it was common knowledge.

"Naturally," Xue said, "it raised certain questions. For example, had the victim served in military units or had he been involved in violent protests?"

The director sat silently for some moments. He looked at Kaj with sad eyes. "Are you asking if Ajeet was involved with the shooting at the palace?"

"We already know he was not the shooter," Kaj said quickly. "We want to be sure he was not the primary target of the shooting."

"Rather than the royal family? You have come here because you want to know if someone was willing to sacrifice five other lives to kill a single Sikh man?" The man looked horrified.

"You did not seem surprised about the scarring on his back," Kaj reminded him.

"I was not. There are many others who have suffered similarly. It is part of our history. But I am sure you did not come here to hear about old grievances."

Kaj wrinkled his forehead ruefully. "It may turn out that is what we have come for."

"And you believe he might have been the target?" The director spread his hands wide. Let me say this," he said slowly, "assassinations are meant to remove or to replace someone. Why would someone want to replace or even remove Ajeet? He was a gracious man who offended no one."

Kaj measured his next question carefully. He knew what the King had already told him, but he wanted Sharma and Xue to receive the information together and from another source beyond him.

"How did Ajeet get injured?" he prompted.

"Ajeet and his father were in New Delhi on palace business when Indian Prime Minister Indira Ghandi was assassinated."

"By her Sikh bodyguards," Sharma broke in.

"Yes," the Director agreed. "In revenge because she ordered the Indian army to remove Sikh rebels hiding in the Golden Temple in Amritsar. That is our most holy site, and the attack on the temple was made on a day when many innocent people, including women and children, were inside. The assault cost hundreds of lives and did damage to the temple that cannot be repaired."

"These rebels were demanding a Sikh homeland they called Khalistan," Xue said.

"They were," the Director agreed. "But they were only a small group. Other Sikhs did not support them. The Indian army that removed them from the Golden Temple included Sikh soldiers. Did you know that? Their general told them that the action was not against the Sikhs but against terrorists. No Sikh soldier declined to participate."

"How were Ajeet and his father caught up in this?" Kaj asked.

"They did not support the protestors in the temple. I assure you of that. But it made no difference to the street mobs who were encouraged by local police and politicians to attack every Sikh they found. Ajeet and his father were dragged from their hotel out into the street. Ajeet's father died there. Ajeet was left for dead. He was found by a French team on their way to climb Everest. They were staying in the same hotel. They hid him and took him with them when they went to Nepal. King Raju II paid for Ajeet's hospital in Nepal and arranged for his return home. Ajeet could not lift his arms higher than his shoulders, so he was unfit for physical work. Instead, it was arranged for him to work in the Palace's office of state banquets. He was so well respected that, in time, he became the King's personal valet. He was known as a man of honor and integrity. He did not deserve to die."

"And he never supported the protest movement for Khalistan?" Sharma persisted.

"No one in this *gurdwara* has ever supported violent means. Of course, we wish for Punjab to be given back to us. It was our homeland for hundreds of years and our land of pilgrimage. But it was convenient for the British to divide Punjab. The young heir to the British throne, the Princess Elizabeth, was to be married. Earl Mountbatten, the man that the British sent to lead the British withdrawal, wanted to settle India's future very quickly. Why not? Prince Philip, the man marrying the princess was Mountbatten's nephew. He wanted to be back in England for the festivities. So, he agreed with the politicians, and the Sikhs had no voice. India was divided according to religion. Where there was a Hindu majority, that was reserved for the Hindus. Where there was a Muslim majority, that was reserved for them.

"There were twelve million Sikhs in Punjab, but nowhere were we a majority, so the British divided Punjab between Hindu and Muslim. Because Muslims persecuted Sikhs in the past most Sikhs chose to join India. Hindus and Sikhs moved east to join India while Muslims moved west to join Pakistan. Some say that a million people lost their lives when they passed each other on the roads. In the later years, a small group of Sikhs demanded that Punjab be returned to them. These are the people you ask about. This temple has never supported the movement. Support has come from groups in Canada and the UK, where people live abroad and do not understand their country anymore."

"Are you saying that no one associated with this temple was ever involved with these political groups?" Xue asked.

"We consider ourselves Kuthani. Our grandparents were clerks with the British Army. They remained after the British left. Generations have been born here. Kuthan has been good to us. Ajeet considered himself Kuthani first."

"Then this *gurdwara* has never discussed history or politics?" Kaj wanted the confirmation to be beyond any question Sharma or Xue might raise later.

"Of course, we discuss history and politics. But if a speaker wanted to recruit young men to fight for Khalistan, we would not permit that person to speak in the temple. If such people came to this *gurdwara*, we would not let them in. If we were approached for money to support Khalistan, we would refuse. But we are human. We still wish that our sacred places in Pakistan were open for pilgrims. We wish that our homelands could be returned to us. But that does not mean that we condone death and violence. If I heard any talk about violence and death and bombing, I would inform the Colonel."

The Director looked at Colonel Pradhan. "I have brought things to his attention."

The Colonel nodded his affirmation.

"Then there has been no violence against the Sikhs in Kuthan?" Xue asked.

"Only a few hundred Sikhs live in Kuthan and this *gurdwara* is the only temple. We would know."

"Have you heard any recent talk about protests?" Kaj's question deliberately threw out a wider net.

The Director stopped and looked speculatively at the Colonel and then at Kaj.

"You must understand that we are always watchful. We are not spying."

"No, none would blame you if you were."

The Director looked troubled and seemed hesitant.

"We heard rumors that there are plans to build a second hydroelectric dam not far from here. I have already advised the Colonel about these rumors. There is much confusion. People say it is being done without consultation with the people whose land will be taken. People are upset. There is talk of protest."

"Only talk?" Kaj prompted.

"Only talk," the Director agreed. "It is hard to tell where these ideas come from. Some say they saw lorries and surveying tools. I do not know what to make of it."

Somewhere in the distance a bell rang and the Director looked up quickly. "I must go," he said. "Come back," he added as he ushered them out of the door. "Share a meal with us. We welcome everyone. And allow me to wish you well in your search for the truth."

The Director then raised his hands in a final namaste. "May your soul shine forth, and your investigation be blessed with light." Then the man was gone.

Kaj, Xue, Sharma, and the Colonel retrieved their shoes and walked out through the hallway with its cascading arches, toward where the palace van waited for them.

"What did you think?" Kaj looked at Xue and Sharma with a questioning eyebrow.

Sharma shuffled uncomfortably for a moment. "Whoever opened that door in the palace tunnel knew modern technology. The temple looks well financed enough. But he is right, Sikhs have served for generations in the Indian army. They still do. It is doubtful that they would have used a rifle with goat hair and sand in it."

Xue looked equally uncomfortable. "What is this dam he is talking about? That needs to be looked at."

"We need to investigate that rumor right away," Sharma agreed. "Rumors become reality in uninformed minds and can become a cause."

Xue nodded. "We have seen that. When truth no longer matters, people believe things that might only be possible. If there is a rumor, it would be a good thing to put to rest."

"I agree with you," Sharma said.

Kaj noted that Xue gave a small smile at hearing Sharma's agreement, "Well, it's a start," he thought. Xue and Sharma had agreed on something

He assumed his non-committal, reserved face as he watched Xue and Sharma climb into the palace van. He glanced at the Colonel to see if he had had a similar insight. With the Colonel, though, it was sometimes difficult to know.

Instead, Kaj shared an oblique thought capable of many different interpretations. "Is anything in Kuthan ever simple?"

The Colonel looked up at the range of the distant mountain tops, alluring and forbidding, misty in the afternoon sun.

"If you can find a place where life is simple, let me know. I would travel there to see what the people are like."

Chapter 28

KAJ FINALLY DECIDED THAT THE trick, if such it was, to international collaboration was creating an occasion where nations would want, even demand, to work together. If the circumstance was not readily obvious, it required careful, insightful people to create it.

He started the afternoon meeting with Jill's report on the hotel meeting.

"When guests check in, they give the usual information: credit cards, passports, and home addresses, and the hotel adds things like room charges, dining room, and special services. They call that the "client" system. We were given that list when we arrived.

"But there's another set of records they call the "protocol" system. That's where the desk staff makes special, coded notes. They record whether the guest is a VIP, and if so how: A guest of the royal family? A celebrity? Someone with a connection to the dam? Someone with business with palace? They also note if there are special dietary needs; specific room requests; or whether security was called for any reason. It's all coded. A young man was assigned to help me make sense of it.

"We went through both sets of records concentrating on who was in the hotel on the day of the shooting. The King's cousins, Kiran and Kanchan were there. They have been frequent guests in the past few months. Each time, they requested the same rooms next door to each other. I asked whether this was unusual. He thought it was. He said they had always stayed in the palace residence before."

"When did they first stay at the hotel?" Cliff asked.

"About six weeks before the shooting."

"Did they give an explanation?" Sharma asked.

"They said they wanted to escape the formality and protocol of the palace. The hotel assumed they wanted to be normal young men partying away from their parents' eyes."

Kaj leaned forward and put his elbows on the table. "Where were these rooms located?"

Jill unfolded the hotel's floor plan. "They were on the ground floor at the far end of a hallway. There was a keyed door next to their room opening onto the rear parking lot."

"How close were the rooms to the storage room in the hotel basement?"

"Almost directly above."

"They were involved," Sharma said exultantly. "We said they would be amateurs."

"But what is their motive?" Nie objected. "Just staying in the rooms is not proof. We need more information."

"We know that. But, Madam, please allow me my moment." Sharma gave her a winsome smile and bowed.

Kaj looked slightly bemused as Nie laughed. It was the first time she had done that since she had arrived.

"We will work the rooms as another pair of crime scenes." Agarwahl looked both gratified and quizzical at seeing a buoyant Sharma.

Kaj understood the feeling of things perhaps falling into place. He looked at Jill. "Are the rooms left as they were?"

"Yes. Everything was put on hold at the King's request.

"We need to find out what those two cousins were up to," Sharma said more soberly. "Do we believe they planned to kill their parents?"

"It would be unnatural and immoral," Nie observed.

"But not unheard of." Xue added. "Royal families have a history of removing rivals to the throne."

"Let's hold on here," Kaj said. "Who fired the rifle? Whose fingerprints were found on it?"

"It was hard to tell." Choudary said.

"What does that mean?" Xue asked.

"What we are saying is that we looked for the most recent set of fingerprints, but we found at least three overlapping and smeared. All we can say with certainty is that the rifle was handled by several people. It may be that the most recent fingerprints are from the one who killed the victims, but we do not have absolute proof. We need the DNA analysis."

Kaj's forehead wrinkled in frustration. "Mr. Agarwahl, when will we have the DNA results?

"Tomorrow."

That was definitive enough. Kaj decided to move on.

"Dr. Xue, Dr. Sharma, and I visited the Sikh temple today. Our primary purpose was to see if there was some reason the Sikh butler may have been the primary target. That seems unlikely now." Kaj looked pointedly at Xue. "But it seems there is some new possible controversy that might be relevant."

"We were told there is a rumor about possible plans to build a new dam in the eastern part of Kuthan. It seems that surveying teams have been seen on site and people are angry because they have not been consulted."

"We plan to make an appointment with the Dam Board," Kaj said. "Dr. Xue has already told me he wants to be there. Who else is available?"

"I will go also," Sharma said.

Kaj noted that Sharma had not made a request. He had made a demand. It remained to be seen what he had in mind. Kaj hoped it was collegiality. Dr. Xue had told Kaj he would like to see the dam because of the Chinese investment. Kaj guessed Sharma might say the same thing whether it was true or not. But it also remained to be seen. The Sikh temple was a good start, but Kaj was a not a betting man. With these two on the same trip, the odds were still not in favor of a positive, conflict free meeting. Still, there was something to be hopeful about.

Chapter 29

KAJ HAD BEEN ABOUT TO call Linda late that afternoon when he was disturbed by a call from the front desk informing him that a package had been delivered. It was a plain, brown envelope containing whatever the State Department was willing to share with him about Mallik's transfer. He retrieved it and took it back upstairs to read.

What had initiated Malik's release from US custody was a handwritten letter from Mallik to King Raju III. The letter's two pages sounded pitiful. Mallik complained about every possible injustice: the food was inedible; the other inmates called him Chinese and harassed him; the guards were disrespectful; and sleep was impossible because the noise violated his tranquility. It ended with his plea to return to Kuthan due to his extreme homesickness. It ended with Mallik begging the King to forgive him. He promised to spend the rest of his life atoning for the pain he had caused.

The next papers dealt with the King's formal request to the State Department for Mallik's transfer. This was followed by the minutes of a staff meeting in DC where the request was discussed. There had originally been an addendum entitled "Talking Points," but that was not included. What was left was a decision to refer the matter to the Honolulu office with a request for advice. The interest must have been compelling because the Hawaii office recommendation was sent back within a week. The Hawaii office urged that the request be granted. The final record was a copy of the official State Department letter to King Raju, informing him that the State Department would comply with his request and would start the process for Mallik's transfer to Kuthani custody. No exact date for that transfer was given, and there was nothing else.

Kaj remembered what Meng had told him about the official dragon imprint on documents issued by the Palace. When he looked for them, there was no doubt. The dragon stamp was present on every palace document. What was lacking, though, was the answer to his main question: Why did the US government approve Mallik's transfer? His prickle went into overdrive. It told him that there was a lot more he wasn't being told.

He laid each of the palace letters side by side on the table in front of him and reread them several times. He looked for evidence of corrections, for places where information might have been removed, and for inconsistencies of any type that could tell his warning feelings to subside. Finally, he saw it. He confirmed it by putting one palace letter's signature over another and holding them both up to light.

The King's signatures were identical on all letters originating in Kuthan.

Kaj was no expert on handwriting, but he had taken a workshop once. What he'd learned was that the complex sequence of muscles required to create a signature was subject to inattention, distraction, and fatigue, among other things. No signatures could be identical. He agreed now with his prickle. He was dealing with potential forgery.

He sat staring at the papers in a morose mood that was not improved when his phone rang and it was Meng.

"Yes," Kaj said curtly.

Meng was not deterred. "I have information on Mallik." He sounded jovial and self-congratulatory. You will like it."

"Do you want to meet?"

"I have a very good idea. And you will like it very much. I promise. You will not even have to travel. Your hotel has a nice cocktail bar, full of orchids and good whiskey. I will meet you there. They have good Ghurkha cigars, and you will want to buy me some. They take credit cards, Visa, Master Card, American Express. Easy."

Kaj sighed. Greg had warned him about the return favors. "What time?"

"Five minutes, perhaps?" Meng said. "I am in the hotel."

There was nothing for Kaj to do but agree. Let Meng enjoy his advantage. There was always the possibility that Meng had really come through. The man's excitement implied that he had. Kaj headed downstairs. He'd work out the finances later.

Chapter 30

Meng was waiting for Kaj at a small table at the rear of the lounge. Meng was right about the orchids. They were everywhere and in full bloom. The space was a cross between expatriate nostalgia for Britain of the 1930s and a sentimental evocation of what European visitors thought South Asian countries were supposed to look like. The serving staff all wore some form of Kuthani costume, but obviously created by some couturier in Paris or Hong Kong. It was the type of bar that would have a famous signature cocktail named for it. Kaj felt self-conscious. Meng fitted right in.

"What have you found out, Meng?" Kaj watched as the man opened the leather menu wallet containing the list of available spirits.

"All in good time. Enjoy the moment." Meng spoke almost dreamily. "Ah," he said, "as I thought. They still have the good single malts. Nothing beats the Scots for whiskey. When I was in London, I took the Flying Scotsman train overnight to Edinburgh and took taxis to the distilleries. Magnificent. Unforgettable."

The waiter came with a basket of popcorn and spiced nuts and began a discussion with Meng over the various brands available. Meng ordered himself a double whiskey with a water chaser. Kaj ordered himself a carafe of coffee. He no longer suspected that Meng intended to enjoy himself for as long as possible, he now knew it.

The single malt came first, and Meng reverently pitched a tiny drop of water into the amber whiskey. He held it up to the light, swirled it gently and sniffed appreciatively. "Magnificent," he said and took a large swallow. When the coffee came, Meng asked about Gurkha cigars. The server brought a wooden box containing dark, ultra-premium cigars. Meng took a handful and tucked them into his coat. He smiled and took another swallow of his whiskey before ordering another double.

"The Russians certainly taught you how to drink," Kaj observed.

Meng was indignant. "I did not learn anything from watching them swill vodka. They drink to forget. I drink for the pure beauty of a whiskey made by a process perfected over hundreds of years. The Scots export their shortbread, their whiskey, and their North Sea oil. The whiskey is the best by far." He nodded happily when the waiter put another glass in front of him.

Kaj's coffee was served in a glass carafe set over a warming stove. Even the milk was warm. He took the first of what he knew would be multiple cups while he wrestled the information out of Meng.

"Now," Meng began. "I told you it would not be easy. Our Singapore embassy was suspicious. I told them I needed to find out who assassinated Kuthan's royal family before you Americans did. I said I was concerned that Kuthan might allow further America concessions if you were successful. That worked. So, the first piece of information is that the soldiers you turned Mallik over to at Changi were not Singapore security at all. We found the date Mallik arrived in Singapore and persuaded the airport to search for the security tapes. Now, getting those tapes was the hard part, and you owe the Chinese embassy in Singapore for making it happen. Or, really me. Mallik was put into a Mercedes-Benz van and driven away. We were able to make out the license plate."

Meng waved to the waiter and pointed to his glass. He let Kaj sit in suspense until the whiskey arrived.

"One more, and then I must be more temperate and switch to singles." Meng smiled a little giddily. "I am starting to get what you might call a little glow. I may start rolling my r's like the Scots do. Wonderful country. Loved the Hebrides."

Kaj looked at Meng blankly. Except for getting sentimental about Scotland, the man did not look or sound inebriated. If Kaj had drunk that much, he would have been under the table.

"The license plate told us that the van belonged to the Kuthani embassy. The soldiers were embassy security."

Kaj almost dropped his coffee cup. "The Kuthanis?"

"None other," Meng said smugly. "The Kuthanis cut out Singapore entirely and captured their own man. Didn't I tell you that the palace had to be involved?" He smiled at his own cleverness.

"Is Mallik still in Singapore?"

"I am getting to that. We shall order something to eat while I tell you." Meng waved the server over and requested the food menu. When it came, it was large and bound in soft red leather with the Kuthani seal embossed on the cover. The menu and its binding looked expensive. It turned out also to be a travel guide to Kuthan. The selections, described both in Kuthani and English, explained in complete detail where each food stuff had been grown or raised. Considerable space was given to Mountain Thunder and Snow Leopard, who seemed to be the prime purveyors of things gourmet and exclusive.

Kaj began silently calculating the costs and wondering who was going to pay. He thought he would send the bill to Greg. The State Department must budget for clandestine activities because no ordinary expense account could cover extremely expensive cigars and half a bottle or more of exclusive, aged single malt. He hoped that what Meng had to tell him would justify the price of getting it out of him.

Platters of curried vegetables, momos, noodles, stews, breads, fruits, and sauces soon arrived at the table. Even Kaj was tempted and ate well. But when Meng insisted on telling Kaj what all the dishes were and how they were prepared, Kaj gritted his teeth in impatience.

Finally, Meng signaled for another whiskey that he diluted and was ready.

"Singapore has strict border controls and likes to track its foreigners. Hush hush, *infra dig*, of course. We asked Singapore to search their passenger lists for someone from the Kuthani embassy traveling north. The embassy did not try to hide it. Mallik flew home the day after he arrived in Singapore. After that? There was no record of what they did with him once they got him here. The speculation is that he is—how do you say—holed up somewhere? Our Kuthan specialists think it may be some monastery. That seems to be the MO, as you say. Kuthan uses its monasteries to bury people."

Meng dabbed his mouth with a napkin that had delicate cutouts around the edge. He looked pleased with himself. "Now Inspector Kaj, you need to be asking why the secrecy and why not involve Changi security? Who else is involved? Worth a little whiskey, no?"

Meng signaled for yet another single whiskey.

Kaj drank the last of his coffee. He would probably be up all night, but by any measure, he was sure he could show the US State Department that the evening had been worth it. He could now confirm that Mallik had almost certainly been in the country when the massacre of the royal family occurred. But, where would he be hiding?

"OK. You have had your whiskey and cigars," Kaj said suspiciously. "So far, so good. But what haven't you told me?"

Meng tried to look innocent. His slightly watery eyes gave him away. He took a gulp of his whiskey and then patted the expensive cigars in his jacket pocket. He smiled at the thought of clipping off the cigar heads one by one, slowly rolling the cigars above a lighter to warm them, letting the tobacco settle for a few moments, and then lighting up and inhaling the blue smoke from one of the world's finest cigars.

"All right. Since you insist. I heard that the directions for the exchange came directly from the Kuthani royal palace. Interesting, no? I told you the palace had to be involved. Look closely at the documents with that Kuthani dragon seal."

"Nothing more specific? Like who was involved?"

Meng ignored the question. As far as he was concerned the commerce of the evening was settled. Fine whiskey, cigars, and a good dinner for good intelligence. Fair exchange. He drained the last few drops of his whiskey and stood up a trifle unsteadily. "I shall have security call me a taxi," he announced regally. He nodded to Kaj, gave a little whiskey burp, and walked away.

Kaj finished his coffee and picked over the last of the food platter. Then he signaled the server for the bill. He was still not sure whether to charge it to the room or sign Dorji's name to it. As it turned out, he did not have to choose. Instead, he was greeted with the most charming of smiles and the information that any charges incurred by the visiting teams were courtesy of the palace. Kaj glanced at the bill. It showed a very high three-figure total in US dollars that had been reduced to zero. He noted that the whiskey had been charged as a full bottle. Meng must have made off with whatever he had not already drunk. Kaj sighed and left a generous tip from his remaining US dollars. The information had been worth it, but he was not sure how pleased the palace would be with the bill or the news. He shook his head in rueful amazement. He had never met someone like Meng who could turn things on their head simply by showing up.

Chapter 31

PERHAPS IT WAS THE COFFEE or just his earlier prickle of warning, but sleep was elusive. Kaj lay dozing, the victim of mentally replaying the scenes from the previous days. The final scene, the one that came just before gray hints of dawn, was the King telling him that the dragon called people for whom it had a message. It seemed like fantasy, but Kaj felt the sudden, overwhelming urge to revisit the dragon pool.

The security guards, Abiral among them, looked surprised when their sleep-deprived visitor told them where he wanted to go, but they brought the van around with their usual smiles. They drove quickly over the empty roads and, as they approached Kalyani, Kaj could see the summit snow of Masakatsu reflecting the half-moon orange of the rising sun.

He moved quickly along the path, breathing more easily than he had on that first day, and sat down on the same bench where he and the King had talked. The now-risen sun cast a hypnotic glow reflected in the water. He felt his eyes go dry from fatigue and his body settle into a strange receptivity as if time had stopped.

The first sign of the dragon was when the deer antlers broke through the water. Then came the elephant snout and the alligator eyes that opened like the lens of a camera. Kaj and the dragon stared at one another.

"What is it you want to know?" the dragon asked.

Kaj looked at the dragon's scales and didn't answer.

The dragon prompted him. "Don't you wonder why you survived while others did not?"

Kaj couldn't deny that. If he had consciously asked a question, he knew it would have been that one.

"It was the luck of the draw." Kaj looked down at the water, recognizing his evasion. He felt vulnerable and guilty.

The dragon snorted. "Luck? The universe has its own purpose. Your responsibility was making the choices you were given. Every one you made has brought you to this moment."

"But that's true of everybody," Kaj objected. "Everyone ends up in the logical place where their decisions take them."

"Logic?" The dragon snorted. "You want to apply reason to the greatest mystery of life?"

"Are you saying that my purpose was whatever happened to me? Isn't that like saying that because I burn my hand in a fireplace, that was my destiny and meant to happen?"

The dragon shook its head impatiently. "Your purpose is not what happened to you. Those were things, like the war you fought in, you could not control. Your purpose lay with what you could control. Your decisions were part of who you were. What did you allow yourself to learn from them?"

Kaj shook his head. "You need to be clearer than that."

"You allowed your father's war experience to shape your life. You never questioned it."

Kaj bristled at the mention of his father. "Is that a bad thing? He taught me duty and honor. Why would I disagree with those values after what he had been through?"

The dragon ignored him.

"Your doctor. The one who is angry at life. What do you see in him?"

Kaj's eyebrows hit his hairline. "You mean Dr. Xue? What am I supposed to see?"

The dragon sighed. "Constrained by his upbringing, trapped by his culture, using his work to earn approval and respect, but destined to fail until he recognizes who he is."

"Are you saying that's what I am?"

"Are you saying you are not?" The dragon sounded almost smug. "Tell me, what were you like as a child?"

"What do you mean?"

"Were you rebellious? Did you have friends? Were you artistic?"

Kaj frowned. "I was pretty obedient. I followed the rules." Kaj stopped with a small chuckle. "If I didn't, I made sure my parents didn't hear about it."

"Because?" the dragon asked.

"Well, I didn't want to disappoint them. My father told me the Kajiwara family descended from a samurai clan. It was important to him that I remembered that."

"He lived by a code of conduct," the dragon said. "Did he ever talk with you about the war he fought in?"

Kaj shook his head definitely. "None of them did, except perhaps when they were alone. I heard about what a hero he was from other people. I was in awe of what he did."

"So," the dragon concluded, "you were constrained by your upbringing into following your father's code and trapped into using his heroism as your definition of yourself."

"I wouldn't put it that way," Kaj said. "He was a worthy role model."

"Tell me about your sister," the dragon said. "Did she try to be like him?"

"I don't know. She was older and she left home when I was young."

"Did you know why she left?"

"Not until many years later. My mother told me what happened. She was the star student of the family. I followed her in school and all I heard was teachers asking me why I wasn't more like her." Kaj grinned at the memory. "She earned a scholarship that covered her expenses at a medical school on the Mainland, but she needed travel money to get there. Dad refused to help. He wanted her to get a nurse's license here and only then go on to medical school. She thought he meant that she was not capable of becoming a doctor and would need to find work as a nurse when she failed. In the end, my mother gave her the money, and she never came back to Hawaii after she graduated. What no one told her then was that Dad had given the money to Ai to give her. He hadn't wanted to lose his only daughter, but there was no healing of the rift until Dad was dying."

"Did you miss your sister?" The dragon gave Kaj a penetrating gaze.

Kaj felt indignant. "Of course, I did. It was lonely with her gone, and Dad became even more distant."

"And you never knew why she had left. Did it ever occur to you that her disappearance taught you something?"

"Now you're talking in riddles." Kaj's voice trembled with exasperation.

The dragon glared at him and hissed. "You thought she must have done something to make your father angry. Was it so strange for you as a child to imagine that if you disobeyed your parents, if you didn't fulfill their every expectation, they might send you away as well?"

"This is crazy," Kaj spluttered.

The dragon rose to its full height. "Open your eyes and stop trying to follow your father's example. He fought a war to prove his loyalty. He was a hero of his times. Things change. Life changes. Don't climb your ancestors' mountain. Find your own."

"How am I supposed to do that? And why should I?"

The dragon snorted emphatically. "You are the hero of another time. You fought a war with his bravery, but it was a political war without a noble purpose. None of you should have been there, and you came home believing you had not measured up to him. Ask yourself now, without the burden of his expectations, what have you done with your life? Or if that is not enough, what are your questions?"

"My questions?" Kaj shook his head in annoyance. The dragon seemed intent on talking in circles.

"Yes. Questions. You ask them when you are investigating a crime. Is this crime like any others? How is it different? Is there a pattern? Why not ask those questions of your life? Or, if you prefer: What fills your days and gives them meaning?" The dragon sank partly back into the water.

Kaj was momentarily startled by the question. *Why isn't catching guilty people enough?*

"No," the dragon said, "catching guilty people is not enough. That is merely what you do. Look deeper into who you are."

Kaj felt invaded. The dragon was reading his mind.

The creature rolled slightly and rose higher in the water. "Why do you spend your time looking for violent people who harm others?"

Kaj waited for several moments before an answer came. "I suppose I am looking for justice for the victims."

The dragon took the opening. "Justice only for other people? Not justice for yourself? You and your fellow soldiers had a saying: 'you have not lived until you have nearly died.' It was your way of saying that surviving was its own comfort, and the experience could be shared. You detect criminals for the same reason. Solving a crime soothes you. It reminds you of your humanity. It makes you feel that your life is not meaningless."

"Are you saying that I use people to make myself feel better?" Kaj spoke his words emphatically. "That's not what I do."

"And what if you did? Does it help? You who do not believe in anything that is not part of the bleak vision you brought back from war. Why have you grieved and continued to relive the death of that young soldier in Vietnam?"

Kaj's face froze. He remembered what the boy looked like when he turned the body over. The loss was still bitter.

"He was a local boy from Hawaii. He was like everyone I'd ever known. I could have played baseball or gone fishing with him. I could not protect him."

"So that made his death worse? Because he was like you? Someone from your tribe? Was that all it took to turn your anger into guilt, make you feel a traitor to your father's values, and blame yourself for his death? Tell me—remind yourself—how all of you survived the war."

Kaj was silent for some time. "We soldiers had one another," he conceded. "No one wanted to be there. We shared things. We talked about the REMFs, the rear echelon mother fuckers who called the shots but knew nothing about the jungles. We laughed together. We didn't feel so alone."

"So, you did the only thing you could control. You stayed close to that young man and did not let him die alone. That was your choice. Your comrades were the key to your survival, and you chose to protect them. But who was there to protect you?"

Kaj sat silently, his mind a confused jumble of emotions. He wanted to run away. Then, somehow, an answer formed.

"Moses Mahi," Kaj said slowly.

"Your friend. The man who served with you and then worked beside you when you came home. He never judged you. Yet, you blamed him for your nightmares and pushed him aside just when you needed him the most. And still, he waited patiently for you to reconnect with him.

Kaj closed his eyes. He hoped he would see an empty pool when he opened them. But the dragon was still there and still judging him. He watched as the dragon shook water from its scales and blew an impatient bubble of air and water out through its snout.

"This is too subtle for me," Kaj finally admitted. "You tell me. Why did I have to be wounded and see others die?"

"You did not become indifferent to death. You kept your humanity. That's what the good ones did. But your tigers are not your father's tigers. He wanted to prove his loyalty to a country that rejected him. You have devoted your life to justice. Justice requires evil to exist but at the same time there must be hope. Hope depends on asking the right questions. Find the difference between truth and fact.

"Truth and fact? Are they so different?"

"As night and day. Truth is what people like you believe because you have been taught it. Fact is what you can see for yourself. Spirit and body. Your race has been talking about this for thousands of years. Look closely at your life, even the political part that you do not value."

"Politics? Really? Do dragons have politics?" Kaj's eyebrows rose in unison. The idea suggested a way to escape the dragon's probing.

The dragon saw the gesture for what it was and slapped its rooster tail on the water in frustration. "Even yaks and goats have politics. Your politicians look for people to blame in order to use it to control. They never question themselves. You can because you feel your heart beating in unison with the planet's vibration. That is the humanity that sets you apart. That is what others see in you. Find your balance. Understand there's no need for you to conform to someone else's values to be a hero."

"That doesn't help." Kaj's eyebrows knitted in frustration.

"That's as clear as you deserve to have," the dragon said. "When you are ready to hear, the universe will show you. Do not mistake it for coincidence."

The dragon opened its eyes suddenly and began to back away from the shore. Kaj looked around but saw nothing. When he looked back, the dragon was gone. He felt the cold stone of the bench beneath him and the whisper of the wind starting to blow through the trees. It was as if time had stopped and was now restarting.

Then he heard the footsteps. This time when he turned around, he saw the Colonel.

"Is everything all right?" the Colonel asked. "I was concerned when they told me you had asked to come here so early in the morning."

Kaj stood up quickly, brushing away a few small leaves that had fallen on him. He knew he owed the Colonel some explanation, but he had none to offer except perhaps to say he might have dozed off in the quiet of his surroundings. He was not about to admit to pouring out his soul to a dragon. Who would believe him anyway?

"I am able to think here," he said instead. "It is a place to have a conversation with myself. Does that make sense?"

The Colonel looked at the pond's still water. "And did you have a good conversation with yourself?"

"I'm not sure what happened. I think it was more of an argument. Colonel, may I ask you a question?"

Kaj stepped down from the terrace and rubbed his arms. He felt suddenly chilled, as if the sun had gone behind the clouds.

"Of course."

"When you were in the British Army, far away from your home, what did you miss the most?"

"I assume you are not talking about the obvious distance of family and friends or the comfort foods of childhood?"

"I am not," Kaj agreed.

"I missed the mountains. In Nepal, they say that the mountains control the weather, the seasons, and even life itself. The earliest people worshipped the mountain as gods. I am not sure they were wrong."

"What did you do when you couldn't see the mountains every day?"

"We were garrisoned in a southern beach town, so I would watch the waves in the English Channel. If you look at the waves in a certain way, they look like ranges of hills and mountains. Water is precious too."

"Did that work for you?"

"Well, in the early years, whenever I had leave, I flew home. I was eager to go back."

"Will you ever go back to Nepal now?"

The Colonel stopped smiling. "I am not sure I can go back. Nepal has changed, and I have changed. I have lived abroad so long that I do not feel I belong anywhere. Perhaps that means I belong to the planet."

"Does that bother you?"

"It saddens me that only my memories survive. But there is joy to be found everywhere if I allow myself to see it. I have always drawn strength from the Gurkha brotherhood. I feel that I belong and their comradeship is the central core of who I am. I will always stand with them."

"May I ask you a further question?"

"You may," the Colonel said with a smile.

"I know you have been reporting our actions to the King."

"I made no secret of it," the Colonel replied without any apology. "If you had asked, I would have confirmed it."

"I did not ask because I didn't want to know. If the King didn't trust us, it would have complicated our job. It was easier to move forward expecting that we had his full confidence."

"It was not lack of trust. The King wanted to help you and your team. You have seen how he comes to meetings unannounced when he has something to say. Before you arrived, he came to one of our meetings and gave orders to protect you at all costs."

Kaj imagined the impulsive king arriving suddenly at a security staff meeting. He could even imagine the hurried scrape of chairs as the men leapt to their feet to salute him.

"I see his point," Kaj said. "A misdirected outside presence could stir up the clans and affect Kuthan's relations with its neighbors. The King took a big chance inviting us to investigate."

"Yes, but a wise one."

"I hope so." Kaj smiled at the Colonel's reassurance. He thought again of Moses Mahi. He did not yet understand the concept of balance, but he suspected it must deal with perspective. Perhaps that's why he was brought to Kuthan and the dragon pool. Perhaps he was meant to see things in a new way. He hoped that one day he would understand.

Both men then turned back along the path that had brought them to the pool. Behind them, the sunlight formed a dappled pattern on the pond's surface and a bird's song echoed in among the trees. Kaj felt ready now to tell the King what he had learned about Mallik.

Despite the path being narrow, Kaj and the Colonel managed to walk side by side.

Chapter 32

THE KING LISTENED INTENTLY AND then picked up the documents Kaj had laid out on the table. He read the text silently, studied the Kuthani dragon seals, and examined the dates and signatures.

"Tell me again how you have these." The King's voice sounded choked.

"At my request, Greg Horne provided copies of correspondence between the US State Department and the palace. You have a copy of the letter Mallik addressed to you requesting transfer to a Kuthani prison on humanitarian grounds. As you see, the US responded by asking about the transfer process. The palace indicated that the exchange was to be made immediately upon Mallik's arrival in Singapore. The US clearly believed that the request to release him to Kuthani custody was legitimate and so moved to comply. The exchange was made at Changi Airport as agreed, but then Mallik seems to have disappeared.

"How do you know he is not still in Singapore?"

Kaj looked down briefly in a gesture of embarrassment. Now he knew how Greg felt when he had to admit that Mallik had been "lost" somewhere. "Well, Sir, I have to admit that I personally asked someone from the People's Republic to assist us in finding him."

"China?" The King's eyes opened in alarm.

"Don't worry," Kaj said quickly. "Any obligations incurred by this cooperation are personal to me and by extension to the US State Department. Kuthan is only involved to the extent of a bottle of single-malt whiskey and some Gurkha cigars. Those were charged to the hotel."

"Who did you work with?" The King's mouth set into a steely line of disapproval.

Kaj had no reason to protect his sources. "Meng."

To Kaj's surprise, the King's frozen face unfolded itself into creases of amusement. "Meng. How did I not know that?"

"You've worked with him before?" Kaj wondered why no one had told him.

"Meng goes where there's trouble. If it is only a few cigars and some whiskey this time, we are lucky. He must like you. He managed an entire case of cigars and several bottles last time. He is a likeable scoundrel. What did you learn from him?"

"Meng said there is a video showing Mallik being driven from Changi Airport in a car registered to the Kuthani Embassy. From there, it seems he was flown to Kuthan, where he disappears."

"And you think he might have had something to do with the attack on the palace?"

Kaj considered his words carefully. "We need to rule that out."

The King sat back in his chair for a long minute. Then, in his characteristic response when he saw a pathway open before him, he took immediate action. He walked over to the heavy sound-proofed door, opened it, and shouted out Dorji's name in a most unroyal manner. He stood by the door until a worried looking Dorji came in. The King shut the door sharply behind him.

"I have just been provided with copies of correspondence between this office and the US State Department regarding Abhinav Mallik. Would you like to explain?"

Dorji's face became ashen and his eyes opened wide with fear. His shoulders hunched and his chest seemed to shrink into his body. He looked as if he was willing himself to suddenly become invisible.

The King picked up the letters and tossed them contemptuously on the table in front of his secretary. "I never saw these. Who signed them?"

The Adam's apple in Dorji's throat rose and fell. He looked as if he was about to burst into tears.

"I used your signature stamp. I wanted to save you from the trouble," he said pitifully.

"What trouble was that?" The King sat down at the head of the table and waited as he would if he were a headmaster surveying the sins of a schoolboy. As Kaj watched, he felt uncomfortable but also interested.

Dorji could hardly get the words out. "When the letter from Mallik arrived, I felt sorry for him. He begged you to save him. He was sure he was about to die. I did not think you would want to be involved since he had killed your friend, Dr. Whitworth."

"You brought him back so he could kill my family? Is that what you were thinking."

"On my honor, no. He could never do anything like that." Dorji was trembling so hard that Kaj wondered how he managed to stay upright.

"And how do you know that?"

"We grew up together. I know his heart. His family came to Kuthan from India long ago. He is a good man. The Golden Tiger clan took them in and his family worked hard."

Kaj began to wonder if Dorji was talking about the same Mallik that killed Harrison Whitworth with a bow and arrow on his driveway, smuggled Kuthani antiquities for profit, and spat obscenities at Kaj and his team when he was cornered

"You say you did this out of loyalty?" The King's scorn was palpable. "Where is Mallik?" His voice was cold and unforgiving.

"When he returned from Singapore, he joined the Temple of the Thousand Steps to Heaven. The monks agreed that his soul would best be healed if he stayed with them. You would never have been troubled with this if there had not been the attack on the palace."

"You would have tried to keep this from me forever?" The King sounded incredulous.

"I never meant to harm you. I would give my life for you."

"That is not the point," the King snorted. "I shall never be able to trust you again. And how am I to be sure that Mallik did not murder my family or that you did not help him?"

At that point, Dorji fell in a heap on the floor weeping copiously.

"Your Majesty," Kaj said quietly. "If someone tells us where the temple is, we'll go there tomorrow."

"The temple is in the hills above Golden Tiger lands. Take the Colonel and as many guards as you need. Ananda, you are under house arrest tonight. You will not talk with anyone about this, and tomorrow, you will accompany the detectives to the temple. Then you are not to return to the palace."

Dorji got on his hands and knees and finally managed to stand upright. "I apologize with all my heart. I thought I was doing the right thing."

Chapter 33

KAJ TOOK HIS TIME DECIDING whom he wanted to take with him to Golden Tiger. It seemed only a matter of fairness to include Nie, since Xue was already set to visit the dam and had visited the Sikh temple. It was a natural decision to include Jill, but then there was the question of the crime lab. His problem was solved surprisingly quickly when Sharma told him that the forensic team was tied up with processing the DNA results. Sharma then suggested Sanjay. "He needs an outing," Sharma said dismissively.

The drive to Golden Tiger would have been a pleasant journey through rice paddies, cultivated fields, and fruit tree groves if the situation had not been so dire. The road was well maintained, and the sun was out. The houses they passed were larger than in Mongarthuā, but they still had the spirit boxes at the end of their driveways and most had outbuildings in the rear for a wide variety of tractors and harvesting equipment. It could have been an outing in any prosperous, agrarian country in the world.

As it was, they drove in silence. The reason for the visit carried the burden of misrepresentation and embarrassment.

Dorji was prostrate with guilt over deceiving the King. The Colonel was displeased with the lapse of security that Mallik represented. Sanjay felt exposed by the dismissive way Sharma had volunteered him yet again. Kaj was worried about how the people at Golden Tiger would receive them. Only Jill and Nie appeared calm. Nie, in fact, said she was looking forward to a good walk up the stairs to the temple.

The Golden Tiger homestead was not a fortress like Mountain Thunder's, nor a lost paradise of a garden oasis as Water Dragon's once was. It was a large Kuthani farmhouse surrounded by others that seemed to have been added as the family's needs grew: another marriage, another family, another house. None of the houses looked exactly alike, but all had similar function: three or four bedrooms, large living area, garages, and chicken coops.

Seeing the farmhouses gave Kaj a memory, not quite *déjà vu*, but enough to be poignant. He and his grandfather were sitting next to the *furu* behind his grandparents' house. The old man was cleaning fish he had caught that morning. His wife had banished him outside so he couldn't scratch her turquoise blue, Formica kitchen countertops. Kaj was listening to his grandfather tell stories of bears, monkeys, warriors, and heroes, while the pile of scales, guts, and fins piled up on newspaper on the ground. The old man died shortly after, so the memory was precious. But, as he looked back now, Kaj realized that his grandfather never talked about the war years in Hawaii. Nobody did. And that included his own father, Goro, who would never talk about the young men who did not return from Italy.

Kaj put his memories aside as they parked in front of the largest house.

Dorji ushered them inside. No matter Golden Tiger's feelings about Dorji, Kuthani culture required that visitors be offered food and drink. Mounds of fruit, bowls of rice with cooked vegetables and butter chicken, momos, and bowls of sauces were waiting. Jill smiled her approval when she was offered White Bone fermented tea rather than butter tea, but there was no mistaking the tension in the room.

The Golden Tiger patriarch appeared to be a farmer of the type known around the world. He lacked the long-distance stare that came with the mountains. His vision was focused instead on long columns of ducks pouring into the rice paddies to gobble the pests. He proudly told them that his rice was sold in America with the description, *Himalayan*. "But it is really Golden Tiger rice," he said.

"We wish to express our sympathy for Anya's death," Kaj said.

The old man nodded sadly. "Too much loss," he said. "Those children she cared for were her life."

"Did she have other responsibilities there?"

"She stayed with the children until they were old enough to go to British boarding school. Then she was a housekeeper for the new hotel. When she retired, the King gave her a small, lifetime apartment."

"Did she care for any other children?"

The old man shook his head. "Only the King and his cousins when they were young."

"The cousins were Kiran and Kanchan?"

The old man nodded.

"Could there have been another cousin? Or perhaps another child about the same age? Abenhav, perhaps?"

"Abenhav Mallik?" The old man's lip curled into a sneer. "Abhinev's family were allowed to stay in Kuthan only because King Raju II, the present King's father, allowed some long-term residents to become citizens. Abhenhav was not suitable as a companion for royal children. His family were immigrant laborers. Not good at all."

The mention of Mallik seemed to be a transition point. The patriarch descended then into unrestrained rage.

"Abenhav Mallik has embarrassed us. I am ashamed of how he abused our hospitality. We took in his family when they asked for help. They were hungry. We fed them. They had no shelter. We gave them a roof. The father asked for work. We provided it. When the palace offered Abenhav a good position, he took it and what does he do? He cheats and kills. Abenhav Mallik will never be welcome in this house."

Kaj sat back uncomfortably and glanced around the room. Everyone was looking studiedly down at the table. When he looked back at the old man, he was suddenly reminded of the vision of Moses coming down from the mountain, fingers pointed at the sinful mortals at his feet, and fire and brimstone filling the sky behind him.

The old man turned his baleful glare at Dorji. "Sending messages in the King's name and to save the traitor who brought shame to this family. Was his betrayal not enough? My own grandson dismissed from the palace for aiding the snake that we had in our midst. And after all that the King has done for you."

The old man turned to Kaj as if asking him to understand that his own loyalty should not be doubted. "I knew nothing of this. I would not have approved if I had known."

Kaj nodded politely. "No one thought anything else."

Then the old man turned back to his grandson. "I am surprised that you had the courage to come back here."

"I have nowhere else to go. I did not mean any harm. I hoped to do a good thing."

"Good?" the old man spat out. "Whose good are you talking about?" The old man took the next few minutes to dissect the question and provide his own answers. Dorji sat like a penitent schoolboy. But, as Kaj noted, this time Dorji did not cry. And then it was over. Gratefully, the group gave their thanks and let Dorji lead them back to the vans.

"That was not as bad as I expected," Dorji said. "My grandfather says what he wants and then forgets. He will never mention it again. The King is not so forgiving."

Kaj had nothing to say. In fact, no one said anything as they took their seats. There had been enough embarrassment to go around. Kaj brought the subject back to the matter at hand.

"I understand that the Master of the temple does not speak English well, who is going to translate?"

"I will if needed."

Kaj was merciless. "Can we trust you to be accurate?"

Dorji stood as tall as possible and spoke with what appeared to Kaj to be some of his lost pride. "The man I most admired and was proud to serve now distrusts me. My only hope is that one day I may return to serving him. My grandfather believes I have betrayed my family. I will translate accurately and honestly because I have no reason not to. I believe you will find that Mallik is a changed man and offered no threat to the King. If you are not satisfied, I am willing to enter the monastery myself because my life is over."

The approach to the monastery was through a large, paved parking area with a marked off section for tour buses. There were several large buildings with the requisite restrooms and shuttered spaces that suggested there was money to be made selling souvenirs on busy holidays. Because there were only a few cars in the parking lot, the van was able to park close to the pathway leading to the access trail.

Jill craned her neck backwards to look up at the monastery. From down below, it seemed to be precariously perched on a narrow ledge far above them.

"How do we get up there?"

Dorji pointed to pathway. "We go this way. This is called the Monastery of a Thousand Steps to Heaven. It is a sacred place. People sometimes follow this path on their hands and knees as a penance.

Kaj wondered quietly if Dorji was going to crawl on this path at some point. The man looked distraught enough.

"It is a good idea to use these toilets now," Dorji added. "There are also large water tanks there to fill your bottles."

When the group had reassembled, Dorji led them to a bridge crossing a water course. There had been rain recently, so water was moving briskly although not at flood stage.

They could see the first challenge immediately. The bridge was not cement like the pathway. It was a rope bridge with a series of metal planks in the base. It was the kind of picturesque and tricky crossing that required patience and practice, and, also, the kind of bridge where the foolish might set it rocking for fun.

"This is a famous monastery," the Colonel explained. "Climbing up to it is considered a spiritual journey. Since the journey between the earth and spirit is individual and private, only one person may be on the bridge at a time. The bridge is considered the start of the pilgrimage."

"Isn't there a road leading up there?" Jill asked. "How do they get supplies?

"No road," Dorji said. "But people make offerings and the monks come down. It is said to have a thousand steps, but there are only eight hundred, and there are flat places to stop."

"Who's going first?" Kaj was prepared to lead if no one else stepped forward. But in this case, there was a ready volunteer.

"I'll do it," Sanjay said enthusiastically.

"Are you familiar with these bridges?" the Colonel asked.

Sanjay nodded, but Kaj gave him one of his blank, disbelieving stares and rephrased the question. "Have you actually crossed one of these?" Kaj did not hear his answer.

"The best way to approach the bridge is with reverence," the Colonel told Sanjay. "Go slowly and get into a rhythm. This one is tricky because it has a rope handrail and side supports. Stay in the middle and put your foot firmly on each metal plate."

Sanjay smiled with the overconfidence of youth and promptly forgot the Colonel's advice. Within five steps the bridge began to sway.

"Slow down," the Colonel shouted. But by then Sanjay was half-way and had decided that the fastest way to get out of trouble was to sprint.

The result was predictable. Sanjay went over the top of the ropes and landed in the water with a spectacular splash. Kaj and the Colonel hauled him out.

"You said you had experience with these bridges," the Colonel told him unsympathetically. "I told you to slow down. Well, you cannot go on wet like this."

"I am not going back. I will dry." Sanjay's teeth chattered.

"I have a change of clothes back in the van," the Colonel said. "If they fit, you can come. Otherwise, you stay down here and wait for us."

"They will fit," Sanjay said with grim determination.

"Is he all right?" Nie asked.

"He is just wet" the Colonel said. "He is lucky it was not melted snow."

The next attempt on the bridge was more organized. Dorji went across first, demonstrating how to sway with the bridge and how to move with a graceful slow motion from plate to plate. The others followed his lead. Sanjay was the last to cross. He was now wearing baggy camouflage trousers with rolled up bottoms and a green t-shirt that came down almost to his knees.

"Remember, it is perfectly safe if you go slow," the Colonel yelled.

Sanjay nodded and took his first step out onto the bridge. He gripped the ropes with white knuckles and placed his feet firmly on the middle of the first metal plate.

"You can do it," Jill yelled.

"Be careful," Nie called. Kaj darted a quick look at her. She had sounded almost parental and anxious.

Sanjay smiled wanly and took his second step. The bridge swayed but not enough to dislodge him. With each further step he gained more confidence and when he was within grabbing distance, the Colonel pulled him to safety.

"See," the Colonel told him, "Even elderly pilgrims can do this."

Dorji then led them to steps cut into the hillside. The steps seemed in good condition except for moss in the seams where the back of the steps met the risers.

"Watch out for the moss. It may be slippery. Use the guide ropes. Most people get up there in just over an hour. There is a bench every hundred steps. Stop if you need to. Our appointment with the Master is two hours from now, so we have time. And even if we are late, he will accommodate us.

Jill looked sardonically at Kaj. "I didn't know it was going to be a marathon."

Kaj did not reply. He was too busy calculating how far he was likely to get before stopping, aikido training or not. As usual, Khutan was full of surprises. But at least they were not doing the climb up in the mountains where they would have had thin air and altitude to contend with.

The Colonel took the lead up the stairs, while Dorji waited to bring up the rear. "Do not look down," Dorji told them as they passed him. "Not until the top. Up there, you will have a wonderful view."

The surprise of the climb turned out to be Nie. She climbed each hundred steps without breaking her pace and passed nearly everyone else.

"What's your secret?" Jill asked her as she panted her way on to the plateau at six hundred steps. Her legs were starting to feel like lead.

"My husband and I hike in the Himalaya range," Nie told her. "He is a busy surgeon and when we have time off, we go as far away from our jobs as possible."

"Have you climbed on Masakatsu?" Jill expected to hear that the mountain was too far or too high.

"Of course," Nie replied. "A beautiful mountain. But we are not climbers. We stay on the lower slopes on the Chinese side."

"Have you hiked on the Khutan side?" Jill held her breath.

"No, it has always been the north side. Kuthan does not permit hikers in the south. Why do you ask?"

"I knew someone who wanted to climb from the south. But I understand that is not possible."

"People who climb on Masakatsu are a small club. Not many get the chance. What was the name?"

Jill hesitated. She wasn't sure how much to say or even what. In the end, she decided that his death was long enough ago that no one could possibly remember him.

"Steven Harkin," she said simply.

"Steven!" Nie's face lit up with recognition. "About six feet, red hair, and blue eyes. We met him on the trail. This cannot be real."

Jill felt her eyes burn. She agreed with Nie's reaction. *This cannot be real.*

"You remember him? It was so long ago."

"I remember him well because he took a picture of us, and after he went home, he sent us a signed copy. We have it framed in our house and see it every day."

Nie turned around to face the steps as Sanjay came panting up. "Nearly there," she told him cheerily. Then she took off briskly up the next flight. Jill and Sanjay each took a couple of deep breaths before they followed her.

The Colonel and Nie were the first to complete the climb and took up position next to a roofed gateway at the monastery entrance. Kaj arrived next, followed by Jill who had slowed down to walk the final flight with Sanjay. Dorji followed close behind them.

Together, as a group, they walked through the gateway and saw the promised tableau of the Kuthan plateau: a swath of agricultural land and beyond that, far in the distance, the ribbon of the river that flowed out to the Bay of Bengal.

"It was a penance to climb up here," Jill said for them all, "but it was worth it for the view. But I am not sure I'll be able to lift my foot into the van when we go back down."

"You should try running up a mountain with 22 kilos of sand on your back," the Colonel laughed. "That was the fitness part of the selection process when we applied to the British Army. We used to train by carrying our friends on our shoulders. Not that I could do that anymore."

"Not that any of us could," Kaj replied with real feeling.

The monastery was a series of buildings one behind the other along a natural ledge that, seen from below, had appeared barely wide enough to accommodate the buildings, a pathway around them, and a wall to keep people from falling off. At this level, they could see that the ledge was wider and the monastery much more extensive than it had appeared. The most striking feature of the various buildings was the exquisite wood carving that surrounded every door and window and ran in a continuous frieze beneath the eaves. It made the monastery look like a series of carved jewelry boxes, one nested behind the other, and each more elaborate than the one before it.

The first building contained a café and a shop selling everything from carved buddhas to triangular face masks edged in gold braid and fur. The next building was the temple with gold painted door frames and upward curving eaves. A seated buddha was visible through the open, double front door, and the air was rich with the smoke from burning incense sticks. The passage beside the temple was cordoned off by a rope indicating that the temple was as far as visitors were allowed to enter.

"We have time," Dorji said. "The shop has been here for a thousand years selling carved images of the Buddha to pilgrims. You'll find wooden prayer beads and wrapped prayer pouches for good luck and health. People buy them as an offering to the temple. The monks bless them, and it is expected that visitors will buy some to take home."

Kaj looked into the shop window and was glad to notice the orange and gold globes and blue and white letters that indicated credit cards were welcome. He had still not converted US dollars to Kuthani rupees, mainly because he had no reason to. He knew he must eventually. He needed to take home a gift for Linda.

They were sitting on benches outside the shop when a monk approached Dorji and told him that the Master would see them earlier than expected.

They were led past the rope barrier and into a building that was far more modern on the inside than its outer architecture would suggest. It seemed the business heart of the monastery because it was equipped with computers and various forms of communication equipment. It could have been an office anywhere except the staff were monks with shorn heads and wearing brown and purple robes. Their slippers slapped on the floor as they walked around.

They were invited into a spacious side room with a low raised platform set with large cushions at one end under a framed picture of the monastery that filled up half the width of the wall. The wall had bamboo siding along the lower half, topped by a frieze of Kuthani dragons that reminded Kaj of the restaurant called Fifty Wise Dragons, back in Honolulu. The floor of the room was spotless and polished to a high shine.

Two sets of low tables spread out on both sides, forming a u-shape with a large, plush carpet in between. The platforms along the sides were slightly lower than the dais. The six visitors were invited to find their places, three on each side.

Dorji took the moment to whisper to Kaj: The Master will answer your question about the history with us all present. Then he will give you a private audience to talk about Mallik. We will wait for you here."

Kaj took particular care not to let Dorji see his eyebrows rise.

Chapter 34

IT WAS ONLY A FEW minutes before the Master and several monks came in and sat cross legged on the platform. Their presence formed a tableau that made Kaj think of Grandpa Lhotse's description of monks coming to convince Mountain Thunder to support the newly formed government in return for their disputed valley.

Kaj could, in fact, be convinced the current Master had somehow defied time and had been the one who revealed his buttocks in defiance. He was a wiry, energetic man with a broad smile and a hint of mischief in his eyes. He sat cross-legged with the agility of someone far younger, and his glance around the room took in every detail of the people he was meeting. Kaj noted how he gave a special greeting to Dorji.

As soon as the Master began greeting the guests, it was clear his lack of English had been greatly exaggerated.

"You want to know about the new government after Kalyani. I was with the Abbot when he asked Azur Lhotse to agree to the new government." The Master gave a sly smile.

"You drove in the truck to Pahāda?" Kaj allowed his voice to show appreciation for the adventure.

The Master chuckled. Both he and Kaj knew what he was laughing about. The others not in on the joke glanced at one another uncertainly. Kaj was not about to tell them.

The Master nodded. "Six of us went with the Abbot. We had a most difficult task. But first, you should hear our story from the start."

Kaj hoped it was not too obvious when he stretched out his leg under the table. The last piece of shrapnel, the one the doctors found too difficult to remove, made itself known if he kept his leg bent for too long. He tried to find a comfortable position.

"This monastery has been here for a thousand years. It has been a peaceful place for pilgrimage and meditation. That was before the British came. There was fighting in India and some rebels escaped across our border. They stayed here and attacked the British Army until they decided to stop them. The British came to turn them out and then stayed to make sure they did not return.

"One day, there were protests for independence in India. The British climbed our steps and told the monks to leave. They said soldiers needed to come here to watch the land below. They said the monks could take only what they could carry. Some monks left for other monasteries. Golden Tiger clan gave some shelter. It was a difficult time."

The Master took a drink from a glass of water on the table. He had covered two hundred years of history in a few minutes. Now came the difficult part.

"Then the British decided they have no further use for the monastery. When they go, the monks climb the steps and find nothing. Not even a pot to cook rice. The British took sacred manuscripts that meant nothing to them. They took pictures off the walls, even the carved wood around the windows and doors. Many people said that the British were thieves, and there was much anger. I am told that the British took millions of dollars in your money from Bengal alone. But they had kept peace. When they left, the clans began to fight again. The Dam Board demanded order but they had no power. The people were frightened and came to the Abbot. Protect us, they asked. I was new then. I saw it myself.

"The Abbot was a wise man. He called people together. Everyone agreed to create a governing council with a king to lead it. It was done. But Mountain Thunder and Snow Leopard were not there. It was a bad winter and they could not travel. No one worried about Snow Leopard. It is a peaceful clan. Mountain Thunder was rich and powerful and warlike. No one knew how to make them agree. In the end, Water Dragon clan said, '*We will give them the valley*.'"

The Master stopped and took another sip of water. He looked around. Everyone looked interested, but Sanjay looked enthralled.

"Someone from White Bone clan said, 'The head of Water Dragon clan, Soöng, thinks of Kuthan for the future. Make him the king.' But other clans said: 'If he is king, he may seek revenge for Kalyani.' But Soöng said, 'Give Water Dragon lands to the city of Mongarthuā to manage. If there is no king or heir, the lands go back to Water Dragon.' It was so agreed. When the summer came, the Abbot and the monks went to talk with Mountain Thunder."

Listening to the jumble of history the Master was presenting, Kaj felt the prickle. *This is too pretty. This is too easy. It's a fairy tale. It's unbelievable. You need to find out who wants you to believe it. The British left Kuthan with a legacy of greed and exploitation. Go ahead: be American. Wait until you are alone with the Master and start asking questions. Don't forget your own mantra: If you want to know, follow the money.*

Chapter 35

After the general meeting ended, Kaj was led into a conservatory furnished only with a cushioned wicker sofa, two armchairs, and a small table between them bearing a large, glass ash tray. He couldn't resist going to the open windows to look down on the valley. The view was out over Golden Tiger farmland, and as far away as Kuthan's border with its southern neighbor. The early afternoon sun had burned off the morning layer of clouds, leaving only the deeper valleys to hold onto their shadows.

The Master joined him after a few minutes and invited him to sit across from him in one of two armchairs. The old monk pulled out a cigarette and paper matches from his robes. He took the cigarette between his thumb and forefinger and lit up, breathing out a satisfying billow of blue smoke.

"I know I should stop," the Master admitted, "but White Bone clan grows exceptional tobacco. At my age, I think I am allowed."

"We all are entitled to a little comfort," Kaj replied.

The old man flicked the ash into the glass bowl, giving Kaj a glimpse of a yellowed nail and stained fingers. The motion was almost meditative. Kaj sensed that the Master was assessing him.

"You thought I told you a fairy tale instead of the truth." The old monk's tone implied statement rather than a question. He took another puff of cigarette and contemplated its tip.

Kaj tried to stifle his surprise at hearing his own words repeated to him, but at the same time he had to admit their accuracy.

"A few days ago, Grandpa Lhotse told me that the Soöng family never gave anything away unless there was something better to replace it. Hearing that they suddenly donated their land for the cause of Kuthan's peace seemed unlikely."

"You mean unbelievable." The Master looked at him serenely. "Well," he said slowly, "you are right and you are wrong. Tell me, have you looked at the map of Kuthan?"

When Kaj nodded, the Master followed immediately with another question. "And what did it tell you?"

Kaj's mind went uncharacteristically blank. He looked through the windows up at the sky and for some reason thought of the dragon.

"Kuthan and its clans are divided by rivers," he said slowly. The regions on this eastern part of the country, Snow Leopard, White Bone, and Golden Tiger, have smaller rivers that irrigate the land but are also likely to flood."

The Master nodded "And what about the other side?"

"The western regions, Mountain Thunder, Water Dragon, and Blue Pheasant, have the Sindhu River that collects water to feed the dam and then releases it through an irrigation system."

The Master took another puff and gave a small cough before he put his cigarette down to rest. He gave Kaj a look of wary reticence.

"Before the British came, the Sindhu River was a small stream. The land looked like the eastern part of Kuthan."

Kaj's eyes widened. "You're saying the rivers were engineered deliberately to become one river?"

"It was done. Now, think again. Who owned the land where the British built the first dam?"

Kaj looked around desperately for a map, but there wasn't one. The room was bare except for the furniture. That forced him to rely on a process of elimination. He knew it could not be Mountain Thunder's land. No one would build a dam in the mountains only to have it freeze every winter. It could not be Blue Pheasant's either, because when their water arrived it had already been through the dam's turbines. That left only one possibility.

"It had to be Water Dragon land." Kaj's mind started the process of putting things into place. Now he understood why Water Dragon fought Mountain Thunder over the valley. The dam had taken so much from the clan already.

The Master agreed. "At first, it was just the area directly behind the dam. Then the British wanted more land for a bigger dam to make electricity. Water Dragon was told to abandon their farmland because the dam would make a big lake. Water Dragon protested, but the British said they must leave and take with them their animals. Then the waters rose. All they could see were the tops of their temples. Soon, those were gone. Only water was left.

The Master took one more pleasurable draw on his cigarette and, regretfully, stubbed it out in the bowl.

"Years later, the Dam Board said they wanted even more Water Dragon land so they could produce more electric power. This time, Water Dragon refused. The Board said they would pay for the land. But they wanted to divide the money among all the clans. The other clans said Water Dragon should agree. Water Dragon refused again. Then Kalyani happened. People said it was because of the dam. People said that the Dam Board had paid Mountain Thunder to attack Water Dragon. People also said that when Mountain Thunder called for men to attack Water Dragon, the other clans sent men because they wanted the money."

Patel's words about the rituals of water came into Kaj's mind. Was Water Dragon sacrificed to serve the greed of the other clans? Darya had hinted at something like this. It also provided an explanation for Grandpa Lhotse's almost compulsive protests of innocence. But he felt the prickle at the back of his neck.

"May I ask why you waited to share this with me? Why not speak out in the earlier meeting?"

"Because there is a lot more, and you have asked to be told the truth."

Kaj's warning prickle became more insistent. He began to wonder whether Kuthan had hidden what really happened at Kalyani.

"With the British gone, people were afraid. They came to the monasteries and asked us to restore peace. The Abbot called for the monasteries to send representatives to a meeting in the city."

The Master looked speculatively at Kaj as if inviting questions. Kaj had none, so the monk continued with the history.

"The monks looked for spiritual solutions first: 'Good values mean good people,' they said. But the Abbot was wiser. He said they needed to find what would motivate the clans to work together."

The Master took out another of his precious cigarettes and fingered it longingly before placing it on the table.

"The monks thought that Mountain Thunder might lay down their arms if they were given the valley they had been fighting for. But should they be rewarded for their aggression? Who knew? The times were difficult. Water Dragon was the second problem. The survivors, the family patriarch and his two sons, needed a guarantee against future violence. There was much discussion how that protection could be provided. The Abbot said the best way was to create a union between Blue Pheasant and Water Dragon. He thought that would discourage Mountain Thunder from claiming more land. Then there was much talk about how to form such an alliance. One solution was through marriage. It was suggested that a Water Dragon son might take a Blue Pheasant wife.

"An arranged marriage?" Kaj's eyebrows rose. "A couple forced to marry?"

"Not so strange. In the past, parents had the duty to find suitable mates for their children. Many arranged marriages have worked well. Blue Pheasant women are beautiful and practical. No one would be forced, but everyone knew what was at stake. There were three available young ladies and Raju and Tranh were sent to visit them. Raju married Aishwarya, the eldest, and Tranh married Dechen, the middle daughter. Pema, the youngest, later married a boy from Golden Tiger. Tragically, Aishwarya died young, but the younger brother, Tranh, was married to Dechen all his life."

"Did Blue Pheasant object to these forced marriages?"

The Master smiled. "It turned out well for them. In return, the Abbot released the Blue Pheasant boys who had made the threats against the dam. They had been sent to our monastery for reformation."

"Imprisoned in your monastery?"

"Not imprisoned. Employed. Wood carving is a Blue Pheasant tradition and we made use of their skills to repair the temple. When that was done, the Dam Board set one of them up in business in the city, where he could be watched. The other married a Snow Leopard lady, moved to the mountains and became a famous painter of mountains and waterfalls. You may have heard of him. He signs his paintings as 'Lama'."

"This is confusing," Kaj said. "You built relationships between these clans for political reasons? And all of this under the watchful eye of the Dam Board?"

"It was a masterful solution. Mountain Thunder put down their arms. Water Dragon had allies and was protected. Blue Pheasant gained husbands for two daughters with the Dam paying their dowries, and the family's sons returned home. Everyone was happy. Everyone agreed to a new constitution, all in the name of unity and peace. Until now, the Abbot's plan has served the country well."

"So that's why the Abbot went personally to negotiate with Mountain Thunder and took you young monks along?"

"He believed that Mountain Thunder was the greatest threat, so we met with them first. They are still the most powerful of the clans, but we believe that Darya Lhotse will maintain the agreement. Each passing year makes the constitution stronger."

"Until now," Kaj objected. "Until the King had to call in foreigners to solve a crime. Was that also an agreement made by the Dam Board and the monasteries?"

"No. That was the King's own decision. But no one would have opposed him if he had asked. We know his heart."

"Sir," Kaj said with a knowing stare. "When the monks received the monastery back from the British, you said that you had nothing left and the buildings were damaged."

The Master nodded.

"May I ask who paid for the repairs? Surely visitor offerings would not have been enough."

The Master picked up his cigarette and made a fuss of striking the match to light it. His hand trembled slightly as he raised the cigarette to his lips.

"You are right. We received generous donations."

Kaj already knew the answer. He went into interrogation mode. "Was the Dam Board also involved in bringing Mallik back to Kuthan?"

The Master looked alarmed. "We have no arrangement with the board." He took an angry puff on his cigarette and coughed for several moments. He then put the burning cigarette out in the bowl.

"I was told that Mallik is here in this monastery," Kaj said grimly.

"He is, and he will speak to you. But he has asked me to explain."

"Explain what?" Kaj's tone was polite but pointed.

"He was in this monastery when the palace was attacked. He was not involved."

Kaj stared at the Master, weighing the possible motives that might lie behind the statement. "Are you willing to swear to that?"

The Master did not like the implication. "I will personally talk to the palace. I will give my word to the King that we followed the directions we were given."

"What were those directions and who gave them to you?"

"We had instructions from the palace to give Mallik a secluded place to recover from his errors and build a peaceful, truthful life."

Kaj controlled his thoughts carefully. He did not want to show his relief at the confirmation of Dorji's story.

"What were his errors?' Kaj didn't expect an answer. He was too used to the clerical exemption to interrogation. In this case, he was wrong.

The abbot looked merely thoughtful as if he was looking for the best way to explain. "Mallik was too much focused on the present. He was impulsive and thoughtless of the welfare of others."

Kaj's eyebrow rose. "I thought that the point of Buddhist meditation was to focus on the present?"

"Only as a place to start," the abbot said sternly. "Observing the present is one way to begin self-awareness. But it is only a gateway. Someone who lives only in the present is incapable of understanding or following the values we teach. If you consider justice, honesty, gratitude, tranquility, and connection with others, none of these are realized without other people. When they are properly understood, these are not selfish qualities. Mallik sees now that his actions served only himself and that he has harmed many others around him. I will bring him in now. You can talk to him alone, and he will tell you."

"No," Kaj said firmly. "I would prefer that you stay. And Ananda Dorji too."

The Master took a small bell from his robe and rang it. The rings were high pitched and left the air vibrating. In response, the door opened and the Master told a monk what was needed.

While they waited, the Master hopefully picked up the remains of the second cigarette from the bowl. He pinched off the black end and lit what was left. Despite Kaj's opposition, he seemed to have relaxed. His hand had trembled only when he talked about the dam.

"Was it difficult for you to tell me that history?" Kaj asked.

The Master looked curiously at Kaj as if seeing him for the first time. "I did not know who you were."

"I'm just a detective trying to solve a crime."

The old monk shook his head emphatically. "No. That is only what you do. I am talking about who you are. You have good will, but I must warn you that to solve this crime means you must come face to face with evil."

The door opened before Kaj could reply. Dorji came in, accompanied by a monk with a shaved head, who sat cross-legged on the floor beside the Master's chair. Dorji took up position behind him.

It took Kaj a moment to recognize Mallik. His aggression had been replaced with something Kaj could only call calm. Kaj remembered what Mallik claimed in his letter to the King: His tranquility was being destroyed in American prison.

"Abhinav Mallik has begun working for his novice ordination," the old monk said proudly. "He has lived with us for four months. He has not left this sanctuary during that time."

The Master inclined his head to Mallik: "Brother, you may speak."

Mallik looked directly into Kaj's eyes. He showed no resentment, only a permeating sadness.

"Every day I was in the American prison, I prayed to be back in Kuthan. My family disowned me. Golden Tiger has made it clear that I can never return to my home. My nephew returned to Kuthan and did not write to me. One man in prison called me Chinese and attacked me. No one cared when I said they were wrong. I had one visitor. I began to feel myself sink into despair."

"Who visited you?" Kaj asked immediately.

"Greg Horne from your State Department. He told me that my mother had died. No one had told me. He asked me if I wanted to go home. Of course, I said yes. He told me to write a letter to the King and ask for his permission."

Kaj stared down fixedly at the ground. He willed his hairline not to jump. This was a detail Greg had neglected to share. Greg did say that they had read Mallik's letter, but not that the State Department had prompted it. Kaj's prickle came back. *Please don't let the US be involved in the palace shootings.* He felt nauseous at the thought. He felt he was back in the days of the Vietnam monsoon, vulnerable and abandoned, not knowing what the plan was or if there ever had been one.

"Did he tell you what to say?"

"He told me to say I was sorry for what I had done. I should say how much I had changed. I should beg him to allow me to finish my prison term in a monastery. I said I would study my behavior and do good things in the future."

"Did you hear back?"

Mallik shook his head. "I did not know if the letter was sent. Then several months later, the guards told me I was to leave. They did not tell me where I was going. Two men came and put handcuffs on me. They drove to the airport. They never talked, but I saw the sign that said *Singapore*. I slept on the aircraft because the prison was noisy, and I could not sleep well. Then we landed in Singapore. We waited until everyone was gone from the aircraft. They put the handcuffs back on and took me into a passage. There were two men in military uniforms waiting. My handcuffs were removed and the soldiers took me to a van. I could not see outside because the windows were dark. They drove into a basement and took me upstairs. Then I could see I was in the Kuthani Embassy, and I started to cry."

Mallik was clearly reliving the moment. A tear rolled down his cheek that he quickly wiped it away.

Kaj turned to Mallik. "Did you write your own letter to the King?"

Mallik nodded.

Kaj turned back to Dorji. "What part did you play in this?"

"When Abhinav's letter arrived, I sent a copy to the US State Department requesting his transfer. I asked Singapore to assist at the airport and asked our embassy there to arrange his transport. I wrote the letter to this monastery requesting his shelter. I used the palace seal and the King's signature stamp on all of them."

"That is a lot of writing and trouble to go through. Why did you do all of this?"

Dorji looked at Mallik. "He is family. We grew up together. I knew the King would sign these letters, but I did not want to ask him."

"Has anyone asked you about him?"

Dorji looked blank and shook his head.

Kaj sat back thoughtfully. "How did you get from the airport to this monastery?" he asked Mallik.

"A Blue Pheasant van was at the airport. I was driven here."

Kaj looked at Dorji with his discouraged stare. This time he came by it naturally and was not using it for stage presence. He had to wonder how many other details Dorji had left out.

"OK, Ananda," he said, "you have more explaining to do. First, how did Greg Horne know to visit Mallik in jail and tell him that he should ask the King to let him come home."

Dorji stammered his reply. "You need to ask Mr. Horne about that." Kaj heard the evasion. He did not pursue it because he already had a very strong suspicion.

"Why did you arrange for Blue Pheasant to send a van to meet Mallik's flight? Why not a van from Golden Tiger?"

"I didn't want my father to know," the man said forlornly. "He was angry with Abhinav. I knew he would forbid me to help him."

"Who did you ask at Blue Pheasant?"

"I asked Kiran to arrange it."

"Kiran? The King's cousin who was killed?"

"Yes."

"And why did he do it?"

Dorji hung his head. "I told him it was a confidential request from the King."

Kaj's prickle became even more insistent. *Who told Greg to talk to Mallik and tell him to write a letter?*

Chapter 36

KAJ BADLY WANTED TO TALK with Jill on the way back down, but she had taken up with Nie, and the two of them had set off down the mountain clearly involved in private conversation. Jill did not look happy.

Sanjay and Dorji followed, leaving Kaj to start the climb down with the Colonel. Kaj stooped under the carved entranceway at the top of stairs and gave an accommodating gesture to beckon the Colonel to go first.

They went down the first three hundred steps before the Colonel sat down on a bench and looked at Kaj.

"You have been silent so far," the Colonel said. "That means you have something you want to talk about."

Kaj sat down next to him. "My question is not so much what I want to ask, but whether you will feel free enough to answer."

Kaj felt he was breaking every rule of protocol and polite Kuthani manners in putting his dilemma so frankly.

For a moment, the Colonel looked confused.

"Sir," he said and thrust his chin out.

"I am having trouble understanding the role of the dam and the Dam Board in this country. Everywhere I turn, I find evidence of the dam's influence. Yet no one ever mentions it."

"I'm only an observer in this country," the Colonel objected mildly.

"But a trusted one with a broad understanding of this country's history. I value your opinion."

"I thought the Master spoke with more authority than I have."

Kaj ignored the suggestion. "But I am asking you."

The Colonel sat back, letting the trees provide a cooling shadow across his face. It took him several moments to formulate his reply.

"After the British left, Kuthan's history becomes like the game of Tigers and Goats we played in Nepal as children. The tigers are the warlord families. They are arrogant and think they are powerful because they have land and private armies. The goats, the city people, have the Dam. But they are only one city. They cannot fight the warlords. They know they must think more cleverly than the tigers or they will lose everything. No one is happy with the fear of more violence. One day there is a rumor that India or China may invade because of the discord. No one can make any reassurances this will not happen. That is when the monasteries must step in. There is still danger because the monasteries may try to impose their form of belief. No one wants that to happen, so the monasteries meet and decide that the families must provide the political leadership through the Kuthani Governing Council. The challenge then is to have the families agree to do this and to make sure that the goats will have a strong voice. The same thing is planned for the Dam Board. There is to be balance. Over time, that is done. The Dam Board is not to be independent or turn into the British East India Company. Kuthan has been very fortunate because The Soōng dynasty has made the tigers and goats work together. You could say King Raju is the balance between them."

"You know a lot about the history," Kaj said.

"I witnessed some of it. But the King has also talked about his father and grandfather. He read British colonial history at Oxford, so he knew what happened when the British East India Company took control of India. He knew that the East India Company tried to buy politicians in London. The Dam Board could not be allowed to take over the country. At the same time, the families could not be allowed to fight with one another, as they had in the past. He is the one who talks for Kuthan."

"With the attack at the palace," Kaj said, "you must wonder what would have happened if the King had been killed?"

"That is why the King must be protected at all costs. There is no one else who can do this work."

Kaj looked at him curiously. "Are you saying governments depend on individuals?"

"It depends on the people. People have the government they have earned."

"A national karma? You get what you deserve?"

The Colonel smiled at Kaj. "Why not?"

"And how does that work?" Kaj asked. "Where does the karma lead to?"

"Ah," the Colonel said, "that is why you study history. Once you know the national karma, every decision will say whether you are on the right path."

Kaj smiled with growing understanding. "You mean that every crime you solve is a step toward a goal."

The Colonel smiled back. "And each step leads you on to the next one. Your goal is not perfection. Your goal is to choose purposefully."

Kaj remembered the dragon's words.

"And know the difference between truth and fact?"

"Very much," the Colonel said. "That is one of the most profound steps."

Chapter 37

AFTER THEY DROPPED DORJI BACK at Golden Tiger, the trip back to the palace was quiet. The Colonel stayed to the front of the van talking with the driver. Sanjay went to sleep in the back, the Colonel's oversized t-shirt wrapped tightly around him and his now dry clothes piled on top as scanty blankets. Nie sat by herself writing notes. Jill sat in front of her, and Kaj could see her confusion, but there was no opportunity for him to ask her in the van, and even less when they reached the hotel and she almost ran upstairs to her room.

He lingered a few minutes thanking everyone for the day before he went up to his suite. Even though it was late in Hawaii, he called Linda.

"Up in the mountains today, visiting a monastery," he told her. "I bought a carved Buddha from a shop that has been there for a thousand years."

"The famous one with all the stairs?"

"It certainly had stairs. It took us well over an hour to get up there."

"Was it worth it?"

"A beautiful view. I took some pictures."

"Still sleeping all right?"

"Very well. It must be the altitude."

"That's good."

He was not sure if she sounded pleased or disappointed. He knew it was time to go home.

Later, he took out the coffee pot and a packet of coffee. It had a picture of farmland with Masakatsu looming in the distance.

As the coffee burbled through the filter, he phoned Jill's room. He had to try several times until the busy signal gave over to a ring. Then it ran for what seemed a long time until she answered.

"Interested in coffee?" he asked her.

"Not really feeling up to it." She sounded indefinite, so Kaj decided to push.

"Fresh pot. Plus, some little packets of sugar. Here's one that says it's from Vietnam. This kitchen is a regular United Nations. Tell you what, I'll open the door and let you smell the coffee. See what you think."

It took a few minutes and then Jill was standing in the doorway. "That smells good," she admitted.

Kaj filled the cups. When he handed one to Jill, she took the cup in both hands as if she had been chilled and was letting the coffee warm her.

"How are you doing?"

She tried to put on her reserved, private face, but she lacked the energy to pull it off. Finally, she gave in. "Not well." In typical Jill fashion, she followed her admission with the proud dismissal. "But I will be fine."

Kaj looked at her puffy cheeks and doubted that. He took a reflective sip of coffee. "Do you want to be just fine?"

She looked at him without comprehending. "Doesn't everyone want to be all right?"

"Well, Jill, there's a difference between being fine and being happy. To me, being fine means you're in a jungle, but you're not being shot at. Happy means having a home to go to and people who want you. An emotional thing."

Jill looked down at her coffee. "I thought I had a home to go to. Now I feel a fool for believing that Greg was different. My father was right. He said never trust anyone in the government. One executive order, 9066, signed by one man, and all rights are gone. All that's left are bleak, drafty places where old and young alike are forcibly relocated behind barbed wire, guarded by people with guns. I hadn't realized until I came to Kuthan how much my life was impacted by that history. It's a hollow, empty feeling. It's the loss of trust and the knowledge that you belong nowhere."

"What happened today," Kaj said softly. "What were you talking about with Dr. Nie?"

Jill stared at Kaj for a moment, then straightened her shoulders in a gesture of acceptance. She was about to talk about things her grandparents hadn't wanted her to know.

"It began when we flew up into the mountains. I knew something was wrong when Darya said climbers were not allowed on the Kuthan side of Mount Masakatsu. Stephen had often talked about climbing there. When I asked her if there were any exceptions, you heard what she said. The only people allowed in the foothills were dam workers and those using the pass between Kuthan and China."

"Did he tell you specifically he had climbed on the Kuthan side?"

Jill frowned. "He certainly gave me that impression. I thought he'd climbed part of it and wanted to make the full ascent. He never corrected me."

"And that was important to you?"

"I didn't think much of it until I learned that Dr. Nie met Stephen when she and her husband were hiking. She said he was with a woman and they looked like a couple. I didn't know what to think, so I didn't say anything. But when we got back to the hotel, I phoned Greg. He had to know about climbing expeditions. They weren't that common back in the day."

"And he did know something?"

Jill smiled bitterly. "At first, he wouldn't answer my questions. He just kept saying that Stephen wasn't doing anything improper. That made me ask him how he knew. Finally, I just demanded he tell me the truth. Then he started talking about Stephen doing something for them. I assumed that meant spying. I realized that there was a connection between Greg and Stephen that I didn't know anything about. It had to mean that when Greg asked me out, it wasn't accidental or spontaneous. It had to be because of my connection to Stephen. It gradually dawned on me that I was being used. I haven't figured out what it's about, but for all I know it's ongoing. I don't like the feeling of being watched. It reminds me of how my family lost control of their lives when they were herded into horse stalls and incarcerated at Tule Lake. My grandfather never talked about it, but my father was angry and told me not to trust anyone in power."

Kaj frowned. "I'm surprised Greg said anything. Most people in that kind of job don't say much. It's a secretive business."

"I told him he could start being honest about our relationship. He finally admitted that his bosses told him to get to know me. That became important after you worked with the Whitworth case with the Kuthani Consulate. What was the State Department afraid of? Did they think that Stephen told me things I shouldn't know? Did they think I was a spy?"

Kaj had no answer. He looked at Jill with the sad recognition of the betrayal she felt.

"Two of them lying to me," she continued. "That's impossible. Why do I attract men with secrets who don't see the harm it's doing to me?"

"Perhaps because you are the only stability they have in their lives?"

Jill looked desperately at Kaj. "But why lie to me? Both of them? Greg could have been honest and told me instead of waiting until I found out."

"Perhaps neither of them thought you would find out. Perhaps they were afraid of losing you if they told you the truth."

"But I did find out."

"True. But sometimes telling the truth is a risk. Before Linda and I were married, I sat down with her and told her what I did in Vietnam. I told her everything. I couldn't let her marry me under false pretenses. If she wanted to change her mind, I wanted her to have time to do it."

"Kaj, you're the only person I know where who you are shines through everything you do."

Kaj smiled grimly and poured them both more coffee. He doubted that the dragon would agree with her.

Jill stared into her coffee cup. "How do I know that anything Greg said is real?"

"What do you mean by *anything*? Did Greg say he was ordered to marry you?"

Jill looked desperately at Kaj. "How do I know that he wasn't?"

"Well, Jill, the interesting thing about human beings is our imagination. It's wonderful when we're building new computers but can be a problem when it comes to judging people. This woman might have been part of Stephen's mission."

"You mean, they told him to get to know her just as they told Greg to get to know me?" Jill looked disgusted.

"That's not what I meant. Stephen came home to you. When I returned from Vietnam, people said that returning vets were crazy and should not be trusted with a gun. They were terrified by the words *Vietnam vet*. Greg is like Stephen. They're warriors in a war that never ends; it just shifts from country to country, and families and loved ones get lost along the way. Let me tell you, though, that for every man I knew, family was the only thing that kept him going. I'm not making excuses for him. I don't like what he said when he answered your questions just now, and I have the feeling that he didn't do it very well."

"He didn't do well," she said bitterly. "He made it worse. And right now, I have a lot to think about."

Kaj sat back. He heard her need to be alone, but he also felt the need to lighten her load.

"You know," he said drolly, "if you really believe you are such an American asset that a man must be ordered to marry you, I might have to reconsider how much crime scene information we allow you access to."

Jill did a doubletake. "What?"

"Just kidding. But if I have learned anything from Kuthan—and I think I can say I have, although it's mostly about myself—I'm seeing that there are two sides or more to everything, and choosing between them is part of us being who we are. After working with Meng, though, I think the two sides might be irrational and absurd."

"I'm going to need time to think about that." Jill couldn't help giving a small smile even though her eyes were sad.

Chapter 38

Greg didn't sound surprised when Kaj called. They met outside the now shuttered teacart. It was getting to be a regular meeting place, only Greg looked unhappy to be there.

"I imagine you've heard that I've got off on the wrong foot with Jill."

"Looks like you're going through a bad patch," Kaj replied laconically. "You have a credibility problem with me as well."

Greg seemed not to have heard the last part. "I'm damned if I do and damned if I don't."

"Do what?"

"Figure out how much I should tell Jill about Stephen Harkin. What did she tell you?"

"Not much. I think the gist of it is that she thinks she's been lied to. You and Harkin both."

"Well, there you are. I tried to tell her enough so that she wouldn't be upset with Harkin. Instead, I told her too much and now she's angry with both of us."

"I see your problem." Kaj looked out into the gathering dusk and the clouds lit from below. Whatever Greg was going through was well deserved. He had shot himself in his own foot.

"If she's going to be angry, I prefer it be for the right reason. She has the idea that Harkin was meeting a woman when he was climbing on Masakatsu." Greg shook his head in disbelief and shrugged his shoulders for extra emphasis. "What are the chances that Jill would meet up with Nie? In the whole wide world, she had to meet up with someone who knew Harkin. It beggars belief."

Kaj shrugged unsympathetically. Greg should have seen it coming. "Did you think she would never find out that you were told to date her?"

"It wasn't quite like that," Greg said peevishly.

"What was it quite like?"

"I told her that Harkin didn't lie about climbing on Masakatsu. He had climbed on it, but, as she found out, it was on the Chinese side. The Chinese were thinking about opening their side of the mountain for tourism. They invited a few reputable climbers to lay out possible access routes to the summit. Harkin was one of those invited. But then, I also told her that Harkin had probably not told her where he was because we asked him to do some work while he was there."

Kaj had heard this part before so he wasn't surprised. "Spying for you?" he asked blandly.

"Not the way you think," Greg replied.

Kaj's left eyebrow lifted. He wondered what possible other ways there were to think.

"It was not our request. Well, I mean it was, but not directly. When China announced the names of the people they had invited, the British asked if we could assist. That's the part I didn't tell her."

Greg looked mournfully at Kaj. "Are the names George Mallory and Andrew Irvine familiar to you? British team who climbed on Everest back in the twenties."

"Didn't they just find Mallory's body last year or so?"

"Yes. But not Irvine, his climbing partner. The two of them were said to be 'climbing strongly' for the summit but then snow clouds moved in and they were never seen again. At least until 1999 when Mallory's body was found. The first official ascent of Everest was Hillary and Tenzing in 1953. Some people believe that Irvine and Mallory summitted first in 1924. The argument goes that they reached the summit and fell to their deaths on the way back down. There was supposed to be a camera that would prove it. There was no camera on Mallory's body, so it was assumed it would be found with Irvine.

Kaj looked quizzically at Greg, wondering about the point of it all.

"In 1960, a Chinese climbing team eventually summitted Everest by the north ridge route. That team reported they saw the body of a European climber with old-fashioned gear not far from the top. Naturally, the British were interested because it sounded like the missing Irving. But when they inquired, they were told by another climber that the body had been removed and was locked away somewhere in Tibet. When the Chinese government announced the names of the climbers they were inviting to establish climbing routes on Masakatsu, one of the women climbers was a member of the same climbing club as the earlier Chinese group. Since Harkin had also been invited, the Brits asked if Harkin would cultivate her and see if she could confirm anything."

"Did you tell all this to Jill?"

Greg hung his head. "No. The less people know, the safer they are. Over-explaining is what got me in trouble. I told her that getting to know someone did not mean seduction. Not necessarily, anyway. I let it slip that I had been asked to get to know Jill because State was worried she might be a target. If Harkin's death had been retaliation for his working for the British, she might be in danger. Now she thinks that Harkin was spying for us, that he lied about it to her, that he had been fooling around, and that I was ordered to have a relationship with her."

"A lot for her to digest," Kaj said neutrally. It was also a lot for him to digest. "Sounds like a lot of explanation needed."

"I know," Greg said mournfully. "I don't even know where to begin."

"At the beginning is usually the best."

"I'm not sure she will even listen to me."

"Greg, are you surprised? You're under every stone we turn over here in Kuthan. It even makes me wonder how much the US government is involved in the massacre of the Kuthani royal family. I follow the evidence, and so will she."

"That's why you were asked to lead this thing. Well, along with your connection to Whitworth and the Kuthani embassy in Hawaii. It is also why the King asked you to do your investigation openly. You thought he meant interference from China and India. But he meant us as well. We didn't want unfounded rumors that the US was involved, and China and India didn't want rumors about them being involved either. That's why they didn't kick up a fuss when the King invited you. China hedged its bets though. They sent Meng to cover China's ass if you found anything."

"I was used too. Is that what you're saying?"

"You see the trouble I get into. I was trying to say you were trusted. All the parties to this mess agreed you should lead the investigation. I can't help it if they all have their own agendas. It was a miracle they agreed on anything in the time frame we had to work with."

"I should be flattered then?" Kaj felt merciless.

"Well, I would congratulate you on sending Meng off to find Mallik. It occupied him nicely. But Beijing didn't trust him or their own team either. You probably don't know that Nie and Xue were competitors for Nie's position. She won, but the Chinese wanted to test her leadership ability, so they sent Xue to see how she would handle him. Liu was added to report back to them."

"And you know this how?"

"I won't say more than I brought John and Chris along with me for a reason. It was a lot to ask of you, particularly without telling you, but that's why India and China sent their best teams and why we stayed away. Official US policy regarding you was hands-off unless requested."

"Now you tell me this?"

"Didn't want to burden you, knowing how much you like politics."

Kaj shook his head in disbelief.

"That brings me to my own issues. I spoke with Mallik today."

Greg's eyes became watchful.

"How was he?"

"Apparently, he's found some form of redemptive god, and he'd signed on with the temple. Conversions are common in prison, but they're usually around parole-hearing times. Still, I'm not going to argue with it. Pragmatically, it seems he has nowhere else to go. He seems sincere enough, and the Master swears that he never left the temple after arriving there. There are eight hundred steps that would make it very obvious if he had tried to take off somewhere. I'm not going to bother with the details since I'm sure you know them all already."

Greg sat silently, waiting for Kaj to continue.

"I was curious about the timing of the letter Mallik wrote to the King. When I spoke with Mallik, he told me you went to see him in prison and told him to write it."

"I don't know why this is an issue," Greg said. "We knew all along Kuthan would ask for his return. It was just a matter of time."

"So why at this particular time?"

Greg gave a frustrated sigh. "With what is happening in Taiwan, we wanted to keep our friends in the region. That's as much as I can say. Everything's interconnected in this region. I told you before that it's like walking a tightrope."

"I believe you told me you had a friend with contacts in the rural villages."

"I'm not going to go into that."

Kaj leaned forward now with interest. "That was Ananda Dorji, wasn't it? The dedicated Golden Tiger secretary who could sign for the King? That was your person."

Greg pursed his lips and said nothing.

"But there's still more to it, isn't there? You went to the prison to start the ball rolling. You and Dorji probably cooked this all up, except that Dorji may not have known what you had in mind. You knew he would intercept the letter and could sign for the King. You also knew that once Mallik was out of prison, he would be buried in an agreeable monastery willing to hide him. Did you tell Dorji that you needed Mallik back in Kuthan so there was a back-up to blame in case we didn't solve the crime?"

Greg sat back with both hands in front of him, still not replying.

Kaj spoke slowly and emphasized each syllable. "Was the US government involved in the attempt to assassinate the King's family?"

This time, Greg exploded into an emphatic denial.

"Absolutely not. We need the King. So does India, and so does China, which is why they sent Meng. The King is the essential hub of stability in the South Asian region."

Greg looked around desperately, but there was no one else in the area.

"We had absolutely nothing to do with the killings." Greg's voice was steely. "Even talking about this is dangerous."

"Were you sent here to make sure we didn't interfere with American interests in the region?"

Greg shrugged as if he had nothing left to lose.

"Part of it, certainly. But it also had to do with your safety. We didn't know who killed the royal family. The King gave us his personal assurances that the Colonel's staff would protect you. But we were still concerned. You have all been under our surveillance from the moment you arrived. I'm sorry if I withheld information. I assumed you would find it out anyway, and you have. But you must believe that I would never have allowed Jill to be in danger."

Kaj sat back. There, at least, was Greg's truth.

"I doubt Jill sees it that way. You must know that the US government incarcerated her family during the war in a relocation camp. They came away from those camps distrusting the government and constitution that should have protected them. She's very private, but I assume she has mentioned this.

"We've talked. It was a damned shame what happened to them, but it was wartime. I've tried to comfort her and tell her it was in the past—that things are different now."

Kaj sighed. "That she and her family should just move on as if it never happened? That's about the worst thing you could have said. You've really given her no reason to trust you now."

Greg shook his head. "I didn't want to mislead her or you. But I had a job to do. We knew you would find out what happened. I told them we might not like what you turned up, but Kuthan is important to us, and we trusted you would be fair. We are still counting on you. But now, we are also counting on your discretion. It could still be dangerous."

"Too bad about Dorji not being at the palace anymore," Kaj said sardonically. "He must have been very helpful."

Greg leaned in conspiratorially. "Don't count him out. The man's suffering from the unrequited love of his employer. He may well find his way back into his good graces."

Kaj's hair jumped over his forehead. "So that's why he stayed in the office when the guards took the King into the safe room. He was going to be a human shield."

"Love does crazy things," Greg said. "But what are you going to do next?"

Kaj looked quizzically at Greg. "Tomorrow I'm going to find out what role the Dam Board plays in this political mess.

If that doesn't pan out, the team and I are going to cast a wider net. But let me tell you this. I am going to hope for all our sakes that the US is not involved because I will not hide it if I find out it's true."

Chapter 39

LONG BEFORE THE DAM ITSELF came into sight, the palace van carrying Kaj, Sharma, the Colonel, and Xue passed a series of relay stations with cables splayed out from them, heading in all directions. These stations became closer together as they neared the dam. In the distance, a cloud of spray was the only indication of where the water was being released on its way south, passing through Blue Pheasant land, and on across the border with India toward Darjeeling.

Sharma and Xue's rapprochement was still clearly in its infant stage, but Kaj was not ready to adopt Darya's "And that is the way it is." He preferred his own "One can live in hope," even if he didn't completely believe it. He sat back as the landscape of rolling grass yielded to the first fences made of multiple layers of electrified fencing. Just before the entrance gate, the van pulled into the parking lot of a modern building of glass and steel that bore the name Strobel Global Engineering Associates.

The Colonel jumped out first and led the way into the building's atrium, an airy room decorated with massive color pictures of Strobel projects around the world. He disappeared into the security office, leaving Kaj and the others to be escorted to the director's office, which was on the top floor, positioned so it had an overview of the dam. Apart from the spray, the dam looked serene in the morning light. There was no sign of trucks or workers, and the distant mountains seemed like a painted backdrop.

"How do you get any work done with this view?"

Strobel laughed at Kaj's question. "You get used to it after a while."

They sat down around a conference table. "I'll be seeing you at the Dam Board meeting this afternoon" Strobel pointed out.

"We know that," Kaj admitted, "but we wanted to ask you about a possible second dam before we meet the board. We've heard rumors about it and possible protests."

"This is probably better answered by the Board. Strobel Engineering is not part of any planning process, so I cannot speak for them."

"But we can ask you about how your company works with them. So, our first question concerns how you would be involved if there were a possible second hydroelectric dam. Hypothetically, if you prefer."

Strobel looked uncomfortable. "Only hypothetical," he said. "And only because the King requested that we cooperate with you. In the case of a new dam, we would become involved only if and when the Dam Board offered us a contract for a feasibility study. It would be extensive and come with environmental impact concerns. It would take a very long time to get up and running."

"But surely you have already given them some advice?" Xue said.

"Our contract calls for five-year operational reports. One part requires us to suggest what is called 'possible further development.' This means ways to make the dam more efficient. Some are obvious such as upgrading existing equipment or updating maintenance. But others are speculative. We are supposed to identify areas where Kuthan could make further use of its geographical advantages."

"Like building more dams?" Sharma asked.

"For the past thirty years, we have made the same point about building another dam. That is a possibility. It always will be. But a new dam is a huge investment and the possibility has not been acted on."

"Do you know why?" Kaj asked.

Strobel chuckled. "The Snow Leopard region says a dam would upset their goats. White Bone says the inevitable water reservoir behind a dam would flood their multi-million-dollar tea estates and tobacco plantations. Golden Tiger might be more receptive because they have the major flooding problems, but they are worried about their insect-eating ducks and rice fields."

"You're saying that it's not going to happen?" Kaj asked.

"History says not. But we still must include it whenever we report to the Board. Last time, we just lifted the language from the previous report and dropped it into the new one. No one noticed."

"Then, why are we hearing rumors that it's being planned?"

"Not coming from us. We would not even talk about it without clear direction."

"Have the Indian and Chinese board members discussed a new dam with you?" Kaj asked.

Strobel gave a very definite shake of the head. "It would be completely improper for any board member to talk with us outside of the established board meetings. We report to the board but take our direction from the King. We would not engage with individual members, and if it happened, I would ethically be required to report it to the King. I can assure you that, to my knowledge, and I have been here for ten years, neither India nor China, board member or anyone else, has ever approached us."

"When was your most recent report?" Xue asked.

"Two years ago."

"Do you think another dam would be a good thing for Kuthan?" Xue asked.

"Off the record," Kaj said immediately.

Strobel gave a deep sigh. "I again emphasize that Strobel Associates has nothing to do with the decision processes of an independent governing board."

"We understand," Kaj said, "but it is a very good question."

"Off the record, then. Do I think that a dam might help mitigate some of the most dangerous flooding occurring regularly in this region—not just in Kuthan but also in Bangladesh and other neighbors? Honestly, I don't know. Despite thirty years of saying it is possible, we have never done feasibility studies or tried to cost it out. But even if we had, my advice to the Board would be to look at every possible type of water containment system before considering a new dam anywhere. I am a strong believer in the law of unintended consequences."

Strobel looked very pointedly at Xue. Kaj sensed that Strobel was determined not be misunderstood. He chose his words carefully.

"The first dam flooded villages that had been there for hundreds if not thousands of years. Livelihoods were ended. People were forced to move. Social upheaval and protest followed. In the section of the report where we mention the possibility of another dam, we always conclude with this question: Is Kuthan prepared to deal with inevitable social and political fallout? For more than thirty years, the answer has been no."

"But if you were asked to design and build one, you would?" Xue knew that Strobel's words had been for his benefit.

"Of course." Strobel replied without hesitation. "We would do everything asked of us. And we would do the very best job possible."

Chapter 40

When the van stopped in front of the administration building, they found themselves looking at a red-brick structure with an inset cement block over the main door bearing the date 1927. The building had small turrets on each end and a double doorway that looked as if it should have opened onto an aisle and an altar. It looked Victorian British, in the sometimes off-handed way that Kuthanis talked about the British occupation: It existed, it enriched Britain at Kuthan's expense, and we don't miss it except when we do. Kaj sensed a certain, slight nostalgia but mainly an unsentimental determination to look ahead rather than back. If buildings could speak, Kaj wondered what this one would say.

Kaj didn't recognize the people waiting to greet them. Fortunately, no one claimed to have met Kaj previously. They introduced themselves as Strobel engineers who said they were to provide Kaj's group with a brief overview of the dam. The Dam Board, they said, was still waiting for members to arrive.

"I'll wait for you outside," the Colonel said and disappeared again.

They were led through various corridors until a final door opened and they stepped onto what looked to be a stage. Kaj stopped in confusion. As his eyes grew accustomed to the light, he saw rows of chairs ascending toward a projection booth, making him feel like a gladiator in the Colosseum before the lions appeared. He didn't like the vulnerability. But when he looked closer, the seats were empty.

Eric Strobel caught up with them at that point and invited them to find their seats. "Your choice. Sit anywhere."

They sat about halfway up and found themselves facing a large screen that would have fitted in an Imax theater. Strobel sat in the row below them and turned around sideways with one elbow on the back of his chair.

The screen had the letters KIHP projected on it, and underneath, the words Kuthan International Hydropower Project. The letters were stylized to look like the blocks of the dam profile. In the lower corner was the tiny word *English.*

Kaj leaned forward to Strobel. "Was your father here when Kalyani happened?"

"No, a few years after. We responded to a request for proposals and were pleasantly surprised to be chosen. We had the equipment and expertise to do the job, but we were bidding against UK, American, and Asian companies with more experience. The rest, as they say, is history."

"So, the decision had already been made to build a major hydroelectric dam before you came on board?"

"Yes. The British had started the process. We did not propose the dam. We responded to an invitation."

Strobel was interrupted by the sound of rushing water and the chirps of birds. The narrator's voice came on. It was smooth with only the slightest hint of an accent Kaj couldn't place. The first scene was a small stream of water.

From time immemorial, the rivers of the vast areas south of the mighty Himalayan range have alternated between devastating flooding or droughts, both causing untold loss of human and wild life. Over the same period, human beings have sought to moderate if not control the vast discrepancy between these two extremes.

Then the stream became a river and there was a snow leopard lapping water, a crane wading through a shallow, and fishes darting under a bridge. The gentle sound of flute sounded in the background.

Kaj stifled a rueful grin. He almost expected to hear the voice say, "And now we say hello to beautiful Kuthan."

The camera pulled back from the rivers and panned up to the mountains.

From these mighty mountains and their glaciers, the waters start as small streams that pour down through foothills onto the vast fertile valleys of Kuthan and the neighboring states.

The scene changed to snow melting into streams and yaks and goats walking across the background of the Himalayan range, with blue sky and wheeling birds above them. Then it panned down over the Masakatsu glaciers before following the river through the foothills.

When the British took over the administration of Kuthan in 1898, the Royal Engineers began laying irrigation channels and linking existing water projects to control flooding. The first dam they built is just upriver from where we are now. As part of this massive undertaking, the engineers decided to reroute a series of smaller rivers and streams into one major source of water that could serve the entire country. By 1910, and with the success of hydroelectric power around the world, the Engineers took on a bigger challenge: to convert the existing dam to produce electricity. When the British left in 1947, they left behind a burgeoning city and prospering regions within the country. Kuthan's products were to become in demand around the world. And there was more need than ever for electricity.

Then came pictures of orchards and a time lapse of planting rice, yaks running through snow, goats on precipices, pictures of people loading crates onto trains, working in offices, and gathering vegetables. Newspaper articles appeared on screen with English subtitles, along with pictures of the proposed dam and pictures of people shaking hands and standing for group pictures. Then there was a map showing the location of the new dam and quite stunning shots of the finished dam that showed the extensive lake built up behind it and the graceful curves of the dam's face.

The dam was designed by Strobel Global Engineering Associates who had worked with similar projects in Australia and the Near East. Strobel Associates supervised the construction of the new dam and the transmission lines and substations. They remain actively involved in the dam and have been designated official managers and consultants to the King and the Dam Board. The dam has been internationally recognized as one of the top ten technological achievements of southern Asia since the end of the British Raj. As nations move forward with their plans, Strobel Global Associates stands proudly beside them, ready to provide assistance and expertise as the continent moves forward to build the future.

The scene changed to the dam's turbine room.

At the end of this presentation, your guides will take you down into the working halls beneath the river. You will be far beneath the river and will hear the powerful rush as the water drives the dam's nine turbines. Your guides will tell you more about how the power generated here comes into your homes.

We hope you enjoy your visit and go away with a new understanding of how this dam makes electricity from the directed flow of water.

The picture showed the face of the dam again and this began to pull away until the dam was placed against the background of the mountains.

Kaj waited for the narrator to say something like, "And so we bid adieu to the wondrous dam of Kuthan."

The lights came up and the three of them stretched in their chairs. Kaj looked inquiringly at Strobel, who was managing a small, almost apologetic smile.

"We usually show this to visitors before we take them on a tour. It was designed mainly for schoolchildren. But I thought you might find some of the historical information interesting."

"Beautiful pictures," Xue said neutrally.

"The children like the animals," Strobel agreed, "but we want them to have an appreciation for what this dam does."

Strobel led them back up onto the stage and then back through the series of corridors. As they approached a pair of double doors, the sound of voices increased. They had arrived at wherever they were meant to be.

Kaj walked through the doors and stopped in his tracks. The room had a large oval table surrounded by high-backed chairs filled with people he recognized. This included the King and Darya. Now he knew why they had been shown the film. It was to entertain them because, most likely, the King was running late. The group would not have waited for anyone else.

The King came over to greet Kaj and Xue and shook their hands. "You look surprised," he said.

"We were expecting to meet with the administration of the dam." Kaj looked at the mixture of suits and mountain coats. "This meeting looks more like the Governing Board."

"Because there is deliberate overlap." The King smiled knowingly. "Come sit down and we'll explain."

Chapter 41

KAJ LOOKED BACK AT THE Colonel, who had magically reappeared, but he was talking with the King's security guards and showed no interest in becoming more involved. Kaj, Sharma, and Xue were invited to seats halfway down the table. The King sat at the head with Eric Strobel sitting beside him.

"Is there anyone here who has not met our Hawaii Inspector?" the King asked. Several hands went up. Kaj recognized the rest even if he could not recall their names. They had been there at the public briefing. The King introduced Kaj for their benefit and then went on to introduce Sharma and Xue.

The preliminaries over, the King got down to business.

"You have questions about the operations of this dam, and I think the best way to answer them, is to share the ideas behind the Board's original charter."

Kaj looked around the room. The Colonel had already given him an overview, but it was going to be interesting to hear the story from another point of view.

"When the monks prepared the charter in 1950, they had the bad example of an unregulated corporation and the corruption it caused. The British East India company failed because it had acted only in its own interests. It taught the monks who wrote our Constitution that corruption follows wealth. Because they realized that building and operating a dam required special expertise, they required an engineering company to build and manage the dam but reporting to this Board. In the charter, the monks deliberately excluded themselves from dam governance and said there was not to be an outside corporate board that might have put profits ahead of Kuthan's needs. The monks decreed that the dam must serve Kuthan, not the other way."

Kaj leaned forward. "So, when the Dam Board supports Kuthan's arts, business, and education, it's really the Kuthan Governing Council that controls how that money is given out?"

"There's not a complete overlap, but there's enough to prevent a conflict of interest and there are enough outside people on the Board to keep it honest."

"It's a worthy experiment, I'll admit," Kaj said.

"Aren't most forms of government?" The King looked quizzical. "Over the centuries governments have come and gone around the world. The monks believed if everyone had all they needed, there would be no violence." He stopped for a long moment. "Recent events say otherwise, so we must adjust."

Kaj looked around the room trying to decide how direct he wanted to be. Part of him felt ambushed, but he knew he was judging Kuthan's structure by American standards. America's government was an experiment too, and even its founding fathers wondered if the people would be able to keep it.

"What do you want to know?" The King sat back and waited.

"We have heard from two separate sources that there may be undisclosed planning for a new dam. Undoubtedly, such a dam would be profitable and perhaps even effective against flooding, but we are also hearing about possible protests."

The King glanced at Eric Strobel before he spoke.

"I understand that you asked our engineers about this today."

Kaj nodded. "Yes. We heard that Mr. Strobel knew nothing about it. Now we need to ask the Board."

The King looked around the room. "Does anyone know anything about this?"

Darya was the only one willing to speak up.

"The only protests we know happened fifty years ago. Nothing recently. But rumors take a long time to reach us in the mountains."

"Do you think the rumors have something to do with what happened at the palace?" The King sat forward and stared at Kaj.

"We can't rule anything out."

"The earliest protests started in Blue Pheasant lands." The King turned to the Blue Pheasant board member. "Lomash, what do you remember about this."

Lomash Lama was a thin, stiffly upright man with dark shadows under his eyes that made him look unwell. His hair was thick and dark and splashed across his head like a storm whipped ocean.

"A long time ago," he said politely. "Memories fade."

"You know what happened," the King said irritably. "It was the time of Kalyani. We all know that."

"A different tragedy, your majesty, the dam was never in danger and no one was killed."

"I remember being told about it," a voice said suddenly. It was the representative Kaj recognized from Golden Tiger.

"My father told me that some people came across the border from India and called the dam a foreign devil. He did not listen, but some of the younger people believed them. My father and some other farmers beat these intruders with sticks and drove them away."

Lomash seemed suddenly to regain his memory. "My father said we knew nothing of threats against the dam. We knew only that the monks came one day and said some of our young people had been plotting to blow it up. The monks took them away with them."

The man stopped and looked anxiously at the King. Kaj caught the glance and was immediately on guard.

"Go on," the King said with a stony face. "Everyone knows. Tell them who these young people were."

Lomash sighed and stated the obvious. "They were Blue Pheasant."

"Who else? There is no need to hide it."

"And Water Dragon," Lomash admitted. "Your own family."

"Both clans are my family," the King said stonily. "My mother was Blue Pheasant."

The room was silent until Xue seized his opportunity. "Does Blue Pheasant still believe that opposition to the dam justifies violent protest?"

Lomash looked shocked. "The family would never support that."

"Then who did?" Xue asked. "At some point, someone in your family once thought that blowing up the dam was a good idea."

Lomash hung his head. "They were young and idealistic. They believed they had no voice in what was happening."

"Do your youth still feel that way?" Xue asked.

"We have lost our youth," Lomash said bitterly. "They are lying in the hospital mortuary waiting for their funeral."

Kaj broke in before anyone could venture further into the palace killings. "Let me ask a different question. Has the Dam Board authorized any work that might give the appearance of planning for a second dam?"

Kaj was surprised when the King turned to Strobel, who stood up immediately.

"Beyond routine maintenance on transmission lines and pylons, we have been working with an on-going project regarding a possible aquaculture development in eastern Kuthan. Our part is providing geologic and topographic assessment of the southern and eastern regions that experience flooding. Our assignment is identifying steps necessary for further flood mitigation."

"Golden Tiger and White Bone lands?" Kaj asked.

Strobel nodded. "White Bone is interested in raising shrimp and prawns. But the problem has been controlling monsoonal weather. Last year, the eastern parts of Kuthan experienced record rainfall. Snow Leopard had minor damage in the mountains. The major flooding was in the foothills and plains below. We were directed by this Board to determine why existing mitigation had failed. We were also asked to identify places where such actions as water diversion, hydraulic barriers, and underground excavation could prevent a repetition of flooding that might devastate aquaculture sites."

"When did you do that work?" Kaj asked.

"Still in progress. Our contract requires that any mitigation projects conform with current land usage. We are working cooperatively with a marine institute in Hawaii. That all takes time."

"The plans do not include a possible new dam?"

Strobel shook his head. "We are looking at land restoration, revetments, water storage, embankments, and water channels, all custom designed to the topography. We made the Board's intentions clear when we did outreach to the affected regions, explaining what our working teams would be doing and why."

"These working teams you have out," Xue said thoughtfully, "what do they look like?"

"Generally, a couple of trucks with staff and surveying equipment. Why do you ask?"

"So, you are not trying to be invisible?"

"No. And it's not uncommon to see our trucks out in the field because we maintain the powerlines and substations throughout the country."

The King looked at the representatives from the three eastern regions. "This Board voted unanimously to request that work. Did anyone not understand what it was for?"

"We understood," the Snow Leopard representative said immediately. "The engineers came and made a presentation. Most of the town attended."

"White Bone?" the King asked.

"We showed the engineers the damage flooding caused to our tea estate and tobacco fields. They told us how we could improve and secure our irrigation ditches. We have no reason to protest. We knew why they were there."

The Golden Tiger board member spoke up without even being asked.

"We welcomed them because we have the worst flooding. But, if we believed our fields were threatened, we would not protest. We would come to this Board immediately and demand that you address our concerns."

A ripple of affectionate laughter went around the room. The man was barely five feet tall and no one could describe him as intimidating.

"Did you provide the same outreach to the three western regions?" The King turned to Strobel who shook his head slowly.

"We assumed their level of interest would be lower as they were not affected by the flooding. Since this Board had unanimously voted support for the work, we thought they had been adequately advised."

The King turned to Lomash once more. "Did you tell your people why we were surveying?"

Lomash's reply was terse and openly defensive.

"Every time the Board meets, I report actions that affect us. But I cannot be expected to reach everyone. It might not have seemed so important to share since our family was not directly involved."

"In other words," the King said sardonically, "the answer is no. So, someone heard about trucks and surveying and made assumptions. A good lesson. We need to do a better job of communicating. Whatever affects one family affects us all."

"Is it possible," Kaj asked, "that someone not connected with the Board might have read the five-year reports prepared by Strobel Associates? These always list the possibility of a second dam. Could they have thought that the project was moving forward and the surveys were proof?"

"Possible," the King replied. "These reports are not confidential." He looked round the room. "Has anyone mislaid their copy in the last few months?"

Lama was the only one who raised his hand. "I had to request a duplicate copy as I could not find mine."

"Communication will be the only agenda item on the next Dam Board meeting," the King said grimly as he stood up.

Kaj glanced at Xue and Sharma as they drove back to the palace, wondering whether this visit to the dam and the board had caused any advance in their relationship. On the plus side, they had seemed genuinely interested in the video, but he couldn't gauge their response to the discussion that followed because they had kept quiet after the meeting with the board. But then, Kaj admitted to himself, he had been quiet as well. Communication was a worthy topic but not one that immediately involved the international partners. Kaj himself had been most interested in the elaborate system of interlocking boards that controlled Kuthan's greatest national asset. He had no idea what the two men were taking away with them. He decided to be direct and ask them.

To his surprise, Xue had nothing negative to say. He said the dam seemed well managed and provided a positive example of international cooperation in service of the region. He didn't mention the historical aspects of governance, but then he had expected to come to Kuthan, perform autopsies and leave quickly. Kaj suspected that he must have complained to his home government about being detained in Kuthan, only to be told to keep his mouth shut and his eyes open.

Sharma was even less predictable. There was no obvious way a highly academic man such as Xue would immediately warm to an ebullient provocateur such as Sharma with his trail of snide comments and patronizing gentility. It was like Aquarian detachment versus Leo exuberance. Sharma's mind was as sharp and clear as Xue's, it was just wrapped in a different costume. Kaj knew this from that first meeting when they started exchanging barbs that weren't even witty. Kaj made little jokes, usually at his own expense, but, after listening to them, made sure that his comments were sharper, more self-deprecating, and wittier than either of them. As he looked at them now, he wondered if he had simply taken on too great a challenge. He stoically awaited Sharma's opinion.

Sharma sat up as straight as the van allowed and bestowed a brilliant smile on them all.

"Oh lord," Kaj thought. "Here we go."

"The dam is a magnificent installation," Sharma said. "It is a fitting tribute to cooperation among China, India, and Kuthan. Aquaculture is critically important for South Asia. This cooperation is the way of the future."

Kaj sank into a relieved, if surprised, acquiescence. He wondered if he should thank the snow leopard and patient yaks from the video.

But, ever the master of the grand gesture, Sharma was not done. He nodded at Xue and said that the work they had started should continue. He said he was sure that their home governments would be delighted. Whether that was true or not, the two of them began a private conversation about how this dam might be a model for future ventures.

Kaj did not feel slighted by his exclusion. Instead, he felt relieved. If he were asked, Kaj might have denied his surprise, if not his shock. As it was, with no one obviously interested, he sat back and listened. His work, in some part was done. For the first time in this investigation, he felt some justification for his belief that one can live in hope.

Chapter 42

THE TEAM MEETING THAT EVENING had a different feeling. Sharma and Agarwahl took it on themselves to start the team meeting without Kaj asking them to. The crime lab staff had busied themselves earlier, removing existing posters and replacing them with new ones. There was excitement in the air.

"We have the DNA results." Sharma stood back to defer to the crime-lab team. He even did this without making his usual flowery promises.

Agarwahl briefly described the procedures used to gather the samples and where they were taken from. The key elements, he pointed out, were the blood trail in the hallway outside the crime scene and the rifle recovered from the drainage canal. The DNA told a consistent story.

Agarwahl turned to Choudhary who took up a pointer and turned to the poster behind him.

"We evaluated the blood relations of the victims. We knew the family relations between victims one, three, four, five, and six. These were the King's uncle Tranh and his wife, Dechen;

Dechen's sister, Pema, and her son, Kanchan; and Tranh's son Kiran. We then evaluated the fingerprints on the rifle and the blood trail in the hallway. We now have that information."

Choudhary cleared his throat.

"We have determined that the shooter's DNA came from a close family member. He is full brother to Kiran. Tranh and Dechen Soöng are his parents. Pema is probable aunt and Kanchan first cousin."

There was silence in the room. Kaj could see why Choudhary might feel the pressure. But there was no way around it. The facts were what they were.

"This unknown family member killed his parents, his brother, his aunt, and a cousin, along with a butler and a nanny? Is this a Greek tragedy?" Jill's voice echoed the deep shock on her face.

"It's a Kuthani tragedy," Sharma corrected her.

"And he is related to the King?" Xue asked.

Sharma nodded. "Another first cousin. At this moment, the only survivors of the Water Dragon family, beside the lady Soniya and her son, are the King and this unnamed family member."

"But who is he?" Cliff held up the King's family tree. "There is no mention of Kiran having a brother."

Kaipo frowned. "And he is not included in the family tree."

"Yes," Sharma agreed. "We must also wonder, if this cousin is not listed, whether there are others we do not know about."

Xue tossed his head cynically. "Royal families do not behave like other people. They discard family if they do not want to share an inheritance or a throne. They fight wars over this."

"Family members can be disowned for various reasons," Nie agreed. "But only a powerful family can completely remove a member from official records."

"If the birth was ever recorded," Cliff said.

Xue frowned: "There must be a record. If Kiran has a birth certificate, so must this brother."

"Unless it was a home birth," Sharma replied.

Nie seemed more concerned about the child: "Was he born deformed in some way? Otherwise, why would a family obliterate a child at birth."

"It's hard to know at this point," Kaj agreed. "Birth records may have been changed. The family may have hidden the child or said he was dead."

"What could the child be or have done to be disowned so completely?" Nie asked.

Sanjay had his own experience to share. "I have friends who were disowned because they disobeyed their parents and changed religion. But that was when they were older."

Cliff nodded. "Sometimes parents do not accept who the child is. Sometimes the child does something that frightens the parents. If the culture is superstitious or deeply religious, they may believe the child is infected with demons. But that requires evidence and happens over time. No one can look at a newborn and predict the future."

"Sometimes parents give away a child because they do not have money to raise it," Choudary said.

"An adoption?" Sanjay asked.

"Or sale." Achari spoke with a dark cynicism.

"But in this case, the family is rich," Kaj said. "You said the missing child is Kiran's full brother?"

Kaj went to the board and flipped over pages until he found one he could write on. "How can we find out if there is a birth certificate? Who keeps the records?"

"I have connections with the hospital," Nie offered. "It might be the place to start, but if the records are not centralized, it may take time to search. We have Kiran's birthdate. This brother may be around the same age."

"I can help you do that," Xue told her.

"We also need to find anyone working in the palace or the hotel at the time when Anya made the complaint about the basement," Kaj said. "Let's see if anyone remembers that fourth child."

"I'll go through the list of current employees and ask about anyone working then," Jill offered. "I've already worked once with the front desk so I feel I know them."

Sharma leaned forward seriously then, this time not posing for the benefit of the Chinese. "The King may find the results hard to believe if he did not know about this cousin. It is a great irony, but this is now one of the few relatives he has left. He may not believe us. The Crime Unit can produce reports to show him. Sanjay, you are the computer genius, you work with us."

"I'll ask the Colonel to arrange for a meeting with Tashi," Kaj said. "She may know or have heard about this missing cousin. The best approach to her might be to ask what would motivate a family to keep a child away from the world. She is a trained professional. Her theories would be very useful if she is willing to share them."

"Or she may not know," Nie said. "It depends on whether the family wanted the child discovered."

"We can already tell a few things about this cousin," Cliff said thoughtfully. "If he is the shooter, working alone, he is not handicapped. He has the physical and mental capacity to hold a rifle and crawl into a restricted space to hide it."

Kaipo nodded. "He also has the intellect to plan. Dr. Sharma said that the attack on the palace was not random. It was premeditated. We are dealing with someone who was able to escape and then avoid detection in the searches afterwards."

Sharma smiled at the recognition. "And someone who knows a lot about the palace. We also know that he may feel no remorse for killing his family."

Nie looked concerned. "It may be dangerous to approach him. If he has been kept away, he may feel resentment and anger for the way his family treated him."

"Which," Kaj said, "may be part or all of the motive."

Kaj then looked around the newly engaged room as he spoke. He felt the emerging sense of common purpose. They were all seeking to restore order to a world where it had been shattered. It seemed a miracle that these diverse people with their own agendas had come together. It was miracle he was glad to have been there to see.

Chapter 43

That night, after he had made the call to Linda and told her that he thought he might be coming home soon, he drifted off in dreams that had a strange rippling effect to them. He felt he was no longer just the observer to them, but had been pulled into the story. He was there, watching it unfold.

The years passed and the couple treated the child as if he were their own. They called him by the dead son's name for his own safety. They saw that he was educated, and they prepared him as best they could for a destiny they knew was his. A beautiful child, he became a handsome and sturdy young man.

Then one day, there was a loud rap at the door. The noise frightened the couple who feared that the wild-eyed man with long hair had returned. Slowly the old man opened the door, but it was not the killer of the boy's family who stood there.

Instead, it was a tall man with piercing eyes that made the old man remember the brightness of the eyes of the long-dead mongoose whose job had been to protect the child. The old man knew that this was another protector of the child. He also suspected why the man had come.

"It is time," the tall man said. "He is grown now. It is time for him to find his destiny."

"Will you come in?" the man's wife asked.

The tall man shook his head. "Your job is done. You protected the child. You raised the boy to a man. What happens now is beyond your knowing. You have not failed. Whatever happens in the future, you have done all that was asked of you. You have done your duty. You will be rewarded. I promise you a peaceful death and there will be many who will mourn you."

"Will he be all right?" the old man asked anxiously as he felt tears start to form.

"His destiny is in his hands," the tall man said. "He faces challenges, but you have done your best to prepare him for them."

"What do you want us to do?" the woman asked.

"When he comes home, tell him to wear the locket that you found him with. He will know what to do after that."

The old man and his wife looked at one another with unspoken questions and sorrow. When they turned back to the tall man, they found he had vanished. Even when the old man stepped out of the door and looked down the pathway, there was no sign of the stranger.

When he went back into the house, his wife had opened the chest and taken out the clothes the child had worn when he was found. She wrapped the clothes in a cloth. She picked up the locket and fingered it. Then she began to cry.

"Can we just not tell him?" she said. "We cannot lose a second child."

But the old man was firm. "We knew he was not ours. He was a loan to us. We could only protect him for the time we were given. Now he has his destiny. It is not ours to tamper with. When he comes home, he must be told."

Kaj woke up realizing he had spoken in his sleep. The air in the room was still vibrating from the sound of his voice. It took him a moment to remember. He had said out loud, "You have done your duty."

Chapter 44

The next day did not turn out as Kaj had expected. Tashi, it seemed, was at her Snow Leopard office and not returning for another day. Since it was critical that Kaj and Kaipo talk with her, they had to go to her, and the Colonel had to arrange it overnight. They would land at the Mountain Thunder airstrip, he told them, and then drive to Snow Leopard. He apologized for the early morning flight, but it was all that was available. They were at the airport and standing at the back of the line for security just as the sun rose over the city.

It did not take them long to spot Darya standing in line ahead of them. Without offering any explanation, the Colonel slipped away and inserted himself into the agents who were checking travel documents. When one of the guards started to salute, the Colonel put his finger to his lips. He kept his head down until Darya approached the table.

While in line, she had not even glanced at the faces of the officials at the desk, so the Colonel knew she had not noticed him. He also knew she would expect to be recognized and waved through. That was what he was counting on.

"Your documents, please, Ma'am," the Colonel said officially as she reached the table.

Darya's head spun around and the words "Do you know who I am?" froze on her lips as she recognized him.

"I've flown through this airport for years," she told him indignantly. "Even the cleaners know who I am." She gave an imperious nod of her head.

"I am sorry, Ma'am, it is regulations. I need to see your identification."

Darya looked around at the line behind her. Conversations had stopped because everyone also knew who she was. There was complete silence as people stared. The distant sound of an aircraft's propellers echoed inside the departure room.

"Oh, all right," she said haughtily. She pulled up her large, black handbag and pulled out her matching Gucci wallet.

Kaj and Kaipo watched along with everyone else. "Do you think she'll throw it at him?" Kaipo whispered. Kaj didn't reply. He was wondering the same thing.

The Colonel took the proffered card and reviewed it carefully. He made her confirm her address. He made her confirm her destination. Then he studied the photograph and looked up at her up several times. "When was this taken?" he asked.

"Are you saying this is not me?" Darya was practically shaking with annoyance. She had chosen the picture herself because she thought it made her look glamorous. She set her lips obstinately.

The Colonel finally held the card up to compare the picture and the original more closely.

"It does not do you justice," he concluded.

It was then that Darya saw the laugh lines crinkling at the corner of the Colonel's eyes and the mischievous line to the edges of his smile. She realized with a shock that he was flirting with her. Her annoyance dangerously weakened. She even forgot for a moment that the guards were smirking at one another. When the edges of her own lips begin to turn up involuntarily, she rushed to hide it with an impatient sigh of disapproval. But the Colonel had seen. So had Kaj and Kaipo.

As she snatched back her identification card, she also tried to take back some of her dignity.

"Am I free to take my flight now?" she asked sarcastically.

"Yes, you are, Ma'am," the Colonel said with a devastating smile, "and thank you for your cooperation." He carefully neglected to tell her that he was also on the flight.

Darya put her head up in the air, looked straight ahead, and marched off towards the gate.

The Colonel followed her progress with his eyes. This was the key moment. Would she stop to look back at him? He had taken his chances. If she looked back, she was interested.

For the next few moments, everyone in the airport heard only the click of her high-heels. When she reached the gate itself and stopped to show her ticket to the crew member, Kaj held his breath.

Just as it appeared she was about to move forward, she tilted her head slightly to one side and glanced back over her shoulder at the Colonel, giving him an expression of reproof.

Then she was gone. Immediately, the airport resumed the usual hubbub of noise and movement.

"Is that how it's done?" Kaipo asked Kaj.

"What's done?" Kaj said innocently.

"He made her notice him. He caught her attention and had a joke at her expense. And she came running."

"Not exactly," Kaj replied. "She *left* running."

"Do you think it would work?"

"Work as what?" Kaj was not about to deal with Kaipo's imprecision.

"As a relationship," Kaipo said more definitely. "After all, you don't go to that much trouble if you don't think something's going to work."

"Like you and Gail?" Kaj asked. "Have you done anything as risky to attract her?"

"No," Kaipo admitted. "Gail has always done that. She's the one who makes the overtures. I've let her because I really don't know what she sees in me."

Kaj looked at Kaipo with open impatience. "Kaipo, your marriage was the failure not you. Your ex-wife said unkind things about you and Hawaii when she left. I understand. But so what? She's allowed to be wrong. At Annie's wedding I heard Gail tell the other bridesmaids to keep their hands off you. You had intrigued her. But until you show her you've got something more to offer than just being passive, she won't know who you really are."

Kaipo gave Kaj a sheepish grin. "That's what my *kupuna* says."

Kaj nodded, "Listen to your grandfather. He's learned something over the years."

"But it's more than what my ex said about me," Kaipo said. "When we got married, she said she loved Hawaii. I think she thought that by marrying me, she'd be part of the culture. I think she wanted to lead some of the protest against the treatment of Hawaiians in their homeland. But she didn't understand that she was a stranger to the culture. She took it personally as rejection. Then she couldn't get a job and she got angry. She said she had cabin fever from living in an isolated island. In the end, she decided that my police work was the problem. She said no one would want to share that life with me. She filed for divorce the next day and left. I'm worried that Gail would never be happy either."

Kaj had to fight the feeling he was interfering in Kaipo's life. He also didn't want to diminish Kaipo's angst by admitting that Linda and he had fought over some of the same issues themselves, particularly the part about the police work's intrusion into their lives. He decided the best approach was to avoid the personal and be practical, which, as he thought about it, was really the best approach to everything.

"Kaipo, look at the differences. Gail was born here, knows the culture, and has a demanding job that will have many of the same pressures as yours. You're miles ahead. She is also a professional woman used to responsibility and management. She will expect you to negotiate issues with her. She will expect you to love her for who she is, and in return she will expect to give you the respect you deserve. You need to move beyond the past and find your place to stand. If you don't, you'll never know what's waiting for you."

My god, Kaj thought as he watched Kaipo take a moment to digest what Kaj had just said. *That's the same advice the dragon gave me and in just about the same words. But I think I understand those words now. The dragon never said that leaving the past behind was going to be easy. It's like climbing up a mountain, just putting one foot in front of the other. There will be blocks, obstacles, and a plan will be needed to get around them. But at least, I know now that it is possible. I can respect the past but not be trapped by it. I think that's where Kaipo is headed. But perhaps that is where we all are.*

His thoughts were disturbed only when he and Kaipo were told to board the aircraft on their way up to Snow Leopard territory. They climbed the stairs up to the cabin door, both lost in thought.

Chapter 45

TO GET TO THEIR SEATS in the back of the aircraft, they had to pass Darya who was settled in the first row, regally pretending to ignore them. Kaj smiled when the Colonel looked back at her and gave a proprietary grin. He wondered what the Colonel was planning next.

The aircraft took off with its customary jerk, making Kaj glad not to be up front where Darya was seated. He did not intend to watch the aircraft come in for its perilous landing. He reached up and turned the air tube vent, releasing a blast of yak-cheese-flavored air across the back three seats.

"Mountain Thunder been making deliveries?" Kaj looked casually at the Colonel, who merely nodded.

"What's that terrible smell?" Kaipo almost gagged.

"Yak cheese." Kaj reached up and turned off the air vent. "They also drink yak milk up in the mountains."

"I hope I don't have to drink it. It must be awful."

"Oh, I don't know." Kaj said. "Something like several-day-old poi. It grows on you, and you can appreciate the subtle changes as it matures."

Kaipo looked at Kaj to see if he was joking. Kaj wasn't. That morning, he had tried the cheese again. It wasn't that he craved it, but it was becoming familiar, just another part of Kuthan life.

One hour later, they were on the ground safely and Kaipo was looking stunned. "They do that every day?" he asked.

"Multiple times," the Colonel said. "But it's not as extreme as landing at Lukla in Tibet."

"I remember you telling me that," Kaj said. "I didn't believe anything could be more hazardous."

"Believe me," the Colonel replied as they walked toward the terminal. They were just in time to see Darya being driven away.

"Here's our transport," the Colonel said as a Land Rover drove up.

Kaj studied the van for a moment and even recognized a couple of scratches where the side door slid open.

"This looks familiar."

"We had it driven up last night." The Colonel smiled benevolently. "We will be driving back to the city. Afternoon wind shears. Remember? Not good flying weather."

After they settled into their seats, the Colonel became their tour guide.

"Snow Leopard's main town is about twelve miles from here. We should be there in about an hour."

"Twelve miles take an hour?" Kaipo asked.

"The roads are maintained and safe enough, but this is mountain driving. The British established summer homes up here for when the weather was too hot in town. There are houseboats on the lake, mansions on the shores, and a town of smaller houses that fills up in the summers. Townspeople like to spend their holidays here."

"What happens in the winter?" Kaipo asked. "If the roads are difficult, is Snow Leopard cut off?"

The Colonel gave a small shrug.

"Mountain Thunder and Snow Leopard keep the roads open to access the airport and the school, but there are snow days. In your country, that means that a student stays home. Here, a snow day means that the student stays at school."

The Colonel turned around and began watching out of the window. Kaj and Kaipo, sitting in the seat behind him, began to watch as well.

There was more to see once they passed the British upper school, a solid brick building that looked like every other bureaucratic building of its age except that it had soccer nets and a cricket pitch. After that, they began a winding ascent until they reached a flat plateau where there was a view of a broad valley with a large lake in its floor. The van then began a meandering descent through a series of switchbacks that slowed progress to a crawl.

Once they passed the tree-line, the landscape began to green with the usual shrubs and trees of the foothills. Farmhouses and livelihoods began to appear and then suddenly there was the town that adhered much closer to Kaj's idea of a Kuthan full of waterfalls and mountains. The houses were a mixture of traditional and modern, all of them substantial and many decorated with murals on an outside wall. There were artists' studios with sculptures outside and cosmopolitan restaurants. Kaj could not decide whether it was an artists' colony or a California mountain town. In the end, he decided it was both.

"We're early," the Colonel said. "We'll take a drive along the lake."

The van turned down a street lined with large gabled houses that looked as if they had been plucked out of some European alpine village.

"These are some of the British summer houses. They get larger along the lakeshore. Some of them have swimming pools, croquet lawns, and tennis courts. Wealthy city people own them now. Others not so wealthy rent the houseboats by the week."

They drove by the houseboats. The long barges were painted in bright colors, gently sleeping on the still water that reflected the white-clad mountains, the steep cliffs of the valley walls, and the deep green of manicured lawns. It seemed out of time.

"Can anyone come here for the summer?" Kaipo asked.

The Colonel immediately shook his head. "Snow Leopard is the main reason Kuthan limits tourism. When someone suggested that the pass between Snow Leopard and Tibet should be engineered to encourage more traffic, Snow Leopard objected so strenuously that the decision was made to expand the one on the Mountain Thunder side instead. Their snow festival here is limited by the number of passes they issue. Some people book their tickets a year in advance to make sure they get one."

Then, just as suddenly as the town and the expensive lake shore housing had appeared, the road turned around a headland and a different village emerged. Here, the houses were smaller although artistically maintained. The residential roads wound along the valley floor. The walls on both sides of the river were terraced in graceful, curving shapes filled with plant life. Given the number of waterfalls along the roadway, Kaj realized that it must be spectacular in the early melt. To Kaj's delight, there were even goats being herded through the street. The sound of their bells filled the air. This was how he had imagined Kuthan to be. But the goats were not bundles of fleece. They had been shorn and were frisking without the weight of their heavy winter wool.

The van stopped outside of another building that looked curiously British and bureaucratic. The Colonel climbed out and helped them down, handing them water again as they passed him.

"This is the hospital clinic. This is where Dr. Dema has her office. We'll wait for you here with the van."

Kaj and Kaipo walked up a flight of cement stairs, noting how the centers had been worn down by constant pressure of feet coming and going. Once they were inside the front door, Tashi appeared as if from nowhere and escorted them into her office. All she could offer them were metal folding chairs, and she did it without apology.

"What brings you here?" she asked with her customary directness.

"We're hoping for your help with a few questions."

"You know my policy on talking about Aki."

"It's not about Aki." Kaj mentally crossed his fingers. "We need to identify another child that Anya might have cared for. It would be contemporary to the King, a one-time playmate who disappeared from the palace."

"A playmate? Surely Raju would remember?"

"We asked him. He remembers the boy but not his name, and he does not know what happened to him."

"Twenty years ago?" Tashi looked more than doubtful. "Don't you have anything more to go on than that? And perhaps I should ask why you are asking me? I hate to say it, but you may have wasted a trip."

"Well, the fact is that DNA indicates that we may be looking for another member of the King's family. I can't go into more detail at this point."

Tashi's eyes opened wide. "You are sure of this? Poor Raju. Does he know?"

"Not yet. And we ask you to keep this confidential until we have more information."

"That's not a problem," Tashi said.

Kaj nodded to Kaipo, who opened a folder and slid it over to Kaj.

"We're going to ask you a set of questions."

Tashi looked at Kaj and shrugged her shoulders.

"Do the words, *taken away*, mean anything to you professionally?"

Tashi leaned forward with her elbows on the table.

"What does the term mean to me? It is not a professional term in psychiatry. If I had to define it, I would say it means that a parent or a medical professional exercised some form of authority. If this involves a child, as you say, the reasons could range from a pattern of misbehavior, to a medical emergency, to a family emergency. I would have no way of knowing."

"Would the words imply to you that there might be some form of disgrace?"

"Well, I would not apply the words to a parent taking a child home after blowing up balloons at a party. I would have to assume something happened that might have put the child or others in danger."

Kaj nodded. "Let's assume that for some reason, the child is an embarrassment or a danger, how would the family handle it?"

"Ah," she let out a sigh. "So that is what this is about. Well, we must look at the history of psychiatry in Kuthan. I am going to assume that psychiatry is somehow involved. As I told you last time we talked, our first mental treatment facilities did not exist until the 1980s. Before that, and you are talking about the 70s, most families, particularly in the countryside, would try to hide their problems. They would not necessarily mistreat an ill person, but they would keep them socially isolated. There simply were no places to seek psychiatric help."

"They might *take them away* then?"

"Your words, not mine. But I suppose it could be seen that way."

"And what kind of treatment might these children be given?"

"Since the traditional approach is to assume an external cause for mental illness—a neighbor's curse, for example—the emphasis might start with a ritual to lift the spell. They might call in the local shaman."

"And the shaman would do what?" Kaipo asked.

"As I said before, I've seen only one ritual. The shaman burned juniper leaves, breathed the smoke to go into a trance, and then began to shake."

"Did it help?"

"The patient seemed to get something out of it. I'll admit that my first thought was that the shaman had an advantage. If the patient improved, the shaman could take the credit. If the patient did not recover, the shaman was not responsible: the curse or possession was just too strong."

"While as a modern psychiatrist you're responsible for treatment either way?"

"Well, it made me wonder about how much of our professional work is based on the power of suggestion. The patient gets the credit for any personal success, of course, but when there is a bad outcome, therapists can fall into the trap of responsibility. I do not underestimate the power of ritual though. There are always things we cannot explain, and I build on strong faith when I find it."

"Then there would be children back in those days who needed but didn't get psychiatric care?"

"Obviously. But during the period you're talking about families were likely to hide mentally ill relatives. It was considered evidence of not living properly."

"Have any of your older colleagues heard of any cases happening in Water Dragon or Blue Pheasant clans?"

Tashi studied Kaj for a moment. "If there was another Soöng child, there would be a record if the birth happened at the hospital. Before the hospital was built, the monasteries collected information. Records are centralized now, but if the mother was not connected to the palace, I am not sure."

"Let's say we locate this child, now grown up. What would be the best way to proceed?"

"I am going to assume you already have someone in mind and it's male. My first thought is that you should have someone professionally trained with you. You will not be dealing with a child in terms of age and size. Mental capacity is another matter. If the family have been protecting this child for years, they may not want to cooperate. On the other hand, they may resent years of having to deal with him. If he has been totally isolated, he could have his own anger issues and resentment, particularly of other children, and may feel victimized or paranoid. He probably lacks direct experience with life. Everything he thinks he knows will be from observing or reading about it. That means he will tend to black and white thinking because his range of experience has been stunted. If he has been over indulged, he will have developed strategies for manipulating circumstances to his own advantage. There could also be serious personality disorders and a tendency to violence."

"Such as?" Kaj asked.

"Hypothetically, anything from Oppositional Defiance through Narcissism, and Psychopathy. But it's folly to start throwing out these labels without case history and interviews. For all we know, the child was nurtured and as an adult is mentally healthy."

Kaj leaned forward intently. "Would you be available and willing to help us tomorrow?"

Tashi frowned for a moment. "It depends on the timing. I fly back tomorrow noon. If you need me, we can meet at the airport. But I do not want to go in without knowing what I am dealing with. I will reserve the right to decide not to participate. I don't want to be caught up in ethical and professional conflicts."

"We will give you everything we have tomorrow. If you decide not to participate, we will understand." As usual, Kaj was prepared to accept whatever he could get from Tashi. "Final question: Can you tell us about the protest movement up here in the mountains? About expanding a pass, I believe."

Tashi looked confused for a moment. "Snow Leopard is not Blue Pheasant. We are not close to the city and do not deal with crowding and urban growth. We also do not deal with the dam except for using their electricity. Our only protest took place in the 60s. There have been proposals to expand a small mountain pass north of us. Given a relatively short building season, it would have been a major construction project over years. Snow Leopard opposed it fiercely. In the end, Mountain Thunder agreed to widen the pass on their side. But they said that no climbing or tourism was to be allowed on Mount Masakatsu. Snow Leopard agreed. Let Nepal and India have the tourists."

"Have you heard about a new dam?"

"People talk but it never goes anywhere. Rich people with the big houses do not want the lake disturbed. And we do not want the goats to be unhappy. Our goats are the national symbol of Kuthan."

Kaj didn't doubt her. He remembered Grandpa Lhotse and the yak named Marta.

"Goats are good," he said with a smile as he stood up. "And may I say that I think Kuthan is very lucky to have someone like you who wants to work with old and new traditions."

Tashi looked at him suspiciously. "Which is why I don't want to leave my profession." She quickly corrected herself. "Not that I mean I am leaving."

Kaj let his smile broaden. He knew the bare bones of her relationship with the King and could sense the rest.

"As you think might happen if you became a part of the royal family?"

Tashi did not look surprised that Kaj knew about her private life.

"Well, it would be traditional, wouldn't it?"

"I wonder sometimes about the word *traditional*," Kaj said in a detached, philosophical tone as Tashi walked them down the hall toward the waiting van.

"Does it mean a hundred years? Two hundred? The US is two hundred years and we keep making changes to our traditions. Kuthan's constitution is fifty years old. Does that qualify as set in stone? Wouldn't there be room for new traditions to be slipped in?"

"New traditions?" Tashi repeated.

"It would all depend on how strongly you believe that a long-term mental health facility is needed in Kuthan. If you believe enough to fight for it, it would mean different roles for professionals, different training, and different staffing by people with a foot in both worlds, people who could make things happen. For someone like you, the challenge would be establishing a tradition of career as well as dynasty for royal wives. Subject to negotiation, of course," Kaj said.

"Negotiation?" Tashi spoke the word as if it was foreign, which it was.

"Always," Kaj said. "That works for us in the States. You define your role and you refuse to accept less than full support."

On the long drive back to the city, Kaj and Kaipo sat in the back of the van occupying themselves in a process of elimination. It did not matter that the Colonel was sitting in front of them. The more minds involved in the case, the better at this point.

"So, who can we rule in or out?" Kaj asked.

"Blue Pheasant has a history of political dissent," Kaipo pointed out.

"At least, they did back in the 60s," Kaj agreed. "According to the Abbot, the Kalyani protestors were ultimately sent back to Blue Pheasant. The current protestors could be their children or grandchildren."

"Why would Blue Pheasant protest a dam that would not even be near them? Are they so altruistic that they would risk their lives to protect White Bone land? Would it matter to them if some tea bushes or tobacco plants or ducks got drowned?" Kaipo shook his head. "I don't get it."

"Altruistic? Maybe not. Idealistic? Perhaps. Some people need a cause. Causes are often spiritual." Kaj was thinking of the dragon's conception of purpose.

"So do we look for shamans?" Kaipo asked.

The Colonel turned around at that point, making no apology for having listened to their conversation.

"If you need a shaman, ask at the hotel front desk. They know everyone. You'll need someone who was active twenty years ago, but who knows when shamans retire? In Nepal they never seem to."

"I can work with Cliff on that when we get back," Kaipo said.

"Just don't take too long with it," Kaj growled.

"Right now, I've got all the time in the world," Kaipo said, his arms wide.

"What does that mean," Kaj said suspiciously.

"Gail laid down the law. I have to get my head together and not phone her until I've done it."

"You didn't mention that this morning," Kaj said irritably.

"I was not ready to talk about it then. But our conversation did make me start thinking about what I was doing."

Kaj leaned back in his seat and thought about Jill. *What is it about Kuthan that makes everyone stop in their tracks and start asking questions? What made Jill suddenly see how her family's past shaped her present? It must be the mountains. They must be emitting chaotic radio impulses that demand you ask yourself "What am I doing with my life?"*

Kaj looked sternly at Kaipo. "So, what are you doing with your life?"

The Colonel took that moment to turn back around to face the front.

"I have no idea. I think you were right before. I am just letting things happen."

Kaj gave his best blank stare. He knew he had started this, and he wasn't sure he wanted to go wherever time and fate and Kuthan were taking Kaipo.

Kaipo saved him the trouble. "After our talk, I can see I'm at a crossroads."

"With Gail?"

"She is so used to making executive decisions that she does not negotiate. She figures out what she thinks I want and then goes ahead without asking me. She's usually right, but it's the not asking that bothers me."

"And have you told her how you feel?"

Kaipo shook his head.

"What did I tell you. If you don't speak up, then how's she going to know what you want?"

"I don't want to ruin things." Kaipo looked discouraged as if this confession had cost him a great deal to admit.

"Well, the Colonel wasn't afraid to take a chance this morning." Kaj tried not to sound too accusatory, but it came out briskly as a form of admonition.

Upon hearing his name, the Colonel turned around and stared at Kaipo.

"You mean he was making a pass at Darya?" Kaipo looked at the Colonel who now looked a little bit embarrassed at listening in. "Really? Is that what you were doing?"

"I was teasing her," the Colonel admitted.

"I thought you were telling her that she was pretty arrogant."

"Well, there was some of that. But she is a strong, proud woman whose mind is on business. I wanted her to notice me."

"I'm no expert, but she noticed you all right." Kaj's eyes creased with amusement this time.

"And that's what it takes?" Kaipo asked the Colonel. "You do something unexpected to get their attention?"

"With Darya, yes. I cannot speak for all women."

Kaj heard the hedging and began to lose patience with romantic mishaps. "Darya noticed you long ago, Colonel. She was trying to get your attention when she was showing us the yaks."

Now it was the Colonel's turn to look surprised. "I didn't see that."

"Well, she was. I promise you. Now can the two of you please get over your women problems and get back to business. We need to find that missing cousin or whoever it is."

Kaj carefully concealed his amusement while Kaipo and the Colonel just looked at each other with knowing smiles.

Chapter 46

IT WAS DARK WHEN THEY got back to the palace. It was the first day without a team meeting, but Kaj did not feel the loss. He was tired and made the call to Linda very short. When he woke up it was late morning, and he felt as if he were still out in the mountains, driving down winding roads, coming home from Snow Leopard. A loud knock on the door disturbed him as he was getting dressed. It was Kaipo.

"The shaman. Remember? Cliff and I were going to find him."

Kaj invited him in and took out the coffee cups while Kaipo looked around at the suite. "You're going to miss this," he said.

Kaj smiled. "I was just thinking that myself. This room must be larger than my entire house. I don't even have to go outside to practice aikido. But it's just as well. If we had a space this large, Linda would want to fill it with things. She's not into minimal living."

"Gail likes sleek and modern, but she's accepted my soft couch. I told her that sofas with wooden legs were probably not going to be heavy duty enough. I sat on one of the dining room chairs and heard it creak. We agreed to spread some of my old stuff around so her antique stuff is kept safe."

"Was she upset about it?" Kaj asked.

"Nah. She keeps the delicate stuff in her office and the rest of it is up for negotiation, which really means the best ways to keep something safe from a tired cop coming home and plopping down on it. That's why I kept my sofa. It's soft and doesn't mind if I spill things on it."

Kaj sat down himself. "OK. Now what about this shaman? How did the hotel know he was the likely one?"

Kaipo looked pleased with himself and drew out the moment.

"The way they described him he's the shaman on call for the palace. His family have been shamans for generations. It goes from father to son, except that he was trained by his grandfather. Once he qualified and started building a reputation, the palace took notice and called him whenever they needed him. He's worked with them for nearly thirty years. That means that anything involving palace personnel and the royal family would naturally include him. The guards drove us there and insisted on going in with us. It seems his English is dotted with so many local words that they didn't think we would understand him."

"Pidgin?" Kaj asked, remembering the language developed on the plantations back home when they all spoke different languages.

"Something like," Kaj admitted. "But the base language isn't English, so we'd have trouble. Anyway, it wasn't far, and we got lucky. He was in his backyard making medicine pouches. He's in his late sixties and still does rituals. I asked if he remembered a Blue Pheasant child and what his name was."

"And he remembered?" Kaj doubted he could recall details from twenty-year-old cases. There were some that were memorable, but always because of something outrageously special.

"He did. I asked him why he was sure because it was a long time ago. He said that the child had been possessed by a particularly strong demon. He remembered because he could not dislodge it. He said it was one of the few times he had failed to help."

Kaj nodded. In his experience, it was the cases he couldn't close that stayed in his desk drawer haunting him.

"He said the boy was called Kamal. He said he was a beautiful child, which made the possession so disturbing. There was no evidence he was being mistreated, but he was pale and there was no evidence that the boy was leaving the house or attending school."

"He was being hidden?"

"He didn't say that. But he did say the child had a peculiar habit of watching people intently. While he performed the rituals and ceremony, he felt the boy was sneering at him. He had never had that reaction from a child that young. He knew right away that he could not help him."

"Did he know who the child was?"

"He knew the name, but that was all. But he could tell from the clothing and an ill-concealed arrogance that the boy came from a wealthy, high-placed family."

"That sounds plausible. It fits with the DNA that says there was another relative in the hall. Now we have a name, there's something to go with. Tell the Colonel that Tashi needs to be picked up at the airport, and then we'll head out for Blue Pheasant."

"I'll make the arrangements, but Cliff and I are still working with the forensics. We still have loose ends to tie up here. Are you OK without us?"

"Go where you need to be," Kaj said. "Tashi and I can handle this. We'll have the Colonel there for backup."

"Are you sure it's no problem?" Kaipo looked worried.

Kaj gave one of his signature eyebrow raises. "I've dealt with a few demons in my time. They all sound the same after a while. Between Tashi and me, I think we will be just fine."

Kaipo nodded uncertainly and walked toward the door. When he looked back, Kaj was standing by the window looking up at the mountains. He was watching the morning sun outline small clouds with a golden aura. Kaj did not hear Kaipo close the door. At that moment, he was thinking that the mountains and the light were what he was going to miss the most about Kuthan.

Chapter 47

The Blue Pheasant farmstead was less than twenty miles from the palace, but the drive seemed longer because no one was in any mood to talk. It was Kaj's first contact with Blue Pheasant and, given the family's history of protest, he had no idea how they would be received, since they came with no warning or even with a clear idea of how or why a Blue Pheasant family member might be involved in the violence at the palace. The Colonel seemed to share his concern. There was a second van following closely behind them carrying members of palace security.

They parked in a semi-circular driveway in front of a stately home that would have been comfortable among English hedgerows and lychgates. The only exotic touches were the architectural curves around the doors and roof that suggested the traditional woodworking skills of Indian craftsman living below Kuthan's southern border. Kaj was not surprised. Dorji had told him that Blue Pheasant was culturally closer to India than the northern clans, which showed the influence of Nepal and China.

They were received civilly and invited to wait in a sunny room with deep bay windows filled with tropical plants. The dam's distant plume of water mist was visible from every window. It seemed a fitting metaphor for how the dam had worked its way into Kuthan history and, even more, into the country's daily life.

The head of the Lama clan finally entered the room. She was an old woman, dressed in loose clothing of an indistinguishable darkness, her thinning grey hair pulled back severely to reveal an almost bullet shaped skull. The dark hollows beneath her cheekbones gave her an air of cold authority.

"What do you want?"

Kaj studied her for a moment. He thought of the artist whose sensitive paintings hung in his suite at the hotel. Confronted with the matriarch's abstract politeness, Kaj guessed that the artist's marrying into Snow Leopard and moving north into the mountains might have been a bolt for freedom. He hoped the man had been happy.

"We need to talk to Kamal." Kaj returned her formality and did not give her the chance to claim that her grandson wasn't there. He wanted her to think they already knew he was.

She did not argue. "I am his grandmother. What is this about?"

"We need to ask him some questions about the shooting at the palace."

"I see." She did not seem surprised. "What do you want to know?"

"We need to talk with him," Kaj said.

"I may be able to give you the information you need," she replied. "My grandson lives a very private life."

"Then let me ask you why his name is not included in the Soōng family tree?"

"Then we should sit down."

The woman invited them to a sofa and armchairs. Their backs were to the windows and the dam. Kaj wondered if the woman was about to try damage-control. He was wrong. The way she talked about Kamal was clipped and unsympathetic.

"I knew someone would ask about Kamal one day. His parents left him here because he could not handle the public pressures of royal life. That's what they told me. It was not my choice, but they said he had nowhere else to go."

"Did they give any more reason why?" Tashi asked.

The woman took a deep breath. "They said that Kamal tried to kill his brother."

Kaj took a deep breath himself. "Kiran and Kamal are brothers?"

The woman nodded. "Fraternal twins. But nothing like each other. Kamal bullied his brother. He lied and blamed other people. He tried to harm him and laughed when he was caught."

"That must have been difficult," Tashi said. "Did his parents realize that he posed a danger?"

"I watched the boys one summer. They were nine. I could see how Kamal treated his brother. I told his parents. I said we were dealing with evil. I told my daughter to call a shaman. She said that was old fashioned nonsense. Her husband, Tranh, would not see that there was anything wrong. They took him back with them when they returned to the palace. I told them they were fools."

"You must have been worried," Tashi said.

"I was frightened for Kiran, and I was right. One day, after they were back, Kamal locked his cousins in a basement and tried to start a fire. He could have killed them. The nanny, Anya, found him there, laughing, while the three other boys were trapped. When she tried to free them, he attacked her and knocked out some of her teeth. When she called the guards, he tried to blame Kiran. The family was ashamed, and Kamal was brought here. After that, his parents called the shaman, who told them that an angry and very powerful demon had taken possession of Kamal. The shaman told them that the demon was too strong for him to drive away. It was telling Kamal to harm his brother. There was no choice then. They sent the one brother, Kiran, to boarding school and left the other here with me."

"And you became responsible for him?"

The old woman looked sharply at Tashi. "What choice did I have? He was family although he did not behave like it. There was nowhere else he could go or that would have him."

"Did he understand what was happening?" Tashi asked.

The woman nodded. "Yes. He was lonely, but he could not make friends. None of the children here were allowed to play with him. That made him angry and resentful. He said Anya and the Sikh butler had lied. He said his parents had abandoned him. He had tutors and caretakers, but none stayed very long. There was nothing I could do until Kamal found a life in his computers. The tantrums stopped. His parents hoped that the demon had left. When Kiran came home from university, his parents asked him to spend time with his brother. I should have refused. I shall regret allowing that for the rest of my life. That sweet boy, Kiran, agreed immediately and taught Kamal how to drive. I should have stepped in. I feel responsible for whatever Kamal has done."

"What do you think he has done?" Kaj asked.

The woman shook her head. "All I know is that my sweet Kiran is dead and my daughters and Kanchan are gone."

"Did he say anything about what happened at the palace?" Kaj asked.

"He said he was there. I knew something was wrong when he drove Kiran's car back."

Kaj and the Colonel exchanged significant glances.

"What did he say?" Tashi asked.

"He said that people had been killed. He said he was in a hotel room waiting for Kiran when the shooting happened. That's all. I should not have believed him. He was never like Kiran."

Given his impressions of this woman, Kaj imagined that Kiran must have been compliant and agreeable, perhaps even sensitive like his Lama artist relative.

The old woman proved him right.

"Kiran was always smiling, never any trouble as a child, obedient and eager to please. You could play games with him and he loved to sit on my lap and be read to. I don't know how two brothers could be so different. Kamal did not like to be touched. He was defiant and told us that he hated us all. How can you love a child like that?"

"Where is he now?" Kaj asked.

Kaj watched a quick shadow of fear and then anger cross her face as she pointed out toward the entrance hall. "His rooms are at the top of the stairs." You can go up if you want.

Kaj looked up at the stairs. They were narrow and curved up and around the entrance-hall wall before disappearing behind a railing at the top. They felt defensive. Someone could stand at the top and easily repulse invaders.

"You don't go up there?" he asked.

"He gets angry if I do. If he wants to be left alone, I am not going to argue with him."

"Does he become violent?" Tashi asked.

"It's easier to just give him whatever he wants." The woman looked grim and stood up.

The Colonel was the first to go to the bottom of the stairs and look up. The stairs were steep, and there was nothing to break a fall if Kamal resisted. He motioned for Kaj and Tashi to wait while he positioned the palace guards at the bottom and walked up the stairs himself. He knocked and then cautiously opened a door. A few minutes later, he came out of the door and nodded for Kaj and Tashi to come up.

The room they went into must once have been a reception or living room for a suite, but it had now converted into a computer room. What looked like thousands of dollars of equipment had been crammed into it. Beyond was a hallway with several connecting doors. Through one, they could see a fully equipped gym. The occupant had not been deprived. In fact, he might have been even more seriously indulged than his grandmother had implied.

The room's occupant initially ignored them but then swung his chair around to face them. Kaj's first impression was that Kamal looked out of place. He dominated the room with glittering, darting eyes and a restless movement of his shoulders that made Kaj imagine a hungry Komodo dragon dropped into a petting zoo. His hands were those of a child and he was at least three inches shorter than Sanjay, meaning that he could have easily navigated the palace flood channel, more easily than Sanjay anyway. His bone structure was delicate but his arms were muscled and his shirt pulled tight across his chest. He looked as if he had spent hours working out.

"I am Inspector Kajiwara," Kaj began.

Kamal interrupted him. "I know who you are. I heard you talking to the old woman."

Kaj did not ask him how he had overheard them. That could come later if it became important. "The people with me are Dr. Dema and Colonel Pradhan."

Kamal ignored the Colonel. "You're the psychologist," he said to Tashi. I read your article on shamans. A lot of people thought you were wrong. Do you know why?"

"You seem to be well-read." Tashi kept her expression neutral.

"You did not prove that mixing Eastern and Western methods of treating mental illness does any good." He gave a scornful, superior laugh. "Do you think you will be powerful if you marry Raju?"

"Why would I want to be powerful?" Tashi's voice was placid.

"Why else would you want to marry him?"

"Is that why people marry? To gain power over them?"

"Answer a question with a question," Kamal sneered at her. "You think you are better than me. Three hours of reading on the computer and I know more than you do."

"Can we sit down," Kaj said.

Kamal shrugged.

They found a couple of chairs. The Colonel remained in the doorway.

"Is all this equipment yours?" Kaj asked.

"The old woman already told you." Kamal gave them a triumphant smile. "She gives me whatever I want."

"She has never refused you anything?" Tashi asked.

Kamal smirked. "She wouldn't dare."

Kaj paused for a moment to digest Kamal's contemptuous gloating.

"What would happen if she did refuse you?" he asked.

"Grandma has an over-active imagination. If I shout at her, she thinks I plan to burn the house. She treats anything unpleasant as if it does not exist. If she cannot ignore it, she throws money at it. I always win."

"She is the one who buys you computers?" Tashi asked as she looked around.

Kamal followed her gaze around the room. "Of course not. I order what I want. She pays for it." He gave the Colonel a challenging glance. "My equipment is better than anything you have at the palace."

Kaj stared into Kamal's black, lifeless eyes and thought of the dragon pool as he had first seen it. He also remembered the shaman had said that the child had a demonic force too powerful to be driven out.

"Kamal," Kaj began, "I'm going to be honest with you. I hope you will be honest with us, so we don't waste each other's time. We already know that you were in the palace hotel on the day of the shootings."

"I know. My grandmother just told you that," Kamal sneered. "She is a senile old fool. Kiran always was her favorite because he was so 'sweet.' But I am more intelligent."

"Your grandmother showed no signs of dementia," Tashi said. "She told us that Kiran taught you how to drive."

"No one has to teach me anything," Kamal bristled.

"Then you know how to open a closed electronic lock." Kaj said.

"I do not know what you are talking about." Kamal crossed his arms and looked sullen.

"What were you doing in the palace?" Kaj asked.

Kamal stared at Kaj calculating how far a denial was likely to get him. He didn't like the look on Kaj's face. "Playing computer games in the hotel room," he finally admitted.

"Was Kiran any good at playing those games?" Tashi asked.

"Not as good as me. I beat him every time. He said I was the king of the computers." Kamal smiled victoriously.

"All the more reason he would ask for your help to open some electronic locks," Kaj said. "The king of computers would know how to do something simple like that, wouldn't he?"

Kamal sensed the danger. He stared at Kaj from under lowered lids and did not respond.

Kaj waited for a few moments and then prompted him. "Only someone very skilled and intelligent could open closed electronic locks without a key. I don't want to underestimate what Kiran could do. Or was it Kanchan who knew how to do it?"

Kamal's face twisted into an angry sneer. "Not in their dreams. Kiran could not find an on-off switch."

"So, it was you. Process of elimination. They couldn't. You could."

Kamal sat back in his chair and looked suspiciously at Kaj. "Why would I want to?"

"Oh, come on. Why wouldn't you?" Kaj allowed a hint of admiration to enter his voice. "What a chance to show off. How often do you get the chance to challenge the programmers and developers who designed the locks? You knew you could beat them. Every lock can be picked, but it would take a genius to open an electronic one. How could you refuse? No one else could do it. Tell me, was Kiran the one wise enough to ask you?"

"I see what you are trying to do. It's not going to work on me."

Kaj chuckled. "Not going to work when you have the chance to play chess with Bobby Fischer? That's what breaking into an electronic lock is like. It's the world class chess of computer hacking. Aren't you a prodigy like Fischer? Don't you see all the mistakes everyone else makes so you can smile and say, 'I know better.' We brought two computer techs with us. They broke into that lock in ten minutes flat."

"Ten minutes?" Kamal sneered. "Amateurs."

"How fast could you do it? And even if you beat them, who ever heard of you? Our guys can go home and write papers about how they did it. They will be famous. Companies will want to hire them for big salaries."

"If I wanted to, I could do it."

"So, what would make you want to do it? Did Kiran say opening the lock meant that you boys could see the passage under the palace where you used to play? It would be an adventure like the ones you used to have as children. No one could blame you for children's play. Plus weren't you curious what these cousins were doing?"

"Opening electronic locks is not easy," Kamal said testily.

"Obviously, Kiran was helpless without you," Tashi said. She flipped her hair back over shoulder and let it fall rippling down her back.

Kamal stared at Tashi, unable to remove his eyes from her. He saw the small pearl earring as she tucked a loose tendril of hair back into place. He looked at the curve of her throat and noticed how her blouse allowed him to see the shadow of her breasts. He felt an urge to run the back of his hand slowly down her arm. He hated Raju more intensely in that moment than he ever had before.

"Kamal," Kaj had to say loudly to get his attention.

"Kiran asked me if I could open the lock. Of course, they could not. They were too stupid."

"How did you do it?" Kaj asked.

"It was nothing. I looked up how to do it. I had it open in three minutes. They couldn't do it even when I showed them. But that's all. Opening locks is not a crime. It was a game."

"You were at the hotel, playing games with the electronic locks on a hotel basement door?"

Kamal glared at Kaj. "Just a game. Nothing more. An adventure like you said for old playmates who wanted to see the tunnels again."

"OK," Kaj said. "Now what about the rifle? We found it in the tunnel. Did Kiran ask you to find that for him?"

Kamal's lizard eyes narrowed. He had not planned on them finding the drainage canal. If they had the rifle, they had his fingerprints. That meant he needed a reason why he handled the weapon.

"Kiran said he wanted to buy a rifle for target practice. He said if I helped him find one, he would take me shooting with him. It sounded different, like fun."

"Wherever did you find it?" Kaj let his voice indicate his surprise, as if finding a rifle was an unimaginable achievement.

Kamal shut Kaj down. "I did not say I found one."

Kaj immediately changed tactics. "Let's say then, hypothetically, that if someone asked you where to buy a rifle, where would you tell them to look?"

Kamal was scornful. "Anyone can search on the computer. There are people in India and in Bangladesh."

"And did you share that with Kiran?"

"I may have told him where to look. But he drove to the border and paid the dealer."

Kaj sat back and let both his eyebrows rise in surprise.

"You trusted him to make the deal? You know how incompetent he is. Why wouldn't you drive with him to buy it, especially if you were going to shoot it yourself later? Wouldn't the dealer try to cheat him if he saw how naïve Kiran was? You wouldn't let a dealer get away with that would you?"

Kamal squirmed and his voice rose insistently. "He was the one who drove the car to the border. I just watched as he bought the rifle. I did stop the man from trying to charge more than he had agreed."

"Ok, Kamal, you say that Kiran took you target shooting. Did he also buy full magazines from the dealer?"

"Why would I know?"

"You were there. You saw what he bought. Then you all went shooting. Was the rifle set on automatic or semi-automatic? Were you firing one shot at a time or holding down the trigger?"

"One shot."

"Ok. How many shots did you fire?"

"Why would we count?"

Kaj frowned. "An AK-47 magazine has 30 bullets. It takes only a few seconds to empty the magazine on automatic. One shot at a time lasts longer. Is that what you did?"

"Kiran told us we had to conserve the ammunition."

"So how many times did you fire?"

"It could be twenty."

"Ok," Kaj said, "that's one mag almost empty. Kanchan probably fired the same and then Kiran. That's 60 bullets or two magazines. So, it's a simple answer: you must have had more than two mags or you would have had no ammunition left. So how many did you have left?"

Kamal shrugged.

"Kamal, come on, be honest. We know you were a very important part of the planning. You were clearly the one who made things happen. You're not responsible for their mistakes or lack of planning. But I know you wouldn't have run out of ammunition. What did they tell you they were planning?"

"It was nothing to do with me. I did not ask."

"Come on. They told you they wanted to practice firing a rifle and they wanted to go into the passages under the palace. You know there are no target ranges down there. Really, Kamal. A smart man like you? You must have wondered what they were planning. I can't believe you would have allowed yourself to be used. Was Kiran that good?"

"I'm too smart to be used"

"So, what was Kiran planning? Was it a brilliant plan that he made without any input from you?"

Kamal's lip curled. "Kiran was not brilliant. He was stupid." Kamal sat back primly. "His plan was stupid."

"We believe you. But we need you to help us understand. Who put the rifle in the drainage canal?"

"Kiran did."

"We've seen that drainage channel. Kiran and Kanchan were much taller than you are. They wouldn't have fit. But you would. You had to be the one who put it there, after you opened the lock beneath the palace hotel. So far Kiran's brilliant plan is working, but only because he has you to do the hard work. Now where are we? The rifle is safely in the drainage channel. It must have at least one full magazine. Just confirm that so we can move on. How many magazines were left?"

"One," Kamal finally admitted.

"OK. Good. We're making progress. I am assuming it was a full magazine. I mean, who would go to the trouble of hiding a rifle if there was no ammunition. Kiran did plan to have ammunition with the rifle, didn't he?"

Kamal nodded.

"Then what happened? The smart plan would be for someone to go up the ladder in the storage room to make sure that the shelving above the trapdoor could still be moved. After all, the whole plan would have failed if you couldn't move the shelving. I'm sure Kiran would have anticipated that."

Kamal sat sullenly but said nothing.

"Now," Kaj said, "help us to understand what was going to happen on the day of the party. Kiran and Kanchan were in the hall with your parents. Somebody had to bring the rifle to the hall. Kiran could not be in two places at the same time."

"Kiran must have left the hall to get it."

"But the King told us that everyone was in the hall. It can't be Kiran or Kanchan. They were using you again, Kamal. You were the one who had to crawl into that dark narrow passage, full of rats and spiders. You had to pull the rifle out, go down the passage, take down the wallboard, and climb up the stairs into the storage room. Only thing I can't figure out is how someone like you got talked into doing all this without knowing why. Didn't they trust you? Did they think you were too stupid to understand the plan?"

"I heard what they said they were planning," Kamal spat out. "It was stupid, just like them. They said they were going to wave the rifle around to make the King order the Dam Board to stop planning a second dam. Kiran was almost crying over a stupid dam and ruining the land."

Kaj leaned in toward Kamal and almost whispered. "You are an intelligent man. Were they going to wave a fully loaded rifle around and never use it? You must have seen through them. Think of it, Kamal. Would you take a loaded weapon into a room and not plan to shoot it? They underestimated you, didn't they? You were the one who deserved their respect for all the help you gave them. What were they were really planning?"

Kamal leaned forward conspiratorially and looked smug. "They wanted power. Kiran planned to kill them all so he could become king."

Kaj felt the hard back of the chair as he leaned back. "Kiran wanted to be king?" he repeated. "How was this going to happen?"

"He was going to kill them all. Then there would be no one left and he would be king."

"You said the plan was stupid. Why was that?" Kaj's voice was conspiratorial.

"Because I was born first. I am older than him. If he had killed them all, I would have been king. That's why his plan was stupid."

"Is that why you went along with him? You knew you would be first in line to the throne?"

Kamal said nothing.

"But didn't Kiran know that?" Kaj asked. "Was he planning to kill you?"

"They would have reason to kill you." Tashi's voice was silk sheets and Chanel Number 5. "But I'm sure you didn't plan to let them."

She fingered the pearl hanging on a gold chain round her neck. Kamal's eyes followed her every move.

Kaj hid his smile. Kamal was out of his depth with a woman like this.

"I had no plan," Kamal said, but his voice cracked with discomfort.

Kaj imagined that there had not been many women around Kamal as he grew up. "It must have been very hard growing up without affection and knowing that Kiran was living the life you should have had. Respect was all you had left. And that had to be demanded."

Kamal tore his eyes from Tashi. "They put me away like rubbish. They lied about me. They wanted Kiran to have everything." He licked his lips with his lizard tongue and went silent.

Kaj focused intently on Kamal. He couldn't remember another case where he felt so driven to get a confession. He knew he was on the verge of getting it. It would just take a few minutes more.

"All right, Kamal," Kaj said. "I said we would be honest. So let me tell you what we think happened on that day. You already told us that you opened the door in the hotel basement. You also said that you retrieved the rifle. We know it had to be you who took the rifle to the hall because Kiran and Kanchan were already there. Now, what we don't know yet is whether you stepped into the hall and started shooting or whether you handed the rifle to someone else. We can narrow things down. Kanchan was not near but Kiran was. Both of you have motive and opportunity."

"I have no motive," Kamal snarled.

"Oh yes, Kamal, you did," Kaj objected. "You've already given us more than one. You hate your parents, you blame the Sikh butler and Anya for causing you to be sent away from the palace, and you think your brother Kiran was favored over you. That's a lot of motive. Did you think that if they all died, you would be the logical choice to be the king because you would be the only one left?"

"What about Kiran? He bought the rifle."

"All we know about Kiran is that he opposed a dam. We don't know what he planned to do once he had the rifle in his hands. Were you supposed to hand it to him?"

"I did. I handed it to him. He started shooting. I did not know what he was going to do. I tried to stop him."

"How did you try to stop him?" Kaj face was set.

"I tried to take the rifle from him."

"Tell me what happened."

"I did what Kiran asked. I brought the rifle to the hall door. He saw me and came to take it from me. I handed it to him. I was supposed to wait until the protest was over and then take the rifle back to the drainage canal. Then I was supposed to go back into the hotel and wait for Kiran and Kanchan to come join me. That was all."

"All right," Kaj said. "That's good to know. Now, let's stop here for a minute. We found blood traces down the hallway. You didn't happen to bang against a door or something when you brought the rifle to the hall, did you? It would make it so much easier for us to believe you. Do you have any wounds that could have dripped blood. That would be very helpful."

Kamal frowned. He wasn't sure where Kaj's questions were heading.

"Did you happen to cut yourself while you were in the hall," Kaj asked.

"I don't know," he said. "It all happened so quickly."

Kaj pounced. "What happened so quickly?"

"Kiran did not follow the plan. Instead of waving the rifle, he opened fire on everyone in the hall. Kanchan ran down to stop him, but Kiran shot him. I tried to seize the rifle to stop him but he hit me on the head with the rifle and threw me on the ground. I crawled away to escape. Now that I think of it, that's where the blood trail you followed came from. My nose was bleeding."

"OK, Kamal," Kaj said. You said you tried to take the rifle from Kiran. But then you said he knocked you down and you crawled away. Which is it?"

"I got up again and tried to take the rifle from him. He resisted and we struggled over it. It was an accident. The gun went off by itself.

"You are telling us that Kanchan was shot in the chest because he was running towards Kiran, trying to stop him. But you, Kamal, you struggled with Kiran twice. Do I have that right? And Kiran was shot during your second struggle. Now, this is important. Where were you holding the rifle when you tried to take it from him?"

"I don't remember. It happened so fast."

"Well, Kamal, there are only so many places you can hold a rifle when you try to take it from someone. Let me see if we can help you. Most people would try to grab the barrel because that way you can try to pull it up and away from you. We found bullet holes in the ceiling. Is that what happened? Were you trying to pull the rifle away from Kiran by holding onto the barrel? That would be the sensible place."

"Yes, yes. Now I remember. I was holding the barrel."

"And then what happened?"

"I was frightened. I had the rifle and had to get away. People would think that I had done the shooting. I ran out of the hall."

"What happened to Anya?"

"She grabbed my shirt. She started scratching and tried to bite me. I had to hit her with the rifle to stop her. Then I ran back into the tunnel and put up the wallboard. I put the rifle back and hid in the hotel basement. I was afraid people would think I had done it. It was Kiran."

Kaj looked at Tashi and the Colonel. Now came the tricky part.

"Well, Kamal, he sighed. Just a few more things. You've been very helpful so far, so I hope you will give us a little more time. You see, we need to make sure we have enough proof that Kiran was the shooter. You said yourself that it could have been either one of you."

Kamal's eyes began to dart uneasily.

"Kiran's wounds were caused during a struggle for the rifle. But he could just as easily have been trying to take it away from you. Now, bear with me. Let me give you another scenario and then we will be able to solve the problem. It has to do with the question I asked you about where you were holding the rifle when you tried to take it from Kiran. I don't think any of you paid much attention when you were shooting at targets. If you had, you would have noticed that the barrel gets too hot to touch pretty quickly. Anyone touching the barrel is going to have some significantly burnt flesh, enough to leave marks on their hands. So, if you were the one taking the rifle from Kiran as you say, we would expect burn marks on your hands. Could you show us your hands, palms up."

"I must have tried to grab the rifle stock. Yes, I remember now. I did not touch the barrel."

"Are you sure, Kamal? That sounds very difficult. The stock fits against the shooter's body. Are you sure that's what you did?"

"I do not remember." Kamal gave out a wail that sounded to Kaj like the cry of a wolf lost in the dark forests at the end of the earth. For a second. Kaj felt compassion for the forgotten child. Kamal's life had not been easy.

The Colonel broke the spell. He came in from the doorway as Kamal put his hands down under his thighs. He held Kamal firmly down with one hand on his shoulder and pulled out one of Kamal's hands. There was nothing there.

"Kiran had burns on the both of his palms," Kaj said almost sadly. "Now that tells us, Kamal, that he was trying to take the rifle away from you."

"It doesn't prove anything," Kamal shouted. "He could have burned his hands when he was struggling with me."

"That's true, Kamal, but it does not explain why you don't have burns. It's over, Kamal. Why don't you tell us what really happened."

Kamal roared in anger. "It was Kiran. It was his plan."

The Colonel spun Kamal around to subdue him then suddenly stopped. "Damn," he said out loud as he looked at the bank of screens fixed on the wall behind the computer. "He has been watching everyone. He has taken control of the palace security cameras." He shouted for the guards to come up the stairs.

Kaj looked where the Colonel had been pointing. One of the screens showed the unmistakable outline of the palace hotel's courtyard. The action was live, with people and cars moving in real time. The other screens showed outside walls and interior hallways, even the food carts where Kaj and Greg had met. Kaj looked anxiously from one screen to the other. He was afraid he would find the team's investigation room. To his relief, it didn't seem to be there.

"Take him and his computer and hard drive," the Colonel shouted to his men. "This man is under arrest for violation of national security."

Kaj was forced to stand aside while guards grappled Kamal to the ground and others began pulling cables from the walls. Kaj felt shocked. He had not finished with Kamal. He wanted the confession the interrogation had been leading. His prickle came back telling him there was something wrong.

"Don't touch my computers," Kamal screamed. "Leave me alone. I have done nothing wrong." The noise echoed in the house as they dragged Kamal kicking and screaming to the waiting vans.

Without any coordination with Kaj, the Colonel followed his men down the stairs and called for the Blue Pheasant matriarch. Kaj and Tashi stood at the top of the stairs, leaning over the bannisters.

"Madam," the Colonel told the woman, "Kamal has been taken into custody. Palace guards will be posted here until we can determine the nature of the security breach this man has caused. We have confiscated certain pieces of his computer equipment. Palace staff will be returning to remove the rest. In the meantime, the room will remain secured and guarded. No one is to enter."

Kaj and Tashi came down slowly after the guards had left. They didn't speak or even look at one another. It had all happened too fast. Kaj felt resentful at the abrupt way that the Colonel had ended his interrogation of Kamal, but it was too late now. It left Kaj without a sense of completion. There could be no resolution without confession.

The old woman turned to Kaj as they reached the bottom of the stairs. "What were they saying? Did Kamal kill them all?"

Kaj could not confirm or deny anything until the King had been informed. "The palace will issue a statement soon," he said to her. "I am sorry for your losses."

"Don't be sorry about Kamal," she said bitterly. "He's taken everything from me. I gave up my relationship with my other grandsons to protect them, not him. And what good did that do me? I have lost my daughters and now I learn that one of my two surviving grandsons is pure evil. This family is cursed.

"Raju is not cursed," Tashi said. "You sacrificed yourself for those boys, but you had no choice. There was nowhere you could turn for help."

Kaj heard the van leave with a squeal of tires on the gravel drive. The sound was final. Kaj looked out the front door in the direction of the distant dam. He had no real idea of what had just happened. Was the palace about to embargo news about the murders? Was the Colonel embarrassed by the breach of the palace's security system? Was Kaj being told he was no longer needed now that there was a viable suspect? Would the team find their suitcases packed and ready when they got back to the hotel? Had their work in Kuthan been just an elaborate charade? He did not know what to say when they got back to the hotel.

"If he had received proper therapy," Tashi said as they walked to the van, "Kamal might have been able to deal with his feelings of powerlessness and avoided the tragedy of his envy of his brother. The Shaman's demon was the repressed anger and jealousy the child could not express. His brother had taken the role of the good child. What was left for him to play beyond being the unfavored brother? If his brother follows the rules, he must behave as if they do not apply to him. If he is being raised by a cold, domineering grandmother, he must diminish her by saying she does not matter. The only way to express his will is through exerting power and the only way he sees to get power is by making people fear him. His grandmother submits to him because she is afraid of him."

"What's going to happen to him now?"

Tashi took a moment to answer.

"I don't know where the Colonel will take him. But, if we can establish the mental health center, we may be able to help him find some sort of peace. What I fear is that we have just changed one type of imprisonment for another. Without intensive therapy, he will always be a threat to Raju."

"Sometimes I hate my job," Kaj said.

"You must be saddened by seeing how much evil there is in the world."

Kaj smiled at her. "I prefer to be surprised by how much good there is."

Chapter 48

KAJ, THE COLONEL, AND TASHI stood in the courtyard outside the King's office, very aware that the moment was both solemn and historic. The Colonel had offered no explanation for the rough way they had removed Kamal nor any indication of where he had been taken. He soon made clear that his primary concern now was how much they were to tell the King.

"Tell the King only the facts," the Colonel urged. "We know that Kamal was at least an accomplice, and he will spend the rest of his life under guard regardless of what the other two cousins intended. If the King asks specifically about the other two cousins, I suggest not talking about Kamal's claim that Kiran wanted to be king."

Kaj frowned. "What exactly do you want me to tell him?" His tone expressed his dismay with the way the investigation had been cut short. "We know the rifle magazine was full when the shooting started and empty when we found it. Whoever fired the shots intended to kill. You prevented me from finding out whose plan it was. I'm finding it difficult to not be honest with the King since you and your officers stopped me from finding out."

The Colonel shook his head impatiently. "Your investigation was complete. You did what he asked of you. You narrowed down the possibilities to Kiran and Kamal. It was enough. The King has suffered the loss of his uncle and aunts and the wounding of his sister and nephew. Does he also need the pain of thinking that the cousins he grew up with wanted to overthrow him?" The Colonel looked at Tashi as if asking her to agree with him. Tashi remained silent.

Kaj stared at the Colonel. "Are you saying that arresting Kamal was close enough to the truth?"

"It depends on how you define *truth*. Pure honesty is a rare thing," the Colonel replied. "But I have never heard that the word *fact* meant the same thing as *opinion* and particularly not *speculation*.

Kaj did not respond to his own words being used against him. "You are asking me, then, to protect the King's illusions."

"The Colonel is saying that we should let Raju grieve for his family without having to wonder about their loyalty," Tashi said. "I can tell him truthfully that Kamal was living in a world driven by his delusions. It is sad how many people have suffered because of them. But that is as far as I can go."

"That is enough," the Colonel replied.

"But is it?" Kaj objected. "I was asked for complete transparency."

The Colonel looked stern. "You proved that the motive for the attack did not come from outside the country. No one was trying to undermine Kuthan. You showed that the protests were caused partly by a lack of vision regarding the dam's role in the life and future of the nation. It's tragic, but that is something the King can address. You also proved that the Dam Board was not involved. He needed to know that. You gave the King what he and Kuthan needed. You must leave the rest to us."

"What exactly is the rest?" Kaj asked morosely.

The Colonel did not reply. He ushered them into the King's office and stood aside with an unsmiling stiffness.

The King greeted them with a mixture of hope and despair. "You know who killed my family?"

"We do," Kaj told the King.

"Did he confess?" the King asked.

"The evidence is clear. His grandmother provided more explanation. It starts with a family secret. That boy whose name you did not recall was another of your cousins. He was Kiran's brother."

"His brother! How could that be kept from me? And why?"

"He was not kept away at first," Tashi said. "It was only after he began to display serious psychological problems. His grandmother said that the decision to send you boys to boarding school and take him back to Blue Pheasant was made once they realized it was not safe for you to be raised around him."

"As far as we can tell," Kaj said as he glanced at Tashi, "he was seeking revenge. He blamed Anya and the Butler for telling his parents about his attempt to harm you boys. He blamed his parents, Tranh and Dechen, for banishing him to Blue Pheasant lands. He hated your cousins because they lived the life he thought he should have. The only one he hadn't planned on killing was his grandmother, and that may be because she was useful. She bought him computers."

"And he wanted to kill me, of course," the King said.

"Because you are who he wanted to be," Tashi said.

Kaj moved quickly onto what he knew as facts. "We think Anya recognized him in the hall and sent the Sikh butler to warn you." Kaj looked sympathetically at the distraught King. "We think she saved your life."

"Anya saved my life? She was the one who said there was an urgent telephone call?"

"Just before she died, she tried to tell the hospital staff who it was, but they thought she was trying to say *camel.* His name is Kamal, except we were pronouncing it as Kamāl. It is pronounced like *camel.* She was trying to say his name."

"But how did he do this? And why? Where did the gun come from and how did it get into the room?"

Kaj sighed inwardly. Here was the hard part. He had to decide how much to disclose. He glanced at the Colonel but the man's face was impassive. Whatever decision Kaj had to make was his alone.

"According to Kamal, Kiran and Kanchan thought they were protesting the rumored eastern dam. He said they planned to wave the rifle around and convince you that you should save the nation from a repeat of the flooding that occurred with the first one."

"A visit to the dam board would have cured them of that idea," the King replied. "They should have come to me."

"I'm not sure they would have believed you. Kamal fed their illusions. He went with them to get the rifle. On the day of your party, he entered the hotel basement, retrieved the rifle from where he had previously hidden it, and then came into the hall. He told us that with everyone dead, he would be the logical and legitimate heir to the throne. He hid until the security search was over and then drove Kiran's vehicle off the premises. No one would question the palace tags on the car."

The King sat silently, his head in his hands. Tashi walked over, sat beside him, and put her hand on his arm.

"Thank you, Kaj, for telling me not all my cousins were my enemies. That is a comfort. But where is Kamal now?"

The Colonel came to life at that moment, turning on his British Army mode. His tone was frosty and official. "He has been detained by Kuthani National Security at an undisclosed location for his own safety."

The King did not ask for further details. Kaj did not know how to feel, so he took his lead from the Colonel and quietly left the room with him. When Kaj glanced back from the doorway, Tashi had her arms around the King.

"I suppose that went as well as it could," Kaj said to the Colonel. "I did not say one thing that was not true. But I still feel that I have not fully solved the crime as he asked me to."

"There is no easy way to know when to stand down. But what good would it have done if you told him that his cousins might all have been plotting against him? We don't know that. You made the best decision you could. I commend you, Inspector Kaj, for fulfilling your duty to Kuthan. You found a place to stand."

"The truth but not too many facts, you mean?" Kaj appreciated neither how the case had been settled nor his role in it. He was wise enough, though, to see the Colonel's point. Justice might not always have to be perfect to be just."

"Sometimes," the Colonel replied, "that is the way it is."

Chapter 49

THAT EVENING, KAJ STRETCHED OUT on his bed and stared around his luxurious suite. On his pay, he doubted he would ever see the likes of it again. It was fun while it lasted.

He couldn't see the mountains, but he knew they were there. Then the rest of Akela's story came to him, and he did not have to dream to remember it. It was a story Kaj's mother, Ai, had read to him. They were in the Palolo house, a few streets back from Waialae Avenue. He was young, not more than four, and it was in the days before Goro had overfilled the garden with row upon row of pots on wooden benches, all to provide the stock for his landscaping business. He and his mother were in his bedroom. He remembered the thick layer of cream paint on the walls. It was almost enough to fill in the vertical tongue and groove paneling.

Ai had opened the book to show him the picture of a wild-eyed warrior who had killed a child's family. Kaj remembered the man's long black hair flying out behind him as he galloped a black horse along a tree-lined road. The horse's tongue was thrust forward and its eyes were blood red. The man wore a helmet with a dragon on the front, and his body was covered with rows of metal plates and padding.

"This is the bad man," Ai said. But Kaj already knew that.

"Why is he bad?" he asked.

"Because he has stolen and lied and killed."

"Will he be punished?"

Ai smiled at her son. "He will find karma. Justice will find him."

"How?" Kaj asked. The concept of karma, like death, was far too abstract for him to understand.

And so, Ai read him the rest of the story.

When the young man put the locket around his neck as he had been told, he saw what his parents had seen. He saw the wild-eyed man lead desperate, cruel men to kill the family and their servants. He knew that this man was his father's cousin and that he had killed because he wanted to steal their lands. He also knew that it was his destiny to right this terrible wrong.

He left the old couple crying in their forest home and walked towards the city that had once belonged to his parents. As he approached the city walls, he was stopped by a grey-haired stranger with a long beard, a staff, and eyes as dark and shiny as the long-dead mongoose. It made the young man remember how the mongoose had brought him comfort and how much he missed him when old age took his life.

"Where are you going?" the grey-bearded one asked.

"To the city," the young man replied.

"And what to do there?"

"To seek my fortune." The young man felt the golden locket become warm on his chest.

"Good," the grey-beard said. "You are cautious. You are wise to be. Your task is not an easy one. Go to the palace guards and tell them you heard they were looking for good men. They will be glad to have you join them. Stay hidden for now. You will know when the time has come for you to act."

The young man looked at the city and marveled at how the afternoon sunlight had made the roofs shine like gold. When he looked back, grey beard had disappeared. He gave a shrug and did as he was told. When he gave the palace guard the message he was told to give, he was led into a large room where a burly man stood up to assess him.

"You look healthy enough," the man said gruffly. "I reckon you can swing a good sword. Come outside and let's see how you do."

The guard officer took him to where there was a row of archery butts and handed him a sword.

"Take a swing at the one on the end."

The young man walked down to the butt and stood before it. It was filled with straw and had a surface pockmarked by arrows that had not been able to penetrate far into the thick surface. He hefted the sword and took a practice swing. It was not a great sword. It did not have balance in his hand, but it was sharp enough when he touched the edge. He knew that the sword had been waiting for him. When he stood back from the target and took a large swing, the sword sliced through the target as if the butt were butter.

"No mistaking that," the officer said. "Where are you from? What's your name? Where did you learn to handle a sword like that?"

"I am from the woods. I learned by chopping down trees. My name is Treeman."

When he said no more, the officer merely grunted and told him to get something to eat inside and then report for his uniform.

Many months passed and the young man known as Treeman mastered the weapons used by the guards and proved to be popular with his fellows. During this time, he learned that the wild-eyed man was unpopular. The people were oppressed by heavy taxes and cruel punishments if they disobeyed him. For the time, Treeman did nothing to make himself known outside of the guards. But that changed when there was need for someone to become an officer and he was named by popular acclaim. Now it was not so easy to hide.

One day, the wild-eyed cousin came down to talk with the man in charge of the guards and Treeman was called in to meet him. The cousin looked at him strangely.

"Have we met?" the cousin asked. "You look familiar."

"No, Lord. This city is strange to me. I come from far away."

The cousin frowned and felt a stirring of fear in his breast. When he looked back at Treeman, he recognized the resemblance to his cousin and knew that this was the missing child, the one they did not find that day in the forest. His first impulse was to draw his sword to kill him, but he had heard strange tales about Treeman's strength. He had also heard about Treeman's popularity.

"Young man," the cousin said. "I have heard of you and I am much in need of your services. Would you be willing to undertake a great adventure on my behalf? The rewards will be rich, and you will be famous."

The locket burned on Treeman's chest. He knew he had been recognized.

"I would be honored, even without the reward," he said lightly.

"Good. Then I want you to free this country of a troublesome dragon that lives at the end of the marshes, near where the world ends. You will have a ship to sail there and as many of your fellows as you want to go along with you."

Treeman's heart fell, for he had heard of the marshes and the end of the world. The maps said that beyond the marshes there were demons. But he smiled and accepted the challenge as he knew he must.

As soon as the ship was prepared, Treeman and four guard-friends set off on the quest. After many storms and high seas, they came to the end of the marshes and saw the cave where the dragon was living.

"Wait with the ship," Treeman told his friends. "If I do not come back, tell the story of how we overcame all the obstacles and arrived here. I will go in and talk to the dragon alone."

The friends protested, but Treeman was not moved. He walked to the cave opening and stepped inside. Immediately, he felt the ground give out under his feet and he slid down into a large cavern. The dragon was sitting on a rock staring at him.

"I suppose you have come to kill me," the dragon said.

Treeman picked himself up and sat on another rock, rubbing his legs where they had brushed against the walls.

"I'm not interested in killing you unless you want me to."

"I have a choice?" The dragon looked interested. "This is new. Then why are you here?"

"My life seems to be driven by things beyond my control," Treeman said.

"And, of all the caves in the universe, you end up in mine?" The dragon looked as quizzical as a dragon could.

"I know it doesn't make much sense, but I think I am supposed to learn something from you."

"And who told you that?"

Treeman took out the locket and held it up toward the dragon. The gold glinted in the darkness.

"So, the prophesy is true," the dragon said in shock. "You have come."

"Did you call me?" Treeman asked.

"Perhaps. I suppose I must have. It has been a long time."

"What is the prophesy?"

"That I am to help someone who comes bearing a locket. Have you looked inside?

When Treeman shook his head, the dragon told him to do so.

Treeman was reluctant at first because he had tried to open the locket before but was never able to. This time, the locket opened as soon as he touched the edge. Inside were two pictures. One of a man on the left and another of a woman on the right.

"These are your parents," the dragon said. "Use your real name now. You are Akela. You are to restore the land. And I am to serve you."

Treeman, or Akela, peered suspiciously at the dragon. "If my purpose is to restore, what is yours?"

"Beyond serving you? I suppose I am to support justice. But I am old now. In your years, I am over a thousand. I do not know if I have the energy anymore. You need a younger dragon."

"No," Akela said definitively. "I was brought to you by an old grey-haired man with the bright eyes of a mongoose. You are called just as I am."

And so it was that Akela and the four companions sailed back over treacherous seas to the golden city. The dragon spent the voyage sitting on the top of the rigging and Akela came to know and love the dragon for its wisdom and honesty.

The wild-eyed cousin panicked when he saw the ship coming into the harbor with the dragon sitting on top of the sails. He knew the young man had come back for his vengeance. He called the guards and told them to imprison the young man, but they did not understand why the cousin was hostile to someone who had done his bidding, and they remained loyal to their friend. The wild-eyed cousin rushed down to the stables and tried to saddle a horse to escape, but the horses rolled their eyes and flared their nostrils and would not be harnessed. He ran into the streets, but the people would not open their doors to him. When he saw the dragon flying overhead, about to swoop down on him, he felt his heart burst and pour out all the evil he had done in his life. He dropped dead in the street just as Akela entered the gates.

There were happy celebrations when Akela was recognized as the true heir. Justice had triumphed, and he ruled wisely and well for many years. He rewarded his companions who had gone with him to that dark place beyond which there were demons. He brought the old man and his wife from the forest. When they died, he erected a statue of them with the mongoose at their feet. They were buried in the palace grounds and a yearly holiday was called in their honor.

The dragon was given his choice of land. He chose a piece of property high among the hills with a wide view of the mountains and a large lake for him to swim in. Akela issued a decree that the dragon was not to be harmed and that is why dragons are revered to this day.

Kaj saw how his mother had taught him the culture by telling him stories about loyalty, duty, gratitude, courage, and wisdom. Through repetition, these values had become a part of him. They had united as well as shaped. Yet, they also had confined because they had not taught him that people learn and times change. Akela did not kill the dragon as he had been ordered. Some might say he did not obey orders. Instead, he went by himself to face the dragon and, because of that, he learned what it had to teach him. In the end, Kaj understood, it was the universe that rid the country of the evil cousin.

Kaj began to see that while there was still work to be done, he could see the first of the steps stretching out before him.

Chapter 50

KAJ'S TEAM ASSEMBLED IN THE restaurant outside the palace walls to celebrate before they left. The King and the Colonel were to join them later. The King said they wanted to give Kaj time to say his own goodbyes before they were given thanks and awards for their service.

The food was as good as ever, but now the dark, clandestine atmosphere of the restaurant had transformed into a warm, rustic charm. Kaj looked around at the team he had worked with for the past ten days. He heard Nie tell Sharma that she would like a tour of the crime lab before it drove back to New Delhi. He heard Xue say he also wanted to see it. Sometimes hope won out, he thought, even if it was only a small change in perspective. Thanks to Greg, Kaj knew that Nie had as much riding on the outcome of the investigation as Xue had. It was Liu who was stirring them up and reporting back. It annoyed Kaj that there had been a spy in the camp, and he planned to give Liu a lot to chew on. It was Kaj's parting gift to the doctors.

Kaj clinked his chopsticks against a bowl to gain their attention.

"I want to thank you all for your cooperation and hard work," he began as he stood up. Then he began to single out each one.

"Dr. Nie. You have a disarming wisdom and strength. I want you to know that your efforts were noticed and appreciated. I see why your country places so much trust in your leadership, and it was our privilege to work with you."

Nie kept her composure and offered only a very small, tight smile, but Kaj knew she was pleased.

Go ahead and report that, Mr. Liu. Kaj smiled inwardly with delicious malice. *If Beijing wants scandal or propaganda, it will not be on my watch.*

"Dr. Xue, you were our analyst. You asked probing questions and challenged the team. Have you considered changing careers to become a detective? I think you would make a good one."

Xue bobbed his head awkwardly in thanks, and his cheeks turned pink.

Send that one back to Beijing, Mr. Liu, Kaj said to himself.

"Mr. Liu, you worked on many problems. Thank you." It was the best that Kaj could manage to say and still retain his integrity. Liu gave a nervous dip of his head and looked sideways at Nie.

Hah, Kaj thought, *you'll never know that I knew you were a spy. On the other hand, I hope that Dr. Nie knows I do.*

Kaj then turned to the Indian team.

"Mr. Agarwahl, your efforts and, Mr. Choudhary and Mr. Achari, yours as well were critically important to this case. I shall be conveying my appreciation to your superiors and telling them how much we depended on your work and professional analysis. You did not let us down."

"Dr. Sharma," Kaj began.

"Emir, please," Sharma said.

"Emir," Kaj acquiesced. "Your optimism and dedication to your work played a major part in the success of this investigation. You were never daunted by a challenge and always promised you would succeed, and you did."

Sharma rose to the moment. He stood up and looked around the room. "I speak for the forensics team. Thank you, Kaj and your detectives, for the professional and patient way you dealt with our disagreements and fanciful ideas."

"And Sanjay, of course," Kaj began.

"Sanjay?" Sharma sounded surprised. "But he has done nothing. He has not even chosen his dissertation topic."

As he heard those words, Sanjay stood up suddenly, his face contorted with indignation and his eyes clouded with a shimmer of tears. He looked accusingly at Sharma and shouted.

"I have. I plan to use this investigation as an example of how international investigations can work. You did not see all that I did. I climbed in every hole, went down every alley you told me to, and even fell in the river. All I wanted was the opportunity to learn. I never complained. Not even when you said you did not care if I learned anything. Did I ever tell you that I am claustrophobic?"

Sanjay's rage rose to an anguished climax.

"Someone needs to tell you that you are . . .." Sanjay shook from the effort of standing up for himself.

Kaj could not make out the word that Sanjay used. He turned to Agarwahl and asked what it was.

Agarwahl pulled his lips together in a semblance of a silent whistle and looked down at the table. Kaj thought he detected a slight smile. The other two members of the Indian lab team sat silently with raised eyebrows. Whatever Sanjay had said must have been quite something.

Agarwahl looked sideways at Kaj without raising his head and almost whispered.

"He called him *paagal*. That means *demented*. It is not what you say to a senior professor."

Kaj looked over at Sharma, who had now sat down and was quietly studying the indignant student. He appeared more interested than insulted. For several minutes, there was complete silence in the room.

"So," Dr. Sharma said with great dramatic irony, "I am *paagal*. It is a long time since anyone has called me that. In fact, I do not remember anyone doing so."

He looked sternly at the quavering Sanjay.

"I am *paagal*, is that your decision?"

Sanjay nodded his head so hard that Kaj thought it might fall off.

"If that is the case," Sharma said with another deep, dramatic sigh, "and if you are using this investigation, which I agree is a good research topic, then I suppose I must supervise your dissertation." He rolled his eyes, blew his cheeks out, and the moment was over.

The effect on Sanjay was immediate. He stepped backward and fell over his chair. It took time for him to right the chair and himself. Then he stood stock still, seeming not to know what to do with himself, especially when the Chinese team and the lab crew all stood up and applauded.

"What does that mean?" Kaj asked.

Agarwahl looked knowingly. "Sharma has just assured that young man of an important career. One day he will be a forensics director or a university professor or something even better. Sharma's graduates support and promote one another. Sharma must be pleased that Sanjay finally found some courage."

"It's an apology, then?"

"Oh no." Agarwahl looked at Kaj with a shocked expression. "He never apologizes. He corrects things. The better solution, is it not?

Chapter 51

THAT EVENING, KAJ FOUND HIMSELF in an unaccustomed place. Usually, when a case was completed, there was a ceremonial ending point, a moment of congratulation before moving on. Most often, it was marked by the transfer of the files. Without that finality, something was missing, and he had no idea how to get beyond it. It was a welcome distraction when the phone rang and he was told the King asked for them to meet one final time at the dragon pool. Kaj arrived early to have time alone with the pool.

Once out of the van, he stepped away from the trees to look up at the mountain. It was then that he had his moment.

An aura began to build around Masakatsu's double peaks. It started with an amber flash that ran through a spectrum of colors until it became a transparent frame echoing the mountain's shape. Before Kaj's eyes, the mist shrouding the mountain's summit became a pearly effervescence that broke into shafts of sunlight illuminating the glaciers beneath. He felt the power of the colors. He felt the presence of the universe. For several long minutes, Kaj stood transfixed before the mountain. Then, like fireworks slowly fading, the color ebbed away and the mountain settled back into its life.

His sensei's words came to him. "When you are ready, you will feel your true nature at the bright center of the universe. You will not wonder if there is emptiness or fullness at the core. There will be both at once, and you will simply be." At the time, those words had been inaccessible, stretched beyond any recognizable meaning, and the rational part of him had refused to surrender. He didn't know whether to feel blessed or embarrassed. He only knew that he was changed by what he had seen. It was a moment where his practical Linda would probably say something like, "Kaj, it's time. You need to sort this out."

He sat down on the cement bench and started to do that. He knew he could not relive his father's life, nor should he have tried. His father's time was different to his. Also, he could no longer be the weakness to Linda's strength. That was not good for either of them. He would continue to serve the purposes of justice because that gave him his place to stand, just as the Colonel made his stand on Gurkha loyalty. But he could not be responsible for things that were never his to control. If anything could be said about his military service, it was that he had done what his country asked of him, even if he did not believe in the nobility of the call to duty that sent countless young men to pointless deaths. What he did not know yet was how life would accommodate him when he returned home.

The darting fish in the pools increasingly clear water told him that something was coming back to life. Then he saw the dragon. It swam past him along the edge of the pond, making small ripples that spread out like a vee behind its body. It did not speak to him, but in the wake of its passing, he saw a gathering of people. He saw a much older Linda and himself. They were celebrating what looked like a high school graduation. He knew they were cheering for their grandson. He knew it was a promise. The universe would move forward without his needing to bear the burden.

His reverie was only disturbed when a hand fell on his shoulder. Startled, he broke from his trance and looked up to see the King.

"I am sorry if I disturbed you. This is my opportunity to thank you, while we are alone."

Kaj began to stand up but the King shook his head and sat down beside him.

"I hear that your sister is recovering," Kaj said.

"Yes. It is a great relief. My brother-in-law took Aki to see her. We do not know yet what the future holds, but we have more hope."

The King put his head down and wiped the heel of his hand across his eyes. It was an almost boyish gesture. The King's emotions were escaping only now that his sister was out of danger.

"So much death," the King said as he looked up. "And all about a dam that was never planned. I have already decided that we must find a way to integrate the dam more openly into the life of the country."

"And the wise know the rituals of water," Kaj said.

His prickle took over the rest of his thought: *Whoever talked about the banality of evil was right. It is as drearily commonplace as the dragon said. Kamal's separation from his family isolated him and robbed him of community. In the end, all he had left was exclusion and alienation.*

Kaj brought himself sharply back to the present. "Has it been decided what will happen to Kamal?"

"As the head of security, the Colonel is responsible for all matters of national security. I do not want to interfere with his decisions."

Kaj listened carefully but couldn't tell if the King was agreeing with the Colonel or simply accepting the opportunity to stand upwind of difficult decisions.

"On the other hand," the King continued, "Tashi says we need a crisis center to deal with serious mental illness. I did not believe that Kuthan needed such a formal place to treat the mentally ill. But now, she has convinced me to plan for one. Tashi says Kamal has the mind of a child."

Kaj wondered for a moment what the Colonel had in mind for Kamal. He was glad he would never know. But perhaps Tashi might have something to say about that too.

The King peered intently at Kaj. "Did you see the dragon?"

"I think what I saw in the pool was myself." Kaj looked steadily at the King. "You brought in our team to investigate, but you set out the path for us to follow."

The King did not deny it. "I knew that the monks' theological constitution was incomplete because it was designed to impose conformity. My father warned me about it. He told me that the monks' religion was not a strong enough foundation for a nation. I see his wisdom. But I also admit that we tried to guide you."

"We?" Kaj's head furrowed.

"Colonel Pradhan and I made out a list of the people you needed to meet. We housed you and the Chinese and Indian teams in the palace to keep you together and near us. That way we would always be available. We also wanted you to learn Kuthan's history. Your logical first stop for the history was with Mountain Thunder."

"Darya was part of your planning?"

"Not at all. We knew the Lhotses would be suspicious and demand to meet you before anyone else. But after that, you were on your own. We did not know that Ananda had brought Mallik back to Kuthan. We did not know the Lama family had hidden a child. We should have. But, as you now know, the families have a long history of independence. I respect the challenge that monks faced trying to unite the country. I respect their understanding that a diverse and secular society could not be built on spiritual conformity."

"But the monks were not totally wrong," Kaj replied. "The Master of the Temple of the Thousand Steps to Heaven feared the dam because it was a corporation, and he knew that they naturally promote themselves and think of profit only in the short term. He wanted to be sure that the dam did not become another British East India Company."

"He said this?" The King looked surprised.

"Not directly. I inferred this from what he said about the dam. He seemed quite frightened of the dam's potential corruption."

"I can see why. The monks kept the records and knew how the East India Company plundered India. My grandfather wanted the monasteries to serve on Kuthan's Governing Council but not on the international Dam Board. Unfortunately, that exclusion meant that the Master had no way to know how carefully the dam is managed. We also kept much of the dam operations private to avoid outside influence. But, as it turns out, that meant we were not as open as we needed to be."

Kaj looked once more at the dragon pool. "You asked me once what advice I had to help you to unify your country. I don't know if you still need it. But the Master at The Temple of the Thousand Steps told me people must choose values that reflect who they want to be, not what they are. That made me think about my own work. I recognize now our first ideas about right and wrong come from the stories we are told and what our parents value. As we grow older, and if the laws are wise, they reinforce and interpret what we learn. What I do in law enforcement is to confirm those values by seeking out those who violate them. But, as the monks learned, a unifying vision is more complex than just changing laws."

"Language and meaning," the King sighed. "That's what people say about Patel's poem. It seems that the poem means whatever someone wants it to. But every system I have looked at starts with beautiful words, and all become corrupt over time. My father said that the purpose of government was making people treat one another fairly. Laws are like boundaries, he told me, and governments are the only places where these can be set. But, as we have learned, telling people to follow rules they don't own is an invitation for them to find ways around them. That evasion leads to even more laws trying to plug the evasions, and people hiring solicitors to lobby for their interests. It becomes madness, and we do not want a system that catches only common flies while the hornets go unpunished."

Kaj smiled. He'd never heard that expression before, but he could think of other situations it could apply to.

"The question you asked when I arrived was about encouraging your country to climb the same mountain even when they do not want to follow the same path. It is much easier to get people angry and resentful than it is to have them work together. The first is the way of the demagogue who demands that everyone follow the same way. That is not how I understood your family's vision to be."

At the sound of Kaj's words, the King transformed himself back into the young man of his Oxford days. In the UK, he had been the outsider among the privileged British elite. His social position had bought him inclusion but not acceptance except as a curiosity from a former part of the British empire. Now, with the hindsight of his own history and experience, he was free to think and dream for the future.

"The monks thought that if Kuthan's wealth were distributed equally, there would be no evil left in the world because everyone would have material comfort. It did not work because, as we learned, government by religion is inherently discriminatory. People look for what divides rather than what unites them, and when grievance replaces tolerance, it becomes self-definition: We define ourselves by who we are not."

The King looked discouraged at the folly he was describing.

"A purely capitalist model of private ownership, in the case of the dam, is not what we needed. We wanted it to serve Kuthan rather than a bank of investors. But the monarchy, our current system, is too dependent on whoever inherits the throne and is strong enough to impose his or her will. The British experience with royal families justifies my concern. Their history is filled with violence, including conquest, execution, and civil war. Through it all, it is the people who suffer. Revolutions or not, nothing seems to change for them."

The King sat for a moment, silently watching the water in the pool. Kaj had no idea what the man was thinking. Was he watching the dragon? If so, Kaj wondered what the dragon might be telling him.

"My thought," Kaj began slowly and diffidently, "is for you to restore your family's home at Kalyani. People know what happened here. Even in ruins, it is a symbol of the past you are leaving and the future you want to build. You can create there a neutral place where people can talk about qualities such as *justice* and *loyalty* and what they mean for Kuthan. That discussion is where they need your leadership. They need to become Kuthani before anything else. You represent the very land and history these buildings stand on. You have the moral and mythic authority. They were crying out for your family's leadership when they chose your grandfather as their first king. You are the only one left who has the education and experience to lead Kuthan into the future. Sitting back and allowing it to happen as consensus and without your guidance will not get any of you up that mountain or up the ones you can see from the top."

The King took a moment to think. "When the British left, there was only religion and wealth to unify us but, as you say, neither could bear the burden."

"And the British did not know the customs of trees, nor did they know the rituals of water," Kaj recited.

The King looked startled. "Is that what Patel was saying?"

"Part of it, I think. The part that I can understand without being Kuthani. It is about why the British raj was destined to end. They did not know what they did not know. It takes a wise hand to steer through the reefs of self-interest and greed. It also takes people who are committed to the nation. As I said, you have the education, experience, open-mindedness, and dedication. But, judging from my own experience, please choose your heroes and founding myths carefully because they set the pattern for what the people value, how they judge themselves, and even how they live."

"You mean do not celebrate violence from the days of the warlords, and do not allow loyalty to the clans or religious sects to become larger than loyalty to Kuthan as a whole. I agree. But, also, we should never again allow our young people to think they are voiceless and have no stake in the country's future."

"There always will be tigers."

"You are right, Inspector Kaj. There will always be tigers. There will be those unable or unwilling to come on the journey. We must be aware of them and deal with them. But it is a place to start. Perhaps we could also start to talk about Patel's poem as a national purpose: Let honesty and justice tumble out the things that do not serve us as we seek clarity in everything we do."

Kaj smiled as he listened to the King interpret the poem. Kaj, in fact, had found his own meaning: *The customs of trees. The rituals of water. The earth-bound and the flowing. Nature will endure just as snow melts from trees and water purifies the land, but only if there is balance. There will be as many interpretations as there are readers of the poem, just as there will be many pathways leading up the mountain. What is important is that they walk in the same direction. That is the promise of myth as well as the power of balance.*

They stood up together and looked once more at the pond. Kaj knew he was not a poet like Patel. Solving crimes had a certain symmetry but he would not say there was beauty. Still, it was enough.

Then he and the King turned away and walked back down the path.

Chapter 52

IT WAS THE LAST DAY. Greg and his tech team had already gone home. Jill had not gone with them. Kaj's team was flying out commercial in a few hours. The King was planning to announce his engagement but had already told Kaj that he had "negotiated" with Tashi. He smiled as he said the word. He said the Kajiwaras would receive an invitation to the wedding. Kaj imagined that the invitation itself would be worth framing even if they couldn't attend.

Kaj sat alone in the dining hall at his favorite table by the window. As usual, he was the first one down and the staff had made sure that the puffy momos and orange lentil soup he liked were ready for him. He enjoyed these solitary moments when he could look out at the mountains. This morning, they were pink in the early morning light.

The moment wasn't his for long, though. Someone came into the room and sat down at the table beside him. Kaj was surprised to see it was Meng.

"I hoped to find you alone," Meng told him. "I wanted to say goodbye to you personally. And I wanted to say that I apologize for doubting your methods."

Meng accepted coffee when it was offered but waved aside the milk.

"You Americans are a peculiar combination of inconsistency and delusions. Somehow or other, you get the job done when others cannot."

"Meng," Kaj replied in a weary voice, "you aren't going to dissect America are you? That would make me have to dissect Beijing."

"God forbid," Meng said hastily. "I was about to ask you a question. You and I are of a similar age and have similar professions. I wondered if you had thought about what you will do as you face irrelevance."

"Meng, what is this about? Don't tell me that it's because you worked with Americans. We can't have had that kind of impact on you."

Meng turned to watch as the sun turned the mountains from pink to golden. Then he looked down and stirred his coffee more out of habit than need.

"You have a wit and irony that remind me of the Russians in their better days. The difference between our professions is only a matter of scope. You police Hawaii. I police wherever I am sent around the world."

"I wouldn't call it policing, what you do," Kaj objected.

Meng disagreed. "I would call it detective work in a broad way." He took a sip of coffee and looked up thoughtfully at the waterfall mural.

"I like waterfalls. Did you know there are six different types? I did not know that, but I am not surprised. Once upon a time, embassies were like waterfalls. They collected information and sent it flowing to their home governments. Now the staff on site just process visas and are not consulted on anything."

Kaj studied Meng for a moment. There seemed to be an infinite number of ways to interpret Patel's line about water.

Meng curled his lip into a disapproving sneer.

"It is depressing. And I find the quality of the people I work with now is what you Americans call 'in the pits.' Am I saying that correctly? Embassy staffs are boring technocrats who only push buttons and stare at computer screens."

Kaj took too large a sip of coffee and choked on its heat. He had to cough into his napkin. It took a moment for the burn in his mouth to calm.

"Let me understand you, Meng. Are you saying that you are bored by the intellectual level of the people you work with?"

"See," Meng, said triumphantly, "I knew you would understand. You have the same problem."

"Actually, Meng, I don't. Most people coming into my office aren't literate let alone intellectual."

"But where is the beauty? The symmetry? The existential proof of existence?" Meng looked almost in tears.

Kaj shook his head. "Greg is right. You have been in Russia too long. You need to get a life."

"My job is my life."

"Meng, this happens to us all. I call it the succession of equivalence. Our younger equivalents are hungry to replace us. On the day we leave, they will not write poetry about us, at least not Russian melancholia."

Meng looked disappointed. "Not even gratitude?"

"Gratitude?" Kaj almost laughed out loud. "Organizations don't have hearts or souls, Meng. They are incapable of gratitude. We are just cogs in their machinery."

Meng looked speculatively into his coffee cup before looking at Kaj with a knowing gleam in his eyes.

"Dr. Nie is very complimentary of you. That is a good friend to have. She was prepared to have Beijing recall Xue if he continued to be disruptive. But you made him settle down. When you made Sharma and Xue go together to the Sikh temple, you banged their heads together. That was good for them both. I knew you were different when you issued that order about speculation. But after the Sikh temple business, I knew you were someone to take seriously."

Meng gave a smug, self-congratulatory smile before he continued.

"I saw you do this. But then, as if that was not enough, you neutralized the media, made sure the home nations stayed away, and even managed the families. But I must tell you, that was how the palace planned it, and the palace always wins."

Kaj's eyebrows shot up. "The palace planned it?"

"The palace staff did not want people to think the royal family was corrupt. What would happen to palace jobs and careers if the people wanted another revolution? They watched every bulletin the King's office produced for you. But, more to the point, they made sure nothing happened to you."

"Meng, if you are trying to sound cynical, I can assure you that you are merely sounding alarming."

Meng gave an apologetic non-apology. "Trust that I am being objective and telling you things that your bean counters could not. The King wants to bring change to Kuthan, and he needs the country to follow him. How does he do that when people do not trust the royal family? Never mind the reality. Look at the perception. One mentally ill cousin is bad luck. Three murderous cousins are a criminal conspiracy. No one wants the Soöngs described as Asian Borgias. As soon as you identified Kamal, the palace wanted the investigation ended. The others were dead, and he was guilty enough."

"How do you know all this, Meng?"

"No need to doubt me." Meng looked very sly. "Nepal is not so far from Kuthan."

"Meng, surely not the Colonel?

Meng shrugged. "Communication goes both ways. A useful backdoor for China and Kuthan to avoid official channels. Look what Dorji did to protect the King when Mallik came home. He took the blame for it. Never mentioned your Mr. Greg and the US. Do not underestimate the King's loyal advisors when they want to protect him and their jobs. Palaces are not your usual set of administrative offices. They are full of plots and schemes, but everyone agrees on one thing: protect the King at all costs."

"But Dorji lost his job," Kaj objected.

Meng shrugged. "He's already back at his desk. He is the only one who knows how to operate the King's schedule."

Kaj's eyebrow rose suspiciously. "Why are you telling me this?"

Meng shrugged. "I am near retiring. As you say, I am only a cog. I think I might write a book. I hear the US pays people to give talks. I have stories I can tell. I would have to be outside China, though."

Kaj gave a little shudder. He remembered how the King said they paid Meng in cigars and Single Malt whiskey. He didn't know what that was for. Not knowing was probably for the best.

"What you are telling me is that I and my team were being used."

"Not at all. You and Hawaii were being honored. I thought they handled the matter very well with you. They guided you but also trusted you to deal with anything they could not predict. China and India are pleased they are no longer suspected. Your State Department should be happy that you did not create a diplomatic crisis. The King enjoys a swell of sympathy and has gained a very useful future wife he happens to care for. You fulfilled your purpose brilliantly, as the British say, and even went them one better. The palace was worried about signs that the King was retreating into depression. You gave him hope. Restoring Kayani will distract him nicely. You even pulled me in. Why did I help you? You reminded me of me. You are another detached observer. Probably it was your use of silence. In the old days, I would have tried to recruit you myself."

"Meng, you are getting delusional. I just did my job."

"You are a Kuthani hero."

Kaj's face darkened and his eyebrows knit.

"Meng, people use the term *hero* for doing something no one else wants to. Most heroes are dead. Ask them if they wanted to choose heroism over living. Ask Vladimir Komarov—you admire the Russians—if he wanted to die a 'hero' because no one had the courage to tell Brezhnev that the spacecraft was unsafe to fly."

Meng waved his right hand as if to say all that was irrelevant. It reminded Kaj that he'd used the same gesture when he was recruiting Meng to help with finding Mallik.

"I thought you'd want to know . . .."

"Know what?" Kaj started to feel impatient.

"I had to explain to Beijing why I was looking for information on Mallik in Singapore. I could not say that I was doing it to help the Americans."

Kaj's quizzical eyebrow rose and he looked levelly at Meng. He was not sure he wanted to hear what was coming next.

"I told them one of my sources told me you considered Mallik a person of interest and I wanted to know why. I said my plan was to find the information you wanted and use it for leverage later. They were most impressed that I had a possible connection into the police department in Hawaii."

"Meng, you didn't." Kaj's face took on the look he had when he got off the one rollercoaster he had ridden.

"Clever of me, no? Let me tell you I convinced them that I should spend some time getting to know you better in Hawaii. I told them I needed to learn your methods for getting people to cooperate."

Kaj slumped back against the chair back.

"What exactly does that mean, Meng?"

"They are sending me to Hawaii after you get back. Do not worry. I will tell them you turned out to be a dead end. Too unself-aware to help."

Kaj felt like the frog once it had been stung.

"Do not look at me like that," Meng said plaintively. I needed a holiday and I fancied warmth and palm trees. I thought you would be glad to give me a little payback for the help I gave you. I would enjoy taking the boat out to the Arizona memorial. Perhaps you could arrange for the volcanoes to erupt for me. You might even be grateful enough to give me a tour of the islands and tell me the best places to eat. I will be on an expense account."

Kaj gave a deep sigh. Never mind the palace, Meng had his own corner on corruption. Meng looked sheepish at first and then gave an embarrassed chuckle.

"Meng, do they know you're a scorpion?"

"Of course, they do. They are bigger ones themselves. But I know what they are thinking. When I get back from Hawaii, they will hand me my retirement papers. I want to have a good tan when I get them."

"How will you even get a US visa?"

"There is always a diplomatic visa, but I am counting on my friend, the famous Hawaii inspector Kajiwara and his illustrious State Department friend, Greg Horne, to get a nice six-month visitor visa for me. That way I can travel around. I am sure you can make an elaborate excuse for that. After all I did help you."

"Meng, you're an operator."

"I shall take that as a compliment."

Meng rose and gave an elaborate bow. He picked his coffee cup up and held it towards Kaj.

"To the master," he said. "Until we meet again—soon."

Then, he lumbered off, bowing to Kaipo on his way out.

"What was that about?" Kaipo asked as he sat down at the table.

Kaj shook his head in wonder. "You don't want to know. The ways of international spying make me happy that all I deal with is CID paperwork."

"That much trouble, huh?"

Kaj could only imagine the complications of Meng in Hawaii. If he were ever asked about the challenges of international cooperation, he might answer, "Beware of Mengs bearing gifts." Kaj gave a deep shrug of his shoulders and then laughed out loud. His laughter felt good. He'd deal with whatever came when it happened. *"The wise know the rituals of water. And, shoganai, that is the way it is."*

"I have news," Kaipo said eagerly. "I used the Colonel's example."

Kaj stared at Kaipo blankly.

"You remember? At the airport? Powerful women? Humor and surprise?"

"Oh, you mean the Colonel and Darya."

"Well, I phoned Gail this morning and told her I was bringing something back for her. So, no party. I told her I didn't want anyone else there but us."

"And how did she take it?"

"She was surprised and asked if I had got my head together. I assured her I had. She said she thought I would want to see everyone. I told her we needed to make those decisions together. I also told her that she was the first and only person on my agenda, and I wanted to be that person for her. Then she wanted a hint. I told her, 'Nothing doing. You can wait until I get back. Meet me at the airport, and we'll go from there.' I threw in a bit of mystery and now I'm looking forward to it too."

"After that build up, you'd better have something good in store."

"Like this?" Kaipo reached in his pocket and pulled out a green-velvet ring box carrying embossed gold letters, "Mountain Dragon, Gems and Gold, Kuthan." He set it down on the table in front of Kaj. "I went to Mountain Thunder's jewelry store and talked to Batsa. Go ahead, open it. I want to see your reaction."

Slowly, almost reluctantly, Kaj reached out and opened the box. Inside was a gold ring with a single large pearl in the center.

"Look at the carving in the setting around the pearl."

Kaj picked up the ring and peered at the decoration. "It's a little too fine for my eyes," he admitted.

"I couldn't see it either. I need glasses. But Batsa gave me this." He pulled out a small magnifying glass and handed it to Kaj.

This time, Kaj could see a group of people. It was beautifully done, a real work of art.

"It's a wedding procession. They're walking up Mount Masakatsu. The pearl is the mountain. After we came back from Snow Leopard, I had the guards drive me to Batsa's shop. I told him who it was for and what I could afford. He said that since I couldn't afford a significant ruby or sapphire for the ring the next best thing was to go for something unique and artistic. I said Gail was like Darya and asked if he had anything his sister would have liked. He produced the setting and said the original design was made for Darya. That's when I knew it was the one. He set the pearl for me, and I came back to the hotel to call Gail."

Kaj smiled benignly at Kaipo. "I'm delighted for you. Congratulations to you both."

"Well, hang on, she hasn't said yes yet." Kaipo sat back with an expression that clearly said don't count the chickens.

"I don't think you have anything to worry about. Just let us know when you set the date."

Kaj watched Kaipo snap the lid shut on the ring box and then bound up the stairs to go pack. Then he sat back in his chair and looked for the last time out at the range of distant mountains. When Kaipo showed him the ring, Kaj had not mentioned another green velvet box safely locked in his carry-on luggage. It contained an apple-green jade disk with a gold dragon mounted in the center. He also had asked for a ride to Batsa's shop where he described the necklace he wanted. It had been delivered last evening.

He wanted to believe that he was giving Linda the necklace because he wanted her to have something of beauty. But the enlightened, self-aware part of him knew it was because he wanted to remember that moment in the mountains when Masakatsu revealed itself to him. That made the gift consciously selfish.

That was the trouble with enlightenment: whatever is seen cannot be unseen. But then, as he walked up the stairs to pack his own luggage, "his" line from Patel's poem came to him unbidden: "Everything is as it is and should be." He smiled and hoped it was true.

The End

Afterword

When I began writing the Inspector Kajiwara series, my original purpose was to use the mystery novel structure to talk about higher education during the transitional phase of the 1990s when enrollment and funding issues rocked the campuses. Kaj was to be the window into the wonders and weaknesses of a major research university like (the mythical) "Hawaii State University," which was trying to respond to a new world of new needs.

For that reason, the first novel of the Kajiwara series, The Midas Death, introduced the inspector and his team of detectives and reflected the impact from when campuses were challenged to become more independent of public investment. With this follow-up book, however, I have turned the focus away from the campuses to the personal problems facing the inspector and his detectives. They are challenged to solve a crime far beyond the scope of anything they have faced before, one that will force them to adapt and adjust and, not incidentally, gain a new perspective on their lives, particularly as it involves the continuing generational impact of the unjust incarceration of Japanese-Americans during World War II.

As the setting where these transformations happen, the mythical kingdom of Kuthan turns out to be not a place of romantic dreams. Instead, it is both taskmaster and teacher, and also a place where Eastern and Western myths and history meet in the shadow of the mighty Himalayan mountains who still can be seen as gods capable of interacting with people living in their shadow.

Myths, in fact, played a key role as I wrote Dragon Pool, and I relied on Joseph Campbell's, The Hero with a Thousand Faces as both source and inspiration. The dragon of this story is an Eastern Dragon. This dragon is an imperial symbol. It is powerful, wise, and venerated. It is said to live in lakes and is responsible for rainbows. The Western dragon, on the other hand, seems to exist only for young men to kill it. To me, the Western dragon sounds like an illustration of adolescent vandalism. In my telling of the story, the Eastern dragon with its subtlety and wisdom is a symbol of the universe and the oneness of all creation.

In the story of Akela, I have conflated many myths involving a hero and a dragon. I would like to think Jung would be pleased. My point is that myths and storytelling teach us, perhaps unconsciously, about the world and how to behave within it. They also teach us universal truths common to all people. As Campbell has pointed out, myths are a largely unacknowledged part of how we define what a society values and promotes as virtue.

But I did take a liberty with myth. I wanted to show how it contributes to what Asian tradition calls enlightenment.

While there have been Christian mystics—I wrote about one of them, Professor of Rhetoric and devout Christian philosopher, Aonio Paleario, in my novel, Dream of Shadows—the aims of enlightenment and mysticism differ markedly. Western mysticism aims at the dissolution of the self into an exterior god who promises salvation through the manumission of sin. One of the works sometimes attributed to Paleario, but otherwise quite typical, is entitled On the Benefit of Christ's Death. Eastern practice, on the other hand, trains the mind to find the universal within. One famous teaching is that if you find the Buddha on the road, kill the Buddha. That is because the figure on the road is an imposter: the Buddha lives within. This is the difference between a patriarchal law-giver and the deep reflection required to find one's own interior universe. By now, it should be clear that I agree with Socrates: the unexamined life is not worth living.

In Dragon Pool, therefore, I use the word and concept of enlightenment in the Asian tradition of completely understanding and mastering oneself without being constrained to a single, dogmatic set of steps. According to Buddhist teaching, "There are many pathways up the mountain," and that is how I have used the concept: There are infinite pathways, and they may not be straight or easy. Many have detours, gaps, and even dead-ends where the individual must reconsider whatever pathway has led to that point. But the aim remains self-understanding although it should also be understood that climbing one mountain alone is not the only goal. After completing the lessons of one mountain there will always be another.

I learned this lesson myself climbing Colorado's fourteeners. Reaching the top of the two I was able to complete—Grays Peak and Mount Bierstadt—and the two that taught me humility as I surrendered in site of the top, Long's Peak and Mount Elbert—the mountains retain their mystery as great symbols of challenge and meaning. As Aikido founder, Morihei Ueshiba, teaches, the aim of such striving is to understand: "We become the universe. We are one with the universe." Inspector Kaj comes to understand and exemplify this tradition, and by doing this is finally able to lay aside the horrors he brought back from war.

As I noted in the preface to the first novel in the series, The Midas Death, part of me wishes Kuthan existed. However, even a fictional nation requires congruence and accuracy. South Asia's colonial history, religious conflicts, and relations with its much larger neighbors, India and China, are real, and I have made every effort to respect them. I hope I have done a good enough job that the reader will share my feeling that Kuthan could be possible and very special. In the same way, I hope that Hawaii State University is believable even as it is as mythical as Kuthan. As I said in The Midas Death, no one university can get into that much mischief.

I could not have written this book without the help of many people willing to read the manuscript over the past two years. In particular, I would like to thank my former boss at Windward Community College, Dean Hiroshi Kato, who contributed greatly to the story and who never directly told me when I had something wrong but would send me something pertinent to read. Thank you, Sensei. I would also like to thank my reading group for their endless patience with me: Marquette historian, Dr. Tyler Tichelaar; and artist and biographer, Rosalyn Hurley. Thank you both for sticking with me. Also, my editor, Jonathan Glasscock, who was endlessly encouraging when I hit the many roadblocks; layout artist, Larry Alexander; Inez Kimiko Mann, who remembers the same Hawaii I do; Ruth Stevick Gracey, a fellow instructor in those long-ago days in Kuykendall Hall (still waiting for renovation as I understand); Dr. Gillian Bryant Greenwood, who taught me to only write about what I know; and Jean-Sylvan Negre, who generously shared his experiences with martial arts in Asia. In the way of the Islands, many others who contributed to this book are shy about being publicly thanked. I respect that. I do want to thank them, and I want them to know how much I appreciated the help.

Diana DeLuca

Eugene, Oregon 2025

A Note on Kuthan's Clans

OFFICIALLY, KUTHAN'S REGIONAL GROUPS ARE referred to now as families. Historically, they have also been called regions or clans, depending on who is discussing them. They are the remnants of a feudal past where family groups were led by warlords. Kuthan was not united until the British Army forcefully collected these groups under a single administration.

Mountain Thunder: Northwest Himalayan region bordering on Nepal. The Lhotse family are yak herders, miners, and exporters, the family having thriving international markets for their products. They are also known as the most aggressive and feared of the families.

Snow Leopard: North east mountains, bordering on China and Bhutan. The Dema family shares cultural influences with China because of their shared border. The region is exclusive and provides artists, teachers, musicians, doctors, and professionals of all kinds. They also raise the prized Kuthani goats.

White Bone: Eastern foothills, bordering on Bangladesh and south of Snow Leopard. White Bone is famous for its tea, tobacco, and the hundreds of geese and ducks they use to keep the rice paddies free of insects.

Water Dragon: Western foothills, north of Blue Pheasant. The Soöng family were nearly obliterated at Kalyani, the family home, during an invasion by Mountain Thunder after the British left. Formerly, they raised vegetables and fruit and were in the process of developing a nascent wine industry.

Blue Pheasant: Southwestern plains and closest to India, the Lama family raises tropical fruits and medicinal spices for international markets. The Lama family has a history of protest, primarily against the dam. They have a connection with the Soöng family through intermarriage.

Golden Tiger: Southeastern plains, south of White Bone. The Dorjis produce Himalayan rice on the southeastern plains and are associated with The Temple of the Thousand Steps, Kuthan' largest and most respected religious center.

Forthcoming Inspector Kajiwara in *Moku Mo'o*

INSPECTOR "KAJ" KAJIWARA STOPPED DEAD in his tracks at his first sight of the crime scene. He'd never seen anything like it in all his years at the Hawaii Police Department, and there were plenty of those since he was now about to retire. He and his younger partner, Detective Jill Nakamura, were standing dockside at the Hawaii State University's Marine Institute in Kaneohe, watching a scene play out like a Monty Python comedy skit.

Hawaii Police Department Forensic Director Eagle-Bott was kneeling on top of the Hawaii State University Marine Institute's yellow submersible, looking as if he were praying to some marine deity, while State Medical Examiner Howes, a portly but usually very dignified figure, was clinging precariously to a ladder fixed down the submersible's side. What made it ludicrous was the fact the two men were having an almost violent argument while repeatedly pointing to a pair of feet that protruded out of the submersible's entry hatch. The feet wore athletic shoes with a garish purple stripe down the side and looked like the last remains above sea level of some sunken ship.

The argument between the two directors, whatever it was, must not have been fresh, because Kaj noticed that the respective forensic and medical teams had retreated to the shade where they were sitting on whatever they could find, just watching the submersible. Their faces said it all. They looked frustrated, and Kaj understood. This clash between otherwise hallowed professionals was unprecedented. No one had ever heard of a time when the FD and ME came almost to blows over anything. It made Kaj wonder what made this case different, particularly since the only thing known about the victim at this point was what shoes the body was wearing.

Kaj sighed as he watched. All his boss, CID head Bob Wilson, had told him was to get the team together and get over to the Windward side. Once there, an institute launch would be waiting to take them to the island where the institute was located. Kaj would have liked to know more, but he knew that brevity and evasion was Bob's style: he once admitted that he had created Kaj's four-detective "university crime-investigation team" because university cases were complicated and he didn't want to deal with them himself. He put Kaj in charge because of his seniority, but Kaj suspected that it was really his impending retirement that was the attraction. He was a convenient scapegoat if things went wrong. Still, they had succeeded with the Whitworth murder, and that meant that Bob could step back, take the credit, and assign all future campus crimes to them.

It was not all a bad deal. In this case, the drive over from town to the Windward side had many compensations. The Pali Highway ran through Nu'uanu Valley, an area known for its rain and upside-down falls. After a strong rain storm, the wind blew the waterfalls back up through the rocks, turning the spray into a mist. It was a charming drive even in the damp reality of a tropical forest, and people drove up the valley to watch. Once when driving the road in the dark, Kaj had seen a pueo, an owl, white in the headlights, flying over his car. It made him wonder if he had pork onboard. That was the valley's legend: if you unwisely carried pork over the Pali, your car might suddenly stop. If it did, you had to throw out the pork before it would restart. At Halloween, there were always people who insisted it had happened to them. The only experience he'd ever had wasn't so mysterious. He got a speeding ticket on the downslope where the highway entered the city of Honolulu. Remembering that, he reminded Jill to watch her speed.

Once through the tunnels, the Windward Side spread out dramatically before them. Given the early hour, they were not subject to the notorious traffic build-up as cars from Kailua and Kaneohe and beyond, siphoned into town. Their only hold-up was making the left turn onto Kamehameha Highway at Castle Junction. But Jill was driving, allowing Kaj to enjoy the changing greens of the Koolau range.

They drove on until a sign directed them to turn off the highway onto a residential road that bore a large sign announcing the institute's presence: Hawaii State University, Moku Mo'o Marine Institute, No Trespassing. The sign's directions led them to a steep driveway leading down to a private dock. There, as promised, a tied-up launch, gently rose and fell with the waves. The operator was standing on the dock beside it. He gave them a wave to show them where to park.

"Any sign of Cliff and Kaipo?" Kaj asked Jill.

She looked around the parking lot and up to the road above them. "I don't see them."

Kaj waved back at the launch operator to indicate they'd wait for the others. The man understood, nodded, and disappeared into the launch's cabin

"Kaipo must be driving. Cliff would have been here already." Kaj gave his partner the quirky smile that meant he was making a joke.

Jill smiled back. She knew what he meant. Cliff was detail oriented and almost obsessively punctual. He was also the fashionable one with the pressed suit and shirt. Kaipo, on the other hand, while always presentable, was more interested in people than style and didn't share Cliff's almost obsessive need to be early.

"No point going over to the island until they get here." Kaj looked back up to the upper road. "Did you notice that lookout area up there?" He pointed up the steep driveway they'd just driven down.

"I was too busy getting down that driveway. It was like a rollercoaster."

Kaj smiled. "You did OK. Let's head up there and see what we can see."

They were both slightly out of breath when they reached the top. From below, it had looked like just a patch of grass, but it became more extensive and elaborate the closer they came. There were several wooden benches and a garbage can with a box of bags for dogwalkers, and, as Kaj had hoped, it had a panoramic view of the bay's brilliant turquoise and green water. Across from them, they saw the island's north shore, a large mound of palm trees with drop-offs onto rugged coral outcrops. Standing alone in the bay, the island seemed almost an afterthought, something dropped from the sky on its way to somewhere else.

"Where's the institute?" Jill asked. "I don't see any buildings."

"They're on the other side of the island," Kaj replied. "You can't see them from here."

Jill looked quizzical. "I thought you hadn't been here before."

"I haven't. I've sailed past it now and then."

"You never landed? Weren't you curious about it?"

Kaj shook his head. "They don't encourage visitors. You saw the road sign when we came in. No trespassing applies to boats as well. Whenever I saw the buildings on the other side,

I was out fishing, and I wasn't about to drift near that coral. Boats get ripped in shreds if they get too close."

"I think it looks very tropical," she said. "Like a tourist dream. You don't think about crime happening there. You think about steel guitars and luaus."

Kaj tried to see it from her point of view but couldn't. Maybe it was all the keep-out signs along the shore. He knew he ought to warn Jill that they might not be greeted with welcome leis, but he didn't want to get into a discussion about tourist misconceptions about Hawaii. There was really no point. For over a hundred years, Hawaii had been sold around the world as a tropical paradise. There was no going back now, not when so much of the local economy depended on tourism. But being the world's tropical go-to had its price, and the local community were the ones who paid it.

"Kuthan was beautiful with all those mountains," he reminded her. "But it was also the scene of a brutal crime."

Jill reacted to the meaning behind his comment. She was Mainland. She had no sense of the old days before statehood, and since she had been born and raised in California, local culture didn't run in her veins. After the fact, she realized that what she'd said impulsively was what a tourist might say, someone coming to Hawaii for sandy beaches, romance, and local people living in grass shacks. She cursed herself for still thinking Mainland. She felt embarrassed and was glad for the distraction when Cliff and Kaipo finally showed up.

Cliff was the one who spotted them from the parking lot. He and Kaipo climbed their way up the hill.

"The view's pretty, but where are the buildings?" Kaipo peered across the water looking for the structures that belonged to the institute. "Shouldn't there be docks, working labs, and several administrative buildings on the island?"

"Jill and I were just talking about that," Kaj replied. "They're on the other side. The submersible's on that side too. This side is just a landing wharf. You can make it out if you look carefully."

Kaipo squinted at the island. "I can't see anything but trees. I'd need binoculars."

"You really need to get those glasses," Kaj said.

"One of these days. But if I get them, it will mean the start of cataracts and dentures, followed by bad knees."

"I'm older than you, I don't have those things," Kaj objected.

"My dad does," Kaipo said. "It's in the genes."

As usual, Cliff had done his homework. "I read that the family that owned the island shared it with the university until they were ready to donate it to the State. The institute buildings are separate from the old family house where they entertained. Lots of parties, lots of celebrities. It must have been its own little treasure island."

"Enough with the gossip." Kaj tried to sound all business but was amused. It was only natural to be curious about an apparent, real-life Bali Hai. "We need to get over there and see what we're dealing with."

The crossing took only a few minutes, but it was long enough for Kaj to tell Cliff and Kaipo about his experience with the bay.

"On a good day when the fish are biting and the sun is out, it's a beautiful place to be. But, when the Koolau winds blow and the rain comes pouring down in sheets, you get wet and cold and regret being out on the bay at all."

"I didn't know you fished," Kaipo said. "You should have said something. We have good fishing in Waimanalo."

"Used to. In the old days, when I was younger before I ran out of time for fishing. Too many overtimes down at head-quarters." What he didn't mention was that his wife, Linda, also had something to do with it. "We hardly see you at all," she complained. "Fishing is a luxury. Fixing this house and spending time with your daughter is not."

"Did you ever catch anything?" Jill's face was crinkled with amusement.

"Sometimes. But I had my share of coming home with nothing. Don't tell anyone, but sometimes I bought fish from a roadside stall so I wasn't empty handed."

"Wasn't that dishonest?" Cliff was surprised. He was used to seeing Kaj as an unquestioned ethical icon.

"Not really," Kaj said proudly, not at all upset to reveal his youthful folly. "I looked on it then as preserving my marriage, but also an excuse to keep on fishing now and then."

They were still laughing when the launch tied up a few minutes later. Kaj was the first off and helped the others. The Koolau morning wind had picked up, causing small waves to leak into the institute's wharf area, not large enough to make the launch pitch but enough to require timing and balance to make it safely.

Members of the institute security detail were waiting for them, including the head, who introduced himself as Sergeant Jardine. He was the tallest of them and his uniform was crisply starched with perfect creases on both the shirt and his pants. His words were as crisp as his military-style haircut. Kaj couldn't help himself. He remembered other coldly polite people with manicured appearances who had turned out to be hiding something.

"I was told to give you a tour of the island." Jardine's voice was neutral, his face fixed in what seemed an uncongenial indifference. Kaj extended his hand only to feel the lack of welcome in the handshake that followed. Jardine's grip did not engage.

"Not for me," Kaj corrected him. "Detectives Kahana and Lee will be going with you."

Kaj studied Jardine's response: the sideways avoidance of eye contact, the brief frown that was immediately disguised, and the narrowing of the lips. They signaled a wariness almost verging on resentment. He gave the detectives the impression that they were an unwelcome intrusion.

Jardine did not say anything. He just turned back to Kaj and nodded.

"One of my officers will escort you to the institute dock. Your Medical Examiner and Forensics Director are already on site."

"Thank you." Kaj said this with matching lack of emotion. He watched as Jardine led Cliff and Kaipo into the trees that filled the center of the island.

It was when they were out of sight that Kaj felt the uneasy feeling of irritation. He called it his prickle. It was the product of long, lonely sentry-duty in the Vietnamese jungle. There, it was a warning when things weren't right. Jardine had triggered it. He told himself not to overreact. The man's reaction to the detectives was probably understandable. If his mindset was to keep outsiders from trespassing on the island, it might be difficult to start welcoming them. But it seemed more than that, and Kaj knew that so far the prickle had never been wrong.

More Titles By Diana M. DeLuca

The Midas Death

It's December 1997, and reluctant war hero, Inspector "Kaj" Kajiwara, is asked to solve the murder of Hawaii State University Professor Harrison Whitworth, Hawaii's first Nobel Prize winner, shot through the heart by an arrow on his Manoa driveway. Kaj and his team soon face an assortment of investors, faculty, administrators, and political leaders, all with possible motive for harming Whitworth. Then, to make matters worse, a member of the Consulate of Kuthan is detained at the crime scene. The Kuthani belief in soul connection demands that Kaj find a way to bridge communication between East and West at the same time that he delves deeply both into his own past and also into the history of the complicated, brilliant victim.

A Dream of Shadows

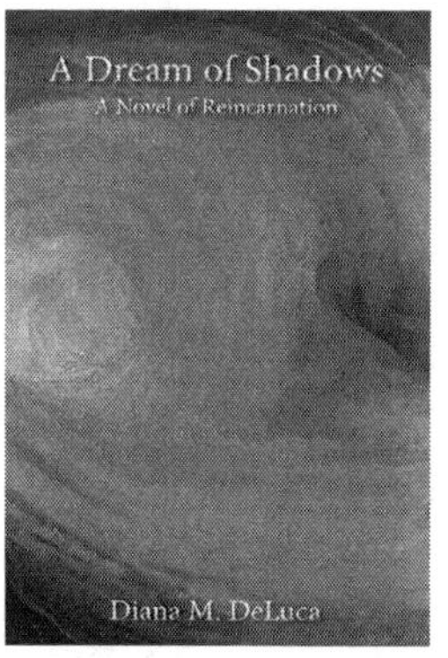

William "Bill" del Vecchio is dying of cancer but has so far refused to go because he believes his life has had no purpose. But then he finds himself in a cave "reliving" not only his own life but that of an (historical) Italian scholar named Aonio Paleario, executed by the Roman Inquisition for heresy in 1570. When he recognizes the same people occurring in both lifetimes, he faces the greatest mystery of human life. Will it be enough to convince him that no one has the right to consider himself inconsequential?

Made in the USA
Monee, IL
10 September 2025